THE SWEET SCENT OF BLOOD

THE SWEET SCENT
OF BLOOD

Spellcrackers.com

SUZANNE McLEOD

GOLLANCZ

LONDON

The right of Suzanne Gillespie to be identified as the author
of this work has been asserted by her in accordance with the
Copyright, Designs and Patents Act 1988.

First published in Great Britain in 2008 by
Gollancz
An imprint of the Orion Publishing Group
Orion House, 5 Upper St Martin's Lane
London WC2H 9EA
An Hachette Livre UK Company

3 5 7 9 10 8 6 4 2

A CIP catalogue record for this book
is available from the British Library

ISBN 978 0 575 086135 (Cased)
ISBN 978 0 575 084285 (Trade Paperback)

Typeset by Deltatype Ltd, Birkenhead, Merseyside

Printed and bound in the UK by
CPI Mackays, Chatham ME5 8TD

The Orion Publishing Group's policy is to use papers that
are natural, renewable and recyclable products and made
from wood grown in sustainable forests. The logging and
manufacturing processes are expected to conform to the
environmental regulations of the country of origin.

ww.orionbooks.co.uk

Chapter One

The vampire looked a beautiful, dangerous cliché. Jet-black hair tied back in a French plait emphasised the pale angles of his face. Shadowed grey eyes stared out with moody promise. Black silk clung to hard abdominals while soft leather stretched down long, lean legs. An ankle-length coat pooled across the stone steps on which he sat so it seemed he existed in his own well of seductive darkness. Behind him, the ferris-wheel silhouette of the London Eye, backlit by exploding fireworks, added a less than subtle suggestion to the scene.

The picture was splashed across the front page of every national newspaper: a celebrity story made more sensational than the norm thanks to the mix of murder and vampires. Other than providing a few moments of idle interest, the news had nothing to do with me.

Or so I thought.

London was in the middle of a late September heat-wave and the bright sunshine blistered hot into the city as I sat at my usual corner table in the Rosy Lea café, staring at the vampire's picture. Outside the tourists that normally thronged Covent Garden huddled in the shade under the stone canopy of St Paul's Church. Even the street entertainers had succumbed to the heat, leaving the expanse of cobbled paving deserted. Inside the empty café was no better. There was no air-conditioning and even with the doors wide open, the hot, heavy air pressed against me as if it were something solid. If nothing else it was peaceful.

I work for Spellcrackers.com – *Making magic safe!* – and

I'd spent a long, frustrating morning chasing pixies through a crowded Trafalgar Square. A pack of them had been attempting to animate the huge bronze lions. The magic was way out of their league of course, but this was their fifth attempt in a month and I had to give them points for persistence if nothing else. Thanks to the pixies, I'd missed lunch, and I'd been hoping for a quick bite before my next job. But Katie, the waitress, had other ideas.

She pulled more papers in front of me. 'Check these out, Genny!'

I cast a long-suffering look over the headlines.

CELEBRITY VAMPIRE ARRESTED IN GIRLFRIEND'S MURDER screamed one. TIME RUNS OUT FOR MR OCTOBER'S DATE was another. And the very snappy, ONE BITE WAS ENOUGH! None of them likely to win any prizes for headline of the year, but they were definitely eye-catching, if only for the font size.

Katie pointed to the picture of the vampire and sighed. 'It's so tragic.' Her fingers stroked her blue heart pendant, the one she always wore. 'Mr October ... isn't he gorgeous? That's the pic they used in the calendar, y'know.'

'Uh-huh,' I muttered. Katie's teenage obsession with vamps was one I didn't participate in.

'The calendar showing all the touristy places?' She nudged me for emphasis. 'Y'know, the vamps dressed up all historical? There was this fab shot of this handsome Cavalier standing in front of Buck House – ooh, and Mr April, the Roman centurion, now he's hot, but not as hot as—'

'Talking of hot,' I interrupted, 'you couldn't get me my orange juice, could you, Katie? I'm dying of thirst here.'

'Ha, Ha. Very funny, Genny.' She swung away to the counter, looking cool in her floaty skirt and strappy top.

Briefly, I closed my eyes. Then, concentrating on that part of me that sees the magic, I *focused* on Katie as she disappeared into the kitchen. A deep cobalt blue shimmered around her in the place I imagined her aura would be if I could actually see it. Relief settled in me. The protective warding spell I'd bought and attached to Katie's heart pendant was as strong as ever. Covent Garden Market is London's Witch Central; you can buy anything, from a bad-hair-day remedy to a noisy neighbour muffler to an anti-Congestion Charge charm – even if the last is illegal. And working there has its advantages, but it still pays to be careful. Upset a witch and they don't just shout at you ... angry red boils is never a good look.

'Isn't this weather just too much?' Katie's voice drifted out into the empty café as she chatted to Freddie, the cook. 'They were saying on the telly it hasn't been this hot for at least ten years, y'know.'

I fanned myself with the menu, the slight breeze disturbing my hair where the short ends stuck to the back of my neck. The cream linen waistcoat I wore was cool enough, but the black trousers had been a mistake. Trouble is, I've never been much for skirts, and shorts just don't have the right professional image. I scanned the café interior, checking for any other stray spells that might be lurking. It took a whole chapter of coven witches – all thirteen of them – to produce a warding complex enough for business premises, and that was way too rich for Freddie's pockets, so, in return for the occasional bacon sandwich, I tidied up on a regular basis instead.

The café was clear of magic, but I glanced down and caught a faint glow coming from my phone. Crap. I snatched up the phone and with a sense of resigned inevitability peered at the thumbnail-sized crystal on the back. A fracture like a black splinter lodged in the crystal's centre. Damn pixies. Even being careful, I'd still managed to *crack* the phone's protection spell when I'd cleared up all their dust. Now I'd risk frying the phone next time I defused a spell if I didn't buy another crystal, and they weren't cheap.

Could my day get any worse?

I dumped the phone on the table and gave the newspapers an irritated look. It wasn't the crystal, although that was bad enough – London is expensive, even with the rent subsidy I got with my job. And it wasn't the weather, my clothes or even the pixies that had me on edge. It was the vampires. They'd deviated from their self-imposed 'politically correct' script. And I hadn't a clue why.

Over the last few years, the vampires had crawled out of their coffins (not that I'd ever known one to actually sleep in a coffin) and brushed the dirt from their public image. They'd poured new blood into British Tourism and transformed the more presentable among themselves into A-list celebs.

It's amazing what a collection of glossy pictures and a no-expense-spared marketing campaign can do. With a steady diet of tourists and infatuated youngsters like Katie satisfying both their physical and financial needs, the vampires pretty much had it all dished up on a plate. Even the current feeding frenzy about the murder had less to do with the accused being a vamp and everything to do with him being a hot property among London's nightlife. I sighed. At least the newest round of government legislation meant sixteen-year-old Katie had another two years before reality could legally sink its fangs into her media-induced crush.

I'd been fourteen when it had happened to me.

I rubbed the phantom throb at the curve of my neck, then dug my fingers into the smooth skin, trying to ease the annoy-ing sensation that the memory had raised. Fourteen was ten years and a different lifetime ago, and the law and the vamps had never been overly concerned when it came to the likes of me.

'Here you go, Genny.' Katie plonked my juice down and lifted another paper.

The juice slipped down my throat and spread a chill through my body instead of the warmth I craved. I'd have to wait until later for that. I flicked a finger at the paper Katie was reading. 'Don't suppose there's any news of my bacon sandwich, is there?'

'Uh-huh,' she muttered, half ignoring me, 'in a sec.'

'Hope you're not expecting a tip,' I added.

'Freddie's doing it.' She gave me a superior look from around the edge of the paper. 'And anyway, Freddie says I'm a much better waitress than you ever were, so there.'

'Means nothing,' I grinned. 'He says that to all the girls.'

Katie sniffed and snapped the paper back up between us.

A quiver of awareness crept across my shoulders. A tall gangly youth not much older than Katie stood in the kitchen doorway, watching. I stared back. He jerked as if I'd burnt him before ducking out of sight.

I shrugged. It's my eyes that do it: amber-coloured, with oval pupils, rather like a cat's. And my hair doesn't help – it's the same odd shade. London has its fair share of fae – and others – living in the city, but even so, my eyes still freak people out. They're the only part of me that doesn't look human.

'Who's the new guy?' I asked.

'Gazza, he's the pot-washer the agency sent. He started yesterday.' She lowered the paper. 'He's a bit of a drip, really. Keeps asking me what sort of stuff I like, y'know, movies, tunes …'

'I wonder why?' I opened my eyes wide in mock surprise.

'Ha. Ha. Anyway, like I'd *so* go out with him.' She wrinkled her nose.

'Course you wouldn't,' I agreed, matter of fact. 'He's not old, hasn't got pointy teeth, and isn't interested in your blood. He's … nice.'

'Well, *I* don't think he's nice.' She bent closer. 'He said he's never seen a faerie before. 'Course, I told him you were sidhe fae, not a *faerie*.' She threw a baleful look behind her, then carried on, 'And Freddie doesn't think he's nice either, I heard him telling Gazza he'd wash his mouth out with soap, it was so dirty. So he's not gonna be here long, anyway.'

I didn't need to ask what else Gazza had been saying. Witches are human, vampires had been human once. But the fae are a different species, like the trolls and the goblins. The humans just lump us together as 'Other'. The less polite call us Freaks or Subs, a nice little abbreviation for sub-human. And we fae are a minority, we're not always pretty, and we're often dangerous. I say we, but even amongst the city's fae community, I'm in a minority of one: the only sidhe living in the whole of London.

And if Gazza's mouth wasn't polluted with prejudice, there was always the other option. The fae are rumoured for their Glamour – or in more prurient terms, faerie sex.

Either way, Gazza wasn't worth the energy it took to notice him. Freddie would sort him out soon enough and Katie wasn't a pushover; I'd seen her dump hot coffee in more than one idiot's lap when he didn't take the hint.

Katie pointed at the newspaper on the top of the pile. A picture of a pretty, smiling brunette covered half the front page. The headline read **VAMPIRE ROBERTO KILLS HIS 'JULIET'**.

'What does that one say about him?'

I unfolded the broadsheet and read snippets from the text. 'It's got some quotes from the undead Lord, the Earl: "crime of passion, regrets the dreadful waste of two such young and promising lives … wants to reassure the public that becoming a vampire is safe … condolences to both their families … full support for the police—"' I looked up at her. 'That sort of thing. Same as all the rest.'

'It's so romantic, isn't it?' she sighed. 'They loved each other so much, y'know, they wanted to be together forever. Only the Gift didn't work and now he's probably gonna die too.'

I snorted. 'Don't be daft, Katie. She probably wasn't his girlfriend at all. He just lost control and then tried to give her the Gift as a cover-up. It's just a PR pitch to make sure the other vamps don't catch any grief over it.' I tapped my finger on the paper. 'Look, she only died yesterday. Last night is too quick for the police to have caught him. I expect the other vamps had him all trussed up ready to go.'

'He didn't try to run. Roberto didn't even know she was dead, Ms Taylor.'

Katie and I both looked up in surprise. A man was standing between us and the entrance. The afternoon sunshine slanting behind him threw him into shadow and for a moment his face appeared a twin for the vampire staring out of the newspaper.

My heart skipped a beat and fear prickled down my spine. Katie gasped, her hand fluttering to my shoulder. Then sense kicked in. *No vamps until after sunset.*

I relaxed slightly as the man stepped forward, his hands clenched at his sides. The navy suit he wore was rumpled, his shirt collar undone and his tie loosened. Grey salted his short dark hair and the lines fanning from his eyes and mouth etched deep into his skin, making him look older than the forty-eight years the papers claimed. Even so, it was obvious where Mr October had inherited his good looks from.

Katie let out a soft breath next to my ear and straightened up.

I looked up at the man, considering – he might be a human but his son was a vampire – it made me want to tell him to go away, to leave me alone, but my father taught me that threats are better dealt with in more practical ways. So instead I asked, 'What do you want, Mr Hinkley?'

His lips thinned briefly, then he took a deep breath. 'I want to hire you, Ms Taylor.'

'Because of this?' I laid my palm on the pile of newspapers. He nodded.

'You're wasting your time. I work for Spellcrackers.com. It's a witch company. Witch Council rules are clear about jobs involving vampires. We don't accept them.'

'I know,' he said, voice quiet and controlled. 'I've already spoken with Stella Raynham. Your boss told me you would be here.'

'I'm surprised she told you where I was?' I made it a question.

'Stella and I know each other,' he said, then paused, letting that statement hang in the air. 'Can I talk to you? Please?'

I shrugged and pushed the newspapers to one side. 'Take a seat. Stella's name means I'll listen, nothing else.'

Katie hovered behind me. 'Tea or coffee?'

He sat down. 'Coffee. Black. Please,' he added belatedly.

She bustled away but not before widening her eyes and silently mouthing an excited *ooh!* behind the man's back.

'You're not a witch, Ms Taylor.'

That's obvious. 'No. I'm not.'

'I know you've worked for Spellcrackers for just over a year, Stella employed you, even though you've never had any known affiliation with the Covens.' He reached out and pushed the salt cellar neatly in line with the pepper pot. 'You're not bound by Witch Council rules.'

'Did Stella tell you that?'

'Not in so many words.'

'Why don't you tell me exactly what Stella *did* say to you, Mr Hinkley?'

'Alan. Please.' He fished in his jacket pocket as he spoke. 'I'm a financial journalist. I did an article on Spellcrackers a couple of months ago, about the proposal to franchise the business.' He laid a newspaper cutting on the table with his by-line under the headline SPELLCRACKERS.COM CRACK THE MAGIC MARKET.

The penny dropped, plugging a large deficit in Stella's publicity budget.

'Okay, I begin to see the picture now. I'm amazed Stella didn't come with you.'

'I asked her not to. I didn't want to put any pressure on you.'

Yeah, right. 'So, Alan, what is it you want me to do?'

He indicated the newspaper picture of the smiling victim. 'I want you to come and see Melissa.'

I frowned, surprised. 'I'm not clear how that's going to help.' Not when Melissa was already dead.

'Roberto and Melissa ...' He shook his head and spoke quietly, almost to himself. 'No, I won't call him that. My son's name is Bobby. Roberto isn't even his given name, it's just the one he took with the Gift.' Moisture glistened in his bloodshot eyes and he blinked it away. 'Bobby and Melissa were going to be married.'

So maybe Katie's romantic notions weren't so far off the mark.

'That's one of the reasons why we want to hire you,' he rushed on. 'Bobby didn't kill Melissa, he couldn't, he loved her, she ... She was a great girl.' He tapped the pepper pot. 'Someone else killed her. We think it's another vampire, but we can't prove it.'

'Who is "we"?'

'Bobby and me.' He grimaced. 'Everyone else is sticking to this ridiculous "doomed lovers" story.'

'What about Bobby's blood family? What do they think?'

The vinegar sloshed as he almost knocked it over. The acrid smell rose between us. 'You're right about that, Ms Taylor. The only aspect of Bobby's current predicament that concerns the vampires is the PR angle.'

I narrowed my eyes. 'Doesn't Bobby have a solicitor looking out for him?'

Alan's lips thinned again. 'I didn't feel confident in the first solicitor. He's a vampire, and I'm not sure he has Bobby's best interests at heart. The one I've hired hasn't dealt with vamps before. Ms Taylor, we need as much help as we can get.'

I didn't disagree, but I didn't want to get involved and so far I'd heard nothing that would make me. 'That still doesn't tell me why you think *I* can help you?'

Alan dropped his gaze to the table. 'My wife died six years ago of a rare blood disease.'

'I'm sorry.' I offered inadequate sympathy.

'Bobby was a teenager when she died, and he went through a rough patch afterwards.' He looked up. 'Now, Bobby is – *was* – training to be a doctor. He thought if he had enough time he could help find a cure, so he accepted the Gift three years ago.' His fingers clamped around the pepper pot. 'I might not agree with his lifestyle choice, Ms Taylor, but he is still my son. He's the only family I have left.'

I looked at him for a moment, then said softly, 'Mr Hinkley – Alan – I'm sorry, but I really can't help you. Even if another vamp did kill Melissa … I find spells, then break or neutralise them. That's all I do.' I didn't like to say but there is nothing magical about a vampire sucking you to death.

He rolled the pepper pot on its edge. 'That's it, though: we want you to look at Melissa and check for magic. The coroner says that the evidence points to just one vampire partner, Bobby, but we think that the other vamp has covered up his bites with a spell.'

Straws and grasping came to mind.

He placed the pepper pot back next to the salt. 'Not only that, you work for the Human, Other and Preternatural Ethics Society at their vampire clinic—'

I interrupted him. 'The clinic's not just for vampire victims. HOPE treats all types of magical attacks.'

'Yes, but you're used to seeing vampire bites, more than the coroner.'

Except the victims I saw were usually still alive.

Alan twirled the vinegar bottle. 'We thought that once you've uncovered the bite, you might be able to identify the other vampire.'

My stomach tightened into a hard knot. 'Mr Hinkley, even if there is another bite hidden by magic, and even if I managed to find it, there is no way I could pinpoint the biter. I doubt even the coroner could do it, not without an actual sample bite to compare it against. And even then, vamp DNA only points to the bloodline, not the individual vampire.'

He looked straight at me. 'But we thought *you* could do it with magic.'

My pulse sped up. I didn't like where he was heading: vampires thinking I could use magic to identify their bites? That along with everything else would *not* be beneficial for my health. 'Then you thought wrong, Mr Hinkley. I can't use magic like that, and I doubt that it's even possible.'

His face fell. Then he tapped his thumbnail against the vinegar bottle, making a tiny tinkling sound, and his mouth twisted into a hard line. 'I can pay you whatever you want.'

I sighed. Not that I couldn't do with the money, but the answer was still no, even with his *association* to Stella. She might have pointed him in my direction, but Stella wasn't about to let one of her employees work for a vampire, even once removed. The witches and vamps 'live-and-let-live' thing started in the fifteenth century – it was one of the more gruesome and sensational parts of history lessons, what with the witch hunts, the inquisition and everything – and anyone who'd been to school could've told Alan Hinkley I wasn't about to say yes to his job. So why was he being so persistent? And why hadn't Stella come with him? Something about that didn't add up. Unless she was leaving it to me to turn him down just so she wasn't made out to be the wicked witch in this sad little scenario. If that was the case, Stella was going to find out I didn't appreciate being cast as the bad-tempered faerie, and soon.

'It's not about money,' I said slowly. 'I don't want any involvement with the vampires. It's one of the main reasons I work for Spellcrackers.com, so I don't have to. Vamps don't give the fae the same respect as they do humans.'

'I'd heard that, but I wanted to talk to you anyway. I'm sure it wouldn't cause you a problem just to look, Ms Taylor. It wouldn't take long.'

I kept my eyes on his, a suspicion forming in my mind. 'What happens if I say no?'

His forehead creased in puzzlement. 'I don't understand.'

'C'mon, Alan: you've waited all day so you can speak to me away from the office. You persuade my boss to let you talk to me, but you don't want to put any pressure on me by having her here while we chat. We've been down the sympathy route.' I leaned forward, took the vinegar bottle from his fingers and lowered my voice. 'Your only son, a vampire, is accused of murder. If he's found guilty, he's not going to sit in jail for the next twenty-odd years. They'll send him to the guillotine, burn his remains and scatter them over running water.' I slammed the vinegar bottle down on the table. 'Why don't you tell me the real reason you think I'm going to help you?'

He flinched and sat back, crossing his arms. 'I'm not the bad guy here, Ms Taylor. I'm just trying to save my son.'

I didn't bother to say anything, just waited for the rest of it.

'Okay,' Alan's shoulders hunched, 'Bobby said to give you a message, but only if you said no. He wouldn't tell me what it meant. He said it was better if I didn't know.' Desperation filled his eyes as he went through some internal struggle, then he spoke again, his voice hard and flat. 'My son wouldn't do anything wrong.'

'Then you'd better give me the message, since I'm supposed to be the one that understands it.'

He glanced round the café, but it was still empty. Even Katie hadn't returned with his coffee yet.

'Siobhan's brother sends his regards,' he said quietly.

Adrenalin rushed through me. The hairs on my arms lifted.

Siobhan's brother.

Fuck, I should've known. What was the bastard playing at this time? Alan was watching me, a horrified expression on his face. 'It is blackmail,' he murmured, almost to himself. 'Bloody hell, what a mess—'

I swallowed, trying to ease the tension in my jaw. 'No, it's not blackmail. Not exactly.'

It might not be blackmail, but I still didn't have a choice. I'd made a bargain, and the fae don't make or break bargains lightly; the magic demands too great a price. But it had never entered my mind that this particular debt would be called in *for* a vampire, rather than one of their victims.

Chapter Two

It was a stubborn, sticky spell, though wrapped around the fridge handle it looked as innocent as a tuft of candyfloss. Except candyfloss doesn't pulse virulent green – spun sugar is *much* more wholesome. I grasped a flimsy strand between my thumb and forefinger and gently pulled. The stench of rotten eggs hit the back of my throat, making me gag. I dropped the magic, watching it curl and twist back into the spell.

'Bad, bad brownie,' I muttered. I tried again, upping my concentration. This time the magic stretched and separated and I let it drift back into the ether.

The job at the swish Kensington bistro was supposed to be an easy one, but thanks to Alan Hinkley's request for help, my mind kept asking questions I didn't have the answers for – like what the fuck was Siobhan's brother up to? And was the *request* really from him? Or had Bobby, aka Roberto, aka Mr October, discovered a secret he shouldn't and decided to use the knowledge for himself? I looked towards my phone, but it wasn't coming up with any answers either. I'd left it near the front door, a safe distance away from the magic, and despite all the messages I'd sent it was disappointingly silent. So failing any sort of reprieve, I was meeting Alan later, at the morgue.

I turned back to the restaurant and made my way through the tables. The air-conditioning hummed like an anxious bee, and gave the place a chilled, cave-like feel. I suppressed a shiver. Low level light makes the spells easier to *see*, and Finn, my co-worker – and future boss, if the rumours were true – had shut the blinds before I'd arrived. I'd have preferred the sunshine.

Gripping the edge of a marble table, I crouched, checking for any tell-tell glows along the floor. Nothing. The black and white tiles were clear. No more magic-induced slips or spell-trapped mice running backwards in frantic circles.

A quick scan of the ornate plastered ceiling revealed no magic lurking in the shadows. I sighed, relieved. The glass-fronted counter running the length of one wall was empty too, no elaborate cream-filled cakes, no hip-expanding pastries, and no lingering nasty leftovers. Hexed or otherwise.

The door to the kitchen swung open, breaking my concentration again, and Finn sauntered through. 'Hell's thorns, that kitchen's a mess.' He stuck his hands in his trouser pockets. 'Manager reckons it's a grouchy customer dropping a spell instead of a tip, at least that's what the brownie's told him.' He shook his head. 'And he believes her.'

I ignored the stupid little leap of pleasure inside me at the sight of him – *so not going there, not when there's no point* – and said, 'Why not? The restaurant's a family business; the brownie's probably been with them for decades ... although it's odd she'd cause this much trouble.' I tapped my fingers against the table. 'Unless it's the manager who's got *her* all miffed and just doesn't want to admit it.'

Finn shrugged, then lifted his arms above his head and stretched gracefully.

Every time I see Finn, I try hard *not* to imagine him with his trousers off. I blame his horns, the office gossip, and my rebellious libido. Finn is a lesser fae, a satyr; his great-great-whatevers were worshipped by the Greeks as one of their gods, Pan, the half-goat, half-man one. Finn's butt looks normal when he's dressed, with not even a hint of a tail or furry thighs, and there's never been a single confirmed rumour to the contrary in all of the three months he'd been with Spellcrackers. Even so, my mind just keeps on—

'How're you doing in here, Gen?' He rubbed one of his horns. They're the colour of dried bracken, sharp and stand a good inch above his wavy blond hair. Add in his poster-boy good looks and Finn should've been an ad-man's wet dream – only the horns mean he doesn't look human enough to sell products to the masses. He had to be wearing a glamour-spell to alter his appearance, but so far I hadn't managed to *see* past it.

'*Cracked* everything except the coffee machine,' I said.

'I could do with a hand in the kitchen when you've finished,' he said with a suggestive grin, 'if you're willing?'

In answer I gave him the look I'd been giving him for the last few weeks, ever since he'd started hitting on me – a half-amused, half-tolerant smile that told him no way did I take his flirting seriously – and then turned my back on him smothering a sigh.

Lifting the counter-top, I *focused* on the machine. The industrial-sized contraption glowed bright enough to cast a sickly orange glare up the wall. The levers were the worst. Of course, it would take only a second to *crack* it rather than tease it apart, but true spellcracking involved blasting the magic – and that also blasted apart whatever the magic was attached to. Collateral damage isn't an option – customers tend to object – so instead I pinched the spell and started to unravel it. Hot steam jetted over my hands and along my arms. Shit. Suppressing a whimper, I shook my hands to get rid of the sensation. The pain was real but the steam wasn't, so there'd be no burns, just the nasty release of power.

'Ouch. That's gotta hurt.' Finn's tone was sympathetic. 'But that's what happens when you take it too fast.'

I snorted. 'Like I don't know that.'

He grinned. ''Course you do, but hey, this is one seriously cranky brownie. Glad it's not me she's pissed off with.'

Gingerly, I poked at the spell. 'Sounds like you're talking from experience.'

'Oh yeah, a whole month's worth.' He winced at the memory. 'Whenever I opened a honey jar, a bee flew out and stung me. Everything I ate tasted burnt, and she hid every single one of my left socks.'

'There's no such thing as a left sock,' I pointed out, delicately unpicking more of the spell. 'They're all the same.'

He laughed. ''Course there is! It's obvious, you always put your right sock on first, so the missing one's got to be the left one.'

'Ha ha.' The magic shredded into tiny filaments under my fingers and finally dissipated. 'So, were you just your usual self or did you do something in particular to annoy her?'

His shoulders lifted in a careless shrug. 'Can't remember now; think it was probably her witch more than the brownie I actually upset.'

Of course, there had to be a witch involved, didn't there? The witches at Spellcrackers had descended on Finn like excited kids playing pass-the-parcel, each of them grabbing to be the next one to unwrap the present when the music stopped. And Finn seemed to be enjoying the party, amazingly keeping everyone happy with his equal-opportunity flirting. I'd been invited to play, but it wasn't an invitation I felt able to accept.

Not that I wasn't attracted. I was, and then some. And there was the whole fae thing going on, which meant the magic was always trying to nudge us together, just to add to the complications. No, my problem was that Finn was almost too appealing. More and more I just wanted to sink my teeth into him, and that was *so* not a good idea. So I swallowed down the disappointment instead and tried hard to keep him at a distance.

He gently touched my hand where the spell had phantom-burnt me. 'Want to talk about what's bothering you?'

I looked up, surprised at the concern in his eyes. 'It's nothing.'

'Yeah? You're usually much more careful with the magic.'

He was right. I was. 'Bad morning,' I said, 'y'know – pixies, and then I managed to crack the crystal on my phone.'

'Ah.' He gave me a thoughtful look for a moment and

then smiled. 'Problem solved then. I just found a new crystal supplier on eBay. The initial quality's good and the prices are reasonable. I'll tell Toni to sort you one out as a trial.'

A pretty gift-horse yawned in front of me, but I ignored it in favour of having my distraction work. 'That's great,' I said, 'thanks.'

Finn dropped a casual arm round my shoulders. 'Heard the latest gossip? Stella left early, supposedly for the Council meeting, but Toni thinks she's got a fancy man.' His breath warmed my hair. 'Apparently he's been on the phone three times this morning and wouldn't give his name, just said Stella'd know who he was.' The faint scent of blackberries curled around me. 'But Toni says she's sure she recognises his voice.'

I slid out from under his arm before I let myself get too comfortable. If Stella was at a Witches' Council meeting, that explained why she was ignoring my messages, and it didn't take much for me to guess who Toni, our office manager, had been talking about.

Finn lent against the counter and winked at me. 'She's certain it's that journalist chap who interviewed Stella. Tall, dark, good-looking. Don't suppose you saw him, did you?'

I gave him a teasing look. 'Worried about competition in your little witch harem, are you?'

He chuckled. 'Hell's thorns, Gen, he's human. Where's the competition?' His face turned sly. 'Just wondering whether Tall, Dark and Handsome is your type as well as Stella's.'

'Don't wander, it doesn't lead anywhere.'

'Don't worry, I know to stay on the path.' He reached for my hand and traced a finger across my palm. 'C'mon, Gen, can't blame me for being curious. I'm a fertility fae.' His thumb stroked gently over my wrist, causing my pulse to throb. 'And you're sidhe fae, your heart beats for passion. Imagine what music we could make: the very birds and bees would sing along with joy.' He lowered his voice. 'It would be a grand opera, rich enough to rival Mozart.'

Laughing, I twisted my hand free, stuck two fingers in my mouth and *accked*. 'Pleeeease! Don't tell me that works? That is soooo bad!'

He grinned, teeth white and even against his tan. 'What do you think?'

'No, that's just too awful to contemplate.' I shook my head. 'All those witch groupies you've got hanging around, they actually fell for that?'

He spread his arms wide. 'What can I say, I'm a sex god.'

'Ha!' I poked him in the chest. 'In your dreams.'

His face turned serious. 'Just one question, though?'

I narrowed my eyes. 'What?'

He leaned in close and murmured against my cheek, 'You ever seized the magic at midnight and danced across the stars?'

My breath caught. Shit. He was too close. Anticipation spiralled deep inside me. I could almost taste the ripe blackberry juice bursting on my tongue.

Finn moved back, far enough to study my face. His moss-green eyes filled with male satisfaction. 'One night, Gen.'

I bit down hard until the copper tang of blood filled my mouth and I swallowed. 'Don't tempt me, Finn.'

'Always.' He tucked a strand of hair behind my ear.

I forced myself to move away and laughed, needing to end the serious mood. 'You know what they say about wishes?'

'Wait.' He held up a hand, then gave me a wicked grin. 'Oh yeah, it's too late once the wish comes true.'

I nodded. 'Remember that.'

'I wasn't making a wish, Gen.' He crooked a finger at me. 'That was a promise.' He twirled the finger like he was reeling me in. 'Wishes have to be granted.' I felt a sharp pull deep in my centre as though hooked on the thorny stems of bramble. 'Promises on the other hand' – he touched his lips to his palm, eyes never leaving mine – 'when given' – he blew me the kiss – 'are a sure thing.'

Fuck. 'Don't bet on it.'

Finn smiled but his eyes were sombre. 'Too late.'

A popping noise followed by an irritated cough sounded from behind my head.

'Mebbe when thee and himself have finished blathering, an ole biddy could get a wee word in?'

The brownie sat like a well-dressed doll on top of the coffee machine, her leather ankle boots stuck straight out at right angles from beneath the floral smock she wore. Huge brown eyes glared down at us out of a sandstone-coloured face and little tufts of brown hair sprouted angrily over her scalp.

The sensible part of me was glad of the interruption.

'I think she wants to talk to you,' Finn muttered. 'I'll be in the kitchen.' Tipping his head at the brownie he retreated faster than a troll who's cornered a cat.

The brownie's round face screwed up into a disapproving scowl, her button nose almost disappearing into dried-peach-like wrinkles. 'Himself had better keep his hands offa *ma* wean, else he'll lose more than the odd sock.' She jumped down to stand on the counter: a bristling two-foot-high guard-nanny. 'And thee better take care yerself, thee's supposed to do the courting, not him.'

I got what she was saying, my mind automatically translating 'wean' into 'child' thanks to a year living in Scotland when I was nine. If her wean was pretty and female and no longer childlike, then Finn had already found her. And as for courting – dating – Finn really didn't need any encouragement from me in that department.

My earlier suspicions clicked. I gave her an enquiring look. 'This is all for my benefit, is it? You could have phoned, you know.'

She fisted her hands on her hips. 'Don't hold with those new-fangled mechanicals. Anyhows' – she smiled smugly – 'you're here now.'

No arguing with that. 'So, what's the problem?'

Her smock billowed as she leapt to the floor and held out her hand. 'Agatha Brown, Lady.'

I placed my palm in hers and an old familiar comfort swept over me, like snuggling under cosy covers on a cold winter's night. I crouched next to her. 'Do I know you?'

Her small rosebud mouth parted in a sigh. 'A brownie's touch goes to them that needs it and is ne'r forgotten.' She shook her head. 'Weren't maself, though, would have bin one of ma sisters.'

She cupped my cheek in her small hand and as she did so, the memory returned. I was six. The latest nanny stood over me, her face flushed red, anger spewing from her like vomit.

We'd moved to an old country mansion and it had one of those stone food safes in the kitchen, a heavy wooden lid covering an ancient hole in the floor. Inside was cold and black. And when I stopped screaming, and started listening, it was full of odd scratching noises. I wanted someone to come for me, my father, or any of them, but it was daylight and they were all sleeping like the dead. Then a small hand crept into mine, offering comfort. I've never been afraid of the dark since.

Agatha's large brown eyes were full of anger and compassion as she shook her head. She'd shared something of my memory. I stood quickly, breaking the connection.

The nanny had taken to leaving me in the hole nearly every day, but that small warm hand was always there. Of course, one day the nanny left me there past sunset and my father found me. We moved again that night. We were always leaving somewhere.

Later, I realised he must have killed the woman.

But then he always was a practical bastard when it came to keeping his secrets safe.

I smiled at Agatha, accepting the obligation along with the manipulation. 'Want to tell me why I'm here?'

Her forehead creased into a worried frown. 'It's ma wean, she's awfy poorly—'

The sound of breaking crockery interrupted her and she rushed away through the service doors into the kitchen. I followed her, and we found Finn and the manager staring down at a pile of shattered china plates.

Damn. Looked like Finn had tried *cracking* a spell.

'Mr Andros, this is not what I had in mind when I hired your company.' The manager prodded the pile with the shiny toe of his shoe. 'I expected a quick professional clear-up of the mess. That is what your company guarantees.' He made a point of looking at his watch. 'I have customers in less than an hour.'

Finn threw a malevolent glance towards Agatha, who sniffed and headed for a half-open doorway at the back of the kitchen.

I left Finn to handle the apologies. Whatever the problem was, it wasn't going to go away until Agatha got what she wanted.

The door led to a small staff area furnished with a table, a couple of battered chairs and a row of lockers. Agatha stood, hands clasped, chewing her lip next to a young woman sprawled over the table. 'Ma wean, Holly.'

Holly wore the standard waitress uniform, white blouse and black skirt. She'd abandoned her shoes on the floor and with her head buried in her arms, all I could see was a mass of dark curls that tumbled over the table like tangled vines.

'Go away, Aggie.' The words were muffled by their passage through all that hair. 'Nothing's wrong. Jus' leave me alone.'

'Herself's here, ma bonny.'

'I don't want to see anyone,' Holly wailed.

Aggie tentatively stroked the girl's shoulder. 'Please, Holly,' she entreated.

Holly jerked upright, her face blotchy from crying. 'Get out,' she snarled at Agatha, baring small green triangular teeth. 'You always ruin everything!'

Agatha's expression turned determined and she grabbed

Holly's wrist, holding it out for me to see. 'She would'nae go to the clinic. Tuesday night it happened, an' I've bin worrid stoopid, what with the news an' all.'

Holly snatched her hand back, though not before I spotted the half-healed vampire bite, and burst into fresh tears.

Now I knew why Agatha had booby-trapped the restaurant with spells: this wasn't a magical problem, but one I dealt with every week at the HOPE clinic. Getting Fanged was the current hot fashion for that all important coming-of-age celebration and as a result, we had a constant parade of youngsters dragged in by worried parents once they realised where, and with whom, their offspring had been out partying the night away.

I nodded at Agatha. 'Why don't you leave us to talk to each other?'

Agatha's shoulders sagged with relief and she disappeared with another audible pop.

Holly glared at the vacant space. 'Don't you be listening either, Aggie,' she shouted at the empty air.

Chapter Three

I sat across from Holly and waited while she wiped her tears. She was a faeling, part fae, part human. I couldn't tell what type of fae blood she carried, but her ancestry was evident in her delicate, angular bone structure as well as her teeth.

She hiccoughed, then ran her fingers through her hair, pulling it back from her face. As she did heart-shaped earrings flashed like blue stars against the black.

'You might as well give in,' I said. 'She's not going to stop until you do.'

Holly pouted as she draped her hair over one shoulder. She tucked a strand in the corner of her mouth and muttered, 'She thinks I'm still ten or something.'

'Uh-huh.' I smiled, encouraging confidences.

'Just because I want to go out with my friends, she gets all het up about it.'

'It's not your friends she's worried about.'

Holly glanced at her wrist and shuddered.

'Pretty earrings,' I said.

Her hand half-lifted to her left ear and a wary look flickered across her face.

'I've never been to the Blue Heart,' I said. 'Is it any good?'

'S'okay.' Only she didn't sound too sure.

'Just okay?' I smiled again. 'I thought it was supposed to be the cool place.'

'It was pretty cool.'

'But not all of it?'

Holly lifted her feet onto the chair and wrapped her arms

around her legs. 'Trace and Lorraine thought it was cool.' She rested her chin on her knees, looked at me with disappointed green eyes and held out her wrist. 'Only it hurt when he bit me. It's not supposed to hurt, is it? It didn't hurt Trace and Lor.'

A crash sounded from the kitchen and Holly flinched. Voices rose and fell like angry waves after the brief silence.

I took her hand in mine and rotated her wrist. Two neat holes an inch apart were just about healed over. 'The vampire tricked their minds, made them think it felt nice. Not many of them can do that to you, because you're faeling.'

She frowned. 'He said it was because he wasn't a very old vampire.' She drew her wrist back and plucked at a thread hanging from her skirt. 'He was nice, he stopped as soon as it hurt. Only' – a tear spilled down her cheek – 'I've been feeling tired and a bit dizzy, and having bad dreams.'

Other than the bad dreams, it sounded like post-bite anaemia, but just the neat fang marks on her wrist wouldn't have caused that.

'You need to show me the other bites, Holly.'

Surprise crossed her face and her chin trembled. Then she pushed aside her shirt collar, angling her head away, displaying two more fang marks puncturing the curve between her neck and her shoulder.

'And that's all, just two bites?'

'Yes.' But as she spoke, she glanced down and I knew she wasn't telling me everything.

'Holly, if you want me to tell Aggie everything's okay, you need to show me all the bites.' I bent and peered into her face. 'I won't tell her where they are, okay?'

The metallic bangs and crashes echoing around the kitchen sounded like a dwarf workshop had taken up residence. What was Finn trying to do? Wreck the place?

Holly squirmed, then unbuttoned her blouse.

The vampire had sunk his teeth into the swell of her breasts, just above the lace edge of her bra, and he hadn't been nearly as neat or careful here. Two bites marked her left breast, the holes puckered, skin white and crinkly where he had fed for some time. He'd made a real mess of her right breast. Half-healed inch-long scabs and mottled bruises showed where his fangs had scored through her flesh … almost as if the vamp had been ripped away from her.

I ignored the throb that leapt into life at the back of my own neck. *Bastard sucker.* All I said was, 'Ouch, that must've hurt too.'

Holly looked down at herself. 'Only a little. I felt sorta weird and fuzzy by then.'

At least the bites looked like sucker bites. The vamp had fed, but hadn't tried infecting her. Of course, 3V – Vampire Venom and Virus Infection – isn't the big bad any more; treatment's been available for the past twenty-odd years. And there was that BBC 'Bat on The Wall' documentary a couple of years ago, with its backdoor propaganda that 3V could be the modern elixir of youth and health. The internet hyped the 'benefits' like a particularly virulent game of cyber whispers. Now 3V is actually considered desirable by some, so much so that the public don't want to know that the majority of infected 'human companions' – the current PC label for a vampire's blood-slave or blood-pet, don't live long and healthy lives as advertised, but end up as short-lived 'disposables' in some blood-pub in Sucker Town.

All they're interested in is the Gift.

According to myth, the original Gift was the Gorgon's blood, given by Athena to Asclepius, the Greek god of healing, to help him in his work. Then Asclepius started raising people from the dead, and Zeus took exception, as überGods do, and killed him with a thunderbolt. The sun god Apollo, Asclepius's dad, wasn't too happy either, and he set about rectifying his son's mistakes by burning the undead to a crisp whenever he could find them. Even so, most feel that drinking blood, staying out of storms and doing without the suntan are easy enough sacrifices to make if it means they might hit the immortality jackpot in the game of vampire roulette.

But neither the government, nor the witches, nor – especially – the vampire hierarchy want the place overrun with baby blood-suckers, so the Gift is strictly controlled. It means the tourist clubs are safe enough: after all, when the punters are not just paying but queuing for the privilege of being the *plat du jour*, there's no need to turn your victims into venom junkies to ensure your next meal. All it takes is some mental sleight of hand, or *mesma*, to convince the customers they're getting what they want. After all, anything else would be bad for business.

Only Holly was a faeling, and fae blood, even diluted with human, is a sought-after commodity within the vampire world. I needed to be sure she wasn't infected.

'Holly, you've heard of 3V, haven't you?'

She pulled out a leaflet hidden under a magazine on the table. 'I checked the bites against the photos in the HOPE leaflet.' She opened the leaflet and showed me the pictures. 'See, two holes is okay, you only have to worry about infection if there's four holes, two tiny extra ones in between. That's what it looks like if they bite you with their retractable fangs as well.' She briefly touched the bruises on her breast. 'All of us, we've only got two fang marks. Trace got a magnifying glass out and we checked each other out to make sure,' she finished in a disappointed tone.

'That's great, then,' I said eyes wide to keep the bemused look from my face. 'Nothing to worry about: the bites are healing and once you make up the blood loss, the dizziness should stop and you'll feel better.'

She held out her wrist again with an anxious expression. 'But what about this one?'

The kitchen produced a hissing noise that sounded like a steam-dragon running riot and Finn's curse sounded distinctly frustrated.

I frowned at the neat bite. 'It's fine, better than the others. Should be gone in a couple of days.'

She leaned forward and whispered, 'But *he* did them, y'know, the vampire that's been in all the papers. The one that— the one that killed his girlfriend.'

'Roberto? You mean Mr October?'

She gave a tiny nod. 'Aggie's worried because they've arrested him. The papers say all it took was one bite, and she thinks— Am I going to die too?' Her voice rose, shrill with panic.

I began mentally revising my offer to help the bastard. 'Did he do all the bites?'

'Oh no, I told you, Roberto was really nice. This French vamp, Louis, did the others.' She touched her bruises again. 'Roberto shouted at him and dragged him away. Trace said they both looked really mad.' She tossed her hair back. 'Roberto bought us all those fruit cocktails, the special ones they do, and made sure we got a taxi home.' Her face fell. 'Do you think I'm going to die like his girlfriend?'

'Genny?'

I looked up as Finn appeared in the doorway. Holly squeaked, clutching her blouse to hold it together.

'Sorry, ladies, I'll wait outside.' Finn held his hands up in apology and grinned, then sent me a questioning look. 'I could do with some help out here, Gen, when you're ready.'

'Okay. I'll be with you in a sec.' I turned back to Holly and lowered my voice. 'Listen, one bite from Roberto won't kill you. You mustn't believe everything the papers say. But keep away from the vampires.' I leaned forward. 'Vamps think our fae blood tastes nicer, sweeter, than plain human blood, and some of them won't take no for an answer. I'd stick to going out with humans or fae if I were you. It's less dangerous.'

Holly sighed. 'He – Louis – said I tasted like cherries. He said he liked me best of all.' She bit her lip. 'Human boys don't always— My teeth scare them, or if I like them, they end up ... y'know, Glamoured.'

I knew exactly how she felt. Rocks and hard places had nothing on dating humans if you were a fae or even a faeling with a touch of power.

'Listen, Holly, the bites are fine. You're not going to die. I'll tell Aggie.' I dug a card out of my bag. 'And if you want to talk or anything, just give me a ring, okay?'

I left her chewing a curl of hair and went to find Finn.

He leant against the wall outside the staffroom, hands in his pockets and a disgruntled expression on his face. 'I tried to talk Agatha into clearing up the mess, but she says she's too low on juice to do anything.'

I grinned. 'Feeling stressed, are we?'

'She's got her wretched spell-traps everywhere,' he groaned, 'and every time I try to *crack* one, something else breaks.'

'Uh-huh,' I said sweetly, 'that's what happens when you go too fast.'

'Yeah, touché, Gen.' He pushed away from the wall and slung an arm around my shoulder. 'It's gonna take ages to unravel all the spells. Mr Manager is as grumpy as a blingless goblin.' His voice took on a cajoling tone. 'Don't suppose you could do something, could you?'

'Maybe.' I sighed, thinking about gift-horses bearing crystals. 'But only if you stop using my shoulder as an arm-rest.'

'Whatever my Lady's heart desires.' He gave me a quick hug, then opened his arms wide, a lazy grin twitching the corners of his mouth.

I rolled my eyes at him. Damn. I so knew I was going to regret this – give in once to him, even if it was over something as simple as work – and the next thing I'd find myself sitting in a painful heap at the bottom of the slippery slope.

And if I was going to clear up all the spells in one go, I needed to find them. There were only a couple of lights on in the kitchen but I turned them off so that the only illumination came from the red electronic numbers that blinked on some of the equipment. I took a deep breath, closed my eyes and *focused*.

Shit. There was more magic than I thought. Way, waaay more.

Opening my eyes confirmed it. The room popped and seethed with pulsing fluorescence like a volcanic swamp covered in fireflies. My heart leapt, apprehension warring with anticipation. No wonder Finn had been having so much trouble *cracking* the stuff. Agatha must have gathered every ounce of her anger, frustration and fear for this many spells. I glanced over at where she stood with Holly in the staffroom doorway, dim misted light wrapping itself around them from the room beyond. She clasped Holly's hand tightly, her huge brown eyes gleaming with relief and gratitude as she inclined her head in a small bow. For an instant, something odd nagged at me, then the kitchen claimed my full attention.

I cupped my palms in front of me and *called* the magic.

Power filled my hands, rushing into me. Wind lifted my hair, heat suffused my body, millions of tiny sharp needles stung my skin. The magic gripped me, flung my arms wide, arched my spine, lifted my feet from the ground. I hung suspended, head thrown back, mouth gasping air into my protesting lungs. Black dots danced before my eyes. Pleasure and pain streamed through me in one long scream as the last drop of magic slammed me to the floor.

I wrapped my arms around my head and curled into a tight ball. Less than a minute passed while the magic bubbled with exhilaration though my blood, chasing away the residual aches and soreness, leaving my heart pounding. A burst of golden light spread out from my skin, shimmering soft and dew-like before dissipating in the air.

Who knew brownie magic could feel so good?

'I heard you could do that.' Finn spoke close to my ear, his voice tinged with satisfaction. 'Absorb the magic, instead of *cracking* it or just pulling it apart.'

I rolled limply onto my back, the most movement I could manage with the power still settling inside me, and found him kneeling next to me. I gazed up at him. Tiny emerald flecks flared deep in the moss-green of his eyes. Speculation flickered across his features. And there was something else, some other emotion ... respect maybe, or awe?

'Genny?' His tone was soft and low.

'What?' I murmured, fascinated by the way his mouth moulded my name.

'How much magic can you *call*?' He bent over me, warm berry-scented breath caressing my face. 'More than this?'

I frowned, his questions confusing, unexpected. A thought pricked through the last haze of the power high: *this* had been a lot of magic. But before I could pin my vague suspicion down, Finn scooped me into his arms, stood and held me tucked tight against him.

Adrenalin and need shot through me. 'What the fuck do you think you're doing?' I snarled, pushing my hand against his chest, feeling his heart thump beneath my palm.

'Hell's thorns, Gen, what d'you think I'm doing? That was a lot of juice you took.' Hurt flickered on his face, then it was gone and he grinned. 'I'm only trying to help you, my Lady.'

'Fine. Well put me down. I can stand on my own, thank you.' I glared at him. 'And cut out the "my Lady" crap too.'

'No problemo,' he said cheerfully and placed me on my feet. I decided maybe I'd imagined his hurt look.

Ignoring him, I dusted myself down as best I could, trying to catch the odd thought I'd had, only it was quite gone.

A polite cough behind me made me turn. Agatha stood there, hands clasped primly in front of her, eyes staring somewhere past my knees. Holly hovered behind her, a green toothy grin spread across her face. At least someone was enjoying the show. Mr Manager had a slightly stunned expression on his face, but he must have been one of those humans who just take magic in their stride, or maybe blank it completely, as Finn cornered him easily enough with the paperwork.

'Maself is glad thee came to our aid, Lady.' Agatha twisted her fingers, but didn't look up at me.

I crouched down. 'I was pleased to aid you, Aggie.' She looked up and I caught a glimpse of fear in her eyes. 'Holly's going to be fine.' I patted her shoulder, but when she flinched, I realised I was the cause of her fear, not Holly.

Damn. Nothing like a magical exhibition to let you know your place in the world.

I told Finn I'd wait outside whilst he finished up with Mr Manager.

Standing on the hot pavement, staring at the clear blue of the sky, I let the heat of the day burn away the air-conditioned chill of the restaurant. The magic fizzed and churned restlessly inside me. I dug into my bag and pulled out three liquorice torpedoes, stuffed them into my mouth and crunched down hard, shuddering as the sugar hit my system. The magic ate it up – the sugar makes it easier to control – and I willed it into a sleepy calm.

The trees along the edge of the road rustled in the slight breeze as Finn strolled out and joined me. 'Remind me not to take a brownie job again,' he said, a hint of laughter in his voice.

'If I remember right, *you* didn't.' I teased, but my heart wasn't in it. 'This was *my* job. *You* just came along for the fun of it.'

He stepped in front of me, close enough that I had to look up at him. 'Not for fun, Gen.' He traced a finger along my jaw, an intent, almost hopeful expression in his eyes. 'To get to know you better.'

I dropped my gaze to the base of his neck, my mouth watered and I had to stifle the urge to place my lips on the smooth tanned skin that stretched over his pulse. Shit. The need was getting stronger, less easy to deny. And I didn't know why. But why wasn't the problem here. I took a step back, holding up my hands.

'Not biting, Finn.' Mentally I rolled my eyes at my own Freudian slip.

'Speaking of biting, that was rather interesting, what you told the little faeling.'

'What did I tell her?'

'About how we fae taste to vampires.' His eyes lit up. 'Wonder what flavour you would be?'

'I already told you, don't wander. You'll only get lost.'

'Yeah, yeah.' He looked at me speculatively. 'Oranges, maybe,' he mused.

'Red hair? Oranges?' I huffed, striding off. 'You've got to be kidding. *Soooo* not original.'

Finn matched his pace to mine. 'You're right; oranges are much too ordinary. Umm, what would ... Figs maybe? Now they're supposed to be sexy.' Shaking his head, he slid an arm round my waist and pulled me to a stop, smiling. 'Ah, got it – sweet, exotic, hard knobbly shell – gotta be passion fruit.'

I gave him my hard knobbly elbow in his ribs. It connected with a satisfying thud.

'Speaking of food,' Finn gasped as he bent double, 'how about dinner?'

Only if he was on the menu. I shook my head. It wasn't even a euphemism. I had a moment's fantasy where I said yes: we went out, had fun, and I *didn't* spend the evening wanting to rip into his throat. Then I sighed and came back to live in the real world. No way could I go out with him, or any other fae, not with 3V running riot through my veins. Being fae, Finn would feel its taint in me – if I let him get too close – then he'd run for the nearest faerie hill, not to mention I'd be out of a job.

He caught up with me. 'C'mon Gen, you've got to stop torturing me like this.' With a rueful smile he rubbed a hand over his stomach, then winked. 'Or at least say yes, then you can do whatever you want with me.'

Way too enticing. 'Finn, you're a nice guy, but ...' I trailed off as disappointment darkened his eyes, echoing my own silent regret, then I made myself carry on. 'I'm sorry, but getting personal is not—'

A stiff wind hurled itself along the road, snatching the words from my mouth and rushing up through the branches above us.

Finn placed a finger on my lips, silencing me.

I moved back. 'Look, I'm really not—'

'Genny, it's okay.' He half-smiled. 'I get that you've said no, but it's not that.' He waved an anxious hand at the road. 'It's the trees. I think they're talking about you.'

Another gust whipped past us and the canopy of autumn leaves rustled almost like they were laughing.

I frowned and looked at Finn. 'What are they saying?'

'Hell's thorns, Gen, how should I know? I never learned the language.'

Chapter Four

Dusk coloured the sky like a purple bruise as I headed for my meeting with Alan Hinkley at Old Scotland Yard Police Station, the headquarters for the Metropolitan Police's Magic and Murder Division. The bodies of vampire attacks, like Melissa's, are contained in the specialised basement morgue ever since the mandatory fourteen-day waiting period came into force – just in case they spontaneously do the Lazarus thing. Old Scotland Yard is also the one-stop-cop-shop for vampires. Keeping a vamp incarcerated is difficult enough without adding humans into the mix. The only time it was tried – back in the eighties when the vamps were *reclaiming* their human rights – the riot lasted a week and a vampire ended up on an impromptu bonfire, together with a prison guard and three other inmates.

That the vampire was proved innocent, post-death – a tarnished silver lining or a kamikaze-inspired martyrdom, depending on your point of view – became the catalyst for all sorts of changes.

As I turned off Whitehall, leaving the noise of the traffic behind, a horse's high-pitched whinny made me jump – Old Scotland Yard is also home to the Met's horses – and I slowed, uneasy in the quiet. A tree rustled as I passed it. Was Finn right, were they talking about me? But why would they? Then the leaves of the next tree stirred and the air trembled in response. Goosebumps rose on my skin, even though the heat of the day hadn't dissipated with the night and I looked up into the branches, but they were empty. I blew out a breath.

Damn. I usually avoided being out after dark like this, trees or no trees. You never knew who you might bump into.

I lifted my bag over my head, settled the strap across my chest to free my hands and slowly walked under the archway that led to Old Scotland Yard. Alan Hinkley was waiting by the police station door. Along the pavement, the street lights created pockets of shadow. As I got closer, one shadow was darker, more solid than the others. My heart tripped and I stopped, staring into the blackness.

The vampire stepped out into the light and stared back.

His appearance was almost a relief.

I played statues, counting under my breath, using my own will to force my pulse to a slow steady thump. It was harder to pull off than I thought. Damn, I was so out of practice. Instinct shouted at me to flee. *Bad idea.* Never run from a vamp, gets them too excited, all that blood pumping faster and faster. Better to take the gamble that they won't attack and wait until they're gone. Of course, that attitude does have its minus points.

'Genevieve Taylor.' His chin lifted as he scented the air.

His accent carried a touch of something, not English. Black hair curled into his neck, even blacker eyes glinted, their almond shape hinting of the East. His face was the prettiest I'd ever seen, alive or undead, and a distant part of me wondered why it wasn't plastered over every billboard in town. And why I'd never seen him before.

I shook my head even as I thought it. It didn't matter who he was, not when I could feel his *mesma* brushing against my mind. I looked past him to Alan, but the blank look he wore had 'vampire mind-lock' written all over it. No help there then, not that I had really expected any. In fact, he was going to be more a hindrance if there was going to be a fight.

'Perhaps Mr Hinkley should wait inside?' I said, keeping my voice steady.

Alan turned and disappeared through the door without the

vampire so much as twitching. I was impressed despite myself, and had to concentrate even more to keep my pulse at its slowest beat.

'How interesting.' His voice rolled around me, as rich as sugar-dusted Turkish delight, making my mouth water.

I tilted my head to one side. 'Not from where I'm standing.'

The vampire had obviously been young when he'd accepted the Gift, near my own age. His suit was ubiquitous vampire-black, but he must have pulled the darkness around him to hide his pale face and hands. Even without the evidence of Alan's departure, that trick alone told me he was old, over five hundred, at least. And he looked like he belonged to the classic Armani style rather than the excess of black leather that the younger vamps preferred – not that I could be sure without checking the designer labels, but I wasn't planning on getting that close.

'Your eyes are truly remarkable.' Smooth silk slipped along my skin as his gaze swept over me.

Damn vampire mesma. I gritted my teeth and tried to block it.

'Your website picture does you an injustice. You are so much more in the flesh and ... blood.'

'Sorry I can't return the sentiment.'

He gently shook his head. 'Tut tut, Genevieve.' He took a step towards me. 'You really don't mean that. Not when I have been waiting especially for you.'

I hardened my voice. 'Then you've wasted your time. My visit's with the police, not you.'

He took another step, fast, calculated to spook me. I swallowed hard, but held my ground. He stopped within touching distance. Long slim fingers brushed a lock of hair from his forehead while he studied me. 'Intriguing.' Half-closed eyes gave him a sleepy, enigmatic look. 'Why would you involve yourself in something not your affair?'

'It's really none of your business.'

'But that's where you're wrong, Genevieve.' The words drifted lazy and sweet through the air. 'You see, this really is my business. I am tasked with bringing this little episode to a satisfactory conclusion for all concerned. I will do better without your ... help.'

When what he had said sank in, rather than the dream of his voice, surprise tumbled through me, banishing the feeling of languor that had seeped into my bones. 'Who says your conclusion would be satisfactory for everyone?'

He grinned, letting me glimpse fang, a push of *mesma* inviting me to go along with the joke. 'Why, I do, of course.'

'Uh-huh.' I nodded slowly. 'Sounds good.' I gave him a smile. A wide happy beam of a smile.

Satisfaction lit his face, but before he could speak, I dropped the smile. 'Only it doesn't sound *quite* good enough.' I winked. 'But hey. Nice try.'

He laughed, and the sound bubbled through me like champagne. I shivered even as sweat trickled down my spine. I gripped the strap of my bag with both hands, holding it like a life-line, concentrating on keeping him out of my mind. The longer he talked, the more the back of my neck throbbed, reminding me I was more vulnerable than usual.

'Genevieve.' He shrugged an elegant shoulder. 'What are we to do now?'

I stared at him, surprised. 'You're asking me?'

He indicated the police station. 'Once you walk through that door, you make yourself defenceless.'

For a moment part of me actually felt he cared. I bit the inside of my mouth, hard, to banish the feeling.

'You dispense with all that wonderful witch protection you have carefully cultivated.' He spread his hands wide. 'You are fair game.'

'Tell me something I *don't* know.'

'Are you so eager to offer your blood?'

'What do you think?'

'Such bravado.' He glanced at the door again, a vague anxiety in the action. 'But even your sidhe magic will not shield you from some amongst us.'

'Are you done yet? Because so far I'm not hearing anything new.'

He sighed, the sound coating me with remorse. 'Go home, Genevieve, while you still can.'

'What? Just leave?' I stopped strangling the strap of my bag and clenched my fists, digging my nails into my palms, determined to resist the impulse he'd given me to go home. 'When you haven't even threatened me yet?'

Something dark and sad appeared in his eyes, then it was gone, hidden by the same enigmatic look as before.

'Threats … Coercion … Violence.' The words hung like blades in the still air. 'Is that what you would want?'

I froze, pulse speeding up, unable to move or speak, gazing into his eyes. A voice screamed in my mind, yelling at me to break his *mesma*, but another part of me wanted, desperately *needed*, whatever he was offering.

Cool fingers circled my left wrist and lifted my still clenched fist between us. My hand moved, seemingly of its own volition, opening like a flower before the sun. Blood welled in the half-moon marks across my palm, bright against my skin.

'May I?' His eyes echoed the silken seduction in his voice.

My lips parted in a sigh as my head bowed in submission.

Anger flashed across his face and his fingers squeezed, the bones in my wrist grating with the pain. 'Say. It.'

'Yes,' I breathed.

For an instant his pupils glowed red and my heart fluttered with sudden terror, then he dipped his head. I gazed at the line of his jaw, the long dark lashes, the sleek silk of his hair where it curled round the intricate whorl of his ear, its lobe pierced through, a single gem black against his pale skin. His lips caressed my palm, a shudder rippled through his body and

I felt an answering shimmer resonate through my own. My eyes closed as he licked hot lines along my hand. Sharp fangs scraped my wrist and chill air kissed my bare skin.

Leaves rustled in the stillness and a horse whinnied from the nearby stables, startling me out of my reverie.

I opened my eyes to an empty street.

The vampire was gone.

I stared down at my palm. The cuts from my nails had disappeared, healed over as though they'd never been. A bracelet of bruises around my wrist was the only evidence of his presence.

'Genevieve.' My name whispered through the breeze.

I swung round fast, searching, then stopped, muscles trembling as the terror hit me again.

Fuck.

I hugged myself, breathing in the scent of spice and liquorice that fragranced the air, trying to ignore the sharp, craving ache inside me. Why had he gone? And why had he been angry when I'd offered him my blood? It didn't make sense.

'Ms Taylor?'

I jerked again, spinning towards the voice.

Alan stood holding the door to the police station open. He said something, but I couldn't hear past the pulse thundering in my ears.

Damn vampire. If he thought he'd scared me enough to stop me …

I took a deep breath, rubbed my hands along my arms to smooth the goosebumps, and walked up the steps into the police station.

Chapter Five

'There's a bit of a hitch here,' Alan said anxiously. 'I'm not sure you're going to be able to see Melissa's body tonight.'

'Why not?' I asked, then frowned. Was the vamp still playing with Alan's mind? I reached out, laid my hand over his and sent a tendril of magic into him.

Alan started. 'What are you doing, Ms Taylor?'

'Checking,' I muttered.

His hand was warm, the skin a little rough under my palm, his pulse was faster than normal, but the tangled net of his thoughts told me he was free of the mind-lock. Whatever commands the vampire had given him were done.

I flashed him a relieved smile and gave his hand a quick squeeze. 'Why don't we go inside and you can tell me what the trouble is.'

Alan wrapped his fingers round mine, as if seeking reassurance. 'You will help, won't you?'

I eased out of his hold and patted his arm. 'Yes, as much as I can.' An odd need to hug him and tell him everything would be all right came over me.

He stepped closer. 'Bobby's my son.' Desperation flooded into his face. 'He's all I've got left. I don't know what I'd do—'

'Shhh.' My heart ached for him and I reached up and cupped his face. Golden light spread from between my fingers, pulses of pink and orange flashing through it. The night air filled with the scent of honeysuckle.

Pinpricks of gold sparked in Alan's pupils, his expression

41

smoothed out and a soft smile curved his mouth. 'So beautiful ... glowing ... like sunshine—' Sliding his hands into my hair, he bent towards me, lips parted.

I raised myself on tip-toe to meet his kiss.

Aye, that's right, comfort the poor man.

The words in my head jerked me back.

Shit. What the hell was I doing?

I yanked free, pulling the magic back inside me and backed off a couple of steps. I dug in my bag and came up with a handful of liquorice torpedoes and stuffed them as quickly as I could into my mouth. I crunched down, willing the sugar to quell the brownie's magic.

A brownie's touch goes to them that needs it. Agatha's voice sounded in my mind again.

I swallowed the sweets. Alan's need for comfort might have awakened the magic, but he wasn't a child. Mixing brownie magic with my own was *so* not a good idea: the last thing either of us needed was Alan to be caught in my Glamour. Damn Finn and his quick fix; now I was going to have to deal with the side-effects.

Alan swayed slightly, then frowned. 'I'm sorry. What was I saying?'

I huffed a relieved sigh. 'You were going to tell me why we can't see Melissa's body.'

'Oh, yes. The Soulers have got an injunction stopping any-one from looking at her body, even the pathologist.' Alan held the door open for me, the worry back in his grey eyes. 'They're petitioning for a pre-emptive staking, claiming that Melissa can't have agreed to the Gift because she was under age. My solicitor's contacting a judge he knows to see what he can do.' He tapped his jacket pocket. 'I'm expecting his call.'

The Soulers – Protectors of the Soul – are a right-wing religious organisation who, supposedly, could trace their lineage back to Cromwell's times. They believe humans who become vampires are selling their souls to the devil, albeit at some distant point in the future. Melissa was already dead, and even with the fourteen-day period to allow for a spontaneous change, the circumstances meant it was doubtful the Gift was going to work, so from Melissa's perspective, it really didn't make much odds – except that after the pre-emptive staking, the body was immediately cremated. If the Soulers had their way, I wouldn't get the chance to *look* for magic.

Was it just a coincidence, or something else?

I angled past Alan into the police station, careful not to touch him again. 'Melissa worked for the vampires. Don't they normally sign some sort of pre-death wish thing for just this sort of situation?'

'She did.' He ran a hand over his head, leaving a few hairs standing on end. 'But Fran, Melissa's mother, claims it's not valid because of her age. She can be a bit eccentric at times, but I never thought she was religious. I tried to talk to her, but the doctor's got her sedated up to the eyeballs.' A chirping sound cut him off and he fumbled for his phone. He gave me a relieved smile. 'It's the solicitor.'

Coincidence or not, it certainly wasn't looking good for Mr October.

I moved far enough away to give Alan some privacy. I'd been to Old Scotland Yard – the 'Back Hall' – a couple of times before. Cheerful was not the adjective that immediately sprang to mind: bare bulbs under steel coolie shades hung on the end of long chains from the high ceiling, the floor was a dull expanse of scarred grey linoleum, and uncomfortable plastic chairs for visitors, two of them currently occupied, sat opposite the reception hatch. In fact, the only welcoming thing was the air-conditioning.

Standing under the vent, I let the chill air flow over me. A uniformed police constable – not one I knew – stuck her head up from behind the reception counter, brown curls bobbing and an enquiring look pasted on her plump face. I smiled briefly and pointed at Alan. She stared at me for a moment, then her expression turned less than friendly. She gave me a curt nod and returned to whatever she was doing.

Nice attitude. I mentally shrugged it off and looked over at the occupied chairs.

The man in the sharp suit had a red and black cross pinned to his lapel; obviously the Soulers' representative. He was in his early twenties and sported a well-trimmed Van Dyke that was a slightly darker blond than the tips of his highlighted hair. He perched on the edge of his chair, his fingers tapping the buckle of the briefcase resting on his lap while his alert gaze darted from me to Alan and back again.

Next to him was a goblin. He sat like a muscle-bound child, his feet dangling six inches above the floor, kicking his heels slowly, making the lights in his trainers flash red. Fat ringlets of dyed black hair bounced gently round his liver-spotted face. Wraparound shades protected his eyes. But no one would ever mistake this goblin for a child: his back was straight as a poker and his huge shoulders strained the seams of his navy boiler-suit. A flashing Union Jack badge was pinned to his left chest pocket, under his own black and red cross, while on the right, shiny gold embroidery proclaimed him an employee of *Goblin Guard Security*. As did the baseball bat, neatly covered in shiny silver tin foil, that he held across his knees.

I felt my own shoulders tighten in apprehension: a Beater goblin. I'd forgotten the Soulers hired Beaters, rather than the Monitor goblins most humans use when business combined with magic or vampires. Normally the only place where Beaters are employed is Sucker Town.

I rolled my shoulders, attempting to ease away the tightness in the muscles. As I did, the goblin turned his blank eyes slowly in my direction, his cat-like ears twitching. He shifted his bat and grasped it in his right hand. He smoothed a long finger down the ski-slope incline of his nose, then covered his mouth with his palm for a brief heartbeat.

It was the traditional mark of respect between goblins.

And every goblin I'd ever met offered me, a sidhe fae, the same salutation, whether I knew them or not … although the mouth-hiding bit is considered old-fashioned by most goblins who work in London.

I returned the greeting. He might not be able to see me do it under the harsh lighting, goblin eyes being better suited to dark underground caverns, but he'd nonetheless sense that I had done so.

Then I sighed and dug my fingers into the annoying throb at my neck. It was getting worse, and I knew I was going to have to deal with it sometime soon. How long was this all going to take? Alan's half-heard conversation murmured through the quiet of the hall, the tone of his voice telling me he was getting nowhere fast with his solicitor. My initial vision of breezing in the police station, checking out the body and getting out fast was floundering like a beached water-dragon.

As my gaze passed over the Souler rep he caught my eye. His hand flew to adjust the knot in his tie, while his face lit up with the eagerness of a zealot. *Damn!* That was all I needed. Still, at least he had a goblin with him. That should curb his urge for conversion.

But the Souler sprang up and came towards me, a big bright smile on his face. 'Ms Taylor, isn't it?' he gushed. 'I'm Neil Banner.'

The goblin leapt after him.

Shit. I took an involuntary step back as they both advanced. It looked like Neil Banner hadn't read the handbook that came with his goblin.

'I'm *so* pleased to meet you, Ms Taylor.' His enthusiasm was almost tangible.

I took another swift step back. 'Er, you too.'

The constable stuck her head up over the counter and smiled gleefully at the scene before ducking back out of sight.

Really nice attitude.

I held my hand up to try and stop him. 'You might want to

sit down again, Mr Banner. You're upsetting your goblin.'

He was so intent on sticking his arm out in greeting that he didn't seem to hear me. 'I heard you were coming. I hoped you wouldn't mind talking to me,' he said.

Dammit. He really was going to try and shake my hand. I back-peddled again—

But before he managed to grab hold, the goblin snagged him by the wrist and pulled him to a stop.

I stood with my back braced against the door. Keeping a cautious eye on the goblin and his foil-covered bat, I held my hands out at my sides, palms displayed.

The goblin's grin stretched wider. The sharp tips of his black teeth had been filed blunt and the shiny green sequins stuck to each one glinted in the overhead lights. A goblin grinning is like a dog curling its lips: a warning. It's got nothing to do with showing off their bling, despite what most humans think. The boiler-suit and badge meant the goblin belonged to Beatrice, the goblin queen. They were usually well trained.

Only the sequins worried me.

'No touch.' The goblin's voice was soft, almost a whisper.

Banner blinked in surprise, his eyes flicking between the goblin and me. 'No touch? Why not?'

'He's protecting you, Mr Banner.' I kept my hands where the goblin could see them. 'Goblin workers are very literal beings. You hired him to do a job and that's what he's doing.'

'But that's against the vampires and magic, not you.'

The goblin, his grin fading a tooth or two, put himself in front of Banner. He nodded his head, ringlets bouncing frantically, and twisted the bat in his grip.

'Why's he doing that?' Banner frowned down at the goblin.

'I come under the heading of magic.' I smiled ruefully, careful to keep my lips closed – I didn't want to spook the goblin. 'He won't let anyone capable of magic touch you, or allow you to touch them. Spells are easier to cast with skin contact.'

He tugged at his neat beard. 'Really? I didn't know that. I thought spells all came in little bottles or crystals, like those at the Market.'

'That's witch magic.' I sighed. Didn't the Soulers teach their acolytes anything? 'When you're dealing with the fae or vampires, you need to be more careful. Don't shake hands, and try not to let them get too near you.' I glanced over at Alan, still clutching his phone to his ear, remembering how easily the pretty Armani-suited vamp outside had controlled him without being anywhere near. 'Although that's not going to work with the more powerful vampires; they only need to be in the vicinity to be able to catch you in a mind-lock. But you needn't worry too much, the goblin will watch out for you. They're very good at sensing magic of any kind, and even better, they're immune to it.' That was, after all, the main reason they'd become so popular in negotiations involving vampires – and the goblins were minting it, selling peace-of-mind-guarantees to the humans that they were acting of their own free will and not being ripped off via vampire mind-locks.

'Wow!' Banner's amazed grin made him look younger. 'This is all so fascinating. Meeting you, chatting with Jeremiah here.' He gave the goblin's head a soft pat. The goblin flinched, only Banner didn't seem to notice. 'I've only ever seen the goblins on the Underground before today. Jeremiah's an interesting chap. He's only recently moved to London from somewhere in the north, I think he said.' He rubbed his palms together, then squeezed the fingers of one hand with the other, as if that would contain his excitement. 'His English isn't too good yet.'

The goblin was a recent import? Maybe that explained the sequins.

'I'll have to make sure I introduce myself without the handshake from now on, Ms Taylor,' he added. 'Thanks for the tip. I've only recently found my salvation, but I'm keen to spread the word.'

I groaned inwardly.

Oblivious, he carried on, 'Perhaps we could—'

The door next to the counter swung back and hit the wall with a soft thud. I jerked round at the noise, stomach somersaulting with nerves as I recognised the figure that ducked under the doorjamb and strode into the reception hall.

Damn. I'd been so hoping he wouldn't be on duty.

Now I was for it.

Chapter Six

You need all the front you can muster when facing seven foot of solid granite troll, especially when the troll is Detective Sergeant Hugh Munro. Never mind that he was as soft as faerie moss, he was not going to be happy I was there.

'Genny, good to see you again.' Hugh's voice was a deep bass. He lifted one large hand in greeting and smiled, pink granite teeth gleaming: his bite was way worse than his bark. His shock of black hair grew straight up, two inches above his scalp ridge, contrasting nicely with the deep red of his skin – not sunburn, just his natural colour. Hugh came from the Cairngorms, from the largest tribe in Scotland, and his grandmother was the matriarch.

I straightened my shoulders and returned his smile.

Hugh scanned the room until his gaze landed on Alan. 'Mr Hinkley, Detective Inspector Crane would like to speak to you.' He stepped aside, revealing the plump, curly-haired policewoman. 'If you'd like to go with the constable, please.'

Alan glanced at me, his face etched with worry, then headed off with the curly-haired constable.

Hugh came towards Banner, the goblin and me. 'Mr Banner, I am sorry, but the inspector insists you wait here, not in the morgue.' A firm expression crossed Hugh's face. 'You have her full assurance that the injunction will be complied with fully.'

The goblin broke in with a high chittering sound. An answering rumble came from Hugh's throat. The goblin tapped his bat three times on the floor, finger smoothing quickly down his nose to cover his mouth. Hugh, lips pressed tight together, touched his own nose, nodding with a slightly self-conscious air.

'I hope there isn't a problem, Sergeant.' Banner sounded earnest as he looked from one to the other. 'My minister assured me that the police wouldn't have any issue with a goblin guard.'

'No, not a problem at all.' Reddish dust puffed into the air above Hugh's head, his embarrassment even more obvious. 'Young Jeremiah here is an adopted member of my tribe. He was just saying ... hello.'

Hmm. If that was the case, what was Hugh getting all dusted about?

'That's great.' Banner gave us all a wide smile, still not noticing when the goblin flinched again. 'It's always nice to bump into old friends, isn't it?'

Fine crevices creased across Hugh's forehead as he frowned. 'You're right, Mr Banner. Old friends are always a welcome sight. Please feel free to wait here as long as you want, you and Jeremiah both.' He looked down at me. 'Genny, why don't you come through to the office.'

I stifled a sigh. It wasn't a request.

As I followed him along the corridor, I eyed the precisely ironed crease down the middle of his white shirt, which was tucked neatly into the belted waistband of his black trousers. He didn't look much different in plain clothes, or any older than when I'd first met him ten years ago. Trolls usually lived a few centuries, and I'd worked out that Hugh must be around ninety-odd, for all that he looked half that age.

He stopped, held the office door open for me. I breathed in the familiar fresh smell of ozone that was Hugh and safety. 'How are things?'

'Fine, Genny.' A large, gentle hand touched my shoulder.

'I heard about the new boss.' I briefly patted his arm. 'I'm sorry.'

'So am I,' he rumbled. 'But Detective Inspector Crane has

an exemplary track record, and I'm happy to be working with her.'

I smiled at his diplomatic answer. 'You'd have made a great Inspector, Hugh.'

'Just wasn't the right time for me, Genny. The DI's a powerful witch, got a lot of experience here and in Europe; she's just what the team needs.'

And even though she's a witch, she's still human, I added silently. Hugh might have been the first troll to make Detective Sergeant, four years previously, but he was still a troll. Life sucks sometimes, and not just for vampires.

I walked into the empty open-plan office and headed for Hugh's L-shaped desk. It was easy enough to find – his was the only one clear of all but the essentials: a pile of paper coasters in a pink granite holder, three of the overlarge ballpoint pens manufactured for a troll's fingers, and an electronic photo frame, currently showing a summer landscape of his mountain. Next to a tidy stack of files, his computer screen flashed a screensaver of the same view, this one taken in lightly falling snow.

Smiling, I asked, 'So what's with the goblin and you?'

'Grandmother was concerned about some of the newer goblins being brought into London.' He pointed me to his 'guest' chair as he sat down. 'She asked me to be their *Ardathair*, that's sort of a pastoral figurehead.'

'That's good, isn't it?' I frowned at his troubled face.

'Sit down, Genny.' Hugh placed his hands flat on the desk. 'There's something more important we need to talk about.'

So much for the catch-up. I dropped my bag on the floor, but instead of sitting immediately, I retreated to the water dispenser in the corner. 'Did you want some, Hugh?'

'What do you think you're doing, Genny?'

Getting some water, I wanted to say as I filled the white plastic cup, but I heard the concern in his voice under the reproach, so I didn't. 'Hugh, it's no big deal.' I carried the water back to his desk. 'I *look* at the victim, check her out for spells and let my client know if I find any.' I sat down. 'Job done.'

The cracks across Hugh's forehead deepened. 'There's nothing to find. The standard tests for magic were all clear.' He straightened one of his pens. 'Then when Mr Hinkley brought up his concerns, Inspector Crane put a circle up herself and repeated them, and did some others. She even got an independent witch from another coven to confirm her findings.' He gave me a level look. 'No magic. Nothing.'

'So that's what I'll tell him.' I gave Hugh a small smile. 'Once I've seen for myself.'

'Genny, I shouldn't be telling you this' – he pressed his index finger against his lips – 'but the most recent bites match the boyfriend's dental mould.'

'What about the blood counts?'

'High levels of V1 and V2 as expected, VM3 present but inactive.'

I nodded. Vampire Venom and Virus – 3V – isn't exactly what the name suggests; the scientist who discovered the different components back in the seventies was a fanatical Souler. He identified the clear fluid injected by a vampire's small retractable fangs as a combination of hormones and proteins, only he decided it made more sense to promote it as a poisonous virulent disease, and back then the Department of Health agreed with him.

The Venom – V1 – part is the initial 'infection'. It boosts production of the red blood cells and addicts the victim, which makes for the ideal blood-slave – lots of hot thick blood on tap, and someone who is dying (literally, on occasion) to have a vamp sink fangs into them. As the infection builds, V1 mutates into V2, and the morphogens alter the DNA, upping the slave's immune system to the point that every other disease is killed off. It's a great health benefit – that's if the slave manages to survive the side-effects of the 3V itself. VM3 is the trigger for the Gift, the marker that the original scientist never found.

But then, he couldn't *see* magic, and VM3 is the magic part of the equation.

The high levels of V1 and V2 made sense. Melissa not only worked for vampires, but dated one too. But with VM3 still being dormant ... I frowned, that meant Melissa's death had nothing to do with a botched Gifting.

Something else Hugh had said caught my attention. 'Recent bites?' I asked.

'The pathologist reports that she had multiple bites, inflicted over an extended period of time. He thinks he's narrowed it down to four, maybe five, regular partners. But only the boyfriend matched the bite wounds made in the last week.'

'He must've overdosed her on V1.' I pursed my lips. 'Still, at least she'd have been too hyped-up to know much about it, so what killed her – a stroke or a heart attack?'

'The victim died of blood loss, Genny,' Hugh rumbled. 'Almost drained dry was how the pathologist put it.'

What Hugh was saying didn't tally with Alan Hinkley's tale of true love between Bobby, aka Mr October, and Melissa. Draining someone infected with 3V would be almost impossible for just one vampire. They just couldn't ingest that amount of blood fast enough – unless it was deliberate.

'Shit,' I muttered, 'the sucker must've gorged himself.'

'Exactly,' Hugh sighed. 'Case solved. Except for the father, who just can't accept what's happened.'

Damn.

'Maybe the father just needs to hear it from someone else.' I took a sip of water. 'Someone not connected with the police. I mean, it wasn't that long ago that his son would've been staked and burned almost as soon as you'd nabbed him, is it?'

Hugh's expression turned disapproving. 'Vampires have the same legal rights as any other human, Genny. They have had for the last fifteen-odd years, since the High Court ruled—'

'Yeah, I know,' I interrupted. 'So once the injunction's lifted, there's no harm me *looking*, is there?'

His mouth turned down as he picked up a file. 'Genny, getting involved with this is not right for you.'

I so didn't want to hear this. Not when I agreed with him.

'C'mon, Hugh.' I tried an appeasing smile. 'I checked out a couple of things like this for your old boss.'

More red mica shimmered above his head. Hugh really was dusted about this. 'Twice you worked for the old man, both times the victims were witches. Neither case was connected to the vampires,' he said gruffly.

'What can happen?' I waved at the room. 'We're in a police station. So this has something to do with the vamps, but my client isn't one, and neither was the victim. I deal with vampire victims at HOPE all the time. It doesn't cause me any hassle.'

'You're splitting hairs.' He lowered his voice. 'Genny, you've coped better, these last few years – and I'm proud of you – but any contact with the vampires isn't going to improve matters.' His frown cracks deepened. 'What if one of them decides to take an interest in you? What's going to happen then?'

'I can handle it.' I glanced at the bruises circling my wrist. An image of the Armani-suited vamp sliced through me. I clenched my left hand as something fluttered deep in my stomach. *Yeah, like hell you can.*

Hugh leaned forward, hands flat on the file. 'In the past, so long as a fae didn't venture into Sucker Town, they could be reasonably sure of not falling foul of the vampires. Even then, an adult fae doesn't have much to fear from them. They can't trick you with *mesma*, they can't mind-lock you.' He drummed his fingers insistently, then stopped. 'But that won't stop them from using force if they think it's worth it.'

I kept my voice calm, hiding my exasperation. 'We've been over this—'

'You could end up dead, Genny.'

Of course, dead would be my first choice.

'And don't bother telling me fae are hard to kill,' he

54

continued. 'I've seen it happen before. Injure any fae badly enough in mind and body and they can't help but fade.'

'Hugh, I *know* all this.' I swirled the water in my cup, watching as it formed a tiny whirlpool. 'I don't need a lecture.'

'Yes, I think that's exactly what you need,' he rumbled quietly. 'I've told you, you can't afford to reveal what's wrong with you.'

I pasted an attentive look on my face and tuned him out. Hugh's advice had always kept me safe, and I loved him to bits. But sometimes it felt like listening to his 'advice' was like having a stake hammered through my heart: *Don't get too friendly with the witches. Keep your distance from the fae. Stay behind a threshold after dark. Never Glamour a human, however much you trust them—* Of course, the times I'd actually ignored his advice hadn't ended up a resounding success.

Never mind that if my having 3V became public knowledge, getting the sack from my job would be the least of my worries – I wouldn't have the chance to feel rejected when the fae gave me their collective cold-shoulder. No, the vamps would have me auctioned off to the highest bidder faster than I could shout, '*One sidhe blood-slave, going, going, gone.*'

I tuned back in as Hugh's lecture got to the point I'd been waiting for. '—and it won't take much for the witches to withdraw their protection.'

I took a deep breath, tried for another conciliatory expression. 'Stella knows all about Alan Hinkley and who his son is. She agreed he should speak to me.' Okay, so she hadn't actually expected me to take the job, and she hadn't actually answered any of my texts yet – neither of which I was going to tell Hugh, but hey, sometimes you have to go with what you've got – and so I added the clincher, 'I think they've got some sort of thing going on between them …' I trailed off at his expected horrified expression.

'What sort of thing?' he demanded.

'I'm not entirely sure.'

'It doesn't matter!' he jabbed his finger at me. 'She might be willing to risk her own position, but she's one witch among many. You've got more to lose than she has.'

'Fine.' I lifted my shoulders in a shrug. *Damn.* Why was he so angry? I placed my cup carefully on the coaster and swallowed back my frustration. 'Hugh, all I've been asked to do is look at a dead body and check it out for magic. It will take five minutes, tops. I really can't see how the witches can possibly object to that.'

'Are you sure that's all?'

'Yes, of course! 'Hugh, I know you're worried.' I leaned forward, put my hands over his. His skin felt hot and gritty. 'But I can take care of myself now, and this is just a job.'

He withdrew his hands. 'You can tell me if there's anything else, you know. I'd understand.'

Puzzled, I frowned at him. 'What else could there be?'

His brow ridges lowered as he slid a sheet of paper from the file and pushed it towards me.

I looked down, blinked when I read it. It was an official form of some sort, something to do with a blood visit. I skimmed it, seeing *Roberto October* handwritten next to the section marked *vampire.*

My eyes shot up to Hugh's. 'What the fuck is this?'

'Part of the updated vampires' legal rights. They now have the right to live blood.' He glared at me. 'Obviously they have to provide their own willing donors, so we insist on a waiver of responsibility.'

'I get that, Hugh, but what I want to know is why my name's on it.'

'Why don't you tell me, Genny?' He slapped his hand on the desk. 'Explain to me why a vampire arrested for murder has put you down as his first choice on his nightly menu card?'

Before I could even think of an answer, the door swung open and the curly-haired constable came into the room. She smiled at Hugh, looked at me like I was a toad, and headed towards us.

Hugh smiled back at her, the anger clearing from his face like the sun banishing the shadows.

Shit. Why would a vampire I'd never met think I was going to put out for a free meal? There had to be some mistake. Gritting my teeth, I read down the page again, checking out the various clauses.

'Shall I take Ms Taylor down to the cells, Sergeant?' Constable Curly-hair stopped by the desk and leant her ample hip against it, very obviously giving me the cold shoulder.

'What?' His distracted tone made me look up.

As she patted her hair I caught a flash of pink at the cuff of her uniform. 'Has she signed the form, Sir? The sucker's getting a bit restless.' She threw me a scornful glance. 'Think he might be hungry.'

I narrowed my eyes. Was this why she was so down on me?

Hugh slowly turned back to me. 'Give us a couple of minutes, please, Constable.'

'Sure thing, Sarge,' she said, patting his bare arm as she walked past him. 'I'll get some water. You just shout when you're ready.'

Hugh twisted round to watch her go.

An idea slid into my mind and I bent my head again, skimming down the form until I found the clause I was looking for. Damn. Ignoring the anxious leap in my pulse, I read it again. So *that's* what this was all about.

I leaned forward, tapped Hugh's hand. 'Something going on between you two?' I nodded at Constable Curly-hair, busying herself at the water dispenser.

He shifted his attention back to me.

'You can't keep your eyes off her.'

'Can't I?' Bewilderment fractured his face. 'But Janet's human – a nice human,' he added quickly, 'and I'm a troll.'

I shrugged. 'So? It's not like it doesn't happen.'

Another large puff of dust glinted above his head ridge. 'Human females are very nice, but they're—' Hugh's skin flushed an even darker red than normal. 'They're too slim for me,' he finished diplomatically.

'Shit, Hugh.' I snorted, throwing an unbelieving glance at the overweight constable. 'If you think she's slim, what do you think I am?'

'Oh, you're just skin and bones, Genny,' he blurted out. 'Not as bad as you used to be, maybe, but you still look like a good gust would blow you away.'

And there was I thinking I'd actually filled out, that my curvy bits had finally got enough curves on them to justify the description.

Hugh's face screwed up in dismay. 'I'm sure you look very pretty to another fae, Genny – or even a human.' He was getting flustered. 'Look, I can't let you see the victim, not with this injunction, but let me ask the DI if you can at least see the initial report.' He pushed himself up out of his chair and hurried out of the office.

Suppressing the twinge of guilt because I'd deliberately embarrassed him, I picked up one of Hugh's overlarge pens. Pulling the Waiver of Responsibility towards me, I did my own few seconds of wavering, then signed on the dotted line. Taking a deep breath, I picked up the piece of paper and flapped it at Constable Curly-hair.

She ambled over, a sneer playing round her mouth. Plucking the Waiver form from my hand, she looked down at me. 'What made Hugh dash off like that?'

I looked innocent.

'Never mind, it doesn't matter.' She slipped the form into the folder with a satisfied air. 'Suckers are kept in the basement. You'd better follow me.'

'No problem.'

Time to go have dinner with a vampire.

Chapter Seven

The cell had a dead, airless feel to it, a wrongness that made my chest ache. The white-painted walls and floor should have felt cold, but the temperature in the small box-like room made London's current heat-wave feel like a cool winter's day. Coughing at the faint scent of blood that caught the back of my throat, I *looked*, but there was no magic, not even the flashing pink spell I'd expected to see at the constable's wrist.

The heat was making sweat prickle down my spine ... of course, the fact that it was going to be just me and a murderous vampire, alone together, might be another reason why I was less than cool and collected. The Waiver form had specified total privacy for a blood visit and not even the lawyers were given that. I was gambling that Mr October wasn't just angling for a quick bite, but wanted to tell me his secrets, in secret.

'The heat's keeping the sucker docile.' Constable Curly-hair gave her truncheon a swing. 'Can't have him getting all agitated now, can we?'

Roberto October, aka Bobby, huddled on a plastic mattress against the back wall, long legs drawn up, arms clutched tight across his chest. His eyes were scrunched shut, his face half-hidden by his lank hair. The black leather had been replaced with a white paper coverall that covered him from neck to ankle, leaving his feet bare. He looked more lost boy than dangerous seductive vampire.

'C'mon, Sucker,' Constable Curly-hair crooned, 'wake up. Dinner's here.'

What *was* her problem?

Bobby didn't move, didn't even open his eyes.

'Life and soul of the party, Handsome is,' she smirked. 'Maybe he'll be more fun when you're alone together.'

She was really starting to piss me off. 'Oh, I'm sure he will be,' I said sweetly.

'Right.' She waved at the cell. 'There's a silver lining beneath the white: walls, floor, door and ceiling. So don't bother trying any of your funny magic stuff.'

Mentally, I raised my eyebrows. They were painting the cells in liquid silver now? The new DI must be really busting the budget on that one. Even the HOPE clinic didn't have that particular magical mod con. Still, it explained why I couldn't *see* any magic: the silver was blocking it. And that was why the air felt like sludge in my lungs. I've always reacted badly to silver, more so in the last three years.

Constable Janet held up an electronic keypad and slapped her truncheon against the steel door. 'Just bang when you're finished and I'll come and let you out.' She didn't need to add *if I feel like it*; it was made plain by her tone of voice. 'I'll leave you two lovebirds alone then.' She pressed a button on the keypad and the door slid open.

My gut clenched. Crossing my arms, I walked towards the silent vampire. Was this really such a good idea? He might look helpless, but that didn't mean he was.

'Constable?' I called over my shoulder.

She stopped and turned back to me, scowling. 'What?'

I smiled, like I knew a secret she didn't. 'You won't forget to turn off the CCTV, will you?'

'No,' she snapped, then muttered, not so *sotto voce*, 'sucker slut!' as the door hissed closed between us.

I snorted. The insult was apt, even if she didn't know why ... but I wasn't planning on opening a vein or anything else for this particular sucker if I could help it.

'He said you'd come.' Bobby's voice was rusty, as if he hadn't used it for a long time.

My pulse sped up. I swung back to face him, working to slow my heartbeat. 'Who said I'd come?'

Bobby sat up, arms hugging his knees. 'My Master.' He lifted his face to me. 'He said you'd be able to help.'

Shock sparked through me as I recognised him. I'd been right with my 'lost boy' thought: I'd *met* Bobby, four years ago, and he'd been sitting in the exact same position, saying the exact same words to me.

'They've got her in there.' He lifted his arm slowly and pointed behind him at the blank wall.

The hairs on the back of my neck stood up.

'She's in the basement.' His shoulders hunched over again.

I stared in disbelief. He was either auditioning for an Equity Card ...

'The Master said to wait here, to tell you where she is.'

... or somehow Bobby was reliving the past.

A past that was burned into my brain.

Bobby hadn't been a vampire then, just one of their blood-pets. He'd kept watch all that night, after the girl had been found, waiting for the morning. Waiting for me to come.

'I tried to get her to come out once they'd gone.' His face crumpled. 'But she started screaming ...'

It had been January. I took a deep breath and hugged myself, unwillingly replaying the scene in my mind. The morning sun was a cold disc in a sky streaked with red warnings. The place had been a rats' nest – or rather, a fang-gang's nest – of squalor, right in the heart of Sucker Town. My stomach roiled. Even now, I could still smell the gagging stench of urine, fresh blood and pain ...

Bobby's expression was bleak with horror.

I'd scrambled into the basement to get her. By then her screaming had disintegrated into whimpers. Her rainbow eyes dripped tears of ice that shattered like glass as they fell. After a while, she let me pick her up. Her fingers dug in my shoulders even as she flinched from my touch. I wrapped my coat around her, smearing the ruby dots that pitted her green skin like a macabre sprinkling of bloody sugar balls. The bastard suckers hadn't left her with enough blood for the bruises to bloom.

'How could they do that to her?' Bobby's whisper was harsh. 'Siobhan's so tiny.'

Siobhan, the girl, was Mick's sister – half-sister really – seeing as she was a full-blooded leprechaun. She'd been twelve years old, here on a holiday visit from Ireland to see her brother, too young to fight back when the fang-gang had snatched her from her bed. She'd been gone for five nights when Mick had sought me out and begged for my help. If she'd been human, any hope of rescuing her alive would've died within twenty-four hours, but those with fae blood last *so* much longer.

And even though I'd known it was an inside job – no vampire could've crossed Mick's threshold without an invitation – and that Mick was only the messenger, I agreed to the bargain when it was offered.

Siobhan was the first fae I'd managed to save. There'd been others in need, before Siobhan, but I'd found them too late. After Siobhan, I'd been much more successful, but by then I had my own insider information.

That bargain, the one I'd made then, was why I was now standing in a locked cell with a vampire accused of murdering his girlfriend, and it was why that vampire was taking me on an unwelcome trip down memory lane.

He was delivering an invitation.

So what the fuck was wrong with using the phone?

Chill air crawled over my flesh. I backed up and leant against the door, not sure if Bobby would say any more. He rocked from side to side, grey eyes glazed, mouth half-open revealing a glimpse of fang. He might have hit the jackpot and graduated from blood-pet to blood-sucker over the last four years, but he was still just a puppet, jerking on his Master's strings. It would be decades before Bobby would reach his Autonomy.

I wondered if he'd known what the Gift had meant, or whether, with his looks, he'd truly been a sucker? Poor bastard. But then, he was better off than Melissa, his girlfriend. At least he wasn't lying in the morgue. Yet.

Another blast of frozen air hit me. I rubbed my hands over my arms and shivered again. What had happened to the heating? I looked up at the vents, puzzled. Then it hit me: Constable Curly-hair must've cut the heat. That same heat that was keeping Bobby, the vampire from getting agitated. *Bitch!* I rapped my knuckles against the cell door. Time to go.

Movement caught in the corner of my vision. I turned back to see Bobby on his hands and knees, head hanging down.

This was so not good.

I slammed my hand against the door again.

Bobby started moving, his movements more fluid now as he crawled across the floor towards me.

I kicked the door with my heel, feeling the reverberation of the hard metal. Surely she could hear it out there?

Three feet away, he lifted his head and scented the air.

My heart thudded. I shifted, arms loose and ready at my sides. Maybe I was staying for dinner after all.

Two feet …

Calm. Don't get him excited. I willed my pulse to slow, but the trick wasn't working. Instead, the silver-laden air tightened my throat and panic pumped my blood faster. *C'mon, think calm!*

His hand touched my shoe.

I clamped my jaw to stop from screaming.

He wrapped his arm round my knees, curling into my legs. 'Help her,' he whispered. 'Help Siobhan.'

My head dropped back against the door and I let out a relieved sigh. Bobby was still trapped in the memory. Cautiously, I brushed his hair aside, offered him a reassuring smile. 'It's okay, Bobby, Siobhan's safe now.'

Pink tinged tears glistened in his eyes. 'She is?'

I cupped his cheek, feeling the urge to comfort him. 'She's gone back to Ireland,' I said softly.

He made a quiet snuffle, then turned, pressing his nose against the inside of my wrist. My stomach jumped. His arm tightened round my legs, his hand convulsing around mine, the points of his fangs sharp against my pulse. The back of my neck throbbed in answer. I breathed in the heady smell of liquorice and the venom craving hit me. Need and want flared hot through my veins, drew a cry from my mouth and flooded my skin with a blood-flush.

Damn. I was neck-deep in trouble ... and there was nothing I wanted to do about it.

I closed my eyes, anticipating the sting of his bite—

The pain didn't come.

A tremor shuddered through me.

I stared down at him, and carefully, slowly, pulled my wrist away from his mouth.

He didn't try and stop me, just watched, awareness sliding over his face.

Tension spiralled inside me.

'You're the sidhe.' Anticipation laced his voice. He flowed to his feet, the movement almost faster than I could see, crowded me back against the door, shoved his hands in my hair. The liquorice scent bled into my mind, holding me captive. Hot breath seared my jaw. He bent his head to my throat. Then he hissed, the noise loud and angry, and punched the door next to my face. I flinched and he flung himself away from me, yelling with rage.

I risked a look at the dented door and shuddered. What was wrong? Why hadn't he bitten me? He was young, a baby vamp, and even if he wasn't hungry – which he had to be – no way could he resist a feed that close to a venom-induced blood-flush. He should have broken skin at the very least.

Fuck. And I hadn't been about to stop him.

I almost cried at the irony. How stupid was I, to think I

could deny it twice in one night? So much for telling Hugh I had the 3V under control: the desire to offer my blood was so desperate that I had to fight the urge to scratch at my own bare arms. And there was worse to come.

I gritted my teeth as the cramps hit. I clutched at my stomach, sliding down the wall, tears pricking the back of my eyes.

He crouched in front of me. 'Christ, but I want to drink you down so bad.' He pulled me into his arms, buried his face in my neck. 'You smell fucking wonderful.' Anguish sliced through his voice. 'God, I can feel it, feel your pain, taste it. It hurts, hurts like hell.'

Panting, I grabbed at him, tore at his paper coverall.

Hands caught my wrists, held me still. 'Shh. You smell so sweet, and hot, your skin's burning with blood, I bet you taste better than Her, better even than Mel.' His words vibrated along my pulse. 'I haven't had a decent meal in weeks. All that thin human blood is all He's let me have.'

Hot claws raked inside me as though rending the flesh from my bones. I opened my mouth, screaming with the pain.

Make it stop.

Sharp tips punctured my heart.

Please, anything.

Ripped through my gut.

No more.

Then it was over.

'Why?' I gasped into his chest, limp and exhausted.

'Bastard likes his games.' He laughed, the sound bitter. 'It turns him on. He lets you have a taste, just so you appreciate what you're missing. Christ, I'm rationed to two mouthfuls, even from my own girlfriend – and he has to watch.' He licked my throat. 'Bet he's getting his rocks off right now, watching me drool over sweet sidhe blood, knowing I can't have even a drop.'

'No—' Still weak, I clutched at him. 'Why that memory?'

He pushed me back, frowned at me. 'What memory?'

'Sucker Town.' I gulped in cold air. 'Four years ago. The fang-gang.'

'I haven't the foggiest idea what you're talking about.' His fingers dug into my arms. 'Which means the bastard's been screwing with me again, stealing my memories. Fuck, I hate it when he does that – it's bloody torture when he gives them back.' He looked around the cell, disgusted. 'And I don't even fucking remember where *here* is!'

I slumped in his hold. 'We're in the police station,' I whispered. 'Do you remember about Melissa?'

'Melissa?' He shook me, making my head snap back. 'What—?'

The door opening interrupted him. 'Time's up, sucker.' Constable Curly-hair's tone was gleeful. Something metallic clanged.

Almost as if in slow motion, I saw him react. He grabbed my shoulders, rolling me over, away from the door.

'Hey,' she shouted, 'don't make me use this.' Green light shattered the edges of my vision. 'C'mon, that's enough now.'

Bobby threw himself on top of me, crushing me as a fork of green lightning arced round the cell. Burnt mint assaulted my nostrils. He jerked, limbs moving as though pulled by tight strings. His eyes widened with pain, then fell empty and blank.

I shoved him off me and collapsed, the backlash of magic pounding me like a Beater goblin.

'Sorry about that,' she said, sounding far more satisfied than sorry. 'I tried to miss you, but he was a bit close for comfort.' She brandished a silver pole. A smooth hunk of jade embedded in the end of the pole still sputtered green sparks. 'These new stun-spells of the DI's can be a bit overpowering.'

Wheezing, I glanced at the unconscious vampire next to me. Damn. No chance of any more answers tonight. He'd be lucky if he revived before dawn.

I glared up at the smirking constable.

She gave me a wide grin. 'Oh, sorry, was I too early? Have I spoiled all your fun?'

'You didn't,' I muttered, adding silently, at least not as much as I intend to spoil yours.

Chapter Eight

'How'd it go with the horny bastard then?'

'What?' I slumped in Hugh's spare chair and pressed my phone closer to my ear, my exhausted gaze taking in the still empty murder squad room. I'd got out of Bobby's cell in one piece, no thanks to Constable Curly-hair, and I'd even survived Hugh's disappointed, disapproving concern. I was tacitly blaming the stun-spell for my jitters. And now I had to wait for DI Crane – she had expressed a wish to see me herself, which sounded like more fun than a whole barrel of laughs.

'C'mon, Genny,' Toni's voice teased me over the phone, ''Fess up: did you succumb or not, when Finn asked you out? Remember there's a lot riding on the answer.'

I rubbed the back of my neck and briefly shut my tired eyes. 'Oh, *that* horny bastard.' Now I knew what our office manager was talking about.

I opened my hand, looked at the blister-pack of G-Zav tablets sitting innocently in my palm. I was going to have to give in and take them.

'You knew who I meant!' She tutted in exasperation. 'Don't forget I know what your social life is like – it's as frozen as the South Pole – and if the male of the species was my thing, Finn's hot enough that I'd definitely let him melt my ice caps.' She laughed. 'Now, you know your Auntie Toni's right, so tell me you've put the sexy satyr out of his misery. And remember, your secrets are safe with me.'

That got a weary smile; Toni was the biggest gossip out. 'Nothing to tell,' I assured her, brushing dust from my trousers.

The black linen was starting to look like I'd been rolling around the floor— Oh wait, I had. Twice. 'Finn asked me out, but no, I didn't "succumb", as you so succinctly put it.' Even if he had picked me up. Literally.

Using my thumb, I pushed two tiny black pills out of the packet.

'What is it with you, Genny?' Her disappointed sigh whistled down the phone. 'It's not good to keep your libido locked up like this. C'mon, Honeybee.' Her tone turned pleading. 'There's just three more days before the bet's up. Give in, have some fun with the *sex god*, it'll do you good.'

I let the saliva pool in my mouth then popped the pills between my lips, tipped my head back and swallowed.

'Otherwise, Genny,' Toni warned, 'Team Toni is going to have to treat that bitch – sorry, *witch* – Leanora and her Luvvies to facials plus all the works.'

'Toni—' I exhaled on a strangled laugh, my tongue sparking with the concentrated liquorice aftertaste. 'Toni, how can I put this? *No way* am I going out with Finn, *no way* am I having sex with him, just so as you can find out about his tail and win a bet!'

I missed her next few words as the G-Zav hit. It's like the build-up to great sex, and then … instead of the fun part, someone injects ice-water into your veins, leaving you feeling like crap. But at least G-Zav, the vampire junkies' methadone equivalent, kept the cravings and blood-flushes under control. If you were human, two tablets would work for a couple of nights, but being fae, I'd metabolise them in a couple of hours. Then I had a choice: another dose, and a session with the leeches (real ones, not the doctor or sucker type) – or I took my chances with the next vamp I bumped into.

So not the healthy option.

Then the amphetamine in the G-Zav kicked in and as I started to feel better, Toni's voice faded back in: '—and you're the only one who's got a chance of finding out.'

'Uh-huh,' I murmured absently into the phone.

'So you will!' Toni's voice jumped with eagerness. 'Oh, I could hug you, Genny . That's going to—'

'Hang on a minute,' I interrupted, 'what exactly have I just agreed to?'

'Asking Finn about his tail, of course! I just told you – Leanora's convinced the only way anyone can find out is the fun way – but none of her cronies have managed to get that far,' she gave a derisive laugh, 'and I can tell you, some of the tricks they've tried to get him to do the down-and-dirty, well, I almost feel sorry for him.'

So Finn hadn't been doing any 'succumbing' himself. Strangely, instead of feeling pleased, anger rose, making me want to hit something – the snippet of gossip was irrelevant after all. Anything with Finn had always been a non-starter, never mind Hugh's all-too-recent repeat lecture on the important *don'ts* in my life, or the situation I was in.

'Anyway,' Toni carried on, 'I only need to find out what colour his tail is, and everyone knows *you're* the one he's got a thing for, so maybe if you asked him nicely enough he'd tell you,' she finished in a hopeful tone.

'If all anyone had to do was ask,' I muttered, 'what's with all the fuss that's been going on?'

Toni snorted. 'Leanora's after Finn herself. She was worried about you being competition, so she's been doing that reverse-psych thing on you. She thinks that making the bet all about sex will put you off.'

'Weird.' More mind games. There were a lot of them going around, which brought my mind back to the vampires and Bobby's selective memories, and his guided tour through our shared past. Had he killed Melissa and his Master caused him to forget it? Or was it only her death that had been wiped from his mind? And why bother anyway? Maybe I'd find out when I paid his Master a personal visit. I pressed my palm against my thudding heart. There's nothing like the thought of meeting the head of one of London's four blood-families for giving a girl's cardiovascular system a really fast workout, never mind the blasts of adrenalin the G-Zav was shooting through my veins.

'And the other thing,' Toni carried on, oblivious to my inattention, 'Leanora thinks she can get Finn to jump the broom with her.'

The office door swung open and Constable Curly-hair, the unpleasant smirk still stuck on her face, ambled over to the water dispenser.

I said sharply, 'She's got no chance.'

''Course she hasn't,' Toni huffed. 'I mean, I reckon I'd have more luck with him, and that's with me batting for the other side. Anyway, did that journo friend of Stella's find you earlier?'

'Uh-huh,' I murmured.

Constable Curly-hair brought her water over to Hugh's desk, put it down and picked up one of Hugh's fat pens. She started clicking it on and off.

I stared at the wet ring mark marring the desk's shine.

'Well, you'll never guess!' Toni's voice switched to high-gossip mode. 'You know that vamp that's in all the papers?' She paused for effect. 'Well, the journo guy is his *dad*!'

I snagged one of Hugh's coasters. 'Yeah, Toni, I know.' Leaning forward, I picked up the cup and placed it on the coaster, dead centre.

Constable Curly-hair twirled the pen at me, indicating I should hurry up and finish.

'You know?' I could almost feel Toni's excitement. 'So what did he want you for?'

'Nothing much.'

The constable made a show of looking at her watch.

'C'mon Genny,' Toni pleaded, 'don't tease, it must've been *something*. You know I have to know these things.'

'I'll tell you all about it tomorrow, Toni.' I brushed another

71

speck from my trousers. 'There's a larger matter here I have to deal with first.' I said my goodbyes, dropped the phone back into my bag and leaned back in my chair.

Constable Curly-hair threw the troll-pen down and it clattered over the desk. 'I want a word with you.'

What *had* I done to piss her off so badly? I gave her a level look. 'What, just the one?'

Her lips twisted in a sneer again. 'It's a bloody shame the sucker didn't bleed you dry,' she snapped.

'But we were so rudely interrupted,' I reminded her. 'Good things take time.'

Her face wrinkled in disgust. 'Hugh's a good man.' She picked her cup up. 'He's kind, caring, concerned.' She knocked back the water as though it was something stronger. 'Sometimes he's too kind, and people take advantage.'

Ahh. Now we were getting to it. I smiled, though it didn't reach my eyes. 'Do they,' I said in a flat voice

'Of course, *you* know about the kids he helps.' Crumpling the cup, she lobbed it over-arm into a nearby bin.

I caught the flash of pink magic at her wrist again, then her sleeve covered it.

'The kids he finds on the streets, runaways, and others.' She wiped her hands down her thighs, tugging at her too-tight uniform trousers. 'He tries to stop them stealing, doing dope, turning tricks, whatever.'

I tapped the arm of the chair.

'I know you're one of them, that Hugh thinks he helped you.' Spots of colour stained her cheeks. 'Oh, not that he's said anything, he's too nice for that, but I can tell by the way he talks about you.'

'And you're telling me this because?'

She leaned towards me, ample breasts threatening the buttons on her shirt. 'I know your sort, even if he doesn't. You're just a nasty little slut who thinks she can get anything she wants using magic.' Mascara caked her lashes into unattractive clumps. 'I might be human, but I'm a witch's daughter. When you came in here with the sucker's dad, your magic was all over like him like a nasty rash. I could *see* it.'

A witch's daughter: her father was human, not sidhe. I'd have offered my sympathies if it hadn't been for what she was up to.

She shook her finger at me. 'Glamour spells are illegal, you know that as well as I do. Stay away from Hugh. Maybe then I'll forget what I saw.'

'What, like you forgot to stay outside the cell earlier?' Grabbing her finger, I bent it far enough back to hurt. 'I think you've already *forgotten* enough, don't you?'

'Bitch,' she hissed, breathing bitter coffee-breath all over me. She swung at me, clawed fingers going for my face, but I caught her wrist, yanked her arm behind her and pushed her back against the desk. She jerked her knee up and I twisted easily to the side, using the desk to trap her.

'You think you know a lot, don't you?' I kept my voice low. 'Well, here's something else you should know.' I bent her finger back even more, forcing her arm down. Grunting, she heaved against me, but I shoved her back and shook her arm until her bracelet dropped, the beads chinking. 'Glamour isn't the only type of spell that's illegal.'

She went still and fear flickered in her eyes.

My gut twisted in anger as I *looked* at the bracelet. Every rose quartz bead but one winked with a spell: lust, binding, memory, maybe an-eye-of–the-beholder … not that I could tell what they all were, but I'd seen bracelets like this in the market: True Love spells, the quartz being the affinity gem that ties the magic together – only love is too pure an emotion to be manufactured, so the bracelets are really nothing more than a confidence boost – unless they come with the addition of an illegal compulsion spell. Like the one hidden in the pink bead that appeared empty of magic.

No wonder Hugh couldn't stop watching her.

Cracking the spells would shatter the bracelet into so much pink dust, but if Janet had been desperate enough to buy one in the first place, that wasn't going to stop her.

'What's your new DI going to say when she sees this?' I murmured in her ear. 'And Hugh, how d'you think he's going to feel?'

'You wouldn't—!'

'Believe me, I so would.'

'No! You don't understand,' she whined. 'I love Hugh, only he won't go out with a human. I just wanted him to think about me like that.' Her voice hitched on a sob. 'You can't tell him.'

I shifted so I could look her in the eyes. 'Okay ... but there is one condition.' Shit, was I really going to bargain with her? Probably not the greatest idea I'd ever had, but this was for Hugh, so I ignored my unease and said, 'You remove the bracelet and keep it in an envelope.'

'That's it?' Surprise sharpened her features. 'Nothing else?'

'Agree, and I'll won't tell Hugh, or your DI.'

Her expression turned sly. 'Give your word you won't tell anyone else either.'

Of course she'd think of that one. 'Agreed.'

'And I get to keep the bracelet?'

'In the envelope.'

She chewed her lip and considered the deal. Then she sighed. 'Fine, okay.'

A quiet chime split the air around us.

'Hear that?' I squeezed her wrist. '*Never* break a bargain with a fae.'

'I know that,' she sniffed.

She'd come up with a way to weasel out of the deal; I'd made it too fast to think through all the options, but if it was the wrong way – the magic could be capricious when it wanted – then the magic would take its retribution. I'd be okay, so long as I kept my end of the bargain. I laughed – not a happy sound – and released her.

She threw me a nasty look and massaged her hand. 'You're pretty strong for such a skinny bitch, you know.' She grabbed an envelope from a pile on a nearby desk and slipped the bracelet off her wrist. 'I really get to keep it and you won't say anything?'

'Yes,' I repeated, 'as long as it's kept sealed in the same envelope.'

A devious smile twitched across her lips, then was gone. She knew as well as I did that the bracelet worked best worn next to skin, but even in an envelope it would still have some power … but she wasn't a witch, only a witch's daughter – she'd have a touch of ability through her genes, but it wouldn't be much more than any other full-blooded human. And judging by how overweight she was, she had to be scoffing sugar by the bagful to amp-up what little *sight* she did have. There was no way she'd be able to check the bracelet still had all its spells while it was in the envelope, and until she figured out how to get out of the deal, Hugh would be safe.

As if I'd conjured him up the door opened and Hugh's deep voice sounded from the hall. A tall thirtysomething woman appeared, stopped and scanned the office, then stalked in, her thin body ramrod-straight. Hugh followed behind.

Constable Curly-hair quickly dropped the bracelet inside the envelope, and sealed it closed. She tucked her package safely into her pocket then turned towards the woman, saying brightly, 'I was just getting a coffee. Can I get you one, ma'am?'

I slumped back in my chair – I needed to be sitting down for the next part of my plan – then I *focused* on the pink glow at Janet's hip and *called* the spell. The magic hit me like a fist in the stomach and winded me so badly I hunched over, hugging myself. The grey linoleum floor turned into a swirling sea that threatened to engulf me, bile rose in my throat and I banged my head on the underside of the desk to keep from throwing up. I scrabbled for my bag, then, clutching a hand to my head, I eased upright in the chair.

'Are you okay, Genny?' Hugh's concerned face blurred in front of me.

'Yeah,' I mumbled, 'just banged my head.' I blinked at him. 'I feel a bit dizzy.'

He placed a gentle hand at the back of my skull. 'Put your head between your knees. Take deep breaths.'

I breathed in and out and a shimmer of heat rushed through me. The magic settled. Slowly I sat up and sank back into the chair. As I apologised I noticed the constable had left the room.

'Accidents happen.' The thin woman stared down at me, a deep frown making her patrician features look even more severe. 'I'm Detective Inspector Helen Crane, Ms Taylor.' She smiled and it was like the moon shining in the night sky. Suddenly she was beautiful.

I'd been wondering why no one else had noticed the constable's bracelet. Here was the answer: Helen Crane's jacket lapel sagged under the weight of three gold broaches set with chips of jade. A wide belt glittering with crystals cinched her waist. Long strings of garnets swung from her lobes tangling with her honey-blonde hair, and as she leaned towards me I noticed a sapphire the size of a robin's egg nestled in the deep vee of her black silk blouse.

DI Crane was decorated like an expensive Christmas tree, only it wasn't the fortune in jewellery that had my nerves twitching but the strength of the spells stored in the gems – almost enough juice to fill half the magic stalls in Covent Garden Witches' Market. It made me want to ask her exactly what she was afraid off.

She regarded me with an indecipherable look out of eyes as blue as the sapphire she wore, then lifted a hand, her fingers adorned with enough rings to double as high-priced knuckledusters, and brushed her thumb across the side of my mouth. 'You have a smear of lipstick on your cheek, Ms Taylor.'

'Have I?' I snagged another of Hugh's paper coasters and rubbed at my face.

She took the crumpled coaster from me, tilted my chin and wiped my mouth as though I were a child. 'There.' She gave me a peculiar smile. 'All gone.'

I gave her a half-smile back, not sure whether to be amused or insulted.

Her expression fell back into severe lines. 'Sergeant Munro tells me you want to look at the pathologist's report on Melissa Banks.' She angled her head and looked at me quizzically. 'Why exactly is that?'

I wasn't really all that interested; it had been Hugh's reason for escaping after I'd deliberately embarrassed him. But as I felt another prick of guilt for the way I'd manipulated him, I said, 'As I can't look at the body, I thought it might be a good idea.'

'You misunderstand me,' she said. 'You're not a police consultant. You have no medical qualifications. You don't deal with the dead. So why are you even here?' Her eyes bored into me.

I *had* misunderstood her. 'Alan Hinkley asked me to come.' I accepted the cup of water Hugh was holding out towards me. Red dust shimmered in his black hair.

DI Crane's mouth turned down. 'Do you always do what people ask of you?'

'My job is to find magic, Inspector.' I took a sip of water, looked at her over the rim of the cup. 'If that's what I'm asked to do, then it pays me to do it.'

Spreading the fingers of her right hand, she inspected her rings, then clenched her fist. 'The Witches' Council wouldn't have approved any involvement in this matter from Spellcrackers.com without a police request.' She looked up, stared me straight in the eyes. 'There hasn't been one. Furthermore, there is no need for one. I have personally investigated Mr Hinkley's claims that his so—'

She stopped mid-word, blue eyes going unfocused.

I glanced at Hugh, but he gave a tiny shake of his head, as mystified as I was.

DI Crane grasped her left earring as the colour faded from her face. A thin red line snaked out of her palm and twisted around her wrist, vanishing into her sleeve.

I jumped up, thinking she'd cut herself on her gems, that it was blood, then I realised it was a spell, one so powerful that I'd seen it without needing to *look*.

'Munro.' The DI's voice cracked. She clutched the sapphire pendant with her other hand. 'Sergeant Munro.' The words were firmer, more decisive. 'Reception. *Now*.' She turned and made for the door, saying over her shoulder to him, 'They're coming.'

Who is coming?

I hurried after them into the Back Hall, where a soft slapping sound caught my attention. Jeremiah the goblin, his mouth stretched wide in a grin, his green sequins bright against the black of his teeth, was smacking his bat against the palm of his hand as he stared fixedly at the entranceway.

Behind the goblin stood Neil Banner and Alan Hinkley, looking similarly confused as they looked from the goblin to us to the door.

Then a crawling sensation washed over me, raising every hair on my body, and I knew what – or rather, *who* – was coming. This was *so* not good. Advertising their approach like this was akin to taking an imp to show-and-tell at Sunday School.

Hugh's hair had flattened, giving him a hard, crushing look. Had he remembered about the goblin's bling, remembered how young and inexperienced the goblin was? 'Hugh,' I muttered, trying to catch his attention.

'Not now, Genny,' he said, voice calm. 'Go back inside. This is no place for you.'

Maybe he was right.

But it was too late.

*

The door crashed open. A chill wind rushed in, swirled round the hall, set the lights swinging on their chains and rattled the glass in the windows.

Then all was perfect stillness.

And the sound of the goblin slapping his bat on the palm of his hand sounded as loud as a fire-dragon's jaw snapping closed.

Chapter Nine

Three vampires walked into the police station. It sounds like one of those jokes, except I doubted anyone would be laughing by the time we got to the punch-line.

The first one through the door lived up to the romantic stereotype: he swept his velvet knee-length jacket back with a flourish and posed with one hand on his hip. Ivory lace billowed at his wrists and neck, and a black ribbon caught his tawny hair in a loose pony-tail at the nape of his neck. Aquiline nostrils flared as he cast an arrogant look around the room, passing over Alan Hinkley, Neil Banner and the grinning goblin, all clustered on my right. He stopped when he reached me.

A shiver ran down my spine as his eyes met mine.

It looked like it was the night for all the old ones to surface, though as with the Armani-suited vamp, I didn't recognise this particular vamp either.

A warning rumble issued from deep within Hugh's chest.

The vampire snapped his head round, sniffed with disdain at Hugh, then settled his attention on DI Crane. His expression turned intense, brooding. With his eyes never leaving hers, he extended his right leg and bowed. 'You are very beautiful, Madame.' He spoke slowly, with a thick accent.

Her eyes wide, she pressed her lips together until they disappeared. Her fingers, clenched around the sapphire pendant at her breast, were almost bloodless.

Damn. The new DI was afraid of the vamps – not just a healthy, 'hey, they could be dangerous' type of fear, but what looked suspiciously like a full-on phobia. So what the hell was she doing running the magic murder squad?

I shot a look at Hugh, but he was still glowering at the lace-bedecked vampire.

'Good evening.' Vampire Number Two appeared, moving with effortless grace to stand just in front of Lacy. He smiled, fangs hidden. The smile was charm itself, not vamp *mesma*, just centuries of practise – eight centuries, to be precise, if the media had got it right, except he looked to be in his early thirties. An Oxford-blue shirt accentuated his azure eyes and blond hair, while his blazer, grey flannels and loafers gave the impression he was generally to be found idly punting down the Thames. Instead he played the Godfather to London's Blood Families.

This was the Undead Lord, the Earl.

'I must apologise for the theatrics.' The Earl gestured at Lacy. 'Louis, my companion, is a little concerned about his friend, Roberto October. I am afraid his feelings have rather overwhelmed him.'

I frowned at Lacy Louis. Was this the same Louis who'd sunk his fangs into Holly, the faeling I'd met earlier? The vamp she'd said Bobby had argued with?

Louis was still brooding at the Inspector. 'I *regrette* also, Madame.'

Then the third vampire shuffled in behind, his shoes squeaking across the floor like an anxious mouse. He stopped, hovering halfway between the Earl and Alan's little group. His rumpled suit looked about as comfortable as a hair shirt and his undone shoe laces trailed about his feet. One sharp fang had pierced his bottom lip, and a sluggish bead of blood dripped onto his collar, merging with the rusty stains already there. He peered around, the fretful look of a young child on his thirtysomething face.

The other vamps ignored him. But then, he did kind of spoil the show.

'That's the vampire solicitor.' Alan's muttered comment to

Neil Banner broke the expectant silence. 'He didn't look like that last night. What's the matter with him?'

It was a good question. A better one was why had the Earl brought him along?

'My dear Inspector.' The Earl extended his hand to DI Crane.

She flinched and Hugh moved nearer, his warning rumble again reverberating around the hall.

Shuffle Vamp stumbled backwards.

The Earl let his hand fall. 'My sincere apologies for calling upon you unannounced, as it were,' he said smoothly. 'When Westman' – he indicated Shuffle Vamp – 'explained the situation to me, I felt I had to come immediately.' His charming smile was tinged with sadness. 'Please do forgive me.'

DI Crane appeared to regain her composure. She gave him a small nod. 'Yes, of course, Lord—?'

'I am known simply as the Earl, my dear lady. There is no need to stand on any ceremony. My claim to my title passed some long years ago and I have no wish to inconvenience the current bearer by reclaiming it. Time stands still for no man.' He inclined his head. 'Please do not let me keep you from your duties any more. It is Mr Hinkley I wish to speak to.'

DI Crane frowned uncertainly at Louis until Hugh bent his head down to hers and said something too low for me to hear. She straightened her shoulders, shaking her head.

I rubbed the back of my neck, still uneasy. What was Lacy Louis doing here? That 'friend' story was a load of crap. The Earl turning up full of concern, that was believable; he was probably running media interference ... except that there were no reporters hanging round to scribble down his well-thought-out off-the-cuff remarks.

And that led me straight on to another question: why weren't there any journalists about? You'd think they were an extinct species, going by the lack of news coverage outside Old Scotland Yard. The only hack in evidence was Alan himself

– who was now listening intently to the Earl – and he didn't count.

'Such a terrible time.' The Earl's tone was warm, solicitous, with just the tiniest whisper of vamp *mesma* to boost the feelings. 'And I understand you have dispensed with Westman's services.'

At the mention of his name, Westman shuffled closer to them. He didn't look in any fit state to offer advice – and he also appeared more interested in Neil Banner and his goblin than in his erstwhile client.

I narrowed my eyes, frowning. Why *had* the Earl brought him along?

The goblin twisted his bat in his palm, his head swinging like a metronome from side to side, trying to keep both vampires in range.

I was still frowning when I realised the Earl was moving my way.

'It is wonderful to meet you at last, Ms Taylor.' He smiled and held out one pale manicured hand.

I tried not to tense as I shook his hand. His palm was warm and dry and felt exactly as a hand should. But that was it. There was no annoying throb in my neck. No desire to spill my blood at his feet. The apprehension in my gut went down a notch. The G-Zav was doing its thing.

'I have heard such delightful things about you.' He gave me a benign look from under his flop of blond hair. 'I feel as if I already know you, so I shall call you Genevieve.'

I beamed at him. He could call me what he liked, so long as he didn't think I was going to call him Master.

'You really are extraordinarily beautiful, my dear.' He reached out, traced a butterfly touch along my jaw. I wanted to brush his hand away, but gritted my teeth instead. 'A delicate, yet eminently strong bone structure.' His blue eyes lit with manly appreciation ... only something told me it was more because he thought I expected it than because he actually meant it. 'You have a dancer's figure: slender, muscled, but ultimately feminine. You would look wonderful cast in bronze. I have quite an extensive collection of Degas.' He patted my hand and leaned towards me. 'I would be honoured if you would view it some time.'

I gave a surprised laugh, tugging my hand from his. Were we talking euphemisms? 'I'm not sure bronzes are my thing, but thanks anyway.' Then I frowned. Why were the DI and Hugh still holding their staring contest with Lacy Louis?

'Perhaps you could enlighten my curiosity then, Genevieve.' He adjusted his cuffs carefully. 'Admirable as your offer to help dear Roberto is, I do find it a little strange, given your usual avoidance of the vampire community.' He gave me a conspiratorial smile. 'How exactly did you make his acquaintance?'

'Through Roberto's father, Alan Hinkley,' I said.

'How interesting.' His words came with a push of *mesma* to tell him more. It buzzed round me like an irritating fly. I mentally waved it away and looked over at Alan.

Had Alan repeated that cryptic comment about Siobhan to the Earl? Not that it mattered; Alan didn't know anything else. Now he was talking to Banner, looking anxious. In contrast, Banner was ignoring both Alan and Jeremiah the goblin, gazing past them at Westman like he'd found the last chocolate in the box. And wasn't he lucky? It was only his *favourite*.

Westman stared back, his expression mirroring Banner's. Damn. Westman had hit him with a mind-lock, and not the careful, controlled mind-lock the Armani-suited vamp had used on Alan Hinkley earlier, but a full-out melding, as dangerous for the vamp as for his victim.

This was *so* not good.

Westman licked his lips, took another shuffling step towards Neil Banner.

Shit. Had anyone else noticed what was happening? I looked at Hugh, but he was *still* glowering at Lacy Louis, and

DI Crane was *still* clutching her sapphire – it was almost as if someone had pressed pause on them.

I looked back at the Earl. He watched me with interest, his charming smile full of calculation.

'What are you doing?' I snapped.

'I? Why, nothing, my dear.' He gestured at Westman and Banner. 'But it looks as if they are of like mind, and far be it for me to come between them.'

Banner took a step towards Westman.

The goblin let out a high-pitched howl.

Banner and Westman ignored him.

The DI and Hugh stayed frozen like statues.

Hoisting his bat, Jeremiah the goblin bounced on his feet, trainers flashing red, and charged at Westman. Trapped in his own mind-lock, Westman didn't even see the goblin coming. The goblin's bat slammed into the back of the vamp's legs with a loud snap, bringing him to his knees. The goblin pirouetted with the up-swing, ringlets fanning out in a circle, and swung the weapon round, smacking Westman solidly in the stomach. He doubled over, head thudding against the floor with a sickening crack. Another elegant pirouette, the bat raised high above him, and the goblin was ready for the third and final blow, the one that would smash Westman's skull like an overripe melon.

I have to end this. 'Jeremiah, stop!' I shouted, hoping desperately that he'd heed me.

The goblin hesitated, then froze.

Screams of pain echoed round the hall.

Westman lay crumpled, silent.

The screams came from Banner, who writhed on the floor, fingers scrabbling at the lino, trying to pull himself to Westman.

I grabbed hold of Alan's hand and he started, looking down at me in shock. I pushed him at Banner. 'Keep him away from the vampire,' I cried as I shoved the command into his mind and pointed at Westman. Alan looked dazed, but nodded, and I raced towards the fight.

I slid onto my knees between the goblin and Westman and threw my hands up. The goblin's black plastic lenses stared down at me as the silver-foiled club glinted in the overhead lights. His ski-slope nose twitched once, acknowledging that he saw me.

'Magic not gone.' His soft voice held confusion.

'It's joined together.' I brought my palms together and entwined my fingers, 'Like this.'

He flexed his arms, lifting the bat higher. 'I break it.'

'No.' I shook my head. 'You can't break it. You'll hurt the human you protect.' I banged my hands on the floor, keeping one fist inside the other. 'See.'

A ringlet fell across his face as his head dipped. 'Job bad.'

'No. I can stop the magic.'

His nose twitched again.

'Like this.' I extended my fisted hands and slowly eased them apart until I held them out to either side of me, palms facing up.

He studied my hands for a moment, then whispered, 'Job good?'

I blew out a relieved breath, the tension in my shoulders easing. 'Job good,' I agreed.

The goblin started to lower his bat ...

... a dark blur hit my back, knocking me on my side ...

... hands lifted the goblin up like a garden faerie snatching a dragonfly, swung him round and launched him hard through the tall window into the darkness outside ...

A stunned silence filled the hall.

Louis walked over to the window, placed a finger on a jagged piece of glass and pushed it out of the frame. A faint tinkling noise echoed through the open gap. Turning to survey the hall, he smoothed pale hands over his velvet jacket, a satisfied expression on his face.

'Jesus effing Christ!' A voice I didn't recognise broke the silence and as I swivelled towards it I saw a uniformed constable crouching over Alan Hinkley's body, staring at the broken window. *Damn.* Where was Banner? Two more uniforms, one human, the other a large troll I recognised, Constable Lamber, had their backs towards me; they had someone barricaded in the corner. Constable Lamber held his hands out in a placatory manner as he backed away. And I saw Banner. The Earl was using his limp body as a shield.

Footsteps sounded behind me and I turned to see Constable Curly-hair running towards the front door.

Louis loomed over me and I glared up at him. It was he who'd thrown the goblin out of the window. 'What the fuck did you do that for?' I sat up. 'He'd stopped.'

Louis dropped into a crouch, forearms resting on his velvet clad thighs. '*Fuck.* I like zis word.' He smiled, but his eyes stayed blank, like a dead fish. 'Fuck. Fuckfuck. *Fuckfuck.*'

'Stand up.' Hugh's booming voice echoed throughout the hall. 'Move away from her. Now.'

'Trolls.' Louis spat inelegantly on the floor. 'Not good for *fuckfuck.*'

I slid along the floor, edging away from Louis, happy to put some distance between us.

'Ms Taylor,' DI Crane's words held a thread of panic. 'Be careful.'

I bumped into something. Something soft. Louis smiled his dead fish smile.

'Genny,' Hugh's tone was urgent, 'move. *Now.* He's coming round.'

I started to push myself to my feet—

Too late.

Steel fingers manacled my wrist, pulling me down onto my side, and I stared into Westman's eyes. They were brown, clouded, like an old man's and full of pain and need. Soon the hunger would take over, stripping him of whatever humanity he had left and plunging him into blood-lust. No way did I want to be this close when he fell. I punched up, catching him under the jaw. His head rocked back. I punched again. He blocked me, grabbing my arm. Jack-knifing my legs, I kicked both feet into his stomach. Stale blood-tainted air puffed out of his mouth, making me gag as he slid away from me, hands still clamped around my wrists.

'Ms Taylor,' DI Crane sounded in control at last, 'I'm going to stun him. You might get a backlash from the spell.'

'NO!' I shouted, frantic, 'you can't! He's mind-locked on Neil Banner!'

Westman started pulling me slowly towards him as though I was something large and heavy – he had to be weak from the goblin's attack. I wriggled backwards, but he tugged, and I lost the couple of inches I'd gained. My heart pounded. Had DI Crane understood what I'd told her? Another pull and I slid closer, my shoulders protesting. Surely she had to realise that stunning Westman might kill Banner? Why didn't she just order Hugh and the other trolls to sit on him?

The vamp yanked at me again and I slid faster towards him. Shit, it felt like he was getting stronger. I tried to shout, but my throat wouldn't work. I twisted onto my front and tried to dig in my toes, my elbows, anything, just to get some traction. Snatches of voices stopped and started over me but I couldn't make sense of the words.

Then Westman started coming at me, using my arms to drag himself nearer, his broken legs trailing behind him like a giant leech. Blood swirled over the whites of his eyes. His mouth opened in a snarl; saliva dripped from one pointed canine, his tiny venom fangs glistening needle-sharp below his front teeth—

He'd fallen into bloodlust.

Terror filled me; I was fourteen again. Remembered pain

stabbed the back of my neck, surging through my body, and tears flooded my eyes. I didn't want to be bitten, not like before. It hurt too much.

I banged my forehead on the floor, hard, to stop the panic before it completely overwhelmed me.

'I vill help you.' Louis crawled past me, lace cuffs sweeping the linoleum, and slithered to lie alongside Westman until they were touching from shoulder to hip, then he leaned in and kissed him on the cheek. Westman froze.

My eyes closed, trembling muscles relaxed and I took a deep breath.

'Now ve bargain.'

Shit. My eyes flew open and met his flat, cold gaze. Maybe I should just climb back into the frying pan.

'Wh—?' Licking my lips, I tried again. 'What bargain?'

'I want she-witch.'

'You want what?' My mouth fell open in shock.

Louis stroked Westman's hair and started speaking fast in what sounded like French – a language I didn't understand.

I shook my head.

'Ms Taylor, perhaps I might help?' I jerked as the Earl's quiet voice sounded next to my ear, even though I could clearly see him across the hall from me – he'd thrown his voice, one of the more simpler vamp tricks – if the vamp was old enough. 'Louis wishes me to relay his request,' the Earl continued. 'Please be assured our conversation will be entirely private.'

I turned my head. Hugh's worried gaze was still fixed on DI Crane. Neither of them were moving, frozen again.

'Hugh,' I called, but he didn't respond. My stomach clenched.

'He can't hear you, Ms Taylor,' the Earl continued. 'Unfortunately, while you were dealing so admirably with the goblin, Mr Banner became rather violent in his need to reach Westman, and he attacked Mr Hinkley.' He gave a small cough. 'I took it upon myself to restrain Mr Banner. Sadly,

89

the estimable Inspector appears to have misunderstood my reasons for holding him and I believe she feels she now has a hostage situation on her hands.'

'Maybe you hugging Neil Banner like a long-lost teddy bear has something to do with that.'

'Hmm. Regrettably her various protection spells do not allow me to discuss the misconception with her. I have attempted to communicate with the sergeant, but our abilities are rather ineffectual against trolls.' He sighed. 'They are such *dense* creatures. So I have elected to contain the situation and buy us all a small amount of time, as they say.'

I frowned at Hugh. He still hadn't moved. Was the Earl saying what I thought he was? Was he actually able to selectively stop time and hold individuals in some sort of stasis? Damn, that was some trick – not that I wanted to be impressed – but it wasn't helping me much.

'Okay, I get it. So what's the deal that your *friend* here wants?'

'It is quite simple: Louis wishes you to remove DI Crane's protection spell, the one in her sapphire, without alerting her to the fact.' The Earl's voice was as calm as if he were discussing a walk in the park, instead of doing something that would go against every tenet that both the witches and vampires held dear. 'Obviously,' he continued, 'this is a difficult, possibly even distasteful option for you to consider, but I believe it is a task that is well within your capabilities.'

'Witches good *fuckfuck*,' Louis said with a grin that never reached his eyes. 'Good blood.'

'So, if I've got this right,' I said slowly, 'I can play matchmaker for Psycho vamp Louis and Inspector Crane, or I can let the other sucker here pump me full of venom whilst he attempts to suck me dry.' I'd already been there and burnt the T-shirt on option two, and was *not* looking for a replay. Never again would be too soon for that.

'Eloquently put, my dear.' The Earl paused. 'Westman

needs blood, and without it, he will be unable to withdraw his hold on Mr Banner, and thus avert the unpleasant situation in which we find ourselves.'

'Stop playing games with me,' I snapped. 'Just order Louis to feed the sucker; I'm quite sure that would also avert the situation.'

A pink bead of sweat rolled down Westman's face. Louis leaned in and caught it with his tongue. *Nice.*

'Sadly, that is not a possibility.' The Earl didn't sound quite so unruffled now. 'Louis does not bow to my hand. He owes his fealty to another.'

I didn't try and keep the surprise out of my voice. 'I thought you were the main man around here?'

'Ms Taylor, Westman needs blood soon.' He sounded tired. 'Please make your decision: who will make the necessary donation?'

'Decision made. I nominate you.'

The Earl sighed. 'In Westman's present state, blood from a vampire not of his family would devastate his mind.'

Damn. 'And destroy Neil Banner's along with it.' I finished the unspoken part of the sentence.

'Yes.' Regret tinged his voice. 'I see you understand the situation.'

Westman tugged at my arms again and I slid another inch nearer. I let out a startled yelp, then clamped my lips firmly together.

Louis grinned, showcasing his sharp fangs.

My heart thudded faster against my ribs.

'Even now, Louis is still trying to save you. Whether he succeeds is up to you. Westman is young and horribly injured. Should he attack you, it would hardly be unprovoked, for the goblin did offer the first blow, and you are sidhe fae, Ms Taylor, not human. The penalties are not so severe.'

Different races, different rules. *Damn.* He had it all worked out.

I looked at DI Crane, standing next to Hugh. One hand was still wrapped around her sapphire pendant, but her other hand was now held up, fingers frozen halfway through casting a spell. Had she moved? Then as I watched, her arm jerked, then stilled again. It looked like the Earl had to keep pressing the 'pause' button to keep them in stasis. Another yank on my arms brought my attention back to the vampires.

'I am afraid you really do need to decide, Ms Taylor.' The Earl's voice sounded fainter, as though he was further away.

'I'm thinking,' I snapped. Not that I had a lot of choices. Someone holds a gun – or a vampire in bloodlust – to your head, and what can you do? Give them what they want? That was a no-brainer. Call their bluff? That one only worked if they actually were bluffing, and somehow I didn't think they were. The only other option was to try and get control of the gun?

Shit. Would that even work?

'There is no more time, Ms Taylor.' A pressure in my head that I hadn't even noticed dissolved and noise burst over me like an oncoming wave: Hugh's voice, yelling, growls from the other troll, moans that I guessed were either Banner's or Hinkley's.

Louis shot me a fang-filled grin and crooked his finger. The pull on my arms increased and I started to slide towards him and Westman again.

I *focused* my own magic and shoved it into Westman. Power like a thin steel wire coiled from him to Louis, binding them together, but I ignored it and reached instead for the fat rope of *mesma* that emanated from Westman and stretched towards Banner. I needed to separate the convulsing red and white strands, but there wasn't time ... instead I wrapped the rope in my own magic, encasing it in a tube of golden light and sealing it tight.

'*Putain!*' Louis hissed, almost breaking my concentration. He tried to prise Westman's fingers from my wrists, but I poured more magic around the rope, locking Westman in my

Glamour, his own hands on my bare skin melding the connection. If Louis wanted Westman free, he'd have to break his fingers one by one; that was the only way he'd get Westman to let go of me.

Sweat trickled into my left eye and I blinked it away.

The scent of honeysuckle permeated the air. Tendrils of magic sprouted out like golden shoots from the rope. *Shit*, that wasn't supposed to happen! The shoots twined around the coiled wire between Westman and Louis like some quick-growing vine.

'*Merde!*' Louis leapt up and stumbled backwards, hands slicing the air between us.

Damn ... slapping a Glamour on one vamp was probably about my limit. I was operating blind; I'd only ever done this with a human before, so no way did I want to try Glamouring two of the suckers.

Heart pounding, I tried to pull the magic back, but it kept rushing out, the beautiful golden light twisting up the steel wire, stretching like elastic, getting thinner and thinner.

Wordless shouts ricocheted above me: Hugh's urgent; DI Crane's sharp with warning—

—then green lightening hit Louis in the chest, arcing along the wire, lashing back at Westman and me ...

... and the world exploded into burning green flames.

Chapter Ten

Dust was getting up my nose. I fought the urge to sneeze, and shivered: catching the backlash of a stun-spell twice in quick succession is so not something I would recommend. I tried to snuggle into the warmth surrounding me, but the dust kept choking me, making me cough.

'Genny,' Hugh's voice rumbled through me, 'Genny, are you awake?'

Opening my eyes didn't feel like a good idea.

'Is she coming round?' A woman's voice, impatient.

'I think so.' Heat breathed over the top of my head as Hugh spoke.

'Perhaps you could put her down then, Sergeant Munro.'

'In a minute, ma'am.'

Ma'am? Oh yes, the new DI.

Hugh gently patted my arm. 'Genny, you have to wake up now.'

I didn't want to; I wanted to stay where I was. I buried my face in Hugh's shoulder, feeling the warmth rising off him like sun-baked stone. If I could just go back to sleep ... But there was something I had to know first.

'Neil Banner – the Souler,' I mumbled. 'Is he all right?'

'Yes, the stun-spell missed him,' Hugh said quietly, 'but they're taking him off to HOPE to make sure.'

I sighed and snuggled back up to Hugh, then remembered something else. 'What about Alan Hinkley?'

'He hit his head on a chair when Banner pushed him.' Hugh

patted my back this time. 'The ambulance crew are just waiting to make sure you're okay.'

Frowning, I opened my eyes.

We were on the floor in the Hall, a forest of legs around us. I looked up, half-smiling as I recognised two of the crew from HOPE. Next to them stood Constable Lamber, jagged age cracks marring his speckled troll face. Then I followed the smartest pair of black-trousered legs upwards until I found DI Crane. Her expression made me wish I could just close my eyes again.

'What exactly did you think you were doing, Ms Taylor?' She didn't wait for an answer. 'I appreciate the backlash from a stun-spell isn't pleasant, but I am sure it's better than the alternative.' Her hands clenched, and her expensive knuckle-duster rings glinted as they caught the overhead lights.

'Your—' Another of Hugh's mini dust clouds drifted over me and I realised that's what had been getting up my nose and in my throat. I blew it away. 'You'd have hit Neil Banner with your spell too: automatic vamp defence.' I rubbed my nose, sneezed and Constable Lamber handed me a troll-sized tissue.

'Ms Taylor is correct.' I twisted my head towards the Earl's voice. He sat on one of the plastic chairs, a bone-china cup and saucer balanced in his hand, looking calm and relaxed. 'If your spell had hit Westman, my dear Inspector, Mr Banner would most certainly have suffered along with him, and being human, it is quite possible the damage would have been fatal.'

DI Crane's lips thinned. 'Thank you,' she snapped. 'Ms Taylor, I understand you were concerned about Mr Banner, but perhaps next time you could cast a simple barrier-spell?' She twisted a turquoise-stoned ring. 'Catching a vampire in a Glamour seems extreme to me.'

I gritted my teeth. I'd like to see her put up a 'simple barrier-spell' when she was inches away from a vamp lost in blood-lust, with Psycho vamp Louis holding his leash – not to mention my other little handicap: not being able to actually cast *any* spell, let alone a barrier one. Not everyone got the opportunity to go to witch school. Never mind she should probably thank me, as it was her that Psycho vamp Louis had the hots for.

I opened my mouth and Hugh gave me a gentle warning squeeze. 'I'll try and remember that,' I muttered.

'Inspector Crane?' Constable Curly-hair hurried into view. Her expression when she caught sight of me in Hugh's lap made me glad I was in a police station and she wasn't holding a sharp implement or six.

'Yes, what is it, Constable Sims?'

Her gaze flicked round the hall, then back to the DI. 'The goblin's dead, ma'am,' she said in a hushed voice. 'He landed on the iron railings.'

'Truly dead?' Hugh's shoulders hunched.

Damn. The goblin had been one of Hugh's flock. I drew a frustrated breath, sad for both of them.

She nodded. 'One of the spikes went straight through his heart.'

Hugh let out a deep roar and the noise rolled round the hall, bouncing off the walls. Constable Curly-hair, Inspector Crane and I all clapped our hands over our ears as the other trolls joined in. The sound exploded outwards, signalling their grief, then it stopped abruptly. I shuddered in the sudden silence. Then a distant cacophony of howls echoed in the darkness, breaking the silence and raising the hairs all over my body.

'My condolences.' The Earl's sympathy brushed over me like soothing hands and a soft sigh left Hugh's lips. I looked at the Earl. He was staring at Hugh, intent, power giving his skin a translucent blue sheen like fine porcelain. I frowned. *Mesma* wasn't supposed to work on trolls. Of course I knew the Earl was powerful, that was a given, particularly after the time stunts he'd pulled. But enough juice to affect a troll?

The blue tinge faded from the Earl's face. I glanced round. No one else had noticed; their heads were still bowed in respect.

Then Inspector Crane rubbed her hands together, rings chinking, ending the moment. She looked down at me and sniffed in annoyance. 'Do you think you might let Ms Taylor get up now, Sergeant?'

'You feeling better, Genny?'

I nodded. Cuddling up next to Hugh had dispelled the shivers I'd awakened with. He pushed me carefully onto my feet.

I gave the Earl a sideways look, then scanned the hall, looking for the other vampires. I didn't have far to look: Westman lay curled up about ten feet away, his entranced gaze fixed on me.

Well that answered that question: not only could I Glamour a vamp but the magic appeared to work the same way as if I'd Glamoured a human.

Constable Curly-hair stepped forward in slow-motion. 'Inspector Crane ... can I arrest ... Ms Taylor—?'

'Very impressive, Ms Taylor.' The Earl lifted his teacup in salute. His face was tinged blue again.

'Thanks.' I tilted my head towards him. 'I think playing with time might be even more so.' I waved a hand at the others. 'Are you slowing them down, or speeding us up, or do you just press some sort of metaphysical pause button?'

'Which would you say?' He replaced the cup on the saucer.

I shrugged. 'Where's your other pal?'

'I believe Louis is having a rest, courtesy of Inspector Crane.' He inclined his head towards the broken window.

Psycho vamp Louis was lying face-down on the floor. A circlet of silver, studded with gemstones, banded his head. It made him look like a mediaeval prince. Matching bands clamped his upper arms and wrists and shackled his ankles, and they were all fastened together with a silver chain. Constable Taegrin, a heavyset troll with skin of polished black granite, stood watch over him. Louis was still unconscious, so all the bespelled hardware seemed a bit excessive.

'And why ... would we want to arrest ... her?' DI Crane's stuttering words made me jump.

'For ... casting a ... Glamour, ma'am.'

The Earl smiled. 'Are you planning on enlightening the Inspector about our little conversation, my dear?'

Was I? Probably, but—

I brushed at the dust on my trousers, then wondered why I was bothering. I seemed to be spending more than my fair share of time on the floor lately. Why had psycho Louis taken such a fancy to the Inspector anyway? Somehow I just couldn't see him as the love-at-first-sight type, and I didn't need a calculator to tell me things didn't add up. But the Inspector wasn't the friendliest witch around, and I wasn't entirely sure she'd want to believe me. Maybe I'd run it all past Hugh first, let him decide.

The Earl touched the teacup to his lips again, watching me thoughtfully over the rim.

'What's in the cup?' I asked.

His brows arched in mild surprise. 'Tea, of course. I find it helps to calm the nerves.'

Yeah, right. Vamps might sip the occasional alcoholic drink – neat spirits only – but I'd never heard of one drinking tea before.

He sighed obviously realising he wasn't getting an answer from me and the blue colour disappeared from his face. I rubbed the back of my head, trying to ease the same odd release of pressure I'd felt before.

'Constable Sims, casting a Glamour on a vampire is not a criminal offence. Casting a Glamour on a human is.' Inspector Crane sent me a condemnatory look. 'Should Ms Taylor be guilty of that, then I will arrest her myself.'

'Yes, ma'am.' Disappointment crossed her face.

Well, that was me warned. Either I was being paranoid, or the Inspector liked me just about as much as Constable Curly-hair did.

I beamed at them both. Nice to know I had friends.

The Inspector curled her hand protectively around her sapphire pendant. 'Ms Taylor, please remove your Glamour as soon as possible. I do not want a lovesick vampire in my police station.' She turned on her heel. 'Sergeant Munro, Constable Sims, I'd like you both outside with me now, please.'

I crossed my arms and studied the lovesick vampire in question.

Westman's brown eyes were no longer clouded with blood-lust; I could see the Glamour as a golden pinprick of light deep in his pupils. Lovesick was right: he was a vampire, so he probably wouldn't die if I left him, like a human could, but he might wander about like a lost soul trying to find me. *So* not what I needed.

But to release the Glamour, I had to touch him. And he was still injured.

'You seem to be in a bit of a dilemma.' The Earl smiled. 'Perhaps I can offer some assistance?'

I snorted. 'I don't think so.'

'No strings, as they say, my dear.' The Earl stood. 'It would be my pleasure.'

He walked over to Louis, bent down and grasped the back of his velvet jacket, picking up the unconscious vampire as if he were nothing more than a pile of rags. I watched suspiciously as the Earl dropped Louis' body next to Westman with a soft thud. Westman didn't so much as flinch. The Earl crouched down, lifted Louis' chin with his forefinger and raked his thumbnail down Louis' neck. A sluggish trail of blood seeped out and the Earl wrinkled his nose. Maybe the other vamp smelled bad to him; all I caught was the faint tang of liquorice and copper.

He motioned at Westman and said, 'You need to bring his head down so he can feed, my dear. Then wait for my word and take your magic back.'

I hesitated.

'On my honour, Ms Taylor. No tricks or foul play.'

He was centuries old; no way would he break his oath.

Gingerly, I put my hand on Westman's head – his hair felt thin, greasy – and guided his face towards the crimson trickle at Louis' throat. Westman's nostrils flared as he scented the blood, and he licked his lips then struck, sinking all four fangs into the soft flesh. Louis jerked beneath him, his own lips parting on a quiet groan, and one of the yellow stones in his silver headband glowed for an instant before he subsided. Wet sucking noises filled the air ...

'Now,' commanded the Earl, jolting me from my brief reverie.

I *called* the magic and it returned, spreading heat through my body like in a slow-moving tide.

'Well done, Ms Taylor.' The Earl smiled at me. He bent down and pushed his finger into the side of Westman's mouth, separating the vampires with a muted pop. Westman flopped onto his back, blood dribbling out between his lips. The Earl grabbed Louis with both hands and flung him back towards the window, almost bouncing him off the wall. Maybe Louis smelled really, really bad.

'Thanks,' I said, frowning. His help might not have strings, but that didn't mean it didn't have an ulterior motive.

'Absolutely no need, Ms Taylor.' He dusted his blazer sleeve. 'Mr Hinkley is very concerned about his son.' He pulled a cream handkerchief from his breast pocket and wiped his hands. 'Do you still plan to help him?'

It was the same question he'd asked earlier. 'Again, why?'

'I would be interested in whatever you might discover.'

'Are you saying there's something to find?'

'It is a possibility, my dear.' He briefly smiled and turned to face the Hall's main entrance.

The pretty Armani-suited vampire was standing over Louis' prone body, his face enigmatic.

'Malik al-Khan.' The Earl flourished his handkerchief. 'I

neglected to see you there.' His choice of words suggested the other vampire had been there all along, watching.

My heartbeat sped up. Where had he appeared from? There were no shadows to hide in, not here inside the police station.

'Forgive me.' The Earl gripped my arm before I could evade him. 'I would introduce you, but I believe you and Ms Taylor have already met.'

Damn. I either had to struggle, or stand there like an errant child while the Earl held me.

I struggled.

'Be still,' hissed the Earl.

Then Malik moved, his movements elegant, almost preternaturally effortless, and I forgot all about the Earl and his fingers digging in my arm.

'You play a dangerous game, *Oligarch,*' he said to the Earl. The menace in his voice scorched like hot flames over my bare skin. I swallowed hard, fear fluttering in my stomach like a flight of frantic dragonflies.

The Earl smiled, power staining his skin blue. 'It seems I am not the only one.'

Malik halted, uncomfortably close. 'Be careful it does not bring an end to you.'

I thought he'd been angry outside, but that had been a storm in the Earl's teacup compared to the tempest now raging in his eyes. I held my breath, hoping he wouldn't notice me. Then the heat shifted, teasing around me like a warm summer's breeze, and spice fragranced the air.

The Earl touched his handkerchief to his nose. 'I see you are ever the faithful servant, still playing the voyeur for your Master. It is not a game *I* would find palatable.' He jerked on my arm, extending it like an accusation between them. 'But then, I do not share your somewhat eclectic tastes, and nor do I feel the need to mark my prey, like a brutish animal.'

What the fuck?

I looked down in shock. The bruises ringing my wrist had

bloomed red under my skin and blood was seeping out, encircling my arm: a bracelet of bright scarlet beads. As my pulse beat faster, so the blood trickle increased.

A pale hand closed over my wrist. 'My apologies, Genevieve.' Malik's cool voice invaded me and calm flooded through my body. 'I had no wish to cause you harm.'

I gazed up at him, saw sorrow in his black eyes, tasted his desire to take my blood again ...

But he turned away.

As he walked from me, the harsh light from the ceiling bulbs dimmed. Shadows that couldn't exist leached from the black of his suit, coalesced into darkness around him, and he vanished into nothingness.

Something banged behind me and I swivelled round, startled.

Constable Lamber ducked through the door. 'You still here, miss? Constable Sims said you'd left with all the others.'

Confused, I looked around me.

The Hall was empty.

Damn. 'What happened to all the vamps?'

He shrugged. 'Like I said, miss, they all left—' He glanced at his watch. 'Must be half an hour ago now. That was quite a tussle you were caught up in.' Dust shimmered above his speckled bald head. 'Proper shame about the little goblin fella. The Sarge is real upset about that. He went off-duty ten minutes ago.' His forehead creased into deep cracks. 'Are you sure you're all right, miss?'

No, I wasn't: there were too many questions jumping around in my mind, and no one left here to give me the answers I needed.

But, lucky me, I knew a vampire that could.

Chapter Eleven

The *Tir na n'Og*, or to give it its colloquial name, the *Bloody Shamrock*, is tucked away down a narrow side street off Shaftesbury Avenue. It's one of the oldest Irish bars in London, and it's been a favourite hangout for those of the fanged persuasion for a couple of centuries or more.

Of course, it's only in the last few years that it's actively advertised the presence of the vampires.

I turned the corner and ran straight into the queue of people waiting to get in: about fifty of them standing patiently, corralled behind red velvet rope hung from brass poles. Apart from a couple of leather-clad goths, the dress code was smart casual, mixed with the occasional sparkle of party wear – marking the obvious tourists. At least my black trousers and cream waistcoat wouldn't look too out of place, even if it felt like I'd been wearing the same clothes for a week.

The queue shifted forward as I moved past it to the front. A high, nervous laugh, quickly stifled, punctuated the low hum of voices. My pulse sped faster, but with the G-Zav in my system, there was no way I could slow it. Still, there'd be plenty of other hearts beating fast right alongside mine, so it shouldn't matter.

And *I* was invited. The invitation offered a guarantee of safety, that old 'Death before Dishonour' thing.

I reached the start of the line. A neon sign in the shape of a cloverleaf cast a deep red glow over the entrance. A gaggle of girls surrounded the doorman; one, a blonde in a red leather mini-skirt and matching sequinned boob tube, had her hand on his shoulder. As she stretched up, balancing on tiptoe in her red wedges, the criss-crossed straps bit into her calves. She murmured in the doorman's ear. He moved aside and waved her in. She turned to her friends, bright red lips smiling in triumph, and caught me watching her. For a moment she hesitated, then she tossed her long hair over her shoulder and followed her friends through into the bar, leaving me to face the doorman.

The top of his black hair was cut flat as a table. He wore a black dinner suit, complete with shamrock-green silk cummerbund and matching bowtie. But underneath the smarts he was all sumo wrestler. I stepped in front of the rope holding back the waiting punters and saw my own face mirrored in his dark glasses. I smiled nice and wide.

He looked down at me, nostrils flaring as he took a good long sniff.

'Hey, there's a queue here,' someone grumbled.

Sumo slowly turned his head in the direction of the voice. He glared at the sandy-haired guy who'd grumbled, then leaned forward and hissed into his startled face.

The guy swallowed with an audible gulp. 'Sorry, man ... was just saying, y'know—'

Sumo's mouth split open, his fangs gleaming. The neon sign started strobing above us, plunging the doorway into darkness, then light, then dark again. Now you see him. Now you don't. It was a nice touch. Gasps and shivers of jumpy excitement rippled through the waiting humans but I was just disappointed his dickie-bow didn't spin.

I sighed and gave Sumo a sharp poke, just above his cummerbund. 'Cut the dramatics, fang-boy.'

His head did that same slow-turn thing back to me.

Ignoring my leaping pulse, I treated him to my best so-not-impressed look. 'I'm here to see Declan. Tell him Genevieve Taylor got his invitation.'

The sign stopped flashing, leaving us in a pool of red light.

I made a twirling motion with my hand. 'Hurry it up. Night's not getting any younger.'

Sumo's lips twitched, then he produced a miniature phone and spoke, staccato-fast, in some Asian language. He listened a bit and snapped the phone shut. Then he ushered me towards the entrance, saying in a surprisingly soft voice, 'All right, luv, you can go in. Mr Declan will be seeing you.'

The tight feeling in my stomach went up a notch. I ignored it and gave Sumo a wink as he held open the door for me.

I heard the music first: a lilting Irish melody, background to the conversational buzz that filled the room. The smells, heavy on the Guinness and the Thai snacks the place served, hit me next – odd for an Irish bar, but hey. I walked up three wooden steps and looked around, letting my eyes adjust to the muted light.

The place looked pretty much like any other pub on a Friday night: lots of tables, a long bar down one side of the room, and with the added extra of a central staircase leading up to a dimly lit galleried area. People were chatting and laughing, all of them looking like they were having a great night out. In fact, the relaxed ambience was at odds with the nervous jitters I'd felt outside. I frowned. Maybe it was the music, or some sort of vamp *mesma*? But if it was, I couldn't sense it.

I also couldn't sense any vampires.

What I could see was a lot of green, interspersed with tiny crimson shamrocks. It was everywhere: green glass lights, emerald-green walls and, when I glanced down, yep, the carpet was green too, complete with its random splattering of blood-red clovers, just great for hiding those pesky drips or spills.

Now that *was* a nice touch.

I hadn't immediately noticed the waitress making straight for me. She was dressed in an oriental-style uniform, green of course, with a fist-sized red shamrock embroidered over her heart. She placed her hands together in the prayer position and bowed. 'Please.' It sounded more like *plis* in her clipped accent.

'Mr Declan, he has business. You wait few minute. You like drink, yes?'

Surprise pricked at me as I followed her. She hit my internal radar as a witch, but I hadn't heard any gossip about him having one on the payroll. She deposited me at the quiet end of the bar, next to a tray of empty glasses.

I hoped it wasn't symbolic.

Banging her hand on the counter, she shouted, 'Mick, house drink.'

A short man, ginger hair gelled into a quiff, appeared through an open door behind the bar. His black muscle vest left the freckled skin of his arms bare and was tight enough over his skinny frame to outline his ribs. A leather bandolier stuffed with corks crossed his chest and a belt studded with bottle tops hung low on his hips. He looked even thinner than the last time I'd seen him, but at least he was alive and well – even if he was a gutless bastard.

I smiled, showing lots of teeth. Being a cluricaun, a relative of the leprechauns and the Irish goblins, Mick would, of course, appreciate my toothsome grin. 'Make it a vodka, Mick, Cristall if you've got it.'

His green eyes bugged and he clutched the edge of the counter, the suckers on his fingertips flushing pink and flattening out against the wood. 'What are you doing here?' he whispered.

The music changed to a lively jig.

I looked at him, my eyes wide, innocent. 'Let me see now … having a drink? Visiting old friends? Maybe wondering why you haven't been returning my messages?'

His Adam's apple bobbed as he swallowed. 'I couldn't. He wouldn't let me. Now go away. Leave me alone.'

'How *is* Siobhan, Mick?' I asked sweetly. 'Still back in Ireland? Still *well*?'

He nodded, opened his mouth to speak—

The band played a fanfare, a hushed gasp rippled through

the room behind me, and Mick stopped looking at me and stared at something up over my shoulder.

I turned round. Up in the gallery, one of the Shamrock's vampires was leaning over the handrail, staring down at the crowd. For a moment I thought it was Declan, but then I realised it was one of his brothers, Seamus or Patrick. All three shared the same dark Irish looks, but Declan was the Master. Together they were the Shamrock's main attraction.

There was another gasp as the vampire moved, seeming to suddenly appear at the top of the stairs. It wasn't a vamp trick; he'd just moved too fast for the humans to see. His black hair curled around his handsome head and a moody look on his face put me in mind of Heathcliff, only he'd got the costume all wrong. He wore a red muscle vest like Mick's, tucked into tight black denims. Still, it matched the red outfit of the blonde now walking up the stairs towards him, the girl I'd seen at the entrance. He held his hand out to her and as she took it, her expression reverential, her knees dipped in an unconscious curtsey.

He bowed with a flourish and kissed the pulse point on her wrist.

A dozen people stood up, clapping their hands together over their heads and Mick made a strangled noise in his throat.

I turned back to him. I knew which brother it was now. 'Seamus is busy tonight.' Pasting a frown on my face, I added, 'Only I'd heard he wasn't into the ladies, just a certain red-headed barman. Something *you've* long neglected to mention.'

His face closed up. 'I was told not to.'

I laughed, but there was no mirth in it. 'Like I couldn't work that one out for myself, Mick.'

Another waitress slid a tray of empties onto the bar. 'Refill, plis,' she said, ignoring me.

Mick threw her a nasty look and muttered, 'Bugger off, Chen.' He scowled as she scurried away.

I glanced upwards, but Seamus and the blonde girl had disappeared into the dark shadows on the balcony. ''Spect that'll put a bit of a crimp in your love life.'

Mick's mouth turned sulky. 'We don't do sex here.'

'Bet that disappoints a few punters.'

'Not at all, Ms Taylor. I can assure you that all of our customers are very satisfied.' I swivelled towards the woman's voice and saw luminous grey eyes, short white-blonde hair and salon-perfect makeup. 'I am Fiona, the proprietor of *Tir na n'Og*.' Her dress was spectacular, form-fitting black silk with what looked like very expensive ruby and diamond catches holding it together. There were more rubies sewn onto her elbow-length evening gloves. 'If you'd like to follow me, Declan is waiting.'

I beamed. 'Let's not keep him any longer then. Lead on.'

As she turned and headed for the stairs, Mick grabbed my arm, his suckers pulsing against my skin. 'Be careful up there,' he whispered. 'Declan doesn't take too kindly to the Gentry.'

It was an apology. Of sorts.

Chapter Twelve

I'm off to meet the vampire ... The words beat out the tune in my mind as I followed Fiona up the stairs, or rather, followed her shoes: red suede courts with four-inch heels, studded with more rubies. The ruby extravaganza made my spine crawl. Fiona had hit my radar as human, so why was she blinged up like a witch or a goblin queen?

I *looked*, checking her out for magic. There was nothing on her. But I did see the blue shimmer of a ward at the top of the stairs. I walked through it. It clung like a garden cobweb, sticky but insubstantial, but whatever it was supposed to stop, it wasn't me.

'This way, Ms Taylor.' Fiona turned to the right.

Horseshoe-shaped booths, set at odd angles like a static fairground ride, lined the deep balcony. They were empty, though a faint candle-like glow rose over their high sides. As we passed them, the noise and light from the bar below receded as if a heavy curtain had dropped. Up here was full of peace and quiet and secrets.

Mesma. I bit the inside of my mouth and the sharp pain cleared my senses. So it was *mesma* working downstairs, manufacturing the relaxing ambience – but it had been so subtle, so insidious, so almost-normal, gliding quietly by me like a snake ... which was ironic, seeing as St Patrick was supposed to have cast that particular beastie from Ireland's shores a long time ago.

What if I'd missed something else?

I *looked* at Fiona again. Still nothing. Except ... The little hairs on my nape stood to attention ... Had the jewels on her shoes winked? Or was it a trick of the light? *Damn.* There was something about rubies, something I couldn't remember ...

Then I realised she'd stopped.

I stared up into laughing blue eyes full of warmth and welcome.

'Well, Genevieve, me darlin'. It's good to meet you at last.'

He looked to be in his mid-forties, so he'd accepted the Gift later than most. He was the archetypal handsome Irishman: straight nose, firm chin with just a hint of a cleft and a shadow of dark stubble. A slender gold hoop pierced one ear and more gold glinted at the neck of his collarless white-linen shirt, which fell loose and casual over his black moleskin jeans.

I smiled back at him before I could stop myself. He radiated happiness; it wrapped round me like the heat of a log fire, the steam rising from a hot toddy, the scent of bread baking in the oven, all the comforts of home.

Only my home had never had those sorts of comforts.

I dropped the smile. 'How could I refuse the invitation when it brought back *so* many old memories?'

Declan gave a deep chuckle, the corners of his eyes crinkling attractively. 'And memories can be of such significance in our lives.' He reached out, took my hand in his.

I let him. I was stoked up on G-Zav, after all.

'Céad míle fáilte.' His fingers were cool. 'That's a hundred thousand welcomes to you, in case you're not for understanding the Gaelic.' Turning my palm upwards, he bent, touched his lips to my pulse and inhaled deeply. 'Ah. Sugar and spice ...'

I wanted to pull my hand away, but my mind couldn't work out why I should. He was like an old family friend, a favourite uncle and I gazed down affectionately at the silver-grey strands threading his hair ...

My family wasn't the friendly type.

And I'd had enough of his games.

I gave an impatient sigh. 'C'mon, Declan, cut the crap,'

Fangs pressed against my skin.

My pulse skipped and distant need itched in my veins, muted by the G-Zav, but still there. Shit. Maybe he wasn't playing after all. I suppressed the urge to smash my knee up into his face. 'Draw blood,' I warned, 'and I'll make sure your nose never sits straight again.'

Moist breath caressed my wrist.

'Declan.' The soft note of warning in Fiona's voice sent a shiver down my spine.

He lifted his head. His eyes were black orbs, his skin stretched tight over the hard bones of his skull, all four fangs glittered needle-sharp in his open mouth.

My heart pounded. *So not good.* Fiona looked more pissed off than anything, but it wasn't her neck on the block. She returned my gaze with an undecided expression, one that brought to mind a Roman emperor debating the merits of thumbs-up, or thumbs-down.

Somehow I couldn't foresee a lasting friendship in our future.

Finally she gave a loud sigh. 'Men and their egos, Ms Taylor. Not even a set of sharp teeth can rip them apart.'

Declan threw his head back and laughed. The sound exploded out into the air, a release of power that lifted my hair and demolished the quiet that had blanketed the gallery. My ears popped – or maybe it was just my nerves snapping as I wondered just how close I'd come to being Declan's next bloody meal.

Bursts of his laughter bounced back from the bar below.

Declan gave me a wide grin, his eyes sparkling blue again, no longer doing his overly dramatic impression of a death's-head. 'Our guests will surely be enjoying the craic tonight!'

I swallowed in relief. His quick change from scary to just-your-friendly-neighbourhood-vamp told me more than I wanted to know about just how much juice he could pull. I was betting he could give the Earl or even Malik a run for their dinners. No need to let him know he'd got me rattled, though.

I clapped my hands together slowly. 'Nice show, Declan. Maybe you should consider going on the stage. I hear you enjoy a memorable performance now and again.'

He released my hand and winked at Fiona. 'There you see, me love, and didn't I tell you she had a sense of humour?'

She pursed her perfectly outlined ruby lips. 'And that's a good thing, for both of you.' She turned smartly on her ruby heels and said over her shoulder, 'I'll bring some refreshments.'

Looked like Fiona was the one with all the good ideas.

Declan blew a kiss at her departing back, then murmured, 'The perfect hostess.' Turning to me with a mischievous grin, he waved towards the semi-circular seat. 'Why don't you make yourself at home, me darlin'?'

The deep patch of darkness behind the high curved back of the bench made the hair on my neck stand up, but something told me the skirmishes were over, for now at least. I sat down at one end of the horseshoe, sinking into the plush green velvet decorated with its tiny red shamrocks.

Declan sat opposite, a half-smile on his mouth. 'You'll have been to see my boy then.'

'Yes, I saw your boy.' I tilted my head. 'You could've used the phone, you know. It would have saved all the drama.'

He chuckled. 'But all those shenanigans make it so much more interesting, me darlin'.'

I pressed my lips together. Maybe for him they did.

'And you'll not deny it's an interesting situation we have,' Declan carried on. 'There's my boy accused of killing Melissa, the poor wee bure.' Sadness filled his face. 'A pretty girl she was too, nearly twenty-one, getting ready to make some big changes in her life, if you take my meaning.'

Twenty-one. The legal age of consent for the Gift. I frowned. 'And your point is?'

'The boy knew those changes were planned, he and the

wee girl were looking forward to them. He wasn't about to try offering her the Gift himself. Why would he be taking that risk, when he knew there was no need?'

'Declan, no one in the know believes the story the papers are touting,' I said, then realised something. He didn't seem to be 'in the know' about how Melissa had been killed, that her death was nothing to do with a botched Gift, otherwise why try and convince me. Did that mean he hadn't searched Bobby's memories for her death? Or did it mean Bobby had no memories for Declan to find because he hadn't killed her?

'But,' I said slowly, fishing for answers, 'that doesn't mean your boy didn't kill her. Maybe he just got greedy?'

'Why would you be thinkin' I wouldn't know if he killed her, me darlin?' He smiled. 'He's mine, after all.'

That told me, didn't it?

'So if the boy didn't do it, someone else did,' Declan carried on.

I narrowed my eyes as I considered him. 'Whether your boy killed her or not, involving me in this situation isn't part of our bargain, Declan.'

'Now why would you be thinkin' that?'

I leaned forward. 'The agreement was you'd notify me when a fae or faeling needed help, and in case it's slipped your mind, your boy isn't fae: he has a nice shiny set of fangs. So you'll have to find someone else to be your own personal private detective.'

A broad smile widened his mouth and he flashed his own sharp set of pearly-whites, looking entirely too pleased with himself. Damn. There was something else, some catch. I sighed inwardly. Telling him I wasn't going to do the job because it didn't meet the terms of our bargain had been a long shot, but at least I could console myself with the thought that I'd tried.

'But what about the wee bure?' he said softly. 'Surely you wouldn't deny her your assistance, not when she's got the blood of the fae in her?'

Melissa was faeling? Why hadn't Hugh mentioned that? Still— 'Even if she was,' I said, 'I think she's past helping, seeing as she's dead.'

'Is she now?' he said, the smile still on his handsome face.

'The police and the pathologist seem to think so,' I said. 'Are you saying she might not be?'

His smile disappeared, replaced by a puzzled frown. 'Did you not see her body?'

'No, her mother's got the Soulers involved.'

His frown deepened. 'Now why would she do that?' he said, more to himself than me.

'Who knows?' Fiona joined in the conversation as she slid a heavily laden tray onto the table. 'Maybe she got one of their silly mailshots.' She twisted the cap off the bottle of vodka and poured a generous amount into a heavy-based crystal glass which she placed in front of me. 'The woman is a flake at best. She probably believes all that rubbish they spout.'

Beyond Fiona I could see the Asian witch-waitress, standing at the top of the stairs. She wove her fingers in a complicated dance and the ward shimmered back into being. The noise from the bar fell silent again. For a moment, I felt a pang of envy at her effortless spell-casting.

Fiona splashed whiskey into another glass and offered it to Declan. He swirled the toffee-coloured liquid, nostrils flaring as he sniffed. 'Jameson's in Waterford crystal: two of Ireland's finest.' He saluted me. 'Slàinte, Genevieve,' then with a sly expression he added, 'that'll be me, wishing you your continued good health in the Gaelic.'

I picked up my own drink and acknowledged the implied threat. 'Likewise.' Draining the glass, I savoured the cold burn. Pleasantries over, I asked, 'So is Melissa alive, or not?'

'The wee girl was ready to accept the Gift. There's always a possibility I could still perform the ritual …' He paused, then continued after a moment, 'If the boy and his father have the right of it, and there's some sort of spell involved, without knowing what the magic is, the ritual would be too risky.'

'The police say there's no magic involved,' I said.

'Me darlin' Genevieve, as to whether there is magic or not, it's your word I'll be trusting over that of the police.'

I put down my glass. 'What about Roberto? Our bargain doesn't extend to him.'

'Well, if you find the wee bure died from magic, then he'll be innocent, and it'll be a joyful time for everyone,' Declan pointed out. 'But the sooner the ritual's done the better for the wee girl.' He stared into his drink. 'We've maybe a night, two at the most.'

So, no pressure then. A question popped into my head. 'What was Melissa doing working at the Blue Heart anyway?'

Fiona smoothed her dress with one crimson-tipped hand. 'Melissa was working temporarily at the Blue Heart whilst Roberto was making appearances there.' Her nail polish matched the large princess-cut ruby ring she wore. She'd taken off her long evening gloves. I frowned, uneasy. 'Melissa was to have returned here after accepting the Gift. Declan was to be her sponsor, weren't you?' Her tone was so neutral that it almost disappeared into the background.

'So I was, me love.' His voice matched hers and upped the stakes.

I looked at them with interest. Was I sensing an undercurrent here?

'So once you get to see the poor wee bure's body, you'll come back and tell me all about it, won't you, me darlin'? And in the meantime—'He leaned forward, a sly expression on his face, 'Maybe you'll be telling me how you do it?'

'How I do what?'

'Why, how you've been rescuing all these poor fae and there's never been even so much a whisper about you. I was hoping you'd be regaling me with your secret.' He waved his glass towards Fiona and the bottles. 'And we could be toasting your continued success.'

I gave him a happy smile. 'I'd be delighted to toast my future success, but sadly, I can't divulge my secret.'

'And why's that, me darlin'?'

I leaned forward, and said in a low voice, 'Because then it wouldn't be a secret any more, would it now?'

His eyes lost their warmth for a moment, then he threw his head back and laughed. 'Fiona, me love, another drink for the sidhe, if you please.'

She hesitated, then held out her hand for my glass. Whatever she was feeling was buried deep beneath a smile of pure courtesy. 'Ms Taylor?'

As I gave her the glass, our fingers touched.

She shuddered, eyes going wide and unfocused, hand spasming, dropping the expensive crystal—

In one quick move Declan caught the glass and placed both it and his own back on the table with a soft thud.

My throat tightened. I'd felt nothing other than the heat of her skin.

'Me love?' There was a thread of something like command riding beneath his quiet concern.

Fiona sank onto the seat next to him, her face pale as rice-paper. Another shudder racked her body and she gasped, drawing in a deep breath.

He took her hand in his. 'Show me.'

She hesitated, shooting me a fearful look from under her lashes, then she leaned in towards him and kissed him full on the mouth.

I got the feeling it was way more than just your standard kiss.

I stared at my glass, sitting unbroken and empty on the table, and finally remembered what it was about rubies. Witches use gems to store their spells, but some humans use them to enhance and control other talents. Rubies were for intuition, empathy, clairvoyance: with a touch Fiona might see the past, or pluck a memory from a mind, or – more rarely

– perceive the future. And right now I was betting Fiona was one of the rare ones. And Declan would be able to taste her ability in her blood. Add that to Declan's handy knack for stealing memories and the old adage *You are what you eat* had to be working overtime between the two of them. The look she'd given me had held fear and horror, but underneath there had been a gloating satisfaction.

Fuck. What had she seen?

'Blood—' Fiona's voice was a harsh whisper. 'So much of it ...' She trailed off with a quiet whimper.

Declan stroked Fiona's face with a gentle hand. 'Forget, me love. Sleep and forget,' he said quietly, insistently.

She relaxed against him, her head dropping to rest in his lap, her eyes fluttering closed with a soft sigh.

This was not good. Picking up the vodka, I poured myself another drink and knocked it back.

'Well, this was *nice.*' Shame I'd have to drink at least another full bottle before the alcohol had any effect on me. Damn sidhe metabolism. I slid the glass onto the table. 'Sorry to break up our little tête-à-tête, Declan, but it's time I was going.'

He looked up at me, the blue of his eyes as chilled as the vodka. 'A warning for you, Genevieve.' He trailed a finger down Fiona's neck, hooked it under the ruby choker she wore. 'Your bargain is with me.' He twisted the necklace. The stones dug into Fiona's pale flesh. 'So you'll be staying away from the Earl and Malik al-Khan.'

My heart thudded in my chest. I got his message loud and clear – Fiona might be important to him, but after all, he considered her his property and he'd hurt, or even kill her if he felt the need – and he'd try and do the same to me.

'Let's get one thing straight, Declan.' I clenched my fists. 'We may have a deal going on here, but that's all we have. It doesn't give you any rights. I belong to no one but myself. Is that crystal-clear enough for you?'

He smiled and gave another sharp twist to the ruby choker.

Fiona whimpered in her sleep, one arm half-lifting in supplication.

I stood up. 'Thanks for the drink, Declan.'

'Slàinte, Genevieve. You'll be sure and let me know as soon as you discover anything.'

The band played 'Danny Boy' as I left.

Chapter Thirteen

Five flights of stairs, the after-effects of too much G-Zav and a visit with Declan at the Bloody Shamrock, never mind the dread weighing me down after Fiona's little fortune-telling show are not the best way to end an evening. I set myself at the last flight of stairs and clutching my keys, grabbed the wooden handrail and climbed. As I stood at the top, head down and heartbeat pounding like a bass drum in my ears; I tried to get my breathing back under control. This was one of those times when I wished I lived on the ground floor instead of in a converted two-room attic – never mind that the night wasn't over and I still had miles to go—

'You look like you could use a few more visits to the gym.'

I yelped and dropped my keys.

Finn was leaning next to my door, shoulder propped against the wall, arms folded. 'Sorry, Gen.' The faint moonlight through the landing window cast a tall shadow of his horns and gave him a slightly menacing air. 'Didn't mean to scare you, I thought you'd realise I was here.'

I would have – should've sensed him – if it wasn't for the G-Zav. Damn stuff always screws me up. I looked at him, but the usual stupid thrill of seeing him was muted by other things: Hugh's little lecture, the mess I was in, and the fact it was getting harder and harder to say no to him.

'Now's not a good time,' I sighed. 'I'm too tired, Finn.'

He frowned. 'You do look sort of hot and bothered.'

Yeah, well, so would he if he was halfway to another venom-induced blood-flush.

'Anyway,' he pushed himself upright, face concerned, 'I need to talk to you.'

'If it's about dinner or—'

'It's important, Gen.' He bent and picked up my keys. 'I've found out what the trees have been talking about.'

Oh right. In all the excitement I'd forgotten about them. 'You'd better come in then,' I said, resigned.

He unlocked the door and stood back to usher me through. 'After you, my Lady.'

I flicked the light on and as I walked across the room, I reached up out of habit and set the light's long strings of glass beads tinkling, then headed for the run of white cabinets along the one wall that makes up my kitchen. I pulled open the fridge, snagged the vodka from the ice-box and grabbed a glass. Then I remembered my guest. 'Want a drink, Finn?' I asked, turning round.

Finn was looking round, taking in the surroundings with interest. I gave the room, my living area, a quick once-over. It all looked as I'd left it – the mound of cushions and throws heaped against the wall, one of Katie's glossy mags lying on the rug, the bundle of bills and junk mail piled next to my compu-ter on the floor – not that I'd expected it to look any different, of course. I didn't have the benefit of a resident brownie, like Agatha ...

... the memory of gift horses bearing crystals and way too much brownie magic surfaced and I frowned at Finn, doubts crowding my mind.

'Great place, Gen.' He grinned and waved up at the vaulted ceiling with its black wooden struts. 'It reminds me of being in the woods on a clear winter's day.' He set the light tinkling again and the long drops of amber and gold and copper beads flashed kaleidoscopic colours over the white-painted walls. 'You know, when the sun shines and sparkles through the naked trees.'

'You didn't come round to look at my décor, Finn,' I said

slowly as the doubts tripped into suspicion. 'Just tell me about the trees.'

'Hey,' he grinned, 'I like the place, it's cool—'

'Fine!' Suspicion fell into anger. 'Let yourself out when you've finished admiring it.' I splashed vodka in the glass and knocked it back, feeling the icy chill deep inside me. 'I need to get some sleep.'

'C'mon, Gen—'

I slammed the glass down. 'No, you *c'mon*. You set me up today, Finn, and I don't like it.' I closed the distance between us. 'If you wanted to know how much magic I could absorb, you only had to ask. But no, you decided to give me a little test instead.' I thumped my hand against his chest. 'The half-dozen spells in the restaurant I could understand: they were just a ruse on the brownie's part to get me there. But I couldn't work out why she'd blitzed the kitchen like that, why she would risk hurting her family's business – only it wasn't her, was it? It was you.' I gave his chest another thump. 'You set all those spells, didn't you?'

'Okay, okay, I admit it.' He held his palms out, face full of remorse. 'And I'm sorry, I was wrong. But it was only brownie magic, Gen, nothing drastic. A lot of people find it useful—'

I threw my arm out, indicating the room. 'Does it look like I clean and tidy and bake, Finn? No! I don't have any furniture; I don't even have an *oven*. I eat all my meals at the Rosy Lee. And you know what else your *nothing drastic* brownie magic is doing? It's leaking out at inconvenient moments, and it's pulling my Glamour with it.' I clenched my fists. 'I nearly Glamoured a human – a *man* – just because I felt sorry for him. No way do I call that *nothing drastic*.'

'Hell's thorns, Gen.' His eyes widened in shock. 'Why's it doing that?'

'How the fuck should I know?' I shouted. 'I've never absorbed brownie magic before, and I can't just let the stuff out, can I? I mean, the spells weren't exactly user-friendly to begin with, and I'm sure my neighbours would be *so* impressed if I turned their kitchens into mini-war zones.'

Alarm flashed across his face. 'Can't you just re-shape the spells, tell the magic to tidy or polish or—?'

'Finn!' I threw up my hands in disgust. 'How the hell am I supposed to do that? Stella must've told you I can't cast spells, let alone re-shape them.'

'Well, yes, she did, but this is brownie magic, Gen. I didn't think—'

'Well, *do* think!' I snarled. 'They're still spells, Finn.' I shoved him again and he stumbled back, looking at me in dismay. 'Get it now, do you?'

'Gods, Gen, I didn't realise—' He took a deep breath. 'My apologies, my Lady. Please forgive me.' The words were stiff and formal, and totally unlike Finn. 'I would never aim to harm you.'

I stared at him in disbelief. I'd half-expected him to try and charm me, but not this strange apology. What the hell was he playing at? I raked my fingers through my hair in frustration; I'd had enough of games for one night. And it wasn't really *all* Finn's fault, was it? I knew absorbing spells came with a price and I'd neglected to mention the possibility of side-effects to him.

'Fine! Apology accepted,' I snapped and turned away to pour another drink, the oncoming blood-flush making my hand shake. Damn brownie magic. I'd have to get one of the witches to put up a circle tomorrow so I could defuse the spells – and that was going to be a fun way to spend the day, wasn't it? Still, that's what I got for being stupid.

Finn touched my shoulder, and I jumped, the drink sloshing. Grabbing a cloth, I gave him a cold stare. 'I think you should leave.'

'Gen, I really am sorry.' A frown creased his forehead. 'If there's anything I can do to help?'

The tiredness rolled back over me, washing away my anger

and leaving behind jagged grains of hurt. 'Dammit, Finn, why would you *do* that? Why couldn't you just ask?'

His face closed up and his eyes went blank and unreadable. 'It was a mistake, Gen. It won't happen again.'

'Oh fine.' I threw the cloth down. 'If you don't want to explain yourself, then you can just get out.' I marched over the door and yanked it open.

He came and stood in front of me and I refused to meet his eyes. 'I'm not leaving,' he said, his stance determined. 'Not yet, not until I've told you about the trees.'

'Get on with it then,' I snapped.

'It's not good, Gen.' He lowered his voice. 'There's a vampire watching you.'

Not really a surprise, considering. 'What's the vamp look like?' I asked, my voice flat.

'They said he's dark-haired, and a bit eastern-looking.' He looked worried. 'He's been hanging around the market, between here and the office.'

The description fit the Armani-suited vamp outside the police station – Malik al-Khan. I glanced at the bruises on my wrist, fear fluttering inside me. Why had he been watching me? Was it just the Mr October business, or was something else going on?

Finn gripped the edge of the door, his hand almost touching mine, and out of the corner of my eye I saw gold light spark between us. 'Gen, I know you're under witch protection,' he said carefully, almost hesitantly, 'but maybe you should be a bit more cautious than usual.'

'Thanks for the heads-up, Finn.' I took my hand off the door and crossed my arms. 'But it's probably nothing more than some vamp getting a bit curious.' I shrugged dismissively. 'It happens sometimes.'

'I care for you, Gen—' He paused as I snorted. 'I know that's hard for you to believe, after ...' Anxiety threaded his voice. 'But I wouldn't want anything to happen to you.' The scent of blackberries sharpened with his fear curled through the air and I felt the brownie's magic soothing the hurt that he'd tricked me. I sighed and looked up at him as the urge to ease away his fear rose within me. Suddenly, too tired to resist, I lifted my hand and cupped his cheek. 'Don't worry, okay? I'll be fine.'

He gazed solemnly down at me, moss-green of his eyes darkening as his own magic responded to mine and he gently clasped my shoulders. I gave into need and traced the arch of his brows and stroked my fingertips along the sharp angle of his cheeks. Brighter gold light shot through with green danced from beneath my skin and I held his face in my palms.

And wanted him.

I blew out a breath, and closed my eyes, dragging the magic back. He was fae – my Glamour couldn't hurt him like a human – but the 3V tainting my blood could harm us both.

'You need to go, Finn,' I whispered as I slid my hands from him.

He caught my arms, gentle fingers circling my wrists, and his thumbs smoothed over the sensitive pulse points, making my breath hitch. 'Gen, don't send me away—'

I shook my head.

'Gen.' He sounded insistent.

Something clutched inside me.

'Feel that,' he murmured. 'Feel the connection.'

Desire spiked, so fierce it almost made me scream. I gasped and opened my eyes wide. 'The magic is just trying to push us together, Finn. Yours, mine, the brownie's, it doesn't *mean* anything.'

'Of course it does! You think this happens between every fae?' He rested his forehead against mine. 'If you do, you're wrong. I've never felt anything this strong before.' His warm scent twisted through me, heat flooding into my very centre. 'Just think how we could take the magic ...'

I looked up at him. Emerald chips, and something more, glinted in the dark-green of his eyes. Drawing him down, I lifted my lips to his. He brushed his mouth over mine, light, teasing, then pressing harder, using teeth and tongue, burning into fierce demand, his unspoken question searing through my body.

I ached to say yes—

Then my heart shuddered and the coming blood-flush, stronger than before, itched through my veins. I had my answer.

I pushed him away. 'I can't. I'm sorry.'

His chest rose and fell, breathing hard. He threw his head back, horns looking darker, longer than before. I stared transfixed at the rapid pulse jumping in his throat. Then he stepped back, the need in his face smoothing out. Skimming his fingers down the vee of my top, he slipped open the first button, then the next. Want shivered through me again. He touched his fingertip to the heated skin over my heart. 'In here, you can. Think on that, my Lady.' Then he turned and left.

Tears pricking my eyes, I closed the door slowly behind him and slid down to huddle against it, listening as the sound of his footsteps—

—was lost, swallowed by pain and anguish as the blood-flush raged through my body.

Chapter Fourteen

I headed for Sucker Town, or Greenwich as it's known by daylight, the heart of the mean times. I'd left my flat using the back way: over the roof and down the fire escape ladder into the garden of St Paul's Church. A rush of hot air at Waterloo Station signalled the arrival of the tube train. Dropping into a seat, I rubbed the back of my neck, heart labouring in my chest. My body felt like I'd climbed Hugh's mountain with a bad attack of the flu; I was weak, itchy and craving. I'd have been making the trip anyway, even if I hadn't wanted to hear the gossip.

I gazed, exhausted, at the train's tunnel-darkened windows and, stifling my regrets over Finn, made a promise to myself that that was an end of it. No more wishing for something that couldn't be. I slumped in the seat and checked out my reflection: black baseball cap hiding the telltale amber of my hair, tinted glasses over my eyes, loose black T-shirt, charity shop jeans, heavy motorbike boots and a knee-length black jacket that had me sweating in the stuffy heat. My only accessory was the pearl-handled flick-knife that nestled against my spine: six inches of silver-plated steel.

Apart from the knife, my venom-junkie outfit fitted in right along with the other occupant of the carriage.

The goth leaned against the doors, arms folded loosely across his chest. Only he wasn't the real deal, just a cheap copy. His ankle-length coat was PVC instead of leather, his dye job was patchy and safety pins featured heavily in his attempt at low-cost adornment. Heavy-handed eyeliner gave him the naïve panda look, and the black, round-necked T-shirt shouted out his inexperience. A true sucker wannabe would've worn a muscle vest. Or nothing. As I'd stumbled past him onto the train, his lip had curled, showing crooked teeth, and I'd recognised him. Cheap Goth was Gazza, the dirty-mouthed pot-washer from the Rosy Lee Café. No prizes for guessing why he was off to Sucker Town.

Ignoring him, I closed my eyes, tucking my hands under my arms to stop from scratching.

The goblin woke me.

I opened my eyes to the blank stare of his dark wraparounds and was reminded of Jeremiah, the goblin who'd died at the police station. But this one was smaller, with his pale grey head-fur crimped into artificial waves and fanned out like a miniature peacock's tail. His white translucent ears flicked like a rat's and he clutched a gold lamé satchel tight to his chest, almost obscuring the London Underground badge on his navy boiler-suit – a gold embroidered 'G' that marked him as a Gatherer.

He slid a thin grey finger down his twitching nose. 'Rubbish, miss.'

My disguise wasn't good enough to trick a goblin, or even a vamp – not that it mattered. It was only the witches I was trying to fool.

I shook my head at the goblin, then touched my own nose in reply.

He patted the flap of his satchel. 'Thankee, miss.'

The goblin clomped along to Gazza, his trainers flashed green with every step. 'Rubbish, mister.'

Gazza sneered again. 'Bugger off, you little creep.'

The goblin grinned up at him, baring black serrated teeth, three of them studded with square-cut garnets. He opened his mouth wide, leaned forward and snapped his teeth together with a loud crack, right next to Gazza's cheap PVC-covered groin. 'Rubbish, mister,' he demanded.

Huddling against the door, his eyes wide, Gazza fumbled in his coat pocket, found something and offered it warily to the goblin. A stick of chewing gum, still wrapped.

Thin fingers plucked at it, then tucked it away inside the gold lamé satchel. 'Thankee, mister.' The goblin stamped his feet, leapt onto a seat and curled up in a ball, his arms hugging tight around his bag.

Gazza subsided like a pricked balloon.

I tucked my chin down, hiding a smirk.

Two stops later, the doors hissed open at Sucker Town North and Gazza jumped out and raced along the platform, coat flapping behind him like the Night Hunt was nipping at his heels.

Following at a slower pace, I shambled onto the escalator, closing my eyes briefly against the headache pounding behind them. I stuck my hand in my pocket and smoothed my fingers over Jeremiah's Union Jack badge I'd found outside the police station, then touched my fingertips to the other two just like it that I'd picked up from home.

My lucky charms.

Reaching ground level, I fed change into the turnstile and pushed through into the ladies. A miasma of bleach, ammonia and sickly-sweet weed clung to the white brick-laid tiles and my stomach roiled. I shuffled along the row of cubicles, gave each door a push, checking for the cleanest.

Two girls, one with dirty blonde hair, the other a more brassy yellow, sat on the counter facing each other, bare feet in one of the washbasins. Giggling, they took it in turns hitting the tap and splashing water over their toes. Brassy threw me a quick furtive glance, decided I wasn't anyone to be bothered about and took a long drag of her spliff.

Dirty gave me the finger. 'Piss off, cow,' she hissed.

Ignoring her, I choose a so-so cubicle at the end and locked myself in. It wasn't the nicest place to change, but it was the most convenient available. The poster on the door advertised

HOPE, and warned against 3V and the perils of Sucker Town.

I hung my jacket over it.

My heart started palpitating and I braced my hands on my knees, and panted shallow breaths until it calmed down. I wiped the sweat from my face and neck, pulled off my boots and then stripped down to my underwear: Lycra black crop-top and hipster shorts. Once I'd donned my jacket and boots again, I'd be good to go as Gazza the Cheap Goth's twin.

Easing down the shorts, I stared at the spell-tattoo on my left hip. Its hard black ridges stood proud against the honey-colour of my skin. Licking my lips, I traced the knotted Celtic shape, and a shudder of power echoed through me.

A door banged, making me jump.

'Give it 'ere, you silly mare,' one of the girls shouted.

'In a min,' the other sniggered back, 'but I wan' some more first.'

I pulled out my knife and flicked it open. The silver gleamed sullenly in the stark light of the fluorescents. Resting my left hand against my thigh, I hesitated. Was using the spell the reason I wanted so badly to sink my teeth into Finn's neck? Was that why his blood smelled of berries? I'd never had that happen before with a fae. And why now? Had something changed? The doubts edged their way into my mind, until something wild and eager and alien pushed them away. I was too far gone to turn back now. I sliced a deep diagonal cut down the bone, bisecting my life line in two.

Nothing happened.

No pain. And no blood.

'Fucking G-Zav,' I breathed out in a whisper.

I chewed my lip, trying to decide whether to tap the vein in my arm – then hot, viscous fluid seeped out of the wound like blood-coloured tar. Inhaling the rich honey scent, my heart beat with shallow thuds. I watched as the blood pooled in my palm. I took a deep breath, then smeared the sticky blood across the spell on my hip. It ran liquid into the knotted design, flooding out over the black ridges and misted in a thin red haze around my body.

My heart stuttered, and stopped thudding in my chest.

A moment's vertigo made me lurch.

The heat fled my skin, my flesh tightening as though I'd walked out into a chill winter's day.

My heart wouldn't beat again now until I fed.

'Open the bog door,' a girl's voice screamed, followed by loud thumps. 'Open the bogging bog dooooor!'

I could smell them, smell their blood, hear the fast rat-tat of their hearts in their chests. Running my tongue cautiously over my teeth, I touched the sharp points of my fangs. I could almost taste the girls: hot and salty and coppery. My jaw ached with need and my stomach pinched with hunger.

'I can see you,' the girl sing-songed.

Stretching my arms, I flexed muscles like a cat.

'I can see you too.' More giggles tumbled out.

I wiped the knife clean on the T-shirt and swung my hair forward so glossy black waves settled over my shoulders. I didn't need to see my eyes to know the colour was like frozen blue gentians. I checked my hand. The wound had already healed to a thin pale red line; it would be gone in another few minutes – part of the expensive spell package: injuries healed fast, even those caused by silver. I pulled up my shorts, smoothing them over my wider hips, and pressed a hand flat against my stomach as another cramp hit. I tugged at the Lycra top, stretching the material over my fuller breasts, tracing the map of blue veins under the paleness of my skin. Lifting my chin, I inhaled, drawing the girls' blood-scent deep into my body. Anticipation hardened my nipples and wet heat throbbed between my legs.

'C'mon.' The whining tone grated like nails on a blackboard. 'You goootta give me it. It's my turn nowww.'

I tucked the knife against my spine and shrugged into my jacket. Leaving the old clothes behind me, I opened the door of the cubicle. Brassy was kneeling on the floor, arse in the air, arms reaching under a cubicle door.

I hissed, lips drawn back.

She peered at me over her shoulder, mouth falling open as she saw me. 'Fuckin'ell,' she gabbled and scrambled back on her haunches, 'there's a bloody sucker out 'ere.'

I crouched next to her. She didn't move; the drug suffocating any fear. I stroked my finger along the blue vein under her jaw, felt her pulse jump, then pushed back a straggle of her hair. The skin covering her neck was smooth, unmarked, virgin. My gut spasmed again. I stood, inhuman quick, and snatched my hand away.

She had nothing I needed.

And everything I thirsted for.

Brassy fell forward, fingers crawling over my boots. 'Wan' some blood, sucker?' She flung her arm up, waving her wrist in the air, shrieking, 'Bloodsucker!'

I ran, her cries of *bloodsucker* chasing me through the night.

Chapter Fifteen

Crowded terraced houses blurred into unkempt semis with junk-filled gardens and peeling paintwork. Light spilled around half-closed curtains to pool on the pitted, uneven pavements. Graffiti-scarred tower blocks thrust into the night sky like giant tombstones and here and there houses squatted like waiting nightmares, their windows shuttered with blank steel plates. Sucker Town in all its midnight glory.

I stopped running, not even winded from my sprint.

A large pub, the Leech & Lettuce, complete with plastic Tudor beams, dominated one corner of the crossroads. The sign above the entrance creaked, even though the air was hot and still. Baring an impressive set of sharp cartoon fangs, the Leech on the sign was poised, ready to sink them deep into the plump juicy lettuce leaf it slithered across. A large blue heart thumped in the leech's slimy breast.

I'd reached my destination.

Gold script above the pub's door proclaimed *Archibald Smith is Licensed to Sell Beers, Wines and Spirits to be Consumed On or Off the Premises and Licensed for Vampiric Activities.*

It wasn't one of my usual hangouts: they didn't need to be licensed. But then, not all the vamps in Sucker Town are as law-abiding as the Leech's locals.

As if my thoughts had conjured them, a hoard of Beater goblins trotted past, trainers flashing red, blue and green, their foil-wrapped bats hoisted on their shoulders: one of the squads from Sucker Town's private security force, paid for by the vampires. It's not as strange as it seems, since goblins are all about the job. I watched them warily as the leader, his red hair in tight Shirley Temple curls, threw a glance my way. But I was on my own and close enough to a blood-pub that he didn't stop to challenge me.

I pushed through the Leech's door into a fug of alcohol, blood and deep-seated staleness. The clamour of voices and heartbeats almost drowned out the Eurythmics singing 'The First Cut' on the jukebox and I almost staggered from the overload on my hypersensitive vampire senses. I stopped breathing and concentrated – like any other vampire, I need oxygen, but like everything else a vamp needs, my body filters the oxygen direct from my blood, not from sucking it in through my lungs. Half-a-dozen non-breaths later and my senses were tuned back to comfortable levels. After three years of using the spell, muting was coming easier. It had taken me six months to get it right; I might have mastered it sooner, but black-market magic doesn't come with instructions.

I looked around. The Tudor theme continued with more fake beams criss-crossing the low ceiling and hunting scenes chasing each other round the walls. The booths in the rear bar – partitioned by high wooden panels – were busy, but the tables in the open area were mostly empty. A line of hot and cold bodies propped up the counter, the humans burning bright to my eyes as their venom-thickened blood pumped round their bodies. The vampires were almost shadows by comparison. Scanning the cool faces, I saw one I recognised: Mr June, another of the Blue Heart's Calendar vamps. He stood with two other vampires. Oddly, they were the only group not chatting up the menu options.

I picked out the perfect spot, near enough to listen, far enough away not to be noticed … only my perfect spot was already taken by a hot black-leather-clad body hulked over his drink. About the only thing that doesn't change with the spell is my height. I'm still five-five. I tapped the leather-clad shoulders and they straightened up and turned towards me, giving me a view of a chest that would've looked at home on the cover of a romance novel – the ever-popular throat-ripping kind, going by the fang marks that trailed from his left nipple down to disappear beneath his leather waistband. Lucky me. I'd found a *real* goth.

His handsome, chiselled face was framed with tawny waves of hair, also model-perfect. He smiled down at me, human teeth gleaming and eagerness lighting up his hazel eyes. 'The name's Darius and the answer's yes.'

Mentally I rolled my own eyes: not just eager, but cocky with it. 'You haven't heard the question yet.'

His hand skimmed down the trail of bites. 'Doesn't matter, it's still yes.'

I ran the tip of my tongue over my fangs. Maybe I should just get this part of the night out of the way – not that willing humans were hard to find in Sucker Town, but *strike while he's hot* flashed in my mind. Given that a couple of his bites were obviously recent, Darius was nothing if not on fire.

As I stroked my fingers over the little red wounds his smooth skin trembled under my touch. My hand brushed his stomach ... *there*. I found what I wanted: the bite was swollen with venom and radiating heat like a furnace. Pressing my palm flat against it, I felt him sigh.

'Anything,' he murmured, his eyes fixed not on my face but lower down my body.

Of course he'd noticed my enhanced assets. The mounds of my breasts swelled above the Lycra, the blood-starved veins under the pale flesh like a blue lace bodice. Darius – or anyone else – could tell I needed to feed just by looking.

He shifted closer, pushing against my hand.

I slid my hand lower. He had his own enlarged assets. Sex was obviously available as a side dish. But then, it usually was. It also made the medicine go down *so* much better. I placed my lips over the bite near his heart and the faint taste of liquorice sparked across my tongue.

I caught a glimpse of Mr June and his pals out of the corner of my eye and shook my head: business first. There was always another Darius, or Roberto, or whatever name they'd chosen.

'Move.' I shoved him away.

He gave me a mock pout. 'Tease.'

I jabbed my index finger into his sternum.

'Okay, okay. I get it.' He gave me a hopeful look. 'Later?'

'Maybe.' I flashed fangs at him.

He grinned. 'Cool.'

Leaning my elbows on the counter, I gestured at the bartender, a sky-born goblin judging by her lack of black wraparound shades. She flipped her glass cloth over her hefty shoulder and hurried across. 'What can I get you, luv?'

'Stoli,' I said, 'Cristall if you have it.'

She adjusted the floppy bow on her acid-yellow blouse. The colour matched her bulging eyes. 'Got the new Blueberi flavour in, if you're interested?'

I shook my head. A lot of vamps liked their spirits sweet, even added sugar to the alcohol. I preferred the pure stuff.

Extending her arm, she snapped her fingers. 'Coming up in two shakes of a lamb's tail.' Then she tilted her head, her stacked coils of plaited white hair threatening to tip over, like a top-heavy wedding cake. 'Don't recognise you for a regular, luv, so I'll just let you in on the rules round here.'

Rules? I raised my eyebrows. The place was more civilised than I'd thought. A coaster materialised on the counter between us. It looked like a playing card, the King of Hearts, except the hearts were blue.

She tapped it with her yellow-varnished claw. 'Most of my vampire clientele belong to the Heart bloodline, but I don't discriminate.' Her chin wrinkled, the long thin cats' whiskers curling and uncurling. 'So long as there's no trouble.'

'Not what I'm looking for.'

'Good to hear it, luv.' An empty shot glass, frosted with condensation, appeared on the coaster. 'Now, if you find yourself a compatible guest, alcoves are for wrists or necks only. We've a nice selection of private rooms underground if your taste runs elsewhere, rates are very reasonable. There's a credit card deposit against any medical expenses and check-out time is one hour before dawn, otherwise we charge for a second night.'

'I'll remember.'

The glass filled with clear liquid, then slid towards me. It was standard brownie magic, except that part of the whole 'not being affected by magic but able to sense it' usually meant that goblins couldn't use magic themselves. I was curious enough to want to check it out, especially after my own brownie-magic problems. Maybe brownies sold their magic like the witches? Not that I'd heard anything like that. Only I couldn't, not in this guise – the sidhe magic part of me shuts down. That's probably why goblins never recognise me like this, or grant me the usual greeting.

'First drink's on the house, luv.' Her lips parted in warning, letting me glimpse sharp silver-plated teeth studded with citrines. 'Enjoy.'

'Cheers.' I touched my fingers to the chilled glass and nodded, but didn't drink.

An age-spotted mirror behind the bar offered a panoramic reflection that included the three vampires, as well as me. That old myth about vampires not reflecting in mirrors is just that: a myth. I didn't even have to turn my head to watch them, or the rest of pub. Mr June looked like that fifties movie star, the Grant guy. His shorter pal had the round cheeks of a cherub. The last of the trio had zigzags shaved into his close-cropped hair and a gold dumbbell through one eyebrow. Something silver-coloured would've looked better against his black skin, but hey, maybe he couldn't afford the platinum-plated stuff.

Concentrating on listening, one of the vamp tricks I *had* managed to master, I cut through the noise in the pub and tuned into their conversation

'Me, I like a young, tasty bit of totty,' Zigzag said. 'I mean, look at the knockers on that one, man: big enough to suffocate in if I still needed the air.'

I checked out the object of his affections. Her black leather corset offered her full venom-flushed breasts on a plate. I could see why the vamp was impressed. Perched on the edge of her seat, hand grasped round an Alcopop bottle, her examination of the room would have put searchlights to shame. It wasn't just the vamps that hunted in Sucker Town.

Cherub Cheeks shook his head. 'Know wot really gets on my wick nowadays? Science, innit. Sumfings jus' ain't right. Ended up back at this bird's place las' night, I tell you, mates, she was sumfing else, tits big as bleedin' melons they was.' He grinned, jiggling his hands in front of his chest. 'You'd 'ave luvved 'em, mate.'

Zigzag leaned in, fangs making small indents in his bottom lip.

'So I tell you, I sunk me points right in one of them juicy tits.' Cherub Cheeks paused for effect. 'Sunk 'em right in, I did, 'spectin; a nice bit of the hot stuff.' He clapped Zigzag on the shoulder. 'And know wot I got? Bleedin' silicone, that's wot.' His face screwed up in disgust. 'Bleedin' melons was nuffin' but pumped-up bleedin' boob balloons.'

'Shit, man.' Zigzag almost pierced his lips in shock.

'I tell you,' Cherub Cheeks patted his own flat chest, 'I'm stickin' to fried eggs from now on, 'cos that stuff tastes like a bleedin' troll.' He shook his head sadly. 'Bleedin' science.'

A tingle of awareness slid across my back. It reminded me of Gazza watching me earlier in the Rosy Lee. I glanced behind me, almost expecting to see his Cheap Goth persona, but it was Darius, leaning against the jukebox, leather coat slung over one shoulder. He pressed a button and 'I Want You Now' – Depeche Mode – blasted out. I ignored him. At least in the Rosy Lee my meals didn't try to proposition me.

'Do you know what I hate?' Mr June combed his hand through his thick dark hair. 'Those awful Blue Heart cocktails!

I mean, fruit juice and no alcohol? Give me a gin drinker any day.' He let out a soulful sigh. 'I used to hunt this district back in the eighteen eighties. It was full of dockworkers in those days. You could stroll down any street after sunset and pretty much take your pick, no need to even mind-lock them to forget. They were all pickled by the gin.'

'And what's with all that fizzy pop they drink now?' Zigzag joined in. 'Shit, man, it gives me the hiccoughs.'

'You know another aspect of the Blue Heart that I hate?' Mr June brushed a hand down his black silk shirt. 'That bloody awful uniform they make me wear. Authentic Second World War it might be, but the material scratches like the devil. You'd think Rio would let me have it lined in silk, but "Oh no," the bitch says, "The customers would take exception." As if they would know?'

'Man, stop grumbling.' Zigzag sniffed his brandy glass. 'You're one of the star attractions, you get well-paid for wearing itchy finery and you get your ugly mug stuck up all over the shop.'

I took a sip of Stoli, then caught movement in the mirror as the girl in the corset stood up, revealing a satin and net skirt. She fluffed it up, then, extending one slender leg, she smoothed her hands from her ankle to her thigh, adjusting her fishnet stockings. Looking up under her lashes, her eyes met mine and a slow smile spread across her face.

'I suppose it has its compensations.' Mr June's words were faint in my ear. 'I just wish Rio would serve alcohol. At least that would improve the blood on offer.'

Corset Girl straightened, gathered her long dark hair in her hands and clipped it in a loose bundle on top of her head.

'Wot abaht that bleedin' Mr October then, mate?' Cherub Cheeks said. 'Fink 'e did it?'

My ears pricked up and I dragged my attention away from the girl.

'Bit of a rum do, I must say.' Mr June lowered his voice. 'I heard he had a bit of trouble with the girlfriend. She took a fancy to the Frenchie, and he to her. Ah, the Eternal Triangle causes yet another crime of passion.' He chucked Zigzag under the chin. 'You would have liked her: she was a real looker, and generous with it.'

'I saw her.' Zigzag grinned, fangs white against his skin. 'She worked in the private bar, one of Rio's specials. Very sweet, mate, verrry sweet indeed.'

The pub door opened and the mirror reflected another familiar face: Gazza, the Cheap Goth, only he wasn't alone. As he headed straight for the alcoves I glanced at the vampire with him, but something made my eyes slide away. I frowned, tried to look again, and the same thing happened. Then I was staring at Corset Girl and Gazza slipped from my mind.

She smiled, fingers tracing the blue ribbon lacing her leather corset, then she tossed her head and started walking towards me.

'Didn't the girlfriend work at the Bloody Shamrock? Declan's always got an eye fer the good stuff. That weird bird, 'er as belongs to Declan, weren't there sum sorta scrap between 'em? Maybe she got jealous an' she bleedin' done 'er in.'

The voice grew fainter as the girl distracted me. She sidled in next to me. 'I saw you looking,' she murmured. Blue streaks layered the brown of her hair. 'Thought I'd come over.'

'Shit, that's all old news, man,' Zigzag said scornfully. 'You know who else was sniffing round the girlfriend? Old Red Eyes himself, Malik al-Khan. Maybe he killed her.'

I tipped back the vodka, letting the alcohol sear my throat.

Corset Girl pulled a length of hair from her loosely piled topknot and draped it down her cleavage. 'You're not one of the Blue Heart vamps, are you?'

'No.' I gazed at her. She glowed rosy with heat, the blood flowing fast beneath her skin.

'... *Malik and the Earl were arguing about it, loud enough that I could hear ...*'

'I saw you talking to Darius earlier.' She gave a sideways glance towards the jukebox where Darius was still standing, forehead creased in a deep frown. 'Good job you blew him out. He's a nice guy, but he's Rio's latest toy.' Her leg nudged against mine. 'None of the regular vamps'll touch him.'

I took a couple of non-breaths, tried to ignore her.

'... and the Earl told him to get lost, well not exactly, but he said he didn't need him here ...'

'Rio gets really possessive about her toys.' Corset Girl picked up my glass, sniffed. 'Is this the new blueberry one?'

I shook my head.

She sipped at the dregs anyway. 'The last toy, before Darius, got something going with this other vamp, y'know?'

I tried to concentrate on Zigzag's voice.

'... told him to stop playing at Machiavelli ...'

'... then Rio issued a Challenge to the other vamp, and killed him.' Corset Girl leaned in, slid her hand under my jacket. 'Said she was making a promise to anyone else who even thought about touching her property.'

'... then he said, death happens all the time. That the traditions we live by were more important ...'

Hot fingers slid round my waist. 'Your skin's really pale, y'know, like cream.' Tilting her head, she offered her throat. A half-moon of four tiny fang marks, the bite swollen hot with venom, marked her neck.

'... that the status quo had to be maintained ...'

Hunger cramped my stomach. Her heated, sweet scent pulled me in and I licked over the hot bite, scraped my fangs over her flesh. Liquorice taste and copper filled my mouth.

She shivered under my lips.

Swallowing hard, I recalled the bartender's rules and looked up, searching for an empty booth.

Gazza strolled past, arm wrapped around—

I blinked. My eyes refused to focus, skating onto Darius instead, now lounging on one of the fake leather benches.

"*eads up, mates.*' Cherub Cheeks' words intruded. '*Bleedin'* *take-away time, innit.*'

Corset Girl's hand stroked up my spine. 'We could get a room.' Pressing closer, she murmured, 'I've never been with a female vamp before.'

My head thundered with her pulse, the ache in my jaw intensified and frustration burned in my chest.

Mr June followed the others out of the pub.

Fuck it.

Gazza had found himself a fang-gang.

Chapter Sixteen

I found the fang-gang in a narrow passage way behind The Leech. Standing in the shadows, I peered down the alley. There was just enough moonlight to boost my vampire sight. Cherub Cheeks, Zigzag and Mr June were gathered in a semi-circle facing Gazza and another vamp with long platinum-blond hair wearing a red poet's shirt. He had his arm slung over Gazza's shoulder. He'd been the one my eyes kept sliding away from in the pub. Was it just a neat vampire trick I hadn't come across before, or some sort of magic?

They'd picked their site well: escape routes at either end, no windows above to shed any light and the half dozen large bottle-skips parked along the alley's brick wall to give them some privacy. Only another vamp might notice them, and depending on their inclination, they'd either ignore what was happening or join in. It was the Beater goblins and their silver-foil covered bats the fang-gang wanted to avoid.

I clenched my fists. I knew what was coming next, and I couldn't stop it, not yet – four against one meant the odds were definitely not in my favour. I could alert the Beaters myself, but Gazza didn't have that much time on his side and all it would gain him would be months of treatment at HOPE and a lifetime popping G-Zav pills.

If he even survived.

So I watched, frustration and hunger eating away like acid at my insides.

Red Poet vamp wrapped his forearm round Gazza's neck. 'Party time,' he crooned.

'What—?' Gazza's startled cry fizzled out as his windpipe and vocal chords were almost crushed.

'Shhh.' Red Poet stroked Gazza's cheek, then shoved his head back at an awkward angle. 'C'mon boys,' he said to the other vamps, 'time to play.'

Gazza's arms flailed, fingers clutching at the empty air.

'My turn now, man.' Zigzag grabbed the edges of Gazza's PVC coat and wrenched it down, trapping his arms against his body.

Gazza's boots scuffed along the gravel.

I dug in my pocket, removed the Union Jack badges.

'Gotta bleedin' luv it, mates.' Cherub Cheeks gave a low whooping laugh as he yanked Gazza's PVC trousers to his knees, effectively hog-tying his legs.

Gazza's lower body jerked, hip bones sticking out like chicken wings above tiny red satin briefs.

I shrugged out of my own jacket and spread it out on the cobbles at the end of the alley. Hiding the badges under it, I flicked on their switches.

Mr June fisted his hands in Gazza's T-shirt and hissed as he tore it apart, exposing Gazza's thin, safety-pin-decorated chest. He ripped a pin out of Gazza's left nipple, held it up to check it, then tossed it over his shoulder. 'We're okay, chaps, its stainless steel.'

Gazza's ribs heaved with each frightened breath.

Red Poet reared back, all four fangs glistening in the moonlight.

I hugged myself, pressed my lips hard together, trying to ignore the excitement frothing through my own veins.

A high, thin squeal, like a pig having its throat cut, pierced the night, sharp scents of blood and venom tainted the air and harsh wet sucking noises permeated the darkness.

I scrunched my eyes tight and leaned back against the brick wall, listening …

Muffled whimpers, the low hum one of the vamps made as he

fed, the rapid beat of Gazza's heart as fear and venom-induced adrenalin pumped his virgin blood faster and faster …

I wanted to blank out the sounds of the attack, but that was too dangerous. If I was to save Gazza, I had to get it right. *Shit.* This part of Sucker Town was supposed to be safer. I was going to have to extend my own hunting territory in future. After a while I opened my eyes and stared up at the stars blinking wearily through London's light pollution, waiting.

'Bleedin' fantastic, mates.'

The voice made me jump. I took a cautious look down the alley.

'Takes the taste of troll tits right outta yer mouth.' Cherub Cheeks smacked his lips.

Showtime.

I snatched up my jacket, shoved it on. The three badges were still bravely flashing their little batteries out.

'Beaters,' I called in a loud whisper, keeping to the shadows. 'Beaters are coming!'

'Bloody hell!' Zigzag's head shot up and he looked towards me.

Cherub Cheeks slapped Mr June and Red Poet on their shoulders. 'Oi, up, mates, git a bleedin' move-on. I can see their bleedin' trainers!'

All four rose as one and almost silently sprinted away in a rush of disturbed air, disappearing out the other end of the alley.

I scooped up my badges, flicked off their lights and walked over to Gazza. He was lying as the vampires had left him, eyes wide and unfocused, held prisoner by his own clothes. Shivers racked his body and dark blood streamed from the bites, four of them in total. I'd only given the vamps enough time for one bite each, but I still counted them, to be sure.

My mouth watered. *Shit.* I turned away and kicked one of the large skips full of empty bottles, then punched it several times, denting the steel. As I slowly licked the blood from my knuckles I felt the craving recede.

I knelt and checked the pulse in his neck. It battered away, fast and shallow, like the heart of a terrified rabbit.

'Not what you were expecting, was it, Gazza?' I murmured.

The four vamps had taken him out to dinner, and then some. He was lucky his heart was young and healthy – but he was still losing blood, and if the bites weren't closed, he'd bleed out. And be just as dead.

I gave him a mocking smile. 'And we wouldn't want that, would we?'

Bending over him, I licked at the bite in the crook of his arm. The metallic taste of his blood burst over my tongue. The adrenalin made it sweet and frothy, like a fizzy drink. The stream slowed then stopped as my vamp saliva speeded up the clotting process. I took a non-breath and forced myself to spit out his blood, rather than do what I really wanted to – roll it round my mouth … and swallow.

I tore a strip off his ruined T-shirt and bandaged it round his arm. He let out a quiet whimper as I carefully pulled his coat up and over his shoulders. I turned to the bites on his legs next. He had one on the inside of each thigh, high up, close to the groin. His red briefs were wet with his own blood.

I sighed. 'Shame they couldn't have picked a less awkward spot, Gazza,' I muttered, though of course I knew the answer to that one: fang-gangs went in for veins in a big way. I closed the first bite and wrapped more material around his skinny thigh. The other was higher, half-covered by the soft bulges in his briefs. Gingerly, I pushed the red fabric lumps out of the way and started on the bite.

Something stirred under my fingers. I rolled my eyes. Males were all the same. What with all that adrenalin and blood pumping round his body, it hadn't taken much for his hormones to spring to life – even if he was halfway to dying.

The blood clotted under my tongue. I sat up and spat it out, then started shredding more T-shirt. His briefs hadn't managed to contain his excitement and he poked out, twitching almost as much as he was shivering.

'C'mon, Gaz, give it a rest, will you,' I muttered. 'Try using that blood somewhere more sensible, like your pea-sized brain.'

In answer, his shivers changed to full-blown tremors.

Damn. He was going into seizure. Red Poet must've shot him up with more venom than I'd thought.

I gripped Gazza's bony shoulders. He jerked like he'd been hit by a massive stun-spell and his knee jolted up, caught me in the chest and sent me sprawling. He panted open-mouthed and his lips started to turn blue – his venom-fuelled blood was rushing too fast through his lungs to consider stopping to pick up oxygen. I flung myself on top of him, using my bodyweight to keep him still.

The venom had to come out, and fast.

His spine bowed, nearly throwing me off again. Grabbing his hair, I wrenched his head to the side. A flash of Red Poet doing the same before he struck left a slimy feeling in my gut. The last bite was high up – it had missed the carotid artery by a goblin's whisker – and clear fluid leaked out of the pinprick marks, not blood. I clamped my mouth down, my fangs piercing the swelling skin. Liquid fire streamed down my throat. The world went silver and shiny and hazy – it felt like every cell in my body was expanding, drinking in the venom, and I was losing the parched, tight, coldness that was my usual existence.

I sucked, mindless as a newly Gifted vampire, revelling in the pulsating heat spreading out through my body. Fingers groped at me and I moaned in pleasure. The jerks beneath me took on a rhythm, old as ages and I ground myself against him, wanting more. Hot breath panted in my ear, smells of salt and sweat teased my nose, metallic copper taste filled my mouth ...

I snapped my head up, awareness returning with the first

swallow of blood.

Gazza grunted, his hands clutching at my back and then his chicken-wing hips jerked one last time. For one frozen moment I looked at him. His black eyeliner was smudged beneath his eyes, angry red spots dotted his chin, and with each exhalation a gob of snot ballooned around the safety pin in his right nostril—

I'd blown out the male model and Corset Girl for this?

I really was a sucker.

Rising onto my hands and knees above him, I spat, trying again to get rid of the taste of his blood. His heart beat fast and shallow under his thin ribs, but it no longer pounded at the same dangerous rate as before. I closed my eyes briefly. My own heartbeat had restarted, a slow strong thud in my chest, but frustration and need still clawed inside me. Even now, sated with venom, I wanted more. A voice in my mind screamed at me to take what I wanted – what I *needed*.

Fuck. Fuck. Fuck!

I had virtually raped him, a kid – never mind I'd probably saved his life, never mind that he'd probably enjoyed it. He hadn't been in a position to choose. A buzzing started in my ears, my stomach heaved ...

A hand grabbed my hair, nearly ripping it from my scalp, and I crashed into the wall of the alley. My skull cracked against the brick and stars exploded in my head.

Chapter Seventeen

There was a naked foot inches from my face. It seemed to have more than the requisite number of toes. I blinked and the toes resolved themselves into the standard five. I moved my head, then stopped as pain jabbed into my skull. Ignoring the foot, I cautiously touched the back of my scalp, and bringing my hand back in front of me, I stared at my fingers – it looked like I'd dipped them in red paint.

Shit. So not good.

I tried to get up and more pain jabbed along my side, making me gasp. I slumped back, wishing the spell would hurry up and heal my injuries.

'How disappointing.' Hot thumb-tacks marched over my skin. 'That I should find you like this.'

I recognised the voice, recognised the not-quite-English accent. Malik al-Khan.

Why wasn't he wearing any shoes?

His feet were narrow, elegant. A thin band of jet ringed one of his toes. I stifled an almost overwhelming urge to reach out and touch and instead looked up. Black trousers, loose black silk shirt, I hesitated at the tantalising glimpse of pale skin at his throat and lifted my gaze further, straight into a pair of shadowed black eyes, punctuated by glowing red pupils.

My heart lurched with terror, and something else. 'What the fuck did you do that for?'

Malik dropped into a crouch. The movement was as elegant as his feet. It brought his eyes closer. I pressed against the brick wall, not sure it had improved matters.

'The human was near death.' His voice was a soft threat.

My gaze flicked to where Gazza was lying, still unconscious. I concentrated, listened to his pulse. It had slowed and now his heart was beating steadily; he obviously had the stamina of a cart horse. Relief eased the snarl in my gut. 'Not any more.'

Malik shook his head, the movement abrupt. 'Feeding in such a way is dangerous. It is this' – his hand sliced towards Gazza – 'that escalates their fears, turning them into maddened vigilantes. That is why it is forbidden.'

An irritated part of me wanted to say, *I didn't start it, I was just trying to help,* but then if I'd been the one I'd discovered sucking on the damned evidence, I probably would've found me guilty too.

'Thanks for the lecture.' I started to edge to one side. 'But really, it's not needed. Believe me, I get all that PC stuff.' The movement jarred my skull. I blinked away the pain, it wasn't as bad now, so at least the spell was doing its thing. 'Now, I'm just going to clear up my little mess and we can forget all about it.'

He sighed, the sound sliding wearily round me. 'You are mine, Rosa. I cannot *forget.* Nor can I allow you to continue like this.'

Confused, I frowned. 'What did you say?'

'I have been informed you had become feral, Rosa.' He ran fingers through his dark hair, pushing it from his pale, pretty face. 'I did not believe it so.' The black gem still pierced his lobe. 'Until now.'

Shock raced through me, the hairs at the back of my nape standing to attention. Why was he calling me Rosa? Was it some sort of game? 'My name isn't Rosa,' I said, grateful the words came out calm. 'You're mistaken.'

'No mistake, Rosa. You are blood of my blood.' The glow in his eyes flared, then snuffed out, leaving them empty obsidian pools. 'I gave you the Gift of this life.'

I stared at him in horror. He thought he'd *Gifted* me? Why? This was just a spelled disguise ...

Wasn't it?

Damn. Exactly what sort of black-market magic had I bought?

I shook my head, the pain almost gone. Stupid question. It didn't matter, not right now. Digging my nails into the gravel, I swallowed back my doubts. 'No, you're wrong.'

'Do not think to deny me,' he said. 'You may have gained your autonomy, but it is still within my right to destroy my own creation,' his beautiful lips thinned, 'should I feel it necessary.'

So not what I wanted to hear.

He carried on, 'Why did you leave your home, Rosa?' He reached out, sorrow in his eyes, and brushed his thumb across my mouth. 'Why did you leave your companions?'

My lips tingled, swelled. A shiver rippled through me, flooding me with need. Remnants of venom-infused lust swirled through my body, muting my pain with the anticipation of pleasure. I parted my mouth, touched my tongue to my lips and tasted rich spice.

'I told you, you've made a mistake, I'm not your Rosa.' But my voice sounded thin, uncertain, even to me.

He gave me a sleepy smile, leant in until he was just a breath away from me. 'I know this body, how to raise it to ecstasy.' Gentle hands clasped my face. 'I know how to drown it in power.' Heat pooled in my belly. 'I know how to promise it pain.'

My lips trembled against his. My body knew what he meant, and it wanted that pain, would claw through hell to get it. Lost, I swayed forward, sighing against the coolness of his mouth.

He caressed my neck, traced the line of my jaw, pressed his thumbs against the pulse jumping in my throat. 'I should rip this pretty head from its body,' he murmured against my mouth.

Far away, deep in the back of my mind, a voice started screaming in panic. I shoved the voice away and listened only to the frantic desire thrumming through my heart. Needing to be closer, I moved to kneel between his legs and slid my hands around his waist, feeling the cool silk of his shirt beneath my palms and breathing in his dark spice scent. His hold on my neck tightened, and with a sigh, I lifted my mouth to his—

In one quick motion he took us both to our feet and slammed me back against the wall, breaking me out of my daze. 'But first,' he whispered, 'you will tell me what has happened to this body's true owner.'

'I am not this Rosa.' I choked the words out around his hold on my throat.

He tilted my face up to his. 'Would you have me hurt you?' His tone was soft, inviting.

An odd feeling spiked low inside me, tipped over into desire, and I wanted him, needed to fill myself with him. Closing my eyes, I stayed still, clenched my jaw and struggled to ignore the feelings ...

... *struggled not to beg.*

'Or would you have me pleasure you?' His hands skimmed over the swell of my breasts, teased me to aching tightness. Cool palms slid low over my hips, moulding my flesh, sending heat singing through my veins.

It's not real. I shook my head against the wall. *It's only mesma.* Rough brick scraped across my scalp raising a far-away pain. *It's not real. It can't be.*

'No,' I whispered, opening my eyes.

The sensations stopped, leaving me empty, yearning.

'Ah. So she is truly gone.' He kissed my forehead sadly. 'Rosa could not resist my touch.'

Grief washed over me like a wave and spilled hot tears down my cheeks.

He bent his head, licked the tears from my face. 'These are precious jewels, not to be wasted.'

My heart quivered beneath my ribs as his mouth met mine. His tongue invaded my mouth, slipping between my fangs, tasting me as though he was starving and I were a banquet for him alone. I welcomed him, drinking him down with a desperate thirst. His body shuddered under my hands, the echo of his heart thudded against my breasts, the solid length of him pressed into my belly sending me liquid and willing and eager and reaching for him to fill the aching urgent need inside—

He broke the kiss and I whimpered at the loss. He stared down at me with eyes bright with tiny flames. 'You shall not keep this body.' He bowed his head. 'It should not exist without her soul.'

His words reverberated through me, shocking me back to my senses. He was going to kill me. No discussion. No offer of alternatives. No phoning a friend. Just dead. But he couldn't kill *me* – a sidhe was too great a prize for any sane vamp to ever contemplate just killing. Only I wasn't sidhe now, was I? I was just another sucker. Damn! How stupid was I? It wasn't just the witches I'd been relying on for protection, it had been me, myself, what I was. And never mind what I'd always told myself about death being my first choice of options—

I didn't want to die.

Malik's hands slid through my hair, holding me still. 'For you, Rosa, for your love.' His murmur wrapped around me, tying me with the finest chains as his mouth moved over my jaw, lips trailing along my skin and cool breath whispered over my neck . . .

I wasn't going to let him kill me.

His fangs pierced my throat.

The pull on my neck was delicate, the sting diffusing into delight. The pull turned seductive as bliss spiralled through my body. His mouth grew more demanding, drawing pleasure and power and pulsing life from me. Shadows swirled like spirits around us, half-seen colours glinting in their darkness . . . *He was killing me* . . . his dark spice scent in my lungs, his beautiful lips taking my life's blood at my throat . . . *Killing me with pleasure.*

I wanted to live.

I dragged my trembling hands from him and flattened them against the wall behind me. I swayed forward, slumping against him, letting him take my weight and slowly, so slowly, felt behind me until I closed weak fingers round my knife.

Could I do it?

I hesitated on the edge of his pleasure, anticipating the plunge into ecstasy until, sobbing, I thrust the knife up between us towards his heart. His mouth at my throat spasmed and I screamed, shoving the knife deeper. He reared back, his eyes incandescent with shock and pain, his mouth stained crimson.

Clutching a hand to my neck, I stumbled back, my eyes never leaving his.

He dropped to his knees, spread his arms wide, *called* out to me, not with words, but with blood.

Blood of my Blood.

I hesitated, wanting to go to him as warm wetness streamed between my fingers, but I clenched my fist and took another step back. My foot caught on something and I stumbled, twisting, arms flailing to break my fall. I landed on my hands and knees, staring down at Gazza.

His eyes snapped open, pupils dilated with fear, and choked out a cry of terror.

'Rosa—' Stone rattling on glass sounded behind me.

I swallowed back my own fear, my own urge to run. There was no way I could leave Gazza, not with a wounded vampire only feet away.

I reached out my hand to him, but he batted it away, wriggling back from me, dragging his trousers up over his hips.

A groan sounded behind me and heart aching, I fought the urge to go to Malik, to heed his *call* still drumming through my blood.

I crawled after Gazza, and he scrambled back again, moaning and swinging his fist wide. Ducking under the blow, I grabbed his wrist. 'Be still,' I hissed, using my touch on his skin to send the command into his mind. He froze, shivering with fear.

'A pretty trick, my love, to spite me so.' Malik's breath burnt along my cheek, I flinched though I knew he wasn't there. 'You always had such pretty tricks ...'

Mesma. It's only mesma.

'*Run home!*' I ordered Gazza, and snatched my hand from his skin.

Gazza staggered to his feet and reeled drunkenly away towards the alley's entrance.

With my heart thudding in my mouth, I turned, curling ready into a crouch. Malik slumped against the alley wall, the pearl handle of my knife a shiny exclamation point in the black shadow of his body.

'S-s-s-silver, Rosa.' He hissed, the accusation sliding over my skin like molten oil.

For one long moment, I stared, desolate ... then I forced my legs to flee.

Chapter Eighteen

I fled with vampire speed, urged on by the predawn light fading the darkness from the sky. My feet flew over pavements, leapt over barriers, careened round corners, buildings distorted before my eyes and the discordant sounds of early morning traffic buzzed in my ears. Half-seen pedestrians blurred as I passed them by, silent and unheeded.

Like Gazza, I was running home.

Had I wounded Malik enough to kill him? My knife was silver and I'd struck for his heart, but had I pierced it? Counting the landmarks that meant I was nearly home, I sprinted past the Law Courts on my right and Somerset House to my left – *but I hadn't felt the life leave his body* – I turned off the Strand and headed for Covent Garden – *not like the last time I'd killed a vampire* – I darted between St Paul's Church and the Apple Market, feet still flying, tiny wings of hope fluttering inside me. Why they should be was something I chose not to think about too closely.

I reached the ladder in the church's garden and sprang up, closing my hand round the cold metal rung. I concentrated on climbing. I had to get to the top before the sun hit the horizon, before the spell reverted, leaving me dead while the new day started. Halfway up my heart thudded, then went silent. I stopped, leaned my forehead against the ladder and closed my eyes. It was a long way back down, nearly thirty feet, and I couldn't risk falling, couldn't risk being found. Closing my eyes, I willed my heart to start again. I needed it to beat now. I needed to get home. It stuttered inside my chest, weak and irregular. I lifted my hand and staring fixedly at the brown brick wall, I climbed.

The wall disappeared.

Confusion made me sway and my fingers clutched the metal rungs painfully hard. I gazed across the gravel in front of me, then the soft scents of lavender and rosemary and lemon balm greeted me and I realised I'd reached the top: this was my roof.

I crawled over the ledge, the sharp stones digging into my hands and knees, and collapsed, too tired to go any further. A bright yellow caterpillar concertinaed past my fingertips, flashing his black inner body. Footsteps crunched in the gravel.

My heart stopped.

I lifted my head and gazed towards the east where the sun stretched pale fingers above the horizon. A shadow fell over me, tall and broad, then as it crouched down and the risen sun spilled over my skin, the fires of the dawn consumed me.

The scent of gardenias drifted over me. I had fallen asleep on the floor, my head pillowed on my building bricks and their sharp edges were digging into my cheek. A hand touched my shoulder, gentle and familiar. I hugged my favourite toy, a grey towelling elephant, and tried to snuggle deeper into dreamland.

'Genevieve, *moy angelochek.*' Hands lifted me into the air and Matilde, my stepmother settled me onto her hip. 'You must wake now.'

I was dreaming of a time when my world was simpler. I knew that time was long-gone, but still I burrowed my face into Matilde's gardenia-scented neck and curled my fingers into her long golden hair.

'Why do you lie on the floor like a peasant, *moy malish*?' Her hand patted my back. 'Is the bed your father gave you not comfortable enough?'

I stuck my thumb in my mouth and mumbled, 'Tired.'

'Too much playtime, I'll guess.' She hitched me higher. 'But now we have a surprise for you, your father and I.'

'Like surprises,' I murmured.

'First we must make you presentable.' She plucked at my brown cord dungarees. 'Little girls should wear pretty dresses, and have ribbons in their hair.'

I took my thumb out of my mouth and gazed sleepily into her large blue eyes. 'Bessie says I get mucky.'

'Mucky.' Matilde mimicked the nursemaid's northern tones and then smiled. 'A bath will wash away the muck.'

I reached up to pat her face and smiled. 'Surprise first, Tildy?'

She laughed open-mouthed, her fangs white and sharp and her eyes sparkling like sapphires. 'No, no, *moy malish*, you will have your bath first. Save your charms for your father' – she kissed me on the lips – 'for I am wise to them.'

'Not want bath,' I pouted.

'I do not want a bath,' she corrected me, sounding out the words.

I stroked her neck, rubbing my fingers over the tender swollen bite there. 'I do not want a bath, Tildy.'

'Very good,' she smiled, and carried me out of the room that was my nursery.

Matilde held me by the hand as she led me down the hall towards my father's study. With each skip I took, I could see my new shiny black-patent leather shoes decorated with their green satin bows, dancing along beneath the flounces of my new green dress. I bobbed my head in time with the *tap, shuffle, tap* sounds that bounced back at me from the grey stone walls.

We stopped outside the dark oak door. Hundreds of candles in wall brackets flickered like fireflies on either side of the doorway.

Matilde slowly crouched down and balancing carefully on

her high heels, smoothed the green Alice-band that tied back my hair. 'Your hair is so beautiful, *moy angelochek*, the colour of fresh blood cascading over our beloved golden domes.'

I leaned in, kissed her pale powdered cheek. 'At the Kremlin, Tildy?'

She smiled, though I could still see the sadness in her face. 'Yes, like my so- beautiful home in Moskva.' Moisture tinted the whites of her eyes with pink. 'One day we shall travel to see it. You and I. Teram Palace, the Cathedral of the Assumption—'

'Ivan the big bell,' I giggled.

She rubbed her nose against mine. '*Da, da, moy malish.*' Then her expression turned serious. She touched a finger to my eyes, my ears, my mouth and my heart. 'Your father has a guest, Genevieve. You must be very much the young lady and remember the manners I have taught to you.'

I touched the black opals that collared her neck. 'What about the surprise?'

Her fingers twitched at my dress, dusted a nonexistent smudge from my shoe. 'You shall have your surprise later, little one.'

We were marooned in an empty acre of grey flagstoned floor, lit by the red glare of a fire I couldn't see. My father, tall and blond and aristocratic, was dressed in his special black suit with the satin lining, the one that matched Matilde's sapphire-blue eyes.

His guest, a stranger to me, stood opposite. The firelight left him alone, as if not wanting to encroach the darkness that surrounded him. I gazed at him, curious to see this new vampire visitor, but his face was hidden by shadows that fell from nowhere.

Matilde gently pushed me forward until I stood between the two vampires.

The stranger's low voice came out of the darkness. 'Is this the child, Alexandre?'

A shiver ran down my spine.

'Greet our guest, Genevieve.' My father's hand pressed down on my shoulder.

I stuck out my black patent toe, clutched the slippery green satin of my dress and bent my knee in a trembling curtsey.

Cold fingers gripped my chin, lifting my face. 'The eyes are truly sidhe fae,' he murmured.

I stared up, but still couldn't see him through the darkness.

He turned my face from side to side. 'Her profile certainly has a look of you about her, Alexandre.'

'She is my daughter.' My father sounded unexpectedly anxious. 'This was reported to your Master at her birth.'

'An achievement indeed.' The stranger was faintly mocking as he released me.

Matilde swept her arm around me, holding me close and I looked up at her. She was staring at my father's guest, and her eyes were wide and scared.

Why was she frightened? Why was my father not happy? My heart pitter-pattered in my chest, and all three vampires turned their attention to me.

'Control yourself, Genevieve.' There was an edge of fear in my father's voice I'd never heard before.

I bit down on my lip, closed my eyes and counted under my breath, 'One elephant ... two elephants ... three elephants ...' My pulse started to slow.

'Impressive in one so young.' The stranger clapped, the sharp noise interrupting my counting.

'... five elephants ...' I opened one eye and glared up at him.

'You have taught her the old ways well.'

'... seven elephants ...'

'She is satisfactory.' The shadows shifted and then settled. 'I am sure my Master will be pleased.'

Matilde's hold on me relaxed.

'... ten elephants ...'

'All that is left is to confirm the contract. I am to take a sample.'

'*Niet.*' Matilde spat out the word.

My father hissed, 'It is but a taste, Matilde; no harm will come to the child.'

'... thirteen elephants ...'

Her fingers dug into my arm, but after a moment she acquiesced and let me go.

'My apologies.' My father offered the stranger a low bow. 'You have the knife?'

'... f— fifteen elephants ...'

The man knelt on one knee and held up a thin blade. 'Forged by the northern dwarves from cold iron and silver,' he said, as the knife gleamed red in the firelight. 'Tempered in dragon's breath. The handle is carved from a unicorn's horn.' Pale light bled from between his fingers. 'And set with a dragon's tear.' An oval of clear amber winked against his palm.

'... s— seventeen elephants ...'

A cold hand circled my left wrist and my arm went numb.

'... e— eighteen ...'

The blade traced an icy-hot slash down my inner arm.

'... n— n— nineteen ...'

Blood ran in thin rivulets to pool on the flagstone floor.

'Stop him, Alexandre.' Matilde's voice was shrill. 'He's wasting it.'

I looked up at the stranger and the shadows fled from his face. He reversed the knife, placed its handle in my palm and clasped his hands round mine to hold it straight and true. His obsidian eyes stared into mine as he pulled on my arms and the thin silver blade stabbed into his chest and plunged into his heart.

'... t—t—twenty ...'

*

Malik stood as he had in the alley, arms outstretched, the pearl-handled knife shining pale against the blackness of his body.

'Genevieve.' Sorrow lanced in his voice. 'See what you have done.'

Matilde and my father stood on either side of Malik, mirroring his stance as blood ran from the gaping wounds in their own chests.

A sharp pain – grief – struck my own heart. I whispered their names.

'Genevieve …' Their voices echoed like ghosts in my mind.

Chapter Nineteen

I woke with a start to find myself tucked up in bed with the sheet pulled up to my chin. Then I realised I wasn't alone, that there was someone else in my bedroom – and fear slammed into me. I froze, squeezing my eyes tight shut and trying not to breathe.

'I can tell you're awake, Gen,' Finn's voice held a trace of anger, 'so don't try pretending you're not.'

The fear slipped away. Taking a shallow breath, I pulled the sheet over my head. 'Huh. He thinks he's auditioning for the part of Big Bad Wolf,' I muttered.

'Try the Big Bad Boss.'

Not yet you aren't, Finn. But I didn't say it, deciding maybe I didn't want to antagonise him, at least not until I'd found out what he was doing here, and what sort of trouble I was in.

I peered from under the sheet and looked at my clock: I'd been asleep for almost five hours, double the time it usually took to recover after one of my Sucker Town outings. Still, at least I felt *so* much better and with the amount of venom I'd taken, the feel-good factor might even last the week – if I could ignore the dream-shadows stalking the outskirts of my mind. I stretched and sighed. I was clean, obviously thanks to Finn. And naked—

I rolled over and stared at him; he was sitting on the floor, arms loosely crossed over his chest and legs stretched out in front. His head was tilted back against the wall, his horns their usual size, and I wondered if I'd imagined them being taller the night before when we'd kiss— *Damn, I'd promised myself*

I wasn't going there. A take-away Rosy Lee Café cup sat beside him and the faint smell of coffee lingered in the air. He looked like he'd been there a while.

I sat up, wrapping the sheet round me, and hugged my knees. 'Why the morning call, Boss?' I asked, my tone as neutral as I could make it. 'I'm not due at work for a couple of hours yet.'

His moss-green eyes briefly met mine and then he looked down, appearing to find the pile of shoes and boots under my bed engrossing. 'I came round about the brownie magic problem,' he said finally, uncrossing his arms and letting his hands fall into his lap. 'I think there's a way you could use the spells up.'

I stared at him, incredulous. Was he just going to ignore how he'd found me, and how I'd got that way? Not that I wouldn't be just as happy *not* explaining, but somehow I didn't think it was going to be that easy.

'The brownie magic?' I asked in the same neutral tone.

'Yes,' he said, a muscle twitching along his jaw, 'it's how they teach the baby witches sometimes.'

Right! So now I'm reduced to nursery games.

'It's not hard.' His hands curled into fists, belying the calmness in his voice. 'Picture something small, something nearby, and cover it in magic. Then *call* whatever it is to your hand as you *call* the magic.' He spoke as if he'd learned the instructions by rote – or as if he was trying not to yell and shout.

'Okay, thanks,' I said slowly. It didn't exactly sound like a quick solution, but hey—

He stood up and flexed his shoulders. 'Great. So I'll see you later at work then.' And he turned to go, *still* without looking at me.

I frowned, tapping my fingers against the sheet. What was going on here? This *reserve* didn't seem like Finn, but then maybe all the flirting and good humour was just the surface Finn – I'd been so busy not getting close to him that I really knew nothing about him – except I did know right now that the trace of anger in his voice was obviously just the tip of a huge, furious iceberg.

Some emotion I didn't want to look at too closely prompted me to speak instead of just letting him go. 'I'm curious,' I said, and he stilled, hand on the bedroom door handle. 'Aren't you going to ask me about what happened?'

He kept his gaze on the door. 'Do you *want* me too?'

Did I? I wasn't sure. Explaining one small thing would just start the first domino falling, and there was no way I could tell him what lay at the end.

'Your silence says you don't' – the door creaked as he turned the handle – 'and I'm not prepared to wait for whatever story you're concocting.'

'I'm fae, Finn,' I snapped. 'Fae can't lie and you know that.'

'Not being able to lie isn't the same as telling the truth, is it, Gen?'

No. It isn't.

He pulled open the door. 'I'll see you later at work.' But he didn't leave. Instead he stood, silent, on the threshold for a moment, then he turned and strode the couple of paces back to the side of my bed.

'Changed your mind?' I glared up at him. 'Want to listen to my stories now, do you?'

His face softened, eyes darkening with concern as he bent and traced a gentle finger down my cheek. 'You were crying in your sleep, Gen.' It was almost a question.

A dream-shadow of sorrow bloomed inside me and I dropped my gaze, hiding my face from him.

'Hell's thorns, Gen—' He sighed, a soft impatient exhalation of breath. 'You know where I am,' he said, 'if you want anything.'

I heard the front door close quietly behind him and I rested my chin on my knees, the sorrow gone almost as fast as it had surfaced. Confusion and an odd disconnected feeling replaced it. Was I suffering from some sort of mild shock, with everything that had happened? But then maybe it was just the hyped-up afterglow from the massive venom hit masking all my worries. I frowned at the picture hanging on my wall.

The scene was of the River Thames, early morning mist layering the grey water, a midwinter sun struggling in the sky, very Turneresque, very bleak and lonely. The artist was Tavish – a three-hundred-year-old kelpie who predated Turner by at least seventy years – and the water-colour had been a gift. He was the only other fae I'd spent any time with; even then I'd minded Hugh's advice and kept Tavish at arm's length. But that hadn't stopped me being more than disappointed when he'd left, ten months earlier, to go prospecting in the Fair Lands.

But it wasn't just Hugh and his advice that told me to keep my secrets, it's who I am. My mother may have been sidhe fae, but my father is – or *was* – a vampire, something that the dream had reminded me of all too clearly. My latent vampire genes were one of the reasons why I'd always thought my vamp-disguise spell worked so well, but now ...

Was Malik right: was I wearing some *stolen* vamp's body? Rosa? Maybe that was why I wanted to sink my teeth into Finn; maybe *Rosa*, my Alter-Vamp, was trying to take over. Sweat broke out over my body and I slammed the thoughts away into the box in my mind and locked it tight.

I looked down at where I'd been pleating the sheet and saw the bruises Malik had given me still circling my left wrist. They should've healed along with all my other injuries when the spell reverted at dawn. My hand flew to my neck – if the bruises hadn't gone, what about his bite? Did I still have the fang-marks? I leapt out of bed and yanked open the wardrobe door, staring at my reflection in its long mirror. But my neck was smooth and unmarked. Then I remembered the Earl's words as he'd held out my arm to Malik: *And nor do I feel the need to mark my prey, like some brutish animal.*

Malik had marked me as his. *So what was new about that?*

I shoved that thought away with all the others, and headed for the kitchen – time to try out Finn's idea for the brownie magic and see if I couldn't get rid of it before it caused me any more problems. If nothing else, it would keep my mind off other less easily dealt with thoughts.

I opened the sweet-shop size jar of liquorice torpedoes I kept on the counter-top and fished out four red ones. I crunched one between my teeth and lined up the other three at the back of the counter. Pulling open the fridge, I grabbed the bottle of Stoli, hesitating as the plastic box in the bottom drawer caught my eye. I shook my head and poured myself a large glass of the vodka. I knocked it back quickly, feeling the chill burn down into my stomach.

Closing my eyes, I *focused* and *looked* inwards. The brownie magic simmered like a multi-coloured soup, florescent wisps of steam rising from its gently bubbling surface. Buried below it were small black pearls, and I frowned until I remembered: they were the compulsion-spell I'd *called* from Constable Curly-hair's 'True Love' bracelet.

Damn. Getting rid of that was going to be even more of a hassle. I'd probably have to wade into the Thames and let the compulsion-spell dissipate into the running water. It was too dangerous to try anything else.

'Right then,' I muttered, opening my eyes, 'let's see if I can do what any self-respecting four-year-old witch can.'

I lifted a ladle of the magic soup and poured it over the sweets, but the ladle kept turning into a sieve, with the magic draining back into the soup faster than I could pour. Each ladle – or sieveful – only managed to splatter pinpricks of the multi-coloured magic over the red torpedoes. I persevered, sweat trickling down my spine, until I finally managed to coat the sweets in the magic. I smiled in relief and *called* them. The sweets moved about an inch, then the magic peeled off and splashed back into the soup.

Damn. Maybe three was too many to start with. I tried again with one torpedo, which eventually moved six inches to the left. Gritting my teeth in frustration, I gave it one more try. This time the torpedo zoomed towards me. I grinned and held up my hand to catch it, then flinched in dismay as it exploded, spraying me with fine sugary dust.

My shoulders slumped. I felt like I'd been for a ten-mile run, but with less to show for it. I decided lesson one was over, and at this rate lesson two might never happen. Why the hell was it proving so difficult? Looked like I'd have to get rid of the magic inside a circle after all. I sighed and opened the fridge to put back the vodka.

The plastic box sat there, waiting.

My chest tightened. This so wasn't a good idea, not when the dream-shadows were already creeping round the edges of my mind. I stood, hesitating, the icy air freezing my naked skin, then before I could change my mind, I opened the fridge drawer and gently removed the box. Biting my lip, I prised off the lid and looked down at the contents.

The gardenia-scented soap, still wrapped in its original waxed paper, rested on a bed of tissue paper next to the thin plait of blue-white hair.

I didn't touch either, just leaned over and inhaled the delicate fragrance of the soap.

Closing my eyes, I saw Tildy as she'd been in my dream, her long blonde curls, the worried blue eyes, and the black opal collar concealing the bite on her neck.

I'd been the count's daughter, his little Russian princess, waiting for my prince to come, just like in all the fairy stories. When he finally arrived, two weeks before the celebrations, I'd been the luckiest princess alive, for my prince was young-looking and handsome and powerful. And on my fourteenth birthday I would take his Blood-Bond – my life and blood and magic given to him to control – and become his faerie queen for ever.

I had been eagerly preparing to become his all my life. I even had my very own lady's maid, Sally. She was pretty, with her pale blue skin and long blue-white hair – her great-grand-mother was a Cailleac Bhuer, one of the Blue Hags. Only Sally wasn't magic enough for the fae, and had too much Other in her for the humans. But the vampires wanted her, even if no one else did.

Tildy had given Sally to me as a present on my twelfth birthday. We were supposed to be inseparable, two young girls growing up together, but Sally was three years older than me, and she wasn't interested in being friends, not with me, anyway, not unless she wanted an audience to listen about her latest conquest.

Then my prince arrived and Sally thought she had snared her greatest prize. But when my prince heard she'd spilled all their bloody details to me, even though I told him I didn't care, the outcome was inevitable.

My prince took five days to kill her.

He had me stand by and watch as he did.

And I'd seen my future in his eyes.

He'd tortured Sally because he could, and because he enjoyed it, but even with her stronger faeling blood, she'd been too fragile to survive for long. But Sally was just an appetiser; I was to be his never-ending feast, my sidhe blood never able to fade and die, no matter how much I might want it too – not after I'd willingly taken his Blood-Bond.

My eyes snapped open at the sharp slash of pain in my hand. I'd broken the glass. The reek of blood and alcohol smothered the scent of gardenia. I threw the glass away and ran my hand under the tap, watching as the thin cut slowly closed itself and scabbed over. The wound would be gone by nightfall. Then, careful not to disturb its contents, I resealed the plastic box and tucked it safely back in the fridge and quietly closed the door.

My skin was sticky with sweat and sugar from the exploding

168

liquorice torpedoes, so I headed to the bathroom. As I stood under the shower, I tried to think about bargains and murder and vampires and what I was going to do next. Only the Pandora's Box in my mind was open, and unlike the plastic one in my fridge, I couldn't get it closed again.

Was the dream right? Had my sleeping mind warped my memories of that long-ago time to remind me of my greatest fear? Had my running away meant the death of Tildy and my father? Tears pricked the back of my eyes and tipping my head back, I let the water stream down on me, trying to wash the dream-shadows away.

Chapter Twenty

I pushed open the door to Spellcrackers.com just after mid-day. The neutral décor – ivory paint, pale wood and chrome coupled with thick sand-coloured carpets – had been designed to make our human customers feel less uncomfortable, more able to cope with the stress that usually accompanied the magical problems they needed us to deal with. Professionalism and calm were Stella's watchwords and the bland backdrop reinforced that. We even had brown twigs in vases, instead of flowers.

Toni, our office manager, batted new pink and purple eye-lashes at me from behind the reception desk. Her outfit matched her eye-catching lashes: a pink blouse under a dark-mauve suit, purple suede court-shoes and pink, mauve and purple stream-ers that curled through her long blonde hair. The streamers reminded me of fireworks at a trolls' New Moon party.

Her get-up wasn't something I'd wear – I don't need to draw any more attention to myself, my sidhe eyes do that all on their own – but it looked great on her. My own clothes were way more conservative; my usual black linen trousers and my favourite green linen jacket. The jacket was for the added confidence boost – the one I was going to need for my next inevitable meeting with Finn. Not that I had a clue what I was going to say to him.

'Love the new look, Toni.' I adjusted the twigs. 'What's that, sixth one this year?'

'Seventh,' she grinned. 'I decided the Cool Blonde look was making me fade into the wallpaper.'

Considering the Cool Blonde look had involved a beige silk shirt-dress, she wasn't far wrong. 'What did Stella have to say when she saw it?'

'Oh you know.' Toni's grin got wider. 'She said it's still an improvement on my Celtic Country look.'

I tried to keep a straight face. 'Really?'

'Nah. What she *really* said was that anything is better than me daubing myself with blue woad.'

'Ah, thought so.' I squinted at her hair. The streamers shone like polished glass. 'You been down to see the goblins again?'

'That Madam Methania is a wonder.' She teased out a pink strand. 'And she's cheap. You should try her.'

'Let a goblin near my hair?' I shuddered. 'No way, I'm not having that slug slime they use anywhere near me.'

'I guess they'd have to use extensions on your hair anyway. You really should let it grow, y'know, it'd look fab.' She looked at me a bit more closely. 'You look a lot better, Honeybee. You've lost that peaky look. And that green jacket looks great with your skin tone.' She waved away my thanks and changed the subject. 'I tried to phone you earlier and it kicked me straight through to messages.'

'Uh-huh, the protection-spell's on the way out. Thought I'd try and save the crystal.'

'That was new only three days ago, and the one before only lasted a week.' She frowned, thoughtful. 'You really are having an iffy time with the magic, aren't you?'

She was right, I realised. The magic had been a bit more off-kilter than usual around me – just one of my occasional blips, or something else?

'Let me have your phone,' she carried on, 'and I'll see what I can do.'

'No probs.' I handed her the phone, wishing not for the first time I could've sorted it myself. Toni had tried to teach me the spell – and I understood the theory, but, as usual with me and magic, the actual *casting* part just hadn't clicked.

Toni popped a square of vanilla fudge in her mouth to give her magic a boost, and peered at the crystal. 'Yep, it's cracked all right – and completely black.'

I leaned against her desk. 'Did Finn say anything to you about the new eBay supplier?'

'Yes, he's left one for you. Just as well!' She rummaged through her desk, took out a wad of small wax paper bags, a pink perfume bottle, her white spell bowl and a black chopstick. She prised the spell-crystal off my phone and dropped it into the jar of salt water she kept under her desk.

I looked down the corridor at the door to Finn's office. Time to beard the satyr in his den. 'Is he in?'

Toni shook her head. 'Nope. Out on a job.' Relief seeped into me.

She poured a drop of clear liquid from the pink bottle into her bowl. 'So, any news to report, hon?' She pointed an accusing finger at me. 'And don't tell me you haven't, because I have it on good authority that a certain horny satyr was clocked exiting a certain sidhe's place of residence earlier this very morning.'

Oh yeah. The bet! 'You should be a detective,' I half-smiled.

'Hah! I knew it! I knew you'd succumb sooner or later.' She waved the pink bottle at me eagerly. 'C'mon, let me in on all the little – or not-so-little – details!'

'Nothing happened, Toni,' I sighed.

'Hmmm.' She pursed her lips, disappointed. 'Well, I can't say you look too happy about it.' She added a pungent sprinkling of dried sage to the bowl. 'Want me to mix you up a nice little *lurrrve* potion? I could always add it to his tea.'

'C'mon Toni, that stuff doesn't really work.' At least not without nasty little additions like a compulsion-spell.

'You haven't tried my special patented recipe for lust yet, have you? I could let you have it cheap, Hon.' A sly look crossed her face. 'It'd only cost you a tiny little snippet of info—'

'Toni, I know you want me to ask Finn about his tail, but … well, let's just say he's not too happy with me just now and leave it at that, okay?'

'Ah' – she looked round conspiratorially – 'I take it he's found out about your visit to the police and a certain Mr October last night.'

I blinked in surprise. 'Didn't take long for that little news item to surface, did it?'

'Well, you know me and gossip. I've got a nose for it.' She grinned and tapped her nose with a long purple fingernail. 'Not that it took much working out, not after all those phone calls Stella got yesterday from his dad.' She shook a crystal into the white bowl and stirred the spell with the chopstick. 'First things first, is Mr October as hot as his calendar pics?'

I flashed back to the memory of Bobby with his paper suit and his lank hair. 'He's a vampire,' I shrugged, 'so of course he's hot. It goes with the job description.'

She gave me an arch look. 'My nose also told me you had a run-in with the Earl and a couple of his vamps too. Bet that was scary.'

'You don't need me to tell you the goss, Toni,' I said with a faint smile, 'not when your "nose" is keeping you so well-informed.'

'Ah, what I'm really after is a full blow-by-blow eye-witness action account straight from the sidhe's mouth.' She waved another wax bag at me. 'C'mon, Genny, pretty please? I'll do your phone with my extra-strong patented buffer spell if you do. I always used to get gold stars for them,' she finished smugly.

Laughing, I said, 'There's not all that much—'

I stopped as the main door opened behind me and Toni stood up, offering a wide welcoming smile.

The woman was in her early thirties. Her blue silk dress and jacket were simple, but expensive. Glossy dark hair framed her face in a perfect bob and understated but effective makeup subtly enlarged her coffee-coloured eyes, sculpted her cheeks and outlined her full mouth. Everything about her shouted well-groomed class. She smiled as she walked towards us over the thick carpet, each step in her high-heeled summer sandals as precise as if she still had the finishing school book balanced on her head.

Her look included us both, but she addressed herself to me. 'Genevieve Taylor?' Her voice matched her appearance: quiet, elegant, with a hint of plum to the vowels.

I nodded, puzzled. She looked vaguely familiar.

'Hannah Ashby.' She looped her handbag over her left arm. 'I am sorry to call without an appointment, but I was hoping you might be able to spare me a few minutes. I have a private matter I would like to discuss with you.'

It wasn't unusual for clients to just walk in. It *was* unusual for humans to ask for me specifically. And Hannah Ashby hit my radar as human.

'Shouldn't be a problem.' I glanced at Toni. 'I've nothing booked?'

Toni shook her head.

I offered Hannah my hand. Hers was warm, and definitely human – no surprises there then. 'My office is along here. Would you like tea or coffee, or water?'

She gave me an odd, amused smile. 'No. Thank you.'

Chapter Twenty-One

My office was a carbon copy of Reception: more sand-coloured carpet, more neutral shades, more pale wood furniture. Holding the door open, I ushered Hannah Ashby in. As she walked past me, I caught her perfume, something sweet. Like her, it was familiar.

She looked briefly around the room then sat down, knees together, at ease despite her ramrod-straight back.

I sat behind my desk, took out a pad and pen. 'How can I help you, Ms Ashby?'

She looked me up and down, her expression pleasant, but with enough concentration in her dark brown eyes that I began to think of bugs, microscopes and pins.

I tapped my pen against the pad, irritated. 'Ms Ashby?'

'Forgive me; you have such an arresting face.' She laughed, a low warm sound. 'Actually, I'm here to help you, Ms Taylor. Or may I call you Genevieve?'

I narrowed my eyes. 'I deal with magical problems, Ms Ashby. You're not a witch, or some sort of fae, so I'm not sure how you can help me, or with what, exactly.'

'I'm sure you don't.' She gave me a wide smile. 'But I *am* here to help you, nonetheless. I am offering you an invitation, in fact.'

'An invitation to what?'

'Let me show you.' She unclipped her bag and took out a small black velvet pouch. She upended it just above the desk and a silver oblong the size of a playing card slid out, landing with a soft metallic slap. Using one French-manicured finger, she pushed it gently towards me. 'Your invitation, Genevieve.'

The 'invitation' gleamed in the sunlight that shone through the window behind me. I'd never seen one before, but I knew what it was, of course.

A VIP pass to the Blue Heart.

And the Blue Heart belonged to the Earl.

I leaned back in my chair. 'Thanks, but I'm not interested.'

Hannah inclined her head. 'The invitation conveys the issuer's full protection, along with their hospitality.' Her voice was businesslike. 'And should you not be fully aware of exactly what that means, then I will be happy to tell you.'

I shook my head. 'No need.' It meant I'd be guaranteed my safety, like my visit to the Bloody Shamrock. But it didn't mean that there wouldn't be any grandstanding. And a lot more vamps called the Blue Heart home, than at the Shamrock.

As if reading my mind, she said, 'During your visit, should you be concerned for your wellbeing' – she laid the velvet pouch next to the silver oblong – 'show the invitation to any vampire and they will be … *deterred.*'

I snorted, casting a judicious eye over the invitation. There was a single black gem in the centre. 'It's not going to *deter* them much if they're too far gone in bloodlust to notice.'

'In that case' – she smoothed her hand down her skirt – 'the invitation has a rather ingenious side to it. It is solid silver, so should one be caught in that unfortunate state of affairs, all one need do is touch it to bare skin. That usually gets a vampire's full attention.'

I laughed, unable to help it. 'I bet.'

Hannah joined me, chuckling huskily herself.

'An expensive invitation.' I picked it up by its edges, ignoring the slight burning in my fingers caused by my sensitivity to the silver. 'So why's the Earl so interested in me visiting the Blue Heart?'

'The invitation isn't from the Earl.' There was a slight derisive edge to her voice.

'It's not?'

She opened her bag, and took out another black velvet pouch. I had a brief moment of déjà vu as she slipped a second silver oblong onto my desk. 'You seem to be in demand, Genevieve.' Her perfectly lipsticked mouth smiled, but her eyes didn't.

Must be my lucky day.

She pointed at the invitation on the table. 'This one is from the Earl.' She tapped her fingernail on the heart-shaped sapphire mounted in the centre. 'The stones are their markers. The one you hold is from Malik al-Khan.'

My stomach knotted as I rubbed my thumb over the black gem. My mind could come up with at least half-a dozen reasons why Malik would want to see me again – none of them good – but ... why invite me to a vampire club? It didn't make any sense. Or any difference, really. An injured vampire – always presuming I hadn't actually killed him – wasn't going to be offering much in the way of protection, was he?

I looked up to find Hannah Ashby watching me with the same intent expression as before.

'Don't suppose you're going to tell me why the Earl thought I might accept, are you?'

Her eyes flashed in amusement. 'The Earl thinks a visit to the club might help in your investigation into the death of Melissa Banks.'

'I'm not investigating her death. The police are doing that.'

'He also mentioned his bronzes. Apparently you showed an interest in seeing them?' She raised her voice in question.

I smiled, slightly in disbelief. 'Are his bronzes a euphemism?'

She arched one of her perfectly plucked eyebrows. 'He does have a beautiful and extensive collection, and he certainly enjoys exhibiting his works of art, but then again, you are an extremely attractive person, Genevieve.'

'Is that a warning?'

Smiling, she took a white business card from her handbag and laid it on the desk. The sunlight lit her features as she bent forward, smoothing out the angles her make-up had created, and I realised where I'd met her before. 'Should you have any questions,' she said, 'please feel free to call me.'

I glanced at her card. She had a stack of letters after her name. The address was in the heart of the City: one of the top accountancy firms in London. 'You're an accountant?' I didn't try to hide my surprise.

Her mouth twitched. 'At present, I'm wearing my Girl Friday hat.'

I wondered how many other hats she had hidden up her sleeve.

'I'll show myself out.' She stood, looped her bag over the crook of her arm.

I waited until she opened the door. 'Ms Ashby. You haven't told me the name of your Master.'

She turned back, the amused expression back on her face. The movement disturbed her hair, confirming my suspicions. Her voice was different, and without the goth makeup, or the blue streaks and the obvious display of breast I hadn't immediately recognised her as Corset Girl, the vamp groupie who'd tried so hard to entice me at the Leech & Lettuce. But the bite was there, high on her neck, where I'd tasted her the night before.

'You're right,' she said. 'I haven't.'

'Not Malik al-Khan or the Earl, then?'

'I look forward to seeing you again, Genevieve.' She stepped into the corridor. 'It should be interesting.'

The door closed with a gentle snick behind her.

Looked like there was another player in the game ... only I still wasn't sure exactly what the game was.

Chapter Twenty-Two

Who was Hannah Ashby – or rather, *what* was she? I swivelled in my chair and stared out the window. Everything about her suggested she was some vampire's daytime flunky – the current PC title was Business Manager. Maybe I would have believed that, if I hadn't seen her last night in her fancy-dress get-up. No way would a flunky be caught slumming as a groupie, not when it meant the kiss of death to their cushy elevated status.

Curiouser and curiouser.

A knock interrupted my thoughts and I nudged my pad over the silver invitations. Katie stuck her head round the door and grinned. 'Hi Genny, thought you might be hungry.' She bounced into the room, blonde ponytail swinging, and plonked a Rosy Lee butty box on my desk along with a large Styrofoam cup. 'BLT, bacon extra crispy, tomatoes thinly sliced, iceberg lettuce and tons of mayo.' She beamed at me. 'Wholegrain brown. Butter. Everything just how you like it. And orange juice, of course.'

'Let me guess,' I grinned, 'you couldn't wait to hear about Mr October, right?'

Katie pulled a shock-horror face. 'Would I be that shallow?' She dropped a wad of napkins next to the cup.

'In a heartbeat.' I pulled the box towards me.

Smirking, Katie kicked off her flip-flops, folded one leg under her and sat. 'So, did you see him, Gen?'

I nodded as I bit into my sandwich, crunching down on the extra-crispy bacon.

'What was he like? What did he say? Did he have his leather coat on? Was he really sad? What are the police doing? Was Mr Hinkley okay?' Katie was almost breathless with excitement.

Holding up my hand for silence, I swallowed. 'Fine, not much, no, yes, nothing interesting, I think so.'

'Gennnnny,' she wailed, 'c'mon, *tell* me!'

I licked mayonnaise off my finger. 'Katie, Mr October's a vampire. Remember? They are *not* nice people.'

'But you are going to help him, aren't you?' She leaned on the desk. 'His dad says he didn't do it. What if he *really* didn't do it? What if the police *have* got the wrong man? Poor Melissa's murderer would *still* be out there, wouldn't he? And *you'd* be the only one looking for him. *You've* got to find him.'

Mouth full, I waved my sandwich at her.

She lowered her voice. 'Did you see *the body*? Was—'

The door opening interrupted her. Toni came in, notepad in hand. 'I've fixed your phone, Honeybee.' She placed it on the desk 'And a job's come in.' She grinned as she tore a sheet from her pad. 'Gremlins at Tower Bridge.'

I groaned. Gremlins would take all afternoon. Still at least they weren't as bad as pixies. 'Thanks Toni,' I mumbled.

Toni leaned forward, her forehead creasing. 'Is that bacon? You can't eat bacon – there's way too much salt in it.' Her voice went up an octave. 'What if you have to *crack* a spell?' She made a grab for the sandwich.

'Hey!' I snatched it out the way. 'That's my lunch – a little bit of bacon's not going to give me any trouble, Toni. I eat it all the time.'

She stopped, hand still outstretched. 'You do?'

'Toasted in a sandwich for breakfast,' Katie chimed in. 'BLT's for lunch, 'cos the salad stuff is green and good for you.' She ticked it off on her fingers. 'And for dinner, bacon, poached egg, medium-soft to dunk the chips in, and grilled tomato,' she giggled, 'cos it's healthier that way.' She pointed my pen at me. 'Never varies, although you don't always eat the healthy stuff, do you?'

'You'd never know you worked in catering, would you?'

'My God, Hon.' Toni's voice was horrified. 'I knew you ate in the café, but don't you *ever* eat anything else but bacon? Does Stella know? She's madder than a cornered cat if she catches us eating even so much as a crisp.'

I put the sandwich down and picked up the phone. 'Toni, really, don't worry. It's not a problem for me.' I turned on the phone and thumbed through to check my messages.

Toni shook her head doubtfully. 'You really eat the stuff all the time?'

'That and liquorice torpedoes—' and, *oh yeah*, vodka, venom and blood, but I wasn't going to mention that out loud.

I had a message from Alan Hinkley: he wanted to meet at midnight in Victoria Embankment Gardens before going to Old Scotland Yard, he'd found an informer, another fae, who would only talk to me. Um. I wasn't sure if that was good news, bad news, or some sort of trap ... well, looked like I'd find out come midnight. Pursing my lips, I texted him back.

'Maybe that's why ...' Toni paused and tapped her pad.

I looked up. 'Why what?'

'Why you can't do witch-magic.' She waved her fingers. 'I'd better get back to the desk.'

I looked after her thoughtfully. Maybe Toni had a point. I'd have to try a few experiments.

Katie picked up my pad and grinned. 'And what would Madame— Oh, way cool!' She grabbed the two silver invitations and waved them in my face. 'Wow, Genny, where'd you get them? What—'

'Katie—'

Katie's face lit up even more. 'These are so you can find the killer, aren't they? Who gave them to you? No, wait, don't tell me' – she held the silver oblongs up to the light and squinted at them – 'let me work it out.'

I gave up, prised the lid of the orange and took a sip. It tasted better than it had the previous day – but then, nothing tasted good when the venom cravings were at their worst. I stifled a shudder as I remembered Gazza: hopefully Katie would be able to put my mind at rest about what had happened to him.

'So what happened to that new pot-washer?' I asked. 'Did Freddie sack him yet?'

'Nah, the creep pulled a sickie.' She turned one of the silver invitations over, studying it minutely. 'Got his mum to phone in for him. Claimed he got beat up or something.'

Relief filtered through me. He'd run home, just as I'd told him to.

'This one' – Katie flicked one of the invitations – 'is from the Earl. It's got his name stamped on the back. And you can tell by the size of the sapphire. Did you know they're made by dwarves in Iceland? And the sapphire's from Ceylon. And they're all limited editions. You've got number thirty-six out of one hundred here.'

'You know way too much about the vamps,' I mumbled past the last of my BLT.

She stuck her tongue out. 'Now this one doesn't have a name stamped on it, and I've never seen it on the website.' She put the invitation back on the desk. 'Guess what edition number it is?'

I shrugged, 'Lucky thirteen?'

'Wrong!' She slid the oblong towards me. 'Look.'

I leaned over and peered at it. Underneath the gemstone was engraved, 1/1.

She blew her fringe up. 'That's what's called an original, I think. What d'you s'pose the stone is?'

I pushed the card back. 'Jet, probably.' Picking up the gremlin job details and my phone, I tucked them in my bag.

'Nah, s'not jet. Its got little red splatters on it, like blood.' She shot me an excited look. 'Hey, I bet its bloodstone – that's really cool.'

'You get all this off the website?'

'Yep.' She held up both the invitations and waggled them. 'So which one d'you think murdered Bobby's girlfriend?'

My mouth fell open. 'What?'

'Well, one of them must've, else they wouldn't have invited you. Murderers always want to find out what the detective knows, in case they've been twigged.'

'Katie, I think the vamps are more interested in the fact that I'm sidhe.'

'Yeah, yeah, I get the whole thing about humans tasting like water and fae like a fruit smoothie.' She pulled her *you're-such-an-idiot* face on me. 'But you've always been sidhe, Genny, all your life, and they weren't sending out invitations before, were they?' She waggled the silver oblongs again. 'So, c'mon, Miss Detective, which one d'you think did it?'

'I am *not* a detective.'

''Course you are! Look, it's easy.' She leaned towards me, her long pony-tail falling onto the desk. 'All you have to do is go there and talk to the staff, y'know, like the tea-boy, or the janitor.'

'I don't think the Blue Heart has tea-boys.'

'Y'know what I mean.' She flicked her hair back. 'I see it all the time on the telly when me and Mum watch murder mysteries together. You just listen to what everyone has to say and put all the clues together and then you work out who the murderer is.' She frowned. 'Either that or the killer bumps you off to stop you blabbing his secret.'

'Thanks, Katie – that is *so* reassuring.' I stood up. 'Anyway, I've got gremlins to deal with, and I expect Freddie will be tearing his hair out if you don't get back soon.'

She ducked below the desk, searching for her shoes. 'Freddie's bald.'

'Exactly.'

'Ha, Ha.' She shook a flip-flop at me, then gave me a pleading look. 'You're going to go, aren't you, and find out who killed Bobby's girlfriend for him?'

'Decision time – let me think: should I visit a vampire club where every sucker wants to drink my blood and turn me into a blood-slave while I'm looking for a murderer who wants to kill me, or not?' I gave her a mildly sarcastic look. 'Definitely a no-brainer, Katie.'

Her face turned serious. 'Well, it's always possible the murderer might try and kill you anyway, unless you can find him first.'

Damn. She was right. And attack was said to be the best form of defence, wasn't it?

'Sometimes you're way too smart.' I took the two silver invitations from her and dropped them into my bag.

She chewed her lip. 'You will be careful, won't you, Genny?'

'As a vampire in a thunderstorm,' I muttered.

Chapter Twenty-Three

I walked into Leicester Square, my heart thudding in my chest. The bright signs of the clubs, pubs, cinemas and restaurants flashed like gigantic goblin badges. It was a couple of hours before midnight and the Square heaved with punters. Their voices hummed against my ears. Popcorn and excitement scented the air, and the hot dryness of the heat-wave coated my skin. I touched tentative fingers to the silver invitations lodged in my jacket pocket and stopped a not-so-comfortable distance away from London's premier vampire nightclub.

The Blue Heart had been a cinema in its former life and the outside still looked much the same. Two-foot-high silver letters hung down over the entrance, with the 'a' in 'heart' replaced by an actual blue neon heart that pulsed like it was alive. Film-style posters advertised the current Vampire Calendar Celebrities: Mr September had top billing as a neck-ruffed Elizabethan, Mr August in his twelfth century Crusader get-up was the outgoing act, while Mr June in his WWII uniform was obviously the understudy for October's absent star.

It had taken nearly an hour on the club's website, and three trawls through my wardrobe, to finally settle on something to wear: a black Lycra top, banded round my neck and waist, that covered my front and left my back bare, and a Lycra wrap-around skirt, also black. It was one of my Sucker Town outfits. But as bare flesh to vampires is like wearing a come-and-fang-me-sign, I'd topped it off with a knee-length bronze silk coat. The shoes matched the coat: bronze Vintage Westwoods with two inches of platform and six inches of thin metal heel. Okay, so they weren't that easy on the feet, but hey, what girl wouldn't suffer for some killer heels?

'Mm-mm-mm: don't you smell just totally delicious,' the contralto voice purred in my ear.

My pulse jumping, I took a step away, then turned sharply to face Rio, the manager of the Blue Heart. I recognised her from the publicity shots on the club's website, and from her fuzz of tight curls dyed her trademark pale blue. What the photos hadn't shown was her height. She had to be an inch or two over six feet tall, but the thigh-high platform boots of electric-blue leather added at least another six inches to her long legs while her blue leather hotpants looked spray-painted onto her narrow hips. She stood grinning at me, her huge lavender-coloured eyes dancing with mischief in her café-au-lait face, while the sheer fabric the blouse tied at her midriff did nothing to hide her almost nonexistent breasts, or her obvious excitement.

Shit. How had she managed to creep up on me? My vamp radar was usually better than that. Maybe last night's G-Zav was still screwing with it.

She brought her hands together with a soft clap. 'Oh, did I scare you?' A pink tongue darted out to lick her full bottom lip. 'I do hope so. Fear adds such a piquant flavour to the blood.'

Trying to calm my speeding pulse, I held up one of the silver invitations between my thumb and forefinger. 'Sorry to disappoint.' I smiled, with just a touch of smirk. 'Invited guest, not part of the catering.'

She made an exaggerated pout as she plucked the invitation from my hand. 'And there I was getting all tingly at the prospect of a sip of sidhe.' Handling the silver slab carefully by the edges, she scraped the metal with a sharp blue fingernail, turning it over and around as though it were something new she'd just discovered.

'An invitation from the Earl, no less.' She offered the silver slab back, then as I was about to take it, snatched it up out of my reach. 'Why settle for second-best?' – she stroked a long finger down her missing cleavage – 'when I could make you a much better offer.'

Giving a loud sigh, I held my hand out.

'As you wish.' She dropped the silver into my hand.

I pocketed it, and strode towards the entrance.

'You really should consider it.' She fell into step next to me. 'Or rather, consider *me*. Something as delightful as you deserves to be *relished*, like the finest dessert, licked and nibbled and sucked' – her voice lowered as she gave me a fang-filled grin – 'and eaten right up, one glorious mouthful at a time.'

Ignoring her, I halted inside the foyer near the semi-circle of ticket booths. The small Monitor goblins manning them were perched on jacked-up barstools. They were only eighteen inches tall, so they needed the boost – not that their size made any difference to their ability to sense magic, of course. The one nearest me, his powder-blue dreads swinging, briefly turned his black wraparounds in my direction while sliding a triple-jointed finger down his nose. I returned the greeting. Then he carefully stamped the back of his lilac-haired customer's hand with a blue ink heart the size of a fifty-pence piece and waved the woman away. She wandered off through the crowd, handbag swinging from her arm, and into the gift shop.

The vamps had more than one way to bleed you dry.

Rio circled behind me like a restless shark. 'Welcome to the Blue Heart, delicious sidhe.' She trailed a finger down my cheek.

A shiver of induced excitement slithered down my spine. *Mesma*.

I stepped away from her and the sensation faded as soon as she no longer touched me. Mentally I downgraded her. She might call the Earl second-best, but in reality she was much further down the pile.

She laughed, the husky sound vibrating through the air, and the people milling about all stopped, their eyes drawn to her.

She spread her arms wide and turned a slow circle, breathing in the scents of the excited clubbers.

'Oh, such a response,' she shivered. 'Aren't humans wonderful?' She cocked her head to one side, looked down at me. 'Here's hoping your visit is as exciting' – she winked a large lavender eye – 'as *I* desire.'

'Don't get your hopes up,' I said, adding sweetly, 'I would *so* hate to ruin your evening.'

'You are going to be *such* fun.' She shook a blue-tipped finger at me and the glint in her eyes turned more predatory. 'So I'll make you a promise, my sweet little sidhe: for your first night at the Blue Heart, there will be entertainment such as you will never forget.'

'*Please*, don't put yourself out on my account.' I gave an indifferent wave. 'I'm not here to do the tourist thing.'

'Oh, but you must—' Her animated expression closed up as she looked over my shoulder.

I turned and saw the Earl. The flop of blond hair remained the same, but he'd ditched the 'boating at Henley' look and gone instead for a navy lounge suit with a pale blue shirt open at the throat, the double cuffs linked with heart-shaped sapphires the size of a thumbnail. His top pocket sported a silk handkerchief the same colour as his shirt. He exuded 'relaxed man-about-town' charisma, but as he strolled towards Rio and me the azure of his eyes shone colder and sharper than the sapphires at his wrists. Something told me he and Rio were not the best of blood-buddies, even though the Earl had been the one to Gift her.

'Genevieve, what a great pleasure to see you again.' He gave me a wide smile that somehow managed not to show his fangs, a practice a lot of the old vamps still followed. 'I am delighted you chose to accept my invitation. I do hope you haven't been waiting long.'

'I haven't been waiting at all.'

Rio gave a snide little chuckle.

'How wonderful.' He held out his arm to me. 'My dear, I shall escort you. I would not want you to get lost' – he looked at Rio – 'or *waylaid* during your time with us.'

Pouting again, Rio sidled up to him and wrapped both hands round his arm, then turned to face me. She topped him by almost a head. 'What a shame. I was just about to show our little sidhe round. I'm sure she would enjoy that much more.'

'Another time, maybe, Rio.' The Earl gave me a gracious smile. 'Ms Taylor is here at my invitation tonight.'

She plucked his handkerchief from his pocket, patted it between her breasts. 'Perhaps we might entertain her together?' she purred. 'That would be fun.'

The Earl's smile didn't change. 'I believe not.'

It was a like watching a big kid poking a snake with a stick, and I really wasn't interested in being anywhere within striking distance. I started to step away, but between lifting my foot and putting it down, the air around me ... *shifted*. I had a moment's disorientation; pressure popped at the back of my head, then I blinked hard and stared in front of me.

Fuck.

Rio was gone. The Earl was still standing there as though he hadn't moved, but the handkerchief was back in his pocket and his smile held a glint of satisfaction.

Chapter Twenty-Four

The Earl had done the same freaky time-pause thing as in the police station. It gave me a hollow feeling in my gut. 'Annoying you, was she?' I asked.

He inclined his head. 'I prefer to spend my time in your company, my dear.' He offered me his arm again. 'Shall we?'

'I'm not sure that's such a great idea – I mean, I really don't think bronzes are my thing, y'know? And that *is* why you invited me, isn't it?'

'Of course,' he said without missing a beat, 'but first I must compliment you.' He reached out and took my hands. 'You look absolutely charming, Genevieve. Such beauty as yours is a pleasure to behold and refreshes the heart.' He smiled, his expression highly amused. 'Although maybe in my case, I should say it could refresh … well, other parts of me.'

Surprised, I laughed. The Earl hadn't seemed the type for innuendos. 'Well, at least you're honest about it.'

'Trite as it may seem,' he bowed over my hand, then turned it and pressed a kiss into the palm, 'I have always found honesty to be the best policy.'

A light flashed to the side of us as he raised his head. 'But forgive me, I get ahead of myself. I feel we should perhaps get to know each other before indulging in such intimacies.'

Sounded good. Of course, that statement was all about definitions, wasn't it?

'Uh-huh.' I gave him a half-smile, my attention snagged by another flash: a Japanese tourist brandishing a miniature camera.

The Earl tucked my hand into his bent arm. 'Sadly, not everyone today is of the same opinion. The whole world rushes past faster and faster, and people appear to be unable or unwilling to consider the long-term consequences of their actions, wishing only to gratify immediate desires.'

'Those desires seem to be gratifying a lot of your vamps just now.'

'It takes time and experience to truly understand what the future holds, and what is necessary to keep it secure.' He sighed, patted my hand. 'The young are unable to understand that our planet is suffering through their cavalier use of its glorious bounty.'

'Uh-huh.' Great, just what I needed: a green vampire, lecturing me on the evils of the world.

'We hope to educate them, not just on the larger environmental—'

There was another flash and the Earl's hand on mine tensed, annoyance flickering across his face. Then a vampire dressed in house uniform – navy trousers and silver-striped navy shirt – appeared next to the tourist and took her arm, removing her camera from her unresisting hold.

'My apologies, Genevieve,' the Earl murmured. 'The staff will ensure the photograph is destroyed. Sometimes our guests fail to fully grasp the Blue Heart's rules.'

'If you don't like photos being taken' – I indicated the posters of all the calendar vamps that lined the club's foyer – 'then what's with all the publicity?'

'You are quite right. It does look rather contradictory.' He led me towards the back of the foyer. 'But it is a lucrative option in this day and age, and of course, like any species, we must evolve as the world around us changes if we are to survive.'

As we walked, people moved aside as though orchestrated to let us pass. I guessed the Earl was using a vamp-trick to subtly clear our way.

'Some among us have spent centuries forging new identities

for ourselves as and when the situation required it,' he continued. 'The invention of the camera, and photographic records, made it increasingly difficult to avoid those humans who were intent on destroying us. So we learnt to evade, and like all habits, it is hard to change.'

Monopolising the conversation appeared to be another of his habits ... and I wasn't interested in the chat.

I was more interested in why he'd invited me here.

We stopped at the swing-doors that led into the interior part of the old cinema. To one side, a Monitor goblin perched on a chrome barstool, his navy boiler-suit decorated with five identical brooches – blue glass hearts – some sort of employee recognition, maybe? He dipped his gelled spike of blue hair towards the Earl, greeted me, then held up his hand, making a low chittering sound.

'You will need to show him your invitation, my dear.' The Earl's voice was quiet. 'And allow him to touch you.' He released me so he wasn't touching me himself. 'It is a condition of our operating licence that all guests enter of their own free will.'

I returned the goblin's greeting, then held the silver invitation out towards him.

The goblin peered at the silver oblong, then clutched at my fingers briefly. He kicked his foot against the leg of his barstool, making his trainers flash blue. 'Okey-dokey, you're cleared to party, miss.' He reached out and pressed the call button for the private lift behind him. There was a ping and the lift door opened and the Earl's hand on my back ushered me forward.

It was a small lift – small enough that two bodies wouldn't have much room between them. I hesitated: not that I'm claustrophobic or anything, but hey, we were adding a vampire into the equation and I didn't like the odds.

The Earl's hand at my back increased its pressure. 'I would like to show you our private members' bar, my dear.' He smiled. 'The lift allows our more select clientele to avoid the crowds. It is more discreet.'

Shit. I so hoped Katie was right about the reason for the invitations, that this was all about the murdered girl and nothing to do with me personally. I took a deep breath and stepped into the small metal box. The floor gave a slight dip, and my stomach went with it. I moved to one side, my back pressed against the wall.

The Earl faced me, an impassive look in his azure eyes as the door slid shut, cutting off the noise from the foyer. The inside of the lift was a dark patterned metal, like an old, foxed mirror. All around us our reflections multiplied and watched us in the eerie quiet. Then I realised why the silence was so strange: the Earl wasn't breathing; his heart wasn't beating. It was almost as if he didn't exist. My own heart sped faster. Did he need to feed? I shot a glance at the open neck of his shirt, but all I could see was pale skin and a shadow of darker blond hair.

Almost as if he could tell what I was thinking, he smiled, amused again, letting me glimpse fang for the first time. 'Alone at last, my dear Genevieve.' He took out a small key, placed it into a hole in the lift's panel and turned it. The power cut off, leaving us in the dim light of a small emergency bulb. 'There, that should ensure we are not disturbed.'

I gripped the silver invitation, tapped it against my chin, concentrating on the slight burn. 'Any particular reason why?' My pulse was kicking like a terrified rabbit, but at least my voice came out calm. 'Or is that a stupid question?'

'Please do not be alarmed. This—' he held his hands open in a placatory gesture '—is just a precaution to ensure our discussion will remain private.'

Narrowing my gaze, I turned his words over in my mind, willing my pulse to slow, or trying to, anyway. Damn G-Zav. 'You don't want anyone to know you're interested in the dead girl, do you?'

His eyes lit with approval. 'Quite so – although my interest isn't in the girl as such, but in the way she died.'

Join the queue! I felt like saying.

'As I mentioned, I believe in honesty.' He looked me straight in the eyes. 'The girl's death was caused by magic, some sort of spell. The incident is an outright attempt to blacken our public image.'

'Going by the punters still queuing to get in, it doesn't appear to have had much effect so far.'

'One death can be labelled a tragic accident, a *domestic*, I understand it is called.' He gestured, dismissive. 'But I have every reason to believe there could be more.'

'What's that to do with me?'

'You have an appointment with Mr Hinkley at the police station later. All being well, you should be able to see the girl's body. I would like you to identify the spell used and, if possible, remove it. And I would appreciate if you would apprise me of your findings.' He adjusted his cuffs. 'In the meantime, I would also like you to carry out some investigations around the club, using your expertise in the area of magic, to see if there is anything else that might shed some light on the matter.'

I didn't bother telling him I wasn't a detective. No one wanted to believe me anyway. 'Is this your way of hiring me?'

He nodded. 'I would have preferred to contact you openly at Spellcrackers, of course, but allowing for the sometimes distrustful relations between vampires and witches, this seemed to be the most expedient way of dealing with the matter. I have obviously informed Inspector Crane about my concerns,' He brushed at a speck on his sleeve. 'But sadly, the good Inspector is new and untried, and is possibly more interested in clearing up a potentially inflammatory situation than finding the truth.'

Talking about inflammatory ...

'So what was with the French Looney-Toon you brought with you last night?'

'A miscalculation on my part.' He adjusted his cuffs again; turning one heart-shaped cufflink the right way up. 'Westman is an excellent lawyer, but sadly, since Louis and he have become enamoured of each other, his mind is not always on his work. As for our foreign guest, I was as surprised as any at his interest in the inspector.' He gave me a rueful smile. 'I do hope it won't influence you against me in this matter.'

I shifted my feet, trying to ease the stretched muscles in my calves. Six-inch heels are not meant for standing still in. 'You do know that the police found no magic on the girl's body, don't you?'

'So Inspector Crane was kind enough to inform me. But she is not only a member of the police, but a witch too.'

Yeah right: so back to the trust thing.

'Even if I find this spell,' I said, 'it's not like I'll be able to tell who cast it, so how are you going to stop it from happening again?'

'The important thing is to find the spell, my dear. Any ramifications can be dealt with later.'

I studied him, then narrowed my eyes. 'Did you know Melissa?'

'She worked here.' His impassive look was back. 'I am sure that we must have spoken at some point.'

'Did you know she was fae?'

'As I said, we might have spoken, but I didn't know her.'

'Did you kill her?'

'Not that I am aware.'

I blinked at that. 'Either you did or you didn't.'

'Sadly, it is always possible that an inadvertent word or gesture of mine at the wrong time may have contributed to her death.' He gave a slight shrug. 'I have always found it pays to be honest.'

I wondered just how *honest* he was really being – he wasn't actively lying; vampires as old as him didn't. They had that whole 'my word is my honour' thing going on. But even I could manage to twist words into the shape I wanted when necessary, and the Earl had a good eight centuries or so on me. So I doubted his *honesty* was the whole-and-nothing-but sort.

Never mind that my bullshit antenna was twitching like a vamp junkie heading for a venom-seizure.

I pursed my lips. 'Is there anything else you can tell me that might help?'

He shook his head. 'I believe not.'

I leaned forward and locked eyes with him. In my six-inch platforms I was the same height as him. 'Not even which vampire you suspect?'

He smiled. 'I never said that I suspected anyone, my dear.'

'You didn't need to.' I leaned back, hands braced either side of me. 'It's no secret that Mr Hinkley thinks that Melissa was killed by another vampire using magic. Or that he's hired me. You've just confirmed that you agree with him.'

As had Declan when I'd visited the Bloody Shamrock. Obviously no one – other than the police – believed Melissa had died of anything other than some sort of magic.

I tapped my foot and carried on, 'The only reason for this little tête-à-tête is just that. No room for anyone to hide and overhear what you've got to say to me. And if all you want is for me to find this so-called spell, you must have a pretty good idea who is responsible for it.' I pursed my lips. 'An invitation, ostensibly to visit your collection of bronzes, isn't going to fool anyone.'

'Although my collection is truly outstanding.' He gave me an appreciative look. 'As are you.'

'So, either you're going to tell me who it is, or you want *them* to think you have.' I took a breath, wanting to slap the patronising approval off his face. 'Which is it?'

'But there is the rub, my dear.' He sighed, turned the key in the lift panel. 'I may have my suspicions, but without the spell, I have absolutely no proof.'

The lights came on and the lift lurched into life. I staggered a little, reaching out to steady myself ...

The air *shifted* and I felt the same disorientation as before.

The lift had stopped. The door was open.

I looked out into the room beyond. It was a crowded lounge bar, and every face had turned to stare my way.

'My dear.' The Earl placed his hand at the small of my back and ushered me from the lift. I stepped out and the lift door pinged closed behind me.

Why had he shifted time again?

Frowning, I turned back, ready to demand an explanation...

But the Earl was gone, and I was on my own.

Chapter Twenty-Five

The private members' bar was crowded with vampires and humans. The vamps gazed with such intensity through the dim light that my heartbeat thudded up a notch. The humans looked on with curiosity. Then they whispered. Then they talked. And glasses clinked and someone laughed a high-pitched laugh and the tension that had filled the air slipped away like a wave flowing back into the sea.

Damn. The manipulative bastard was going fishing, with me on the metaphorical hook. I sighed: so I was bait for a murdering vampire – again! Nothing new about that.

And Katie had already pointed out that I needed to find Melissa's killer – before he found me. Maybe I should be thankful the Earl just wanted to hire me. At least it meant he wasn't the murderer – although he *was* a manipulative bastard so I wasn't totally ruling that idea out – and at best I had a chance at getting paid for something I had to do anyway, thanks to my bargain with Declan. Never mind the fact that whatever Declan and the Earl claimed their reasons were for wanting me to *look* for the spell, those reasons were only the oil-slick obscuring whatever ulterior motives lurked below.

So I looked, and *looked*.

The private bar stretched across the front of the club, along a crescent-shaped balcony. The décor was, unsurprisingly, blue and silver: thick navy carpet woven with silver hearts, pale blue-panelled walls and capacious blue sofas that looked like they could swallow their occupants whole. The vamps had found a theme, and they were sticking to it. Lounging on the sofas were plenty of faces I recognised – not that I actually knew any of them; I wasn't generally on chatting terms with London's glitterati, but it looked as if the local vamp population were, and then some.

And none of them had any spells, not even a glimmer of one – not that I'd expected any; that would've been way too easy. So now it was time to put Katie's investigative tactics into operation and find a talkative tea-boy.

I headed towards the central bar, resisting the urge to tiptoe as I made my way through the sofa obstacle course. The place had an almost crypt-like feel, thanks to the low thrum of conversation and an artificial floral sweetness that filtered out with the air-conditioning.

Something odd pricked up my spine like a half-remembered memory and I frowned, trying to place what it was. Then I realised, the vamps were shut down, like the Earl had been in the lift. I shivered, knowing it stopped them being sent a little crazy by all the pounding pulses and the siren scents of blood. It was what my Alter Vamp did, but it felt weird being on the other side.

As I passed one sofa, a stick-thin model I'd last seen staring out at me from one of the glossies threw her head back, exposing her slender throat. The vamp with her touched a finger to her pulse and she leaned into him, gasping. He winked when he caught me looking.

I gave him a *so-what?* expression back. The menu might be richer, and better dressed, but in reality this place was no different to any of the pubs in Sucker Town.

When I reached the bar I realised my plan was a non-starter. There was no way the human barman, who was flashing his fake fangs like they were a badge of honour, was going to be up for the cosy chat I wanted.

I needed to find someone, somewhere quieter.

I followed the wall of glass that enclosed the balcony-bar, then movement caught in the corner of my eye and I stared down at the bodies dancing in the tightly packed nightclub below. I could just hear the music through the glass, echoing like a faint heartbeat. Then I stopped watching the dancers and focused on the reflections I could see instead.

He stood about ten feet away, arms clasped behind him, doing a really bad job of pretending not to watch me. For a moment I couldn't place him, then his broad shoulders and chest snagged in my memory: the real goth with the romance model's looks from the Leech & Lettuce, the one who'd propositioned my Alter Vamp. Only now his chest, complete with its trail of fang marks, was hidden under a Blue Heart staff uniform.

Darius. Rio's main blood-pet.

Now wasn't that interesting.

Of course, he was an ideal candidate to tag me. I shouldn't have known who he was – and he was human, and staff, so why worry about him when the place was full of big scary vamps?

I started walking again, and saw his reflection following along behind me.

A low cry made me turn and I looked straight into a pair of familiar blue eyes. Declan, from the Bloody Shamrock. My heart thudded faster as he smiled up at me from one of the sofas, his arm draped over the bare shoulders of a blonde in a red-sequinned boob tube. Then I realised it wasn't Declan, but his brother, Seamus. And it wasn't Seamus who was making the girl moan.

Another vampire knelt by her, his head bent over her arm. He was humming quietly as he fed. The sound made me wince with memory. The vamp raised his head and grinned, and I recognised another familiar face: Cherub Cheeks, one of the fang-gang that attacked Gazza.

I filed the scene away and pushed through the exit, then hurried down to the ground floor. Darius's footsteps followed me. Another door led out into the main corridor of the club, where I had a choice of the old cinema's screens one, two or three. A couple of girls ran giggling past me and pulled open door number two, flooding the quiet corridor with loud heart-thudding music.

Glancing behind me I caught Darius coming out of the stairwell. He ducked out of sight and I chose number one – the nearest door – and struck gold, or rather, a pretty girl with a bored expression, standing next to a long, cloth-covered table.

'Hi, I'm Debbie,' she greeted me. 'Welcome to *Fangs for the Memory.*' She smiled, showing off her fake porcelain fangs. 'Tonight we're proud to have the famous Gordon Rackman as our musical director and conductor.' Debbie indicated the stage. The famous Gordon Rackman's pale face glowed under the spotlights as he energetically conducted both the small orchestra in front of him and the dancers behind. The music was guaranteed to make you want to trip around the dance floor ... if you were over sixty. And a good proportion of the room's occupants were, and not because they were vampires.

Right! The tea-dance as advertised on the Blue Heart's website – the club's newest attraction, and apparently popular and therefore lucrative – but then, pensioners have both dis-posable time and income. I just hoped not too many of them had disposable lives.

Under the rainbow sparkles of a huge crystal chandelier, the geriatrics wove and dipped like faded flowers swaying in the breeze. They were mostly female, partnering each other, but a few lucky ones were being swung round in the arms of vampires masquerading as soldiers, sailors and airmen from the Second World War, all looking authentic right up to their slicked-back, Brylcreemed hair – so long as you ignored the fangs. As I watched, the tempo of the music changed and the dancers stopped weaving and instead they rushed past each other across the floor, feet blurring as they executed fast, jumping steps.

'Looks complicated.' I smiled at Debbie.

'It's a foxtrot, I think.' Her nose wrinkled prettily. 'But see-ing as I've got two left feet, I might be wrong. that's why I'm stuck here.'

'Right. Get into many collisions, do they?'

'Nah, most of them are old hands.' The permanent wave of Debbie's brown hair bounced as she laughed. With her bright red lippy matching the hot venom-induced blush in her cheeks, she looked like a throwback to the nineteen forties. Even her heavy green wool uniform with its brass buttons and the sensible laced-up brogues looked like the real McCoy.

She indicated a tray of wide-mouthed glasses. 'Would you like a complimentary Blue Heart cocktail? It's a mixture of blood oranges, raspberries and blueberries.'

The glasses contained a dark red liquid that looked like tired old blood. I picked one up and gave it a tentative sniff, managing not to poke my eye out on the blue paper umbrella. 'No alcohol?'

She shook her head. 'We don't serve alcohol at the Blue Heart. It's part of our healthy living policy to prepare ourselves and our bodies for the Gift.'

'Sounds great,' I said, eyeing the neat punctures on her neck as I handed her the glass back, 'but I think I'll pass.'

The trombone blasted itself into an ending. There was enthusiastic clapping, and the musicians started what even I recognised as a lively waltz.

She gave me an apologetic smile. 'A lot of the regulars don't like it.' She leaned in, whispered, 'Some of them bring their own, y'know, like the old biddy over there next to the pillar.'

The old biddy, her hair rinsed a bright shade of lilac, sat behind her voluminous handbag, topping up her glass from a small silver hip flask. As she carefully screwed the top back, the Blue Heart stamp looked like a dark wound on the back of her hand.

'It's probably gin, or vodka. The cloakroom staff pretend not to notice,' Debbie confided in a low voice. 'I mean, it's not like they're going to get the Gift at their age, is it?' She gave a low laugh. 'Who'd want to spend immortality looking old and decrepit? Not that any of the Masters would sponsor them anyway.'

I raised my eyebrows. 'So why d'they bother coming?

She held up her own stamped hand. 'See, the stamp says you're willing, so it's just a bit of a thrill for most of the old ones, and they get the extra points, along with the health benefits. There's more than enough customers that most of them never get fanged anyway. The last thing the management wants is one of the tea-cosy brigade pegging it from a heart attack or something.'

Looked like I owed Katie one. Debbie was just the person to ask about Melissa … if I could just bring the conversation around to asking about her.

'Y'know, if you're planning on becoming a regular' – she took a sip of the drink I'd handed her back – 'you ought to get yourself a Blue Heart membership card.'

The music headed for a crescendo. A vamp in a white sailor-suit lifted his elderly partner's feet right off the floor, and got a kick in the shins for his consideration.

'It's not just for the points, you get a discount on the entrance fee and in the shop too.' Debbie's face lit with eager-ness. 'And if you save up enough points, you get to pick which vamp you want for a date. I've got my eye on this new French vamp. He looks really cool, wears his hair tied back with a bow, and has these really hot velvet jackets and—'

'Great, but I was wonder—' I tried interrupting her.

Debbie was on a roll. 'I could join you up if you wanted,' she gabbled on with the zealous look of someone ready to clinch a deal. 'You get like a plastic pass card. It's only a few questions and you get to—'

More to shut her up than anything, I produced the Earl's silver invitation and held it up.

Her mouth stopped working, but not for long. 'Oh, wow,

oh look! It's a *silver* one, and it's got a *jewel* in it!' She peered at the card. 'I've never seen that one before. Whose is it?'

I looked myself, saw the black gem. Not the Earl's, then.

'Malik al-Khan.' As I said his name, a sensation like silk brushed over my skin, making my pulse jump. Damn. Maybe speaking his name aloud hadn't been such a great idea.

'Oh, I've seen *him*, yum, he's *totally* cute, but terrifying, if you know what I mean.' She finished her drink with a gulp.

Movement caught my eye. Lilac Hair was doing the finger waggle at someone.

Debbie seemed lost in some inner thought, so I grabbed the opportunity. 'You worked here long, Debbie?'

''Bout four months.'

'So you'll know everyone that works—'

'Oh my God, you're really her aren't you?' She clutched her hands together in excitement. 'Oh my God, this is *amazing*. Your eyes are real, not lenses – I thought you were just one of the fakers.' Her scarlet lips twitched in derision. 'They think it'll get them noticed, but, of course, *they* can tell the difference. But your eyes are really real, aren't they?'

'Last time I looked, yeah.' At last I sensed a way in. I frowned. 'Hey, what about that Mr October's girlfriend? I heard she was a faker.'

She looked puzzled. 'Melissa? No, she—' She stopped, her face closing up. 'Oh, we're not supposed to talk about that, just to say how tragic it was. But' – she glanced behind her – 'there's something funny about all that. I mean, they were an item, her and Mr O, and don't get me wrong, he's really cute, but he's only been a vamp for a couple of years and Mel was aiming a bit higher. She was always lording it, only just lately she'd gone all secretive, kept getting this look, y'know, like the cat that's found the double cream.'

'So you don't think Mr O killed her?'

'Oh yes,' Debbie nodded, 'everyone says he did, 'cause he was jealous. I mean, they all fancied her.' Her expression turned envious. 'The Earl, those Irish brothers, Louis, that's the new French vamp I like, Malik, he's the scary one—' She ticked the names off on her fingers. 'Even Albie hung around her, that's him over there, and he's gay.'

A vampire dressed in the male version of Debbie's green uniform was holding Lilac Hair's hand. Albie had obviously been the recipient of the finger waggle. Lilac Hair looked like she was just as much a chatterbox as Debbie – good thing really, because Albie didn't look the talkative type. Unsurprisingly, he *did* look familiar though – Albie was Mr June – and another fully paid-up member of the fang-gang from Sucker Town.

I wondered briefly whether his uniform still itched.

One of the trumpet players stood and blew a loud blast of notes.

'And there was something else about Mel,' Debbie whispered into the ensuing silence. 'She kept disappearing, like, nobody could find her, then she'd pretend she'd been there all along. She freaked me out once.' She crossed her arms. 'She actually told me something I'd done that I'd thought no one had seen.'

Before I could ask what she meant, more enthusiastic clapping erupted, then the pensioners turned as one, heading straight towards us like stampeding goblins.

Out the corner of my eye, I saw Albie drop Lilac Hair's hand, stand up and stare straight at Debbie. My pulse jumped and I looked back just in time to catch the mind-lock falling over her face.

Shit.

She grabbed my arm, flashed her fake fangs in a grin. 'Break time.' I didn't want to hurt her, so I let her drag me behind the drinks table. 'Better move quick or you'll get run down in the rush.' She pushed me towards the fire-exit. 'Go that way, it's a shortcut.'

Shortcut to where? I looked back at Albie, whose face was pale with strain.

Debbie's grin stretched so wide it looked painful. She gave me another impatient shove. 'Go on. Go.'

Damn. He might push her mind too hard if I didn't do as I was ordered. Taking a deep breath, I wrapped my hand round the steel bar marked 'only for use in emergency' and pushed.

Chapter Twenty-Six

The fire-exit door slammed shut behind me. The shortcut was an empty corridor lit by fluorescent tubes. That and lack of luxurious carpeting on the easy-clean floor, the bare painted walls, unoccupied office, another fire-exit and a cleaning cupboard told me this wasn't one of the public areas.

There was only one other place left to go.

Ornate blue and silver lettering above the double doors read *Le Théâtre du Grand-Guignol*. The twin masks of Comedy and Tragedy looked like the fossilised faces of long-extinct giants. They were thickly coated with silver leaf. One cried a single ruby teardrop the size of a hen's egg, the other laughed wide, showcasing a set of fangs too large to belong to any vampire. There was nothing beguiling about either of the faces, but they left no doubt as to the entertainment on offer.

The Blue Heart's website had listed the Théâtre as open for VIP members only on Saturdays – looked like I'd just been upgraded – but it was odd that someone had spent a lot of money decorating an entrance that no one, other than the club's staff, seemed likely to use.

My gut twisting with unease, I pulled open the doors.

Soft, spine-chilling music floated out of the dark interior, along with the faint copper scent of recently spilled blood. Five or six rows of tables in expanding semi-circles faced a raised stage. All the tables were occupied, but no one looked round as I entered. Every member of the audience was staring in wrapt anticipation at the stage. The set scenery was that of a derelict graveyard. Whatever the play was – and something told me I wasn't going to need more than three guesses – it owed more to the star-struck movie legends than to the less romantic realities of vampiric existence.

I *looked*, but there was no magic to find. Not that I cared that much, but I was beginning to think the Earl was going to be disappointed with my investigations.

'Come in, little sidhe,' Rio's voice whispered. As she spoke, a mist of dry ice rolled out from behind the ivy-strangled headstones and off the stage to swirl around the audience's legs like a malevolent gathering of abandoned ghosts.

I let the doors swing closed behind me and turned towards where Rio's cap of pale blue curls shone in the dim light. She'd gone to enough trouble to get me in here. I hoped it was because of Melissa, and not just because she was hungry, or that she was snapping at the Earl's bait.

'Welcome to the House of Hammer, where terror stalks even the stoutest of hearts.' She cast me a quick sideways glance, before her gaze returned to the stage.

My own heart banged against my ribs. *Comedy time, not!*

'Looks like a popular place,' I said flatly. 'Business must be good.'

Rio put her finger to her lips. 'Shh, the next act is about to start.'

And lucky me, I'd arrived just in time.

I stuck a hand in my jacket pocket and fingered the silver invitations as I scanned the room. It was full of vampires, with an odd scattering of humans. As my eyes adjusted, I recognised most of them from my Sucker Town outings. They were all of them Golden Blade blood, and last I heard, they were still refusing to jump on the celebrity bandwagon, so what the hell were they doing here?

The music struck a chord and a young woman entered stage right, her eyes wide and frightened, the front of her diaphanous white nightgown clutched tight in her hands, loose curls of long dark hair snaking down to her hips. The audience leaned forward almost as one as she stood trembling in the manufactured fog, pinned in place by the beam of a bright spotlight.

I gave a long-suffering sigh, but kept my voice low. 'Isn't this all a little old hat? The graveyard scene's been done to death. I'd have thought you'd have more imagination.'

'Who needs imagination?' Rio's fangs glinted white with her smile.

Suspicion edged into my mind and I studied the human girl on the stage. Sweat glistened on her terrified face as she stumbled to the centre of the stage and thudded to her knees next to a fake stone coffin. She curled up, shaking. She appeared to be completely unaware of the audience who were drinking down her every quiver.

Damn. She was living the scene for real.

'You've got her in a mind-lock, haven't you?' I clenched my fists. 'I thought you weren't supposed to do this type of shit here. Willing victims only.'

Rio chuckled, and the sound crawled over my skin.

Onstage the girl had been joined by a vampire. His classic black opera cape flapped about him in a nonexistent wind – had to be a vamp-party-trick – and his red silk shirt shone under the spotlights. He'd scraped his long platinum hair into a sleek pony-tail, complete with the requisite widow's peak, and with his hooded eyes and thin, cruel lips he was perfect for the part, in more ways than one. The vamp acting the Big Bad Count was none other than Red Poet, leader of the Sucker Town fang-gang.

I felt my pulse speed up a notch.

Red Poet opened his jaw wide, letting the light spark off all four of his fangs, and the audience joined him in a series of loud pantomime hisses.

'Such sweet blood runs through your veins.' Rio held out a hand to me. 'Come closer, little sidhe, for I will enjoy this all the more with your delicious scent teasing me.'

I ignored her. Rio was entirely too happy, which could only

mean one thing: the girl had agreed to – well, whatever was going to happen. She'd probably even signed the deal in her own blood. I looked around for confirmation and found it in the small Monitor goblin sitting in the front row, tapping the red light of his radio earpiece.

I hoped the girl understood what she'd got into, but I was willing to bet she hadn't. Vampires could be as tricky as the fae to bargain with when it suited them.

Red Poet stalked through the mock-graveyard, peering over every headstone, hamming it up big-time. The music crescendoed as his intended victim huddled in full view, tremors racking her plump body.

'Audience participation is such a wonderful thing, don't you think?' Rio's eyes never left the stage. 'What could be more exciting, more thrilling, than to watch, and to feel, real fear?' Excitement laced her voice. 'To actually *feel* the heart beating faster and faster, the blood rushing through your body in a pounding torrent . . .' She took a deep breath. 'What better way is there, when you feel so alive in those moments just before you die?' She let out a gusty sigh. 'True terror is such a rare and precious commodity in these over-enlightened days.' She sent me a sly smile. 'And like any commodity' – she spread her arms wide, encompassing the whole room – 'it can be bought and sold.'

I threw Rio a disgusted look. 'You're all going along for the ride, aren't you?'

She held out her hand again. 'Would you like to join us?'

'Thanks, I'll pass.' I backed off; this wasn't getting me anywhere and I had better places to be. I went to push against the door, but instead of wood, found my hand meeting cool flesh. Rio had moved too fast for me to see and now she stood between me and the exit, arms braced to either side of the door, blocking my way.

'Stay with me, little sidhe,' she murmured.

I stared at my hand flat against her chest, the deep V of

her sheer blouse brushing against my wrist, my own honey-coloured hand looking pale against her darker skin. Her heart thumped under my palm sending little shockwaves along my arm. *Mesma.* I wanted to take my hand away, but I couldn't. The little shocks felt too irresistible.

My throat tightened with fear: she was way more powerful than I'd thought.

Rio pushed closer. Instinct screamed at me to step back. Instead I let my body do what she wanted. I bent my elbow, bringing us nearer, and looked up into her eyes. The whites were as blue as her hair. Her scent, musk, mint and liquorice, clouded my mind and I leaned into her, wrapping my other hand around the back of her neck.

'Well, this is a surprise, little sidhe.' She lowered her head, her mouth parted in anticipation. 'Who'd have thought?'

Our lips met, soft at first, then I pressed mine hard against hers, taking the kiss even deeper. I could feel her heart fluttering fast and frantic under the palm of my hand. I slid my tongue across her cool lips. Hers darted out, eager. The tang of copper mixed with the bitter mint caught in my throat. I dragged my mouth from hers, my hand still against her flesh.

'Is this what you want, Rio?' I breathed the words into her face.

She swayed towards me, arms still outstretched, her hands on the door frame holding her upright.

I trailed my hand lower, touching the trembling skin of her stomach. 'Is this why you rushed out to greet me?'

A small, inarticulate sound issued from her parted lips.

I slid my fingers into the top of her leather hotpants. 'Why you've been so eager for me to join you?'

She shuddered, her breath coming in excited little huffs.

I stepped sharply to the side, stuck my leg out and jerked hard on her shorts. Off-balance, she stumbled forward, her eyes flashing open, her arms windmilling. I thumped my hand between her shoulders and pushed her down. She landed on her front, her chin cracking hard against the wooden floor. Her breath gasped out as I dropped down to sit astride her and I slapped my hands on her arms and leaned my weight on her, pinning her to the floor.

'Or was there something you wanted to tell me?' I leaned down and whispered into her ear.

Then the screaming started.

Onstage, Red Poet had caught the girl and was holding her from behind, trapping her body tightly against his. The audience were transfixed, revelling in her terror. Tears coursed down her face as her struggles grew weaker. He gently wiped the tears away, then lifted her chin, stretching her neck so the large pulse jumped under the skin.

Beneath me, Rio laughed.

He reared back his head.

Shit! *Rio* was controlling him—

'Make him stop,' I shouted in her ear.

Red Poet froze, fangs poised to strike.

Rio turned so our faces were almost touching. 'Shh, little sidhe,' she purred, 'you wouldn't want him to hurt her now, would you? Just a slight miscalculation on his part, and there would be a tragic accident. And of course, she signed the disclaimer of her own free will, all our special guests do ... the Monitor goblin will vouch for that.'

Was she bluffing?

As if she'd read my mind, she whispered, 'Unlike some, our plump little starlet doesn't have the protection of the Earl, or a religious mother, or a celebrity boyfriend – no one would even remember her, if her performance tonight should be her swan song.'

Not bluffing then.

The girl could disappear tonight, and unless the contract called for the Monitor to register her death, no one would ever know. Humans really didn't understand just how literal goblins were sometimes.

'I suppose you want me to move, then?' I muttered.

She gave another skin-crawling chuckle. 'Please don't. This is a delectable situation.'

Okaaay, so she liked being pinned to the floor ... 'Fine,' I snapped.

'Oh, wonderful: now you can enjoy the show, and I can murmur sweet nothings in your tempting ear. Come closer, little sidhe,'

I sighed and bent nearer until my face was next to hers. Vampires do so love their games.

Back onstage, Red Poet had let the girl go and now she was crawling desperately away from him, half strangling herself with her nightgown as she did so. He tiptoed after her, exaggerating every move: a true pantomime villain.

Rio shifted beneath me. 'You've been asking about poor Melissa. A great shame, her death, she was such a delightful pet.'

'I'm not here for the eulogy, so just get on with it, Rio.'

'Very well. Melissa came to me the night before she died and told me she had some information she wanted to sell to me.'

'She was blackmailing you.'

She laughed softly, the sound vibrating through me. 'Melissa was much like me; she had ambitions. She understood that the right word or deed could be used as leverage, or be a very effective weapon.'

Touché. 'So Melissa *was* blackmailing you.'

'She was smart, and she had her eye on a bright and shiny future.' Rio arched one black brow. 'It's always possible she was blackmailing someone, don't you think? I liked her. She was a girl after my own heart.' She winked. 'That's why I agreed to be her sponsor.'

I frowned. Melissa already had a sponsor: Declan at the Bloody Shamrock.

'I see no one's shared that information with you, have

they?' Rio tutted. 'But don't you find it interesting that she had not one, not two, but *three* sponsors? Me, of course, the Earl, and Declan. And there was to be another, but he had still to declare.'

My back was starting to ache. 'Let me guess: that'd be Malik al-Khan.'

'You *have* been busy.' She sniffed the air. 'But I was meaning our other visitor, the Frenchman.'

I needed to clear something up. 'So did you agree to be her sponsor before or after she decided to sell you information?'

'Before, of course.' She licked her lips. 'I declared my intentions some time ago.'

For a moment I'd almost forgotten what was happening a few feet in front of me, but a low moan dragged my attention back to the stage where Red Poet was enjoying himself draping the terrified girl on top of the stone coffin. He flashed a fang-filled grin and tipped her head back, exposing her throat, and started carefully arranging her hair so it wouldn't obstruct the audience's view.

The music deepened ominously.

'So what's this information then?' I asked.

Rio sighed. 'Maybe you'll tell me when you find out, little sidhe. Unfortunately, Melissa was silenced before she could tell me what it was.'

Figured! Rio's little games were just her way of jumping on the spell bandwagon with all the other vamps. And she hadn't even given me much more in the way of information.

The music rose on a drum roll and Red Poet lifted his arms, his cape billowing dramatically behind him.

'Watch this bit,' Rio tensed with excitement, 'this is the best part.'

The music cut out. The audience members were almost out of their seats with anticipation.

A wooden stake bloomed in Red Poet's chest, spraying a fountain of blood—

Light and smoke exploded, obscuring the stage.

I blinked in shock. Had they just staked him for real?

The smoke cleared, unveiling two figures locked in a passionate embrace. The music resumed, this time soft and romantic. The figures broke apart and the girl's saviour flicked back her long red hair and flashed a fang-filled grin. The two of them giggled and took a bow as the audience erupted into loud applause.

'Such a wonderful moment.' Rio sighed with pleasure as the lights cut out, plunging the Théâtre in darkness.

She heaved and rolled and my back hit the floor.

And the lights flared back on to reveal Rio, on her hands and knees above me. 'Happy endings,' she purred, looking down, 'don't you just love them?'

I fumbled in my jacket, my pulse racing. 'Is that what you want?'

Her tongue darted out. 'Isn't it what we all hope for?'

'What about the star of the show,' I demanded, 'can she hope for a happy ending?'

'I'm sure she can. We all need hope, little sidhe, otherwise what is there to live for?' She blew me a kiss. 'Take away hope, and there is nothing left.' Her mouth opened wide in a fang-filled grin, much as the girl's saviour had done, and she started to lower her head.

'Even when hope is gone,' I slammed the silver invitation against her chest, 'there is always retribution.'

She shrieked and leapt back like a scalded cat, hands flapping frantically. Then her mouth gaped and she slid unconscious to the floor. My own mouth opened in shock as smoke wisped between my fingers and the smell of burnt flesh choked my throat, both mine and hers.

Shit. Her reaction was way more dramatic than I'd expected. Coughing, I scrambled round in a crouch, ready to face the audience; they were all staring like it was just part of the entertainment. My hands fisted. What the hell would happen when they realised it wasn't?

Then a dainty blonde vampire in a twenties-style beaded dress stood up: *Elizabetta, head of the Golden Blade family.*

I registered who she was almost without noticing.

This was not good.

She inclined her head graciously, then brought her hands together and clapped.

The rest of the watching audience joined in.

Relief tumbled inside me. I dropped the invitation back in my pocket and swiped the back of my hand over my mouth. 'Thanks for the chat, Rio,' I muttered.

Cue my exit.

Chapter Twenty-Seven

Outside in the empty corridor, I let out a relieved breath. Had Rio been going to bite me? Would she really have given the finger to the Earl and his guarantee of my safety like that? Or had it just been more play-acting? I grimaced at the red burn on my palm, then checked my watch. I still had nearly an hour before my meeting with Alan Hinkley, time enough for some more investigating ... only right now I'd had my fill of playing detective and having vampires taking me for a sucker. Resisting the urge to run, I strode towards the fire-exit, my high-heels sounding like gunshots pinging on the floor behind me.

Fifty feet and I was out of there.

Only I didn't make it.

A shadowed blur hit me and slammed my back against the wall. A hard body pressed against mine, a cool hand clamped over my mouth. My pulse jack-hammered away in my throat as I stared at a familiar black stone in a pale pretty ear.

Malik held me there, silent, unmoving, his dark spice scent invading my senses as he looked not at me, but off to the side, as though waiting. About us the light dimmed and shadows obscured our surroundings, leaving us marooned ... some-where ... or nowhere.

I had a vague thought of struggling, but my body wasn't interested.

'You seem to be having a most informative evening, Genevieve.' He spoke quietly, his jaw hardly moving under his pale skin. 'It is about to get even more so.'

The words slipped over me as I gazed at the dark, silky hair that curled over the neck of his black T-shirt. The taste of Turkish delight melted over my tongue and my heart did an eager dance, swirling my blood through my veins.

'When I remove my hand, you will stay quiet, stay still.' He turned to look at me, pupils glowing red in his almond-shaped eyes.

Part of me didn't want him to take his hand away; the part that was elated to be with him in this nowhere place. Staring into his perfect, pretty face, fear fluttered in my belly that I could even think like that. *Fuck.* I willed the feeling away and concentrated on the small pain digging into my spine – my watch. My right arm was bent and trapped behind me, and Malik was pressed so tight against me that I couldn't get free. Maybe if I sank my teeth into his hand—?

'Genevieve?' His fingers flexed against my mouth. 'You will stay silent?' His hand tightened round my wrist and the bracelet of bruises there throbbed to his touch.

I glared at him. In my heels, we were almost the same height, and close enough that without his hand on my mouth, our lips would have kissed. I couldn't nod, so I blinked.

'Good.' His hand slid down to circle my neck, thumb touching my speeding pulse.

'What the fu—?'

He squeezed my throat, silencing me. 'Look to your left.'

The pressure round my neck gave me no option. I looked.

The shadows shifted, thinning in a small area, almost like watching a slightly out-of-focus TV. Darius, Rio's blood-pet, burst out of the Théâtre and did a frantic check in both directions. He might as well have carried a flashing neon sign advertising that he was searching for me. He dragged a hand through his hair, desperation marring his cover model looks. Then he looked at us and started jogging. I held my breath as he neared, but he ran past us without even a sideways glance, grabbed the bar of the fire-exit door and rammed it.

The door stayed closed.

Damn, it hadn't been a way out after all.

Darius swung round and sprinted back the way he'd come.

Malik tapped a finger on my cheek, indicating that I should keep watching.

Heart thudding fast, I did as he wanted and slowly turned my head.

Darius slid to a halt by the ballroom, banged on the door. For a moment, nothing happened. He thumped it again and this time it opened. He disappeared inside, then barrelled back out almost immediately, frowning. He scanned the empty corridor then, his long legs eating up the floor, he raced back into the Théâtre.

I turned back to Malik. The glow in his eyes had dimmed, leaving them deep pools of black. 'We're ... what? Invisible?'

He gave a small shake of his head, spoke in an undertone. 'Not quite. A smell, a touch, a heartbeat could draw attention to us and we would be seen, although unlikely by a human.'

Okay, so he could hide more than himself in the shadows.

I sniffed. 'You might want to polish up your social skills, y'know,' I muttered. 'The caveman greeting was old even in the Stone Age. Most people content themselves with a handshake nowadays.'

He gave me an enigmatic look, then laid his cheek on mine and inhaled. 'Good evening, Genevieve.' His voice slid over me like hot satin. 'I see you received my invitation.'

Fine, so he wasn't going to hurt me. And he wasn't into handshakes.

'Yeah, and it's been great, but I really must be going, so if you could just move ...' I tried pushing him away, but it was like trying to shift a concrete troll.

'The night is still young, and there is more for us to learn,' he said. 'I have concluded that you could be useful.' Amusement flickered over his face. 'We shall work together on this.'

Who was he kidding? Working together didn't usually mean plastering colleagues against the wall.

I pulled a disappointed face. 'Sorry, prior engagement.'

'Yes, I know.' He turned back to stare at the empty corridor. 'You have an appointment at the police station, but that is not for some time yet.'

Well, if he thought I was just going to stand there ... I wriggled, got a leg free ... he shoved his thigh between mine ... my heel stabbed into the floor, jarring the bones in my leg—

'Calm yourself,' he said softly, not looking at me. 'We have another show to watch.'

'Thanks.' I heaved a frustrated sigh. 'I've seen all the shows I want tonight.' He ignored me, intent on ... whatever. Okay, so he'd got me into a compromising position, but even with my heart thudding like a pneumatic drill, there was no evidence he was the least bit excited about it. And his body was touching mine in all the right places, so that I'd feel, just like I could feel his heart wasn't beating, and he wasn't breathing: he'd shut himself down, like the Earl had earlier. And like the Earl, and Rio, no doubt this was just Malik's way of asking me to find whatever magic killed Melissa – except that he hadn't wanted me to get involved in the first place—

He cut into my thoughts. 'See who is coming now?'

Albie – Mr June – appeared out of the ballroom. He had a good scratch of his thighs through his uniform and strolled to the Théâtre. Before he got there, Rio stalked out, snarling with anger, the burn on her chest like a blistered red brand. An even-more-desperate-looking Darius hovered behind.

My pulse sped faster.

'Slow your heart, Genevieve,' Malik said soft and urgent. 'Slow its beat, as you did before; you will draw their attention otherwise.'

I took a deep breath, concentrated, but nothing happened. I closed my eyes. *One elephant, two elephants.*

'Now,' he hissed, 'or I will do it for you.'

Damn G-Zav. I gritted my teeth. *Five elephants, six elephants.*

'It will not go well if they find us.'

My eyes snapped open, I glared at him and whispered. 'Like that's going to help!'

His hand plucked at my throat. 'Why are you wearing so many clothes?'

'Huh?'

He let go of my wrist, slipped my jacket open and pulled at the Lycra. 'What is this?'

'My top!' I tried to push his hand away.

The glow flared in his eyes. 'Be still.'

I couldn't answer him, couldn't move, couldn't speak, frozen at his command. The flutter of fear returned on great beating wings.

He glanced along the corridor.

'There is no time.' He grabbed the neck band of my top, tore it down. Chill air kissed my naked skin. Incandescent eyes fixed on mine, Malik pressed his palm between my breasts, put his lips on mine. Cold seared through my body like a fast, freezing glacier. I screamed into his mouth. He shuddered, swallowing my screams into silence. Then my heart stuttered, stopped beating. My head dropped to his shoulder, eyes falling shut, body limp. I wondered if I was dying, but the thought was trapped in a sea of ice and didn't matter any more ...

Open your eyes, Genevieve. His voice drifted unspoken through my mind.

My eyes opened.

Rio, Albie and Darius strode past us and through a door further down the hall.

We followed them in ... or we didn't, I wasn't sure, but now we stood against a wall in a spacious office. The room had a hollow feel to it. A desk, a plastic chair, a metal filing cabinet – and a stale rank smell that made my nose wrinkle. *Old blood.*

Malik spooned behind me, his arm tight around my waist, his hand a cold fist over my heart. I knew that my heart did not beat, that my body would do only as he commanded, not as I wanted, but my panic was locked away, a prisoner inside a bubble of ice, and all that was left was calm and coldness.

'Where is the sidhe, Darius?' Beads of pink sweat pearled in Rio's hair. 'How could you lose her?'

Darius stood, arms slack at his sides, submissive. 'I'm sorry, Master.'

She grabbed his throat, lifted him until his feet dangled inches above the ground. 'I gave you a task,' she growled. 'All you had to do was watch her and tell me what she did and who she spoke to.' She shook him.

I almost expected him to rattle.

'You knew I hadn't finished with her yet,' she yelled.

Eyes bulging, Darius let her choke him.

Albie brushed down his uniform, had a sneaky scratch, then said calmly, 'Put him down, Rio. You can play with him later.'

She dropped Darius and backhanded him all in one fast movement, launching him into the air. He hit the filing cabinet face-first, banging it into the wall, and thudded down, blood trickling from his scalp, leaving behind a head-sized dent in the metal.

Ouch! That had to hurt.

'Why are you fussing about the sidhe?' Albie inspected his manicure. 'She must have left.'

'They say not at the front door.' Rio kicked the plastic chair, knocking it over.

'They are such *challenging* things, the fae,' Albie said snidely. 'Maybe she vanished into thin air.'

Rio snarled, lips pulling back from her fangs, 'I told you, she can't do that. She may reek of power, but she lacks any ability to control it.'

Harsh but true. Still I wasn't too happy about the *reeks* bit.

'And you think you are the one to win that prize?' Albie

gave a disbelieving sniff. 'You smell weak enough that I wonder you ever gained your autonomy.'

'Don't push me.' She crowded him, topping him by a good six inches. 'You didn't enjoy it the last time I showed you who's boss.'

A sly look crossed his face. 'I won't help if *He* senses you're this depleted. Remember I'm not the loyal sort. All I'm interested in is my blood-cut and if you can't deliver, then I'll find someone who can.'

'You always were a snivelling parasite,' she sneered at him.

'I prefer to call it judicious pragmatism.' He reached for the door handle.

Be ready, Genevieve, Malik's voice sounded in my head. *I do not wish to stay for the finale.*

He wasn't the only one. Somehow I didn't think I'd enjoy the encore.

'Now if I was you,' Albie pointed a finger at her, 'I'd stop fretting about the sidhe and sort yourself out.'

Rio lunged for him.

But he was gone.

She slammed the door shut, leant back against it and glowered at Darius. He was still huddled on the floor, watching her with wide-open eyes.

Our chance is lost. We must wait until she is otherwise occupied.

A long, low hissing escaped Rio's mouth and she collapsed to her knees. 'Get over here, you pathetic creature,' she ordered.

Darius slowly sat up, then dragged his shirt sleeve across his face, wiping away the blood.

Rio's face contorted in pain. 'For fuck's sake, hurry up!'

He lurched forward as if she'd pulled him, then crawled until he knelt before her, his pupils dilating until they almost eclipsed the brown of his iris.

She stroked his cheek. 'Kiss me.' Her tone lost its stridency, *mesma* giving it promise.

Darius clasped her head in his palms, then mashed his mouth to hers.

Rio looked like she was trying to eat him back.

She's occupied, I tried to shout. *I want to go now.*

Rio reared back, her chest rising with harsh gasps, a rosy bloom in her cheeks. She ran her tongue around her fangs, then laughed, the sound of her pleasure echoing around the room. Darius slumped, a thick trickle of blood running between his lips.

'More,' she purred, pressing her mouth back against his. Her hands reached blindly for his shirt, ripped it open. She scored long blue nails over his pecs, down his abdominals, and thick lines of blood welled up. Moving her palms in ever-widening circles, she spread the blood like jam over his weeping skin.

Okay. I tried to close my eyes, found I couldn't. *This is not good.*

Rio snatched her mouth away and Darius swayed, eyes tightly closed. Her tongue snaked out to lick a smear of blood from his jaw. He moaned, the sound unhappy. She looked down and her gaze turned eager as she tried to lower her head. He stopped her, fingers clamping like limpets to her scalp. A fine trembling started in his body. 'Please ...' The word was an anguished whisper.

She grinned, fangs glinting sharp in the overhead light. 'I know you can beg better than that, my lovely, frightened pet.' Flattening her hand in the wet slickness on his chest, she shoved him onto his back.

Darius lay awkwardly, his legs bent under him, fingers clutching the small blue curls he'd ripped from her hair.

A ripple shivered through the cold that encased me.

Be calm. Malik's mouth breathed ice along my neck.

And the ripple smoothed away.

Rio wiped her bloody hand over the burn mark on her chest, then took a slim mobile phone from her back pocket. Sliding the top up, she thumbed a button and held it to her ear.

'It's me,' she said into the phone. 'There's a problem. It's not going to work.'

She flicked Darius, grinned as he flinched.

'Yes,' Rio said, 'she's been and gone.'

She dug her nails into the tight skin of Darius's stomach, drawing more bright red blood.

He jerked and cried out, but she silenced him with a look.

'Yes, I did, just as you wanted,' she said, her tone placating. 'Only it didn't go as we'd expected. Still, we should've known it wouldn't after that little stunt in the police station.'

Malik's arm tensed around my waist. My ears had already perked up. Now if I could just listen, and not watch …

Phone still pressed to her ear, Rio dipped a finger in Darius's blood, painting streaks over his quivering flesh. 'Interesting.' She tilted her head to admire her efforts.

Darius's wide-eyed stare gave new meaning to rabbits and headlights.

'You really think that's going to make such a difference?' Licking her fingers clean, she listened, then squealed with excitement. 'Oh, that will be so delicious!'

Behind me, another part of Malik stiffened.

Shit. Rio wasn't the only sucker getting worked up. Agitation swept through the calm peace inside my bubble.

'So she could still be useful then.' Rio smiled at the trembling Darius. 'Yes, later. I've got something I want to finish first.'

Be ready, Genevieve.

Rio grinned and said, 'Me too.' She tapped the phone shut, sliding it onto the desk. 'And now, my pet, you can scream all you want.' She bowed as though praying, and sank her fangs deep into his chest and sucked. The noise was loud and painful in the quiet room.

A tear rolled down Darius's face and dripped into the dark brown carpet beneath him.

The office disappeared.

I stood in the round stone room of my memory, the candles

guttering low. The room stank of lust and terror and my legs were cold and wet from my own piss.

Sally's blue-white hair was matted, blackened with her own blood. Her blue skin was pale and lifeless. Her eyes were staring up at me, begging.

And I watched as my prince—

Then the office returned as Darius screamed, the sound shattering the ice that held me frozen. Angry heat rolled inside me. My heart beat once. Pain spasmed through me, splintering every nerve I had.

You must not fight me, it will hurt too much. Malik's voice was urgent in my mind.

A river of molten lava burnt its way through my body: my arms, my legs and my fingers cracked with the heat. My eyes fused shut. Then the itching started, unbearable, tormenting, and I needed to scratch my skin off, but my hands were held frozen in the ice.

'Genevieve, can you hear me?' Blessed cool wrapped itself round my body for an instant. I tried to hold it to me, but the pinpricks needling my body wouldn't let me.

'Genevieve, listen, it will stop soon; it is just your circulation returning. Nothing more.'

Somewhere I laughed. *Nothing more?* Who did the voice think it was kidding?

'Drink this, it will help.' Liquid splashed over my lips.

I opened my mouth; let it pour down my throat.

'That is enough, else you will be sick.'

The itching was back, insects crawling all over my body, nipping me with their tiny sharp teeth.

'What's the matter with her, man?' Another voice, this one heavy, rough. It didn't feel good, not like the cool one. 'She done a bad trip on sumfink?' the rough voice asked.

'Hold her wrists,' the cool voice said. 'Don't let her injure herself.'

'Sure thing, man,' Thick, meaty fingers settled round my

arms. 'You gonna pour some more water over her?'

Firm hands cupped my cheeks. 'Genevieve. Listen to my voice.' The voice wrapped itself round me. It felt like slipping into a still, dark lake.

'Open your eyes.'

The insects gave me a few last bites.

And I looked into the red glow of Malik's eyes. 'What the fuck did you do to me?'

Chapter Twenty-Eight

Tiny flares lit in Malik's pupils, then winked out, leaving his expression enigmatic. 'Good,' he said, 'you are well.'

'Well?' I shouted in disbelief. 'It's your fault I felt crap in the first place!' I tried to lift my arms, but found I couldn't. A thickset man with a lined, saggy face was gripping my wrists like his life depended on it.

I glared at him. 'Let the fuck go of me.'

The creases in his face rearranged themselves into a lopsided grin. 'Sure thing.' He dropped my arms. 'My Rocky was always mad when she came down.' His grin disappeared. 'She's bin dead near three years now, 'course.'

Malik inclined his head to the man. 'Thank you for your assistance. You may leave us.'

The man turned and ambled off.

I stifled an urge to slug Malik and looked around instead. I took a deep breath, then wished I hadn't. Ammonia and the throat-gagging stench of pine disinfectant assaulted my nose. Even if I couldn't see the row of stainless steel urinals, thankfully unoccupied, I'd have still known we were in a public toilet. I grimaced in disgust. The night just kept getting better and better.

Malik followed my gaze. 'We would have been too conspicuous in the Ladies' facilities,' he said.

I snorted. 'And we're *not* in the Gents?'

He gave an elegant shrug.

Oh, just great – and then I remembered the office, and Darius. A queasy feeling settled in my stomach.

'Listen, pal: next time you want to show me something, send me a DVD.' I shoved him out the way. 'Better yet, don't bother.' I headed for the exit. 'If I wanted to watch sucker porn, I'm sure I can find something better than that nasty little effort.'

Malik fell into step next to me. 'Where are you going, Genevieve?'

'None of your business,' I snapped.

'But we will work together.' He grasped my wrist and pulled me round to face him. 'We agreed this, you and I,' and then he smiled. And never mind he was male, he was beautiful, and my heart flip-flopped in my chest and lust pooled hot inside me and my magic almost leapt into life. One smile, and I was ready to jump his bones. Shit. I didn't have enough fingers and toes to count the ways that being attracted to him was such a bad idea. And I couldn't even blame my reaction on *mesma*. He wasn't using any.

I shook him off. 'No. *You* made *that* decision. *I* had nothing to say about it.' I checked my watch. 'Well, I really can't say it was nice meeting you, and we certainly didn't have fun. So please feel free to never call me.'

One side of his mouth lifted. 'As you have not yet given me your number, that is a rather empty request.'

I flipped him the finger and stalked towards the exit, my heels slapping against the tiled floor.

'Genevieve,' he called after me, amusement in his voice, 'you might wish to adjust your clothing before you go any further.'

I looked down. My ripped top was hanging round my waist like an apron and my jacket was flapping open, flashing my tits at anyone interested. Gritting my teeth, I buttoned the jacket – it still left a deep V of cleavage – but at least I wouldn't get arrested for indecent exposure. I untied what was left of the top and shoved it into a nearby waste bin, throwing a toxic glare at a couple of leering teenagers. Threading through the crowds in Leicester Square, I made for the queue of taxis.

I yanked open the taxi door and said, 'Hungerford Bridge,

Victoria Embankment Side, please,' and slumped onto the back seat.

The cabby grinned. 'Right ho, luv.'

The door locks clicked shut, the lights glowing like tiny red eyes in the dim interior.

I shivered and reached for my phone to check for any messages. It wasn't there. Damn I chewed my lip in annoyance. It must've dropped out, probably in all that rolling around with Rio. I sighed, letting my head fall back, and contemplated the roof of the taxi. Well, no way was I going back to look for it now. And what was Rio up to? It sounded like she was plotting some sort of palace coup, but what did that have to do with Melissa's death? My gut made me think it was connected, but there were so many bloody dots appearing on the page that I was having trouble joining them up.

Then I realised the taxi hadn't moved.

I tapped on the glass behind him. 'I'm in sort of a hurry here.'

His head bobbed again. 'Just waiting for your friend, luv.'

'What the—?' Damn vampires! I flung myself back in the seat and a moment later, Malik opened the cab door and gave me another heart-flopping smile.

'Genevieve.' Settling himself on the seat, he stretched out his long legs. His meaning was so obvious even an animated mud-troll would have got it. If I wanted to get out, I'd have to get past him.

The cab rumbled off, diesel engine drowning out my huff of frustration. No way did I want Malik tagging along to my meeting with Alan Hinkley, not with Alan's text about his finding a nervous fae informer who would only talk to me. So I needed to get rid of the pretty vampire – only short of stabbing him again, I didn't see how I was going to make that happen.

I frowned at him. Something was different – he seemed tougher, less sophisticated – then I realised he'd swapped the fancy suit for more of a street-goth look. In the Armani, he'd looked slim, almost slender, but now his black jeans with studded belt and black short-sleeved T-shirt moulded over a body that was hard with muscle. Whatever he'd been when he'd accepted the Gift, he hadn't been a couch potato. A platinum ring set with a black gem similar to the one in his ear banded his thumb. I *looked*, but he had no spells about him. An errant part of my mind wondered what he would look like without the clothes and mentally I rolled my eyes. My mind could imagine all it wanted, but that so wasn't going to happen. Vampires, even hot-fanged eye-candy like Malik, were too dangerous to even think about flirting with, never mind anything else.

So instead I tried to sort through all the nuggets of information I'd unearthed at the Blue Heart, work out which were golden and which were just dross. But in the quiet and dark of the cab, all I could think of was the tear running down Darius's cheek, I crossed my arms and hugged myself and gazed blindly out of the window as we inched slowly through the traffic-clogged streets of London.

As if he knew what I was thinking, Malik said softly, 'If you are concerned about the human, he had already witnessed Rio's particular style of feeding before he chose to become part of her household.'

I sighed. Did that mean Darius had enjoyed being abused like that? It hadn't looked like it – but who was I to know?

'He can always petition for another Master, should he wish,' Malik continued in the same soft tone.

I scowled out at the cars passing in the other direction. 'Like Rio's ever going to let that happen.'

'It would not be up to her. The decision rests with the High Table.' His voice hardened. 'We are a tiny minority compared to humans. It is our capacity to uphold our own customs and traditions that allows us to continue to govern ourselves in these matters.'

'Save the propaganda for someone who cares.' I turned to face him. 'Rio wasn't the only one getting off in there.'

He stared at me, black eyes cool. 'I am vampire. There was blood. What did you expect?'

I gave him a level look back. 'Nothing, absolutely nothing.'

He reached out, traced a finger under my left eye. 'You are no stranger to violence.' He pressed his thumb into the tender spot on my cheekbone.

I tensed at the small hurt, trying not to flinch.

'Or pain,' he murmured.

Something twisted inside me. I knocked his hand away.

'But you would condemn me for that which you yourself desire.'

'This,' I pointed at the bruise, 'was caused by a client, not from some sort of sadistic game-playing.'

'Blood, sex, violence.' His elegant fingers pushed back a fall of black hair. 'You view these with a somewhat human perspective, which is odd in one of your race. You are much like a newly gifted vampire having a crisis of conscience. They feel horror and disgust at their need to feed off their erstwhile companions, but then they discover their almost absolute command over humans, a god-like power of life and death.' He looked at me. 'The knowledge that they can do whatever they desire, and their victim will not stop them. That they can even decide on their victims' emotions: fear, pain, hopelessness, comfort, delight, lust.' He gave no inflection to the words as he spoke. 'These are realisations that most new vampires travel through. It is interesting, do you not agree?'

I narrowed my eyes. 'You're being very chatty all of a sudden.'

'This is true.' He turned the ring on his thumb. 'It has been a long time since I have been able to speak as I wish, to use words without having to weigh and judge each for its impact, if it might give those around me some advantage. It is' – he shot me a glance from beneath his lashes – 'pleasant.'

'Lonely, more like,' I said, my voice flat.

He looked down, considered his feet in silence.

I shifted in my seat, looked out of the window. No way was

I going to feel sorry for him. In front of us, I could see the huge Catherine wheel of the London Eye towering above the Thames, lights bright against the night sky. We were nearly at our destination. Going by the amount of Saturday night traffic, walking the rest of the way would be quicker, but I didn't have that choice.

'You are correct, Genevieve.' His voice slid over my skin like the cool touch of silk. 'I am lonely.' Elegant fingers circled my wrist. 'I have been for longer than I care to contemplate, but it is not an emotion that I would deny, despite it displeasing me.'

The street lights washed his face from shadow to light and back to shadow. Something the cocktail girl had told me about Melissa wormed its way into my head. I narrowed my eyes. 'Is that why you were having a fling with Melissa? Because you were lonely?'

He ignored my question. 'Unlike you,' he said, pulling me round to face him and catching hold of my other wrist, 'I do not choose to lie, even to myself.'

Fear slicked up my spine. With all the chat, I *had* felt sorry for him. I'd half-forgotten what he was, what he might want.

I tried to jerk away and his grip tightened. 'Or was it because Melissa was a faeling?' I spat out. 'Did that make her more of a challenge, more exciting, that you hurt her and didn't have to hold back? Did it make the pain more real for you?'

Bright pinpricks of anger glimmered deep in his pupils.

My pulse pounded under his fingers. 'She saw something, didn't she?' I yelled over the blood racing through my veins. 'When she was with you.' My skin flushed with heat, with need. I gasped, clenching my fists trying to ignore the feelings.

Damn vampire tricks.

'Even now, you lie to yourself.' He turned my wrists, holding my palms upwards. 'You tell yourself that you do not want what I can give, but your body betrays you.'

My fingers relaxed and opened with no conscious thought from me.

'See, Genevieve, this is what happens when you deny the truth. You make yourself weak. How else would I find it so easy to bypass your defences, to bend your body to my wishes, if not by using your own desires against you?' He pulled me towards him, eyes flaring with rage. 'Much as you did with Rio.'

I blinked. Why was he angry? Then I realised what his words meant and my own anger made me lean into him. 'You were watching, weren't you,' I made it a statement, 'in the Théâtre – but that's what you do, isn't it?' I curled my lip. 'You spy on others.'

'It was not wise to tease Rio like that.'

'What, you think yanking her chain was wrong? You heard her, she's ambitious, she already had plans for me, and I'm betting they had nothing to do with my wellbeing. The fact that she's changed them isn't going to make any difference in that respect.'

His hands squeezed my wrists until I thought he would snap the bones. I pressed my lips together to stop myself whimpering. Then the glow in his eyes flickered and snuffed out.

'No, it will not make a difference.' Slowly he loosened his fingers and placed his lips to the throbbing pulse in my left wrist and my stomach plunged into free-fall.

He released me and I scooted back to my side of the cab, trying to ignore the feelings inside me … and the pieces fell together in my mind.

I laughed, short and derisive. 'You knew, didn't you? All that sneaking around, that hiding-in-the-shadows trick you do: you already knew what Rio was planning – only now I've gone and kicked you out of the loop. That's why you're so angry.'

He smiled and my stomach fluttered, not with fear but with warmth. 'The way your mind works is almost as interesting to me as your body, Genevieve.'

Yeah, right, like distracting me is ever going to work. I smirked at him. 'Oh, and thanks for the compliment.'

He arched a brow. 'I didn't know I had given you one.'

Yeah, yeah. 'I bet you know what they're all up to; you probably even know who killed Melissa – and why.'

'If I know so much, then why would I invite you along to help me?'

Ha! That one was easy. 'There's some sort of spell,' I said, 'you all want it, and you all think I can find it.'

He laughed, a deep rich laugh that sent lust fizzing in my veins and heated my blood right down to my toes.

I clutched at the door handle, glaring at him. 'It's not going to work, you know: getting me all hot and bothered isn't going to make me forget.'

Almost in slow motion he reached for my hand, lifted it to his mouth and blew heat on my fingertips, his dark eyes never leaving mine. 'Why would I need you to forget anything, Genevieve? What I want is for you to remember.'

As his words sank in, I frowned. 'Remember what?'

'Why, what I told you before.' He placed a kiss against my fingers, but I felt the touch on my lips. 'I wish to conclude this little episode to my own satisfaction. I do not require knowledge of *any* spell to succeed at my task, so I have no need for you to find it.'

I wet my lips and the taste of Turkish delight sweetened my tongue. Damn *mesma*. Why didn't he want the spell when the rest of them did? And why had he sent me the invitation if he didn't want the spell?

The taxi slowed to a stop. 'That'll be nineteen pounds twenty, please, mate.'

Malik produced a fifty, handed it to the driver. 'Please. Wait here for us.'

The locks clicked open. 'Cheers, mate. No worries.'

'No way,' I said, 'you're not coming with me.'

'Genevieve, we agreed—'

'Go home, Malik.' I repeated his own words to me, and jumped out of the cab.

Chapter Twenty-Nine

I stormed off along the pavement and tried to roll the tension from my shoulders. Damn. Now what? A hot breeze rushed over the River Thames and threw my hair in my face and I shoved it back. I took a deep breath, then wished I hadn't as all I got was a lungful of the ever-present traffic fumes mixed with the fainter scent of water.

Sighing, I rotated one ankle then the next. My feet weren't impressed at having to walk in my high-heels again. I looked around, hoping for some inspiration to help me get rid of the pretty vampire. Along the well-lit Victoria Embankment I could see the RAF monument, its golden eagle perched on top. On the other side of the river the bright pods of the London Eye hung suspended. It might be midnight, but this was London and there were still plenty of people around: walking across the Hungerford Bridge, partygoers out for a smoke on the deck of the Hispaniola boat, a couple smooching under the railway bridge, a man in shorts walking a yappy Pekinese.

Only inspiration and ideas seemed to be in short supply. I sighed and turned around. Malik was standing, feet apart, thumbs hooked into his belt, arrogance surrounding him like a shadowed aura. Even if he wasn't recognised for what he was, he looked dangerous enough that most people would give him a wide berth – like the dog walker who'd obviously turned back to avoid him.

Malik wasn't going to go away as easily as that – but what if I tried the direct approach?

'Look,' I said, walking over to him, 'I don't want you to tag along, okay? Alan Hinkley is my client and it doesn't look very professional if I bring you with me.'

He lifted his chin and scented the air. 'Why are we not at the police station?'

'Old Scotland Yard is just round the corner. Alan Hinkley wanted to meet here first, in private.' I checked my watch. 'If he's not already waiting he'll be here any moment.'

'A street corner is not a suitable place for a private talk.'

'We're meeting in the garden.' I indicated the gate. Through it I could see the gravel path stretching maybe eighty feet to the exit at the other end. Ringed by black iron railings, the garden was mostly grass, with a few large trees, and three statues that faced out towards the river. The buildings behind overlooked it and only a few of the windows were dark, with just the bushes near the railings giving the semblance of privacy. The place was well lit and it was easy to see it was empty.

A line creased between Malik's eyes. 'Why would he choose to meet you here?' he asked, then looked over towards the underground. 'Why not at the station or the café?'

'Okay, enough with the twenty questions.' I let out a frustrated sigh. 'I don't think that Alan Hinkley's too taken with vamps just now, and neither am I. And I don't want you frightening him – so what's it going to take to get you to leave?'

He stood looking at me, expression enigmatic. 'It is not the best place for an ambush, but it could still work. This time of night, not many humans enter the park, and should anyone see or hear something untoward from a window above, they might conclude it to be a lover's assignation and not interfere.'

Apprehension tensed my shoulders. 'You're a scary bastard, aren't you?'

'You should learn to think like your enemy, Genevieve.'

'But to think like my enemy, I'd have to know who he is, wouldn't I?' I jumped, startled, as a jogger ran past, feet slapping hard against the pavement. He veered away from the entrance to the gardens and pounded across the road to sprint along next to the river.

'Why are you nervous?' Malik asked.

'Why the hell do you think?' I snapped. 'Too many vampires taking an interest in me makes me feel like a mouse surround by hungry cats.'

'I shall wait here with the taxi while you have your assignation.' He bowed. 'Rest assured I will not be seen, and therefore I will not "scare off" your client, or anyone else he brings with him.' He smiled, and my stomach flip-flopped again. *Damn.* I was going to have to stop it doing that. And he disappeared.

Mice taste sweet to cats.

I snorted and strode through the gate into the gardens. A cobweb drifted across my face and I swiped it away. 'I hate vampires,' I muttered. The gravel path crunched under my shoes, but otherwise the place was quiet. Not even a leaf rustled. I checked my watch again and gave an irritated thought for my lost phone. Alan should've been here by now. Maybe he'd called it off?

Malik's words sat uneasily in my gut, and I was almost glad he was watching. Slowly I headed for the tree in the centre, the one with its limbs propped up on tall wooden crutches, where I was supposed to meet Alan. Why couldn't I hear the music from the party boats any more? Or the traffic? I shivered. Maybe the sensible thing would be to go back outside. Wait until Alan did finally arrive. I turned—

Wood cracked, the sound loud behind me.

Heart jumping in my throat, I spun around.

A tall, scrawny figure stood under the tree wearing a dirty red T-shirt over stained jeans. He was holding a Beater goblin's baseball bat on his shoulder. 'Say, these things work a treat.' He swung the bat round like he was hitting a home run and demolished another of the wooden crutches propping up the tree.

Fuck: Malik had been right. Tensing, I half-crouched, adrenalin whizzing round my body on overdrive.

Human male, late teens, bad case of acne and no muscle tone: I could take him – except for the bat. The bat sort of knocked my confidence. Only a dead goblin gives up his weapon.

'Yep, a treat. No wonder the little creeps use 'em.' He nodded his shaved head. 'I'm gonna try it on you next, faerie freak. Have us a bit of fun.' Large black letters across his T-shirt advised me to *Remember his name, because I'd be screaming it later.*

I screamed Malik's instead, as loud as I could.

The pizza-faced figure patted the logo. 'That's it, freakoid, get some practise in.'

Why wasn't there a dangerous vampire rushing to my rescue?

I had a nasty thought, so I *looked*. The railings shimmered with green-tinged spells, as equally nasty as my thought – and green meant stun. Crap, no way could I get out, or Malik get in. Even if he'd heard my shout, which was doubtful, he was more than likely lying unconscious outside the gardens anyway. I could try *cracking* the spells, but that would turn the railings into so much shrapnel, so it wasn't worth the risk, not for one scrawny human.

'Freakoid, faerie freak,' Pizza Face sang, swinging the foil-wrapped bat around his head.

And then the night got so much better – *not!* – as another, fatter figure lumbered from the shadows under the tree. His baggy jeans hung from his hips and I could see the flab wobbling under his T-shirt. Small round glasses were stuck like magnifying lenses on his podgy face. 'Ye'th,' he lisped, 'we're gonna show you, faiwy fweak.' A picture of a distorted Dalek blowing a speech-bubble shouting *Exterminate, exterminate,* stretched over his chest and he brandished an arrow-headed pole.

I bit my lip and swallowed a hysterical snort. Exterminating these two felt like a great idea.

Pizza Face moved to the left, putting me between him and Fatboy.

Pulse racing, I back-tracked until I was off the gravel path and on the grass. My gaze flicked from one to the other and back again: who would attack first, Lanky or Lardy?

'C'mon, freakoid, come to me,' Pizza Face called.

Fatboy did a shambling run over to Pizza Face. 'So what're we gonna do, dude?' He waved his pole.

'Do it just do it like I told you, right?' Pizza Face shoved him on the shoulder. 'Now get back over there, y'know, we're gonna be like a pincer action.'

'Oh yeah, yeah,' Fatboy giggled. 'Ni'th.'

I took a breath, concentrated. Pizza Face leapt forward, swinging his bat two-handed. I ducked and it swished over my head. Fatboy swiped low on my other side and I jumped the pole like a skipping rope, my ankles jarring as I landed on the rain-starved grass.

'Hey, thi'th ith fun, man,' he giggled.

Shit. I needed my own weapon. Glamour? I had to get within touching distance for that to work, so it was a nonstarter. But a wooden staff would do, and thanks to Pizza Face, there were plenty lying under the old tree; I just needed to get to one.

Fatboy jabbed his pole at me like a spear and as I swivelled out the way Pizza Face's bat caught me a thudding blow on my shoulder. Pain shot down my arm and I screamed, throwing myself back into a roll that took me away from them. I came up in a crouch, my left arm hanging uselessly at my side.

Fear clamped round my chest – the power behind that blow didn't feel human – and he'd definitely broken something.

'Get her other arm, dude,' Pizza Face shouted.

Fatboy moved towards me, shockingly fast, and jabbed again. I jerked to the side, but too slow. His pole ripped through my sleeve and stabbed into my injured arm. I screamed again, then I almost cried in relief – Fatboy's pole was one of the iron garden railings – and the pain in my arm started to mute as the touch of the iron numbed my flesh.

'Not that one, man, the other one!'

Fatboy raised the iron pole, started to bring it down like an axe. I scrambled back, hoping the numb feeling would last – and the bar thumped the grass in front of me.

'Watch her head,' Pizza Face yelled. 'I tole yer, it's better when they're screaming. Go for the arms and legs so the freak can't run away!'

I staggered up, breath heaving.

Pizza Face tossed the bat in the air, caught it. 'Come to me, pussy, pussy,' he crooned, then he punched Fatboy on the arm, almost knocking him over. 'Get it, dude? The freak's got eyes like a cat, so I called her a pussy!'

Fatboy giggled again. 'Yeah, man, good one! The fweak'th like a little puthy cat!'

They were high or hyped up on something, and it was making them faster and stronger – the odds weren't looking good and I needed to even them up, and for that I needed blood, and enough time to activate my Alter Vamp spell. Blood was no problem; it was dripping down my arm from where Fatboy had stabbed me with the railing. So that just left the time part then.

They were young. They were male.

I held up my good hand, palm out, 'Hold it,' I shouted, standing straighter, 'I surrender, okay?'

Fatboy giggled. 'Yeah, thurrender! *Okay!*'

'Shut up dude,' Pizza Face growled, 'we don't want the freak to surrender, no way. We want to fuck her.'

'And that's just what I'm interested in, boys.' I tried a seductive smile, only it felt more like a pain-filled grimace. 'You've heard about us faeries and sex, haven't you? Like how hot we are? How much we want it, like all the time?'

Fatboy was nodding, his eyes wide behind his glasses.

Pizza Face slapped the bat into his hand. 'Keep talking, freak.'

241

I lowered my hand, slipped the button on my jacket and pulled it open. 'See we can all have a good time,' I shucked the jacket off my shoulder, quickly snatching my good arm out of it, leaving me naked from the waist up. 'No need to beat me up first.'

Fatboy's mouth hung open, his eyes fixed on my chest.

Pizza Face licked his lips. 'This a trick or something?'

'Trick?' I dragged the jacket off my injured arm, trying not to wince. 'Why would I trick you when we all want the same thing?' Taking a deep breath, I expanded my chest, did a little shimmy. 'Anyway, big boy.' I jiggled my foot at him, showing off my heels, then stood legs further apart, bracing myself. 'I mean, it's not like I'm going to get very far if I run away from you, is it?'

Pizza Face nodded. 'You ain't wrong there, freak.' He beckoned with his finger. 'Come 'ere, then, if you want it so much.'

'Nuh-uh.' I stroked my fingers down my cleavage, let my hand fall on the ties that kept my skirt on. 'Don't be so impatient.' The blood trickling down my injured arm had reached my elbow. 'Don't you want to see the rest?'

'Ye'th, more!' Fatboy grinned, dropping his railing.

I tugged at the ties and let the wrap-around skirt drop to the floor. The blood was meandering down my forearm and I was down to black briefs and my shoes. Damn. I should've worn more clothes. They were running out as fast as my time was. I shook my arm, trying to get the blood to run faster.

'Cool tattoo, freak. Got any more?' Pizza Face took a step towards me.

The blood trailed another few of inches. *C'mon, just a couple more.*

'Hang on in there, big boy.' I forced a grin. 'You haven't seen the best bit yet.'

'Looks good enough to me,' Pizza Boy said, breathing fast.

'Me too,' squeaked Fatboy.

Glamour would distract them, gain me a few more seconds, even if I wasn't going to sic them with it. I breathed in, *focused*, and my skin glowed, misting golden light around me.

'Magic,' Fatboy yelled, waving his arms, 'the fweak'th doing magic!'

The blood snaked over my wrist.

'No magic tricks, freak,' Pizza Face ordered. He lifted his bat.

Honeysuckle scented the air. Blood trickled into my palm.

'Stoppit!' Pizza Face leapt at me.

I threw myself to the side and landed hard on my knees, frantically rubbing the blood across my hip into the spell-tattoo. An arm clamped round my waist and yanked me down onto my back. I screamed as the pain exploded in my shoulder breaking my hold on the Glamour. Why wasn't the spell working?

Pizza Face stared down at me, his pupils tiny pinpricks in his muddy brown eyes, and desperation flooded through me as I ground my hand into the tattoo. Where was my Alter Vamp? Pizza Face grinned, flashing sharp fangs. Shock froze me. What the fuck *was* he? He sniggered open-mouthed, curry-breath hitting in my face. I jack-knifed my legs up—

His fist connected with my jaw, and I fell into the dark.

Chapter Thirty

*I*t *was safe in the dark, still and quiet and calm* ... curry, and the coppery taste of blood in my mouth ... *no one could find me* ... hands tugging at my hair ... *nothing hurt in the dark, only the hunger* ... pain sharp at my throat ... *and I wasn't hungry, not yet, not now* ... pain pricking at my breasts ... *the darkness was safe.*

I sank back down, into the cold depths.

'Hey. man,' a voice whined, 'I can't do it like thi'th.'

My eyes snapped open and I froze. Fatboy was kneeling almost astride my head, gripping my scalp. I clamped my mouth shut to stop from screaming.

'Fucking wait then, dude,' Pizza Face snarled. 'I told you, I'm not sticking my nose up your shitty arse.'

I couldn't move my head, but I could just make out Pizza Face crouching between my thighs. Instinct made me clamp my legs together, but his body got in the way.

'Hello, freakoid.' Pizza Face leered up at me. 'We started without you. You can start screaming now if you want.' He grinned, showing bloodstained fangs, and swiped his tongue over his lips. 'Think I'm gonna like this blood-suckin' business. You taste great, y'know, sorta sweet, like honey. I told yer we was gonna have some fun, didn't I?'

Fatboy giggled above me. 'Ye'th, man!'

Bastards. I'd show them fun.

They'd left my arms free. My left shoulder was a mass of hurt – the numbness from the iron had worn off – but my right arm still worked okay. I punched Pizza Face in the mouth and his head jerked back, his fangs scraping my knuckles. Yanking my head from Fatboy's grip, I reared back and jammed my skull into his groin and he squealed, short and high. Pain shot through my shoulder, but I blocked it. Pizza Face swayed unnaturally upright and I brought my knees up tight to my chest as he lunged over me, sniggering. I screamed and kicked out, stamping both metal-heeled shoes into his stomach and shoving him up and away. He was still sniggering as he thudded to the ground, one shoe still impaled in the soft flesh just under his ribs.

Rolling over, I got my legs under me, pushed up onto my feet. The gardens blurred as a moment of dizziness made me sway.

Fatboy was clutching himself, mouth gaping, tears streaming from his wide-open eyes.

I stepped towards him and kicked out, aiming at his temple. With a soft thud, he crumpled to the ground.

I turned back to Pizza Face. He was lying on his back, pink spittle foaming out of his mouth as he gasped for air. There was a dark, wet stain on his T-shirt where blood bubbled out around my shoe. It looked like I'd stomped on him – *oh wait, I had!* But had I hit his heart or just his lungs? As I watched him, Pizza Face frowned down at my shoe, then wrapped his fingers round it and pulled. It came out with a wet popping sound.

He gave another sniggering laugh and threw it at me.

I ducked, and it sailed over my head.

He sat up, grinning like a maniac and pulled up his T-shirt to show me his fast-healing wound.

I took half-a-dozen steps back. Another moment of vertigo made me stumble and agonising pain shot through my injured shoulder. The dizzy thing had to be blood loss, or concussion, or maybe even both. I swallowed, anxiety speeding my pulse. No way did I want to pass out, not while Pizza Face was still alive and kicking.

'C'mon, faerie pussy pussy.' Pizza Face staggered to his feet and grabbed his crotch. 'It's my turn to stick something in you.'

I kicked off my remaining shoe – it wasn't going to help me now – and took another step back. My foot came down on something hard: Fatboy's iron railing. I crouched and picked it up, wedging it between my waist and my good arm like a jousting lance and hoping like crazy I'd get a chance to use it before the spreading numbness from the iron made me drop the damn thing.

Pizza Face giggled as he lurched towards me.

I ran at him yelling at the top of my voice. Pizza Face lurched faster, gaining speed, and the pole dipped, starting to slip. My gut clenched with fear. Three feet, then two, then one, and I shoved the pole at him. The metal arrow-head glanced off his ribs and pierced his side, and I followed through with my good shoulder, knocking him down. The pole jammed into the dry earth, staking him to the ground.

'Fuckin' faerie bitch,' he gasped, struggling to pull it out.

It wasn't going to take him long to free himself. The garden blurred again, this time because of tears. Angry with myself, I swiped them away. *Free.* That's it: I had to get free and get help. I had to *crack* the spell on the railings. I started towards the gate and tripped over something. I looked down: the goblin's bat. I shook my arm to relieve some of the numbness and snatched it up. Weapons were always handy things to have around.

A shuffling noise behind me raised the hairs on my body, and I swung round.

Ten feet away, Fatboy shambled over the grass, slack-faced, his glasses reflecting red. His mouth gaped open over his fangs. It was like a B-movie, the kind of horror flick where the monster just keeps getting right back up. Hysterical laughter threatened to choke my throat.

I tensed and, arm shaking, raised the bat.

Fatboy jerked to a stop. His head snapped to the side and a strange sucking noise, like a turkey leg being wrenched off, splintered the air. Fatboy's body thudded to the ground.

Malik stood above him like some dark avenging angel, flames consuming his eyes. He held Fatboy's dripping head between his hands. The round glasses dangled off one ear. The head's eyes fluttered open, squinted at the ground.

I didn't lower the bat.

'Where is the other one?' Malik's voice sounded rusty, as though he hadn't spoken for a long time.

I jerked my head behind me, then wished I hadn't as the world went painfully out of focus.

'Dead?' he asked.

'No.' My own voice sounded just as rusty.

'I will take care of it.' He turned toward where I knew the river to be and threw Fatboy's head up into the night sky. It flew high through the trees and over the road, disappearing into the darkness. For a second there was nothing, then, in the distance there was a faint splash as it hit the water.

I let the bat fall to the ground as exhaustion washed over me.

Malik took a step back, unsteady, and as the light caught his head, I saw why. Blood seeped down his neck in rivulets from a matted wound at the base of his scalp.

I blinked.

Something, or some*one*, had caved in most of his skull.

Another wave of dizziness washed over me and once again the night rolled away into darkness.

Chapter Thirty-One

Somewhere it was raining. The drumming noise intruded on my sleep. I snuggled my cheek into the soft throw, the comforting scent of honeysuckle telling me I was home, and safe. Jabbing pain shot through my shoulder as I lifted my arm to pull the cover over my head, and I stifled a scream as the memories rushed back. I squinted through my lashes past the bronze and gold of my rug, searching for signs of Malik, but the room was empty. Slowly I moved, wincing as my shoulder complained again, and stared up at the vaulted ceiling lit by its waterfall pendant of amber and copper glass beads.

The rain cut out.

Carefully I sat up. Nausea roiled in my stomach and I rolled onto my knees, retching. Cool hands held my head and stroked the back of my neck and the pain dulled. I heaved again and tasted the sourness of bile as I took shallow breaths and willed myself not to add to the mess I'd made on my varnished floorboards. Shit. At least I'd managed to miss the rug – and Malik's bare knees. The palm of his hand was like ice against my forehead. It reminded me of when he had held me frozen. My heart thudded faster and I shoved him away, ignoring the sharp agony in my shoulder at the movement.

'Get the fuck off me,' I croaked.

'You are hurt, Genevieve.' He bent over me, a coaxing tone in his voice. 'I can help.'

'No way. Keep your hands to yourself.' I wiped my mouth with the back of my hand, grabbed the throw and scooted backwards until I was sitting with my back to the wall. Damn, why had he brought me home?

'As you wish.' Malik sat back on his heels, neatly adjusted the towel that wrapped around his narrow hips. He studied me with a calm look on his face, as if it was nothing out of the ordinary for someone to vomit at his knees. Maybe it wasn't. His black hair was wet, and I could smell the faint honeyed fragrance of my soap – he'd obviously used my shower – and his pale skin gleamed, his muscles lean and defined, his body even better than my errant mind had imagined. The silken triangle of dark hair on his chest narrowed down—

Annoyed at myself, I dragged my eyes up and glared at him. 'How did you get in?'

'Through the window in your bedroom.' He shrugged, and a droplet of water rolled down over his collar-bone. 'It was unlocked.'

'I meant,' I huffed, 'how did you get *in*: I didn't invite you over my threshold.'

'Last night, outside Old Scotland Yard, you freely offered your blood to me.' An odd sadness filled his black eyes. 'I no longer need an invitation.'

Of course! I dropped my forehead to my knees, wondering how much more stupid I could get. Still, one bright point, if whoever wanted me dead did manage to succeed, offering open house to a vampire wasn't going to matter much in the great scheme of things. And that brought the next question to mind. *They'd* had their teeth in me. 3V might be the ultimate zapper for any human infection, but *they* hadn't been human, had they?

I lifted my head. 'What were those things?'

'Revenants.'

'Explain revenants,' I demanded.

He rose in one easy motion, his bare feet silent on the wooden floor as he walked the few steps towards the kitchen counter. 'It is an ancient ritual, forbidden now.' He stood at the sink, his back to me. 'A human can be Gifted in a matter of minutes, without need of the cautious nurturing that we are used to indulging in.'

They'd been a type of vampire. I tipped my head back against the wall, relieved. Vampire bites couldn't hurt me any more than they had already.

'Their prime function was for defence, to delay or divert the hunter.' Water splashed. 'In current terminology, they would be called cannon fodder, although there were no cannons in the beginning. Through the ritual humans gain the strength, the abilities, the features of the vampire.' Glass chinked. 'They have no care for themselves. They will fight until their bodies are no longer able. When they fall, they do not die. Their bodies remake themselves after every injury.' The water cut off. 'The revenant will follow the instructions given by their Maker until they taste their first blood.'

I stared at his back, or rather, at the back of his head. His mention of injuries brought back the memory of his caved-in skull. I frowned. It was completely healed now.

'They will rise night after night, with no other need than to quench the Bloodthirst.' His voice was expressionless. 'Man, woman or child, even beasts: it matters not to a revenant.'

'Just like your average sucker,' I muttered, pulling at the fringe on the throw. 'So far I'm not seeing the difference.'

The towel shifted against his legs as he walked back to me, brushing the fine dark hairs on his calves. Irritated that I'd noticed, I made myself look at the floor instead. 'Even lost in the Bloodthirst,' he continued, 'it is rare for a vampire to actually kill. Once the initial need is satisfied—' He paused, then continued, 'Well, you do not kill the chicken that lays the eggs.' His tone was slightly mocking. 'It is much more effective to practice good husbandry.'

'Oh yeah,' I sighed as his feet came into view. They were as elegant as I remembered. Mentally I gave in. He was eye-candy, no point in denying it, or trying to stop looking, so long as that was all I did – and that I didn't forget what he truly was. I looked up at him, and said, 'A blood-slave is *so* much better than a dead chicken.'

'You are correct.' He held the glass out to me.

I wrinkled my nose, thought about asking for some vodka, then decided I didn't want him rooting in my fridge. I took a gulp, swilled the water around my mouth and swallowed.

'Revenants are where the legends were forged,' Malik carried on, 'shambling corpses crawling from their graves, knowing nothing, caring for nothing, consumed only by their need for blood, until they die again with the sun. They are the true undead.'

I took another sip, and peered at him from under my lashes. More dark hair arrowed up his flat stomach to where a pink starburst of a scar nestled under his left rib. My lips parted in surprise: that was where I'd stabbed him the night before, when he'd mistaken my Alter Vamp for his Rosa. If his head had healed completely, why hadn't that wound?

'Revenants will kill every time they feed.' He met my eyes, and something dark and bleak swam in the black depths of his, then he looked away and stared out of the window. 'They will take three, four, sometimes as many as six or seven humans a night, every night, for as long as the blood-lust grips them.' He headed back into the kitchen. 'It can take months before the lust is fully sated, if ever.'

As what he'd said sank in, I shivered. 'Shit – so those two goons would've gone on a killing spree every time the sun went down?'

'That is why the ritual is forbidden.' He looked back at me, his black eyes now flat and hard. 'Even the most reactionary vampire does not wish to encourage humans to become vigil-antes.'

Snippets of the old myths hijacked my mind and dread cramped my stomach. If the old legends about vampires as ravenous monsters were true, what if one bite really was all it took to become one of them? Pizza Face and Fatboy had bitten me more than once … my hand shook and sloshed my water over the floor – maybe I did have something to panic about after all.

Malik stood over me, an odd closed expression on his face. He held a bowl in his hands.

'They both bit me.' I dropped the glass and grabbed his ankle. 'What's that going to do to me?'

His expression didn't change and I held my breath. Was that why he was here? To stop me changing? To rip my head off like he had Fatboy's?

'Nothing,' he said at last. 'Their bite is to feed only.'

Sucker bites. I blew out a shaky sigh and let him go. The bites were only sucker bites.

Crouching, he placed the bowl down beside me. 'It appears you have become more of a threat than an opportunity.'

I scowled at him. 'Yeah, I sort of got that, seeing as someone sent revenants to kill me.'

He gave me a considering look. He really was beautiful, all lean muscle and pale skin and dark hair, his features just the right side of almost too pretty. And as he mopped up the spilled water and wrung out the cloth into the bowl, twisting it tight between his fingers, even that simple movement seemed more than it was. My pulse hitched and he stilled, tension shimmering through him, then the moment was gone and he wiped the floor again.

Questions started to edge out infatuation in my mind. Who knew I was meeting Alan Hinkley? Everyone, apparently – but who knew the actual details apart from Alan and me? My head was beginning to ache, and not just because of my injuries. I pinched the bridge of my nose, trying to banish it. So it had to be someone Alan had told after he'd texted me. And my phone was lost somewhere at the Blue Heart – anyone could've checked out my messages. As I slumped against the wall, pain jabbed my shoulder again.

I clutched at the throw and held myself still, willing it away. 'So who can do the ritual?'

A wing of damp hair fell over Malik's forehead. 'Here in London? At least eight, maybe nine.' He brushed the hair away, held my look. 'Including myself.'

I licked my lips. He hadn't even had to think about the question. What was he doing here when he was obviously capable of figuring this out all on his own?

I narrowed my eyes. 'Are you always this domesticated?'

He looked at me, black eyes intent.

Heat bloomed inside me, sending nervous spirals twisting through my belly. 'Because it doesn't strike me as being a normal vampire trait,' I said. 'So just exactly why are you here, Malik? What do you want from me?'

He took the bowl back to the sink and washed his hands, then came and stood looking down at me. 'Why did you take me to the Embankment Gardens and not to Old Scotland Yard?'

I frowned, confused. 'Because that's where Alan Hinkley wanted to meet me. I told you that.'

'And yet Alan Hinkley was not there.' His voice was soft. 'Instead, it was an ambush, one that was very nearly successful.'

'Obviously someone used either Hinkley or the information to set me up.'

'No.' He sank gracefully back into a crouch, his forearms resting on his thighs. 'I do not think the attack was aimed at you.'

I snorted. 'You could've fooled me.'

He leaned forward, and my heart thudded with fear. I wanted to shrink from him, but my back was already against the wall and I had nowhere to go to.

'Or did you deceive me, Genevieve?'

'What?' I stared at him in surprise.

His hand flashed out and he gripped my chin. 'The spell

253

that stopped me from entering the gardens stunned me, but it did not stop you.'

I jerked out of his hold. 'Something triggered the spell after I'd gone through the gate and it stopped me getting out.'

'Did it?'

'You know it did,' I spat.

'The spell was powerful enough to knock me unconscious for a few minutes.' His eyes narrowed. 'And that was long enough for someone to take a kerbstone to my head.'

So that explained the caved-in skull, but not what else he was getting at.

'Whoever hit me was fae,' he added, his tone accusing.

Okaaay, so that's what—

'Well, don't look at me,' I snapped, 'I had my own problems, if you remember.'

'Had your scent not engulfed me, I would have known they were there.' He ran a fingertip over my injured shoulder. 'Was I supposed to come into the park with you?' His touch skimmed down my damaged arm. 'Would you have stood back while they attacked me? Would you have watched, and applauded? Was that why they had to improvise?'

'Ri-ight, just because a fae tries to reshape your thick head, you think I've set you up!' I snorted. 'Well, if we're talking stupid ideas, what about the revenants? You just said they could only be made by a vampire, so maybe you made them. 'Cause there's no way I've got anything to do with any vampire.'

'But you *do* have something to do with a vampire, do you not, Genevieve?' His hand circled my left wrist, turned my palm up.

Pain raced up my arm like wildfire and I screamed before I could stop myself. He touched a finger to my palm and the agony was gone, snuffed out like a light.

'See how your body responds to me.' His voice held sorrow.

Another touch, and the pain burnt through my shoulder

254

again – only I couldn't scream; he wouldn't let me. All I could do was stare at him wide-eyed, my heart pounding under my ribs.

Then the pain was gone again and I sagged in relief.

'You will not struggle.' The words were an order. 'Else I will be forced to return the pain. Do you understand?'

'I get that you're into torture,' I ground out.

'No, I am not.' He gave a resigned sigh. 'But I am also not squeamish.'

'Fuck you.'

'Maybe later.' Mocking amusement lit his face. 'But first, we will settle this matter between us?' He made it a question.

Like I had any choice ... I nodded.

'Last night, outside the police station.' Malik stroked my palm. 'I was surprised at how easy it was to enter your mind and influence your body with my thoughts. Why, I wondered, was that?' He glanced down at my open hand. 'You even offered me your blood, almost without demur. It was unexpected, especially for a sidhe.' Blood blossomed, four bright half-moons across my palm.

The sight was just as terrifying as it had been the first time.

But even more terrifying was the lack of those hazy feelings; I didn't feel that desperate need to give Malik whatever he wanted, and I realised just how much he had been playing with my mind, right from the first.

Now he was playing with my body, leaving my mind my own.

He stretched out my arm, brought my hand to his mouth, and I knew it should hurt; I could almost hear the bones grating against each other where they were broken. But I could feel nothing other than his cool breath over my skin, his tongue warm on my palm.

I stared, unable to deny the fluttering in my belly, cursing myself that I could still want him.

'But your blood has already told me who your Master is.'

He sank his fangs into the mound at the base of my thumb, and a shudder rippled through his body.

The sharp sting spiked low inside me, making me gasp with pleasure.

'*The taste of you was of her,*' his voice whispered through my mind. '*Only I would not believe it.*'

'I have no Master,' I hissed through clenched teeth.

He lifted his head and sighed, sounding both sad and threatening. 'She is not strong enough to Bond with such as you, so I imagined I was mistaken.' A pinprick of red glowed in his pupils. 'Only then I found her, and the demon inhabiting her body, trading in her soul.' Keeping his eyes on mine, he fastened his mouth again over the bite on my hand. '*Her taste was of you.*'

Heat sparked between my legs and I dropped my head to my knees, trying to ignore it, trying not to hear the soft sounds of his feeding. His fingers tangled in my hair and he lifted my unresisting head. 'And when she plunged her knife towards my heart' – he took my other hand, pressed, it to the pink starburst scar under his ribs – 'I understood.'

Images and words from the night before slipped like a slide-show into my mind. His insistence that I was Rosa, the pleasure of his bite, the terror that he would kill me, my Alter Vamp stabbing him, the memory of him *calling* me, *calling* to my blood.

'No,' I whispered, my mouth dry. 'I have no Master.'

A bleak expression crossed his face. 'To take you as her Bond, to join with you, is worthy revenge.' He kissed his lips to mine and I tasted my own honeyed blood. 'She knew how much I coveted you,' he murmured, 'but to allow a demon to use her soul is something I can not allow.' His mouth brushed against my ear. 'You shall give her a message from me. It is the only reason I do not kill you.' His words made me tremble.

I saw myself reflected in his obsidian eyes, but I skated as though on black ice, fearful of what might be hidden in their depths. 'I. Have. No. Master.'

He smiled. And my fear dissipated as liquid warmth pooled inside me.

Smiling back at him, I touched my fingers to his perfect pretty face.

He sat and stretched his legs out. 'I carry the True Gift, Genevieve.' He threw back his head, exposing his neck, and drew his thumbnail down the side of his throat. Thick claret-coloured blood seeped from the slash and my pulse beat eager and fast.

His beautiful face filled with peace as he pressed a fingertip into the wound. The trickle ran faster, to pool in the hollow at his throat. 'The blood is strong here, nearer the heart.' He reached out, traced a cool, wet line down my jaw. Tilting my face, I nuzzled into his palm, darting my tongue out to taste. He slid a hand round my neck, his thumb stroking over the pulse thudding in my throat.

'Come. I freely offer you my blood.'

I rested my hand on his chest. His flesh was cold and still. Unease rippled through me, then it was gone. I leaned over him, inhaled the copper and liquorice and sweet Turkish delight of his blood and underneath, a rich, dark spice that was all him.

Shivers pricked over my skin.

The pressure of his hand on my neck increased, pulling me closer.

I looked up. His eyes were black pools, tiny flames flaring in their pupils. Fear made my mouth dry, tightened my stomach.

Come, so I may offer you healing, his voice whispered in my mind.

Need swept through me and I touched my lips to his blood, its rich tang sparking against my tongue. I covered the slash with my mouth and sucked. The glorious nectar slipped cold down my throat, spreading a dazzling chill that frosted over the jagged edges of my pain and burnt it away.

'Enough,' he murmured, hands clasping my head, pushing me away.

Desperate, I sucked harder, teeth biting into his skin, fingers digging into his flesh.

'Genevieve, it is enough,' he ordered. 'You will stop.'

No, not enough. Never enough. The thought scattered his hold on my mind with glittering light and Glamour burst golden. I melted into him, not caring where I ended and he began, wanting more, needing more, taking more—

He shuddered beneath me, the sudden beat of his heart thudding against my breast, a promise of more to come. I lifted my head, spilling my magic over and around him. It was too long since I'd taken the pleasure it wanted. He rolled us until he was staring down at me from above, his hands capturing my wrists beneath my back, his fingers pinching into my skin. Lust and magic fizzed in my veins, demand throbbed hot and wet between my legs. Flames burned deep in the black of his eyes and his lips pulled back from needle-sharp fangs. Through the material that separated us, I felt him pressed against me, hard and ready.

'I am no human or newly Gifted vampire to be caught in your magic, Genevieve.'

'And I am sidhe, and you can't hold me with yours, Malik.' I paused on the edge of the precipice, knowing I wouldn't stop him, that I didn't want to, even as a sliver of terror sliced into my gut. Who would be the master, who the slave? Or would we be neither?

He stayed silent, unmoving. What was he waiting for? Then the knowledge slipped into me. He didn't want to take, he didn't want passive acceptance, he wanted me to offer.

The feeling was curious, tantalising, seductive.

My pulse jumping under my skin, I arched my back, lifted my chin and gave him my throat. Something flickered in his eyes for an instant, then his expression changed, turning dark, predatory, and somehow more desolate. A tremor shivered through me. His hands closed painfully round my wrists as he bent his head and placed his lips to my pulse. I tensed, anticipating the pain. And the pleasure.

Then, too fast for me to even register, he was gone.

I lay there, limp, gazing up at the amber crystals hanging from my ceiling. Other than my own shuddering breaths, the room was silent.

But I could still hear his voice in my head as he spoke his message for Rosa.

An odd quiver of fear chased the lust and magic from my body.

Chapter Thirty-Two

Daylight woke me as a heat-laden breeze drifted through the window and ruffled the white sheet across my bed. The sky was clear and blue, and I wondered why there were no clouds. There'd been clouds in my dreams: black clouds filled with the echoes of Malik's words. Clouds that flowed down my throat and froze me into a solid block of ice that slowly melted, leaving me drowning in a sea of blood. I swung my legs over the edge of the bed and sat up, pressing a hand to my stomach to try and dispel the fear twisting there.

Just dreams, that's all. Nothing more. Just my subconscious processing what had happened.

My bronze jacket, black skirt and even my torn briefs were neatly folded on the chair. I frowned at the small pile. Beneath the chair, my shoes sat side by side, clean. Malik had folded my clothes and polished my shoes. Something about that didn't fit. I opened the wardrobe to put them away and caught my reflection in the mirror. For a moment I stared.

The honey colour of my skin glowed with a warm sheen, my eyes sparkled like polished amber, and my flesh had smoothed out over the angles of my bones. I looked so good I could sell vitamins, never mind that I was healed. If that's what drinking a vampire's blood could do, no wonder they were subtly billing themselves as the new elixir of life and beauty. The only thing marring my new healthy perfection was my breasts. They felt fuller, perkier – but that wasn't the problem. The revenants had made a meal of me, and the evidence was still there.

I touched a fingertip to one fang mark, just above my right nipple. Why hadn't they disappeared along with the rest of my injuries? Then I checked out my left arm. Sweat broke out on my skin. The bruises Malik had marked me with still encircled my wrist, faint but definitely there. A wave of dizziness made me sway. The mound at the base of my thumb was smooth and bite-free. My stomach clenched with nausea and I sprinted for the bathroom and retched into the toilet.

What was the message Malik had given me for Rosa? He'd spoken in a foreign language and I didn't speak anything other than English. But I didn't need to get it translated: I'd understood him, and I didn't even want to think how that could happen.

For my love of Rosa, tell her I will strike the head from her body, rip the heart from her breast and sear her flesh until her bones are nothing more than ashes.

I heaved again, but there was nothing left inside me.

Jerking the shower on, I turned the heat up high and stood under the burning stream. I braced my hands against the tile, letting it scald down my back. Malik wasn't the only one who wanted to kill me. There was last night's little ambush to think about. I doubted Alan Hinkley had been in on the plan – he was probably nothing more than a mind-locked patsy – but I still had questions for him, once I got my phone back from the Blue Heart.

I grabbed a towel and briskly rubbed myself dry, then ran a comb through my hair; it would dry quickly enough in the heat. I scowled at the bites on my breasts. The scabs had washed away, leaving little pink holes.

Who had sent the two revenants after me? A vampire, obviously; but they'd have needed a witch to cast the stun-spell and attach it to the garden railings. And Malik had said he'd been hit over the head by a fae. Well, that combination wasn't such a common one – in fact, the only vamp/witch/fae combo I could think of was at the Bloody Shamrock – but why would Declan want to kill me, a sidhe? There was no reason I could think of, at least none that fitted the larger picture in my mind.

But I was betting a certain cluricaun called Mick would be able to fill in some of the details that my picture was missing. And then there was the update I had for Declan about Melissa's death – getting Mick to deliver the message was a much safer proposition than delivering it to him myself after dark.

Next stop the Bloody Shamrock.

As I stared thoughtfully at my reflection, blood seeped from the fang mark just above my nipple and ran down in a watery pink drop. Crap. I scoured the towel furiously over my chest, chucked it on the floor and yanked open the bathroom door.

I had a visitor.

Finn was standing next to the window, watching the street below. His horns were sharp above his blond hair and he had a glower on his face that suggested he wanted to disembowel something. And the black shirt and trousers weren't making him look any friendlier. Damn, I didn't have time for a repeat of yesterday's 'Big Bad Boss' routine.

I grabbed the towel and wrapped it round me. 'Just exactly how did you get in, Finn?'

'You've got no wards, Gen.' He turned, his gaze flicking over me then settling on my face. 'And the lock wouldn't keep out most humans—'

'Forget it,' Angrily, I waved away his explanation and headed for the bedroom. 'It's my day off. I've got plans, and I'm sure whatever you want can't be that urgent. You can just let yourself back out.' I banged the door shut behind me.

I yanked on a pair of briefs, then delved inside my wardrobe, pulled out a pair of jeans and tugged them on. What the hell did Finn think he was playing at? Twice he'd let himself in now – did he think I lived at Waterloo Station or something?

'I came round to see you last night, Gen.' Finn's voice came faintly through the closed door. 'Toni said you'd had some problems at Tower Bridge, with the gremlins.'

And damn Toni, with her stupid bet! What was she trying to do, play matchmaker? Why couldn't she just worry about her own love life, instead of trying to organise mine? I grabbed a green strappy vest and jerked it over my head.

Finn's voice came again. 'She told me you'd been hurt.'

My anger started to subside and I briefly touched my cheek, then shivered as I remembered Malik doing the same thing in the taxi. One of the gremlins had thrown a spanner and I hadn't moved quickly enough; an accident of course, since he'd been aiming for one of his pals. The bruise was gone now; thanks to Malik healing me. I shoved that disturbing thought away and slipped my leather waistcoat off its hanger and pulled it on.

'But you weren't in,' Finn continued. 'I was worried about you, Gen, especially after yesterday morning. '

Please don't be nice, Finn, I really can't cope with it right now. I sighed and leaned over to fish an ankle boot from under the bed.

'I texted and phoned, then when there was no answer, I let myself in and looked around.'

I dropped the boot as apprehension filled me. Pulling the door open, I said, 'What do you mean, you "looked around"?'

He was leaning, shoulder propped against the wall, just outside the door. His mouth turned down like he'd sucked on some salt. 'You'd left your computer on, so I checked it out.'

And found the Blue Heart website. Damn. I'd been hoping that my evening's entertainment wouldn't get out for a couple of days – looked like my luck was out.

'I came looking for you' – his moss-green eyes darkened – 'and guess where you were? All dressed up and getting into a taxi with a sucker in Leicester Square. Stupidly, I decided to follow you, thinking you might be in trouble.'

The thought of him doing the proverbial knight in shining armour act – however unneeded – made something soften just under my breastbone. Not that it made any difference; any possibilities with Finn had been just wishful thinking, even more so after last night. And now I was beginning to think my job might end up as wishful thinking too.

'Victoria Embankment Gardens, Gen.' His voice was soft, accusing, his anger simmering just under the surface. 'I watched you and the vampire chat, and then I saw you go in alone. I saw those two lads.'

I didn't say anything. I didn't need to. I knew what came next better than he did. I headed for the fridge, the sick feeling back in my stomach.

'I go running in, and next thing I know, I'm taking a nap in the bushes, and when I wake up the place is deserted. But even though someone's tried to wash it away, there's still blood – if you know where to look.'

That had to be where Malik killed the revenants. I grabbed the vodka and poured some into a glass, trying to stop my hand from shaking. The story was nearly over. All I needed to do was let him tell it, give his ultimatum, and then he'd be gone, and I could get back to what I'd been planning.

'Then this morning I heard some interesting news. A jogger found two naked bodies by Hammersmith Pier – human males, in their late teens, early twenties – both had their heads and hearts missing.'

I stilled in shock, then my brain kicked in. What the hell were the bodies doing there? Why *hadn't* Malik burnt them, or at least stashed them so he could do it later? Old vampires were supposed to be good at that sort of thing – after all, they'd had centuries of practise. I frowned, tapping the glass thoughtfully. If the revenants *had* been found, it wasn't because Malik had made a mistake.

Finn carried on in the same quiet, insistent voice, 'Now there are a few things that would take the head and heart – dragons, gargoyles, demons. But what seems to have everyone stumped is that the penis and testicles had been torn off both bodies.'

I blinked in surprise. Head and heart were easy: they'd been vampires, after all – but why the other? Puzzled, I turned to frown at Finn. 'Weird,' I murmured.

He pushed off the wall and started walking towards me. 'Not when you consider it's a vengeance particularly favoured by the *bean sidhe*.'

Then I connected all the dots. I was the only *bean sidhe* in town. I stared at Finn, incredulous. 'You think I did it, don't you?'

'Yesterday at dawn, I find you covered in blood, but not injured.' He stared back at me, his mouth thin with anger. 'Then last night I see you fighting with two lads, and later they turn up dead. That's a lot to put down to coincidence, Gen.'

'Why don't you just shove that idea where it belongs?' I shouted, fear making my own anger rise. 'Even if I had done it, no way would I be stupid enough to leave evidence that pointed right to me!'

'I'm going to ask you, and I don't want to ask it thrice, so no prevaricating. Just give me a straight answer.' Emerald flashed in the hard green of his eyes. 'Did you kill them?'

Shit, I hated the thrice rule. It wasn't just that it forced a fae to tell the truth, but it made you feel so awful.

'No,' I snapped, 'I didn't kill them.'

He took a deep breath, his eyes closing briefly, and the anger seemed to flow out of him.

'Happy now, are you?' I shoved him in the chest, 'Now you've had your little trial and jury scene?'

He stumbled back. 'I'm sorry, Gen. I had to know.' He ran a distracted hand through his blond hair and rubbed his left horn. 'I had to ask—'

'Fine. You've asked. I didn't.' I balled my fists. 'Now if you'll just leave, I can get on with what I was doing.'

His brows came together in a frown. 'I take it the sucker did it?'

Of course, the sucker did it! I took a deep breath, trying to calm myself. I needed to get to the Shamrock, and for that I needed Finn to leave. *Think* … Then something he'd said struck me. 'Were the parts found with the bodies, the heads, the hearts and the other bits?'

'Why?'

'No, of course they weren't,' I murmured, half to myself. 'You said human males. If they'd found the heads, they'd have known they weren't human.'

'They weren't human?' He gave me a quizzical look.

'No, not when they died.' I glanced at the clock to check the time; daylight would disappear too fast for my liking

'So the question is,' Finn crossed his arms, 'why is your sucker friend trying to frame you?'

'I haven't a clue, but I'm not going to find out by staying here, am I?' I moved round him, needing to get my boots. 'C'mon, Finn, discussion time's over for now. I told you I've got something to do.'

'Not yet, Gen. We haven't finished talking.'

My insides felt like they were going to explode, and I almost kicked my bedroom door with frustration. I settled for glaring over my shoulder instead. 'Yes. We. Have.'

'Gen, you keep evading me and changing the subject, or rushing off somewhere.' A muscle clenched in his jaw. 'But we need to talk about all this stuff with the vamps, that spell-tattoo you've got, the murders, whatever it was that happened at the police station. I don't know what's going on, but we're going to sort all this out. Now!'

So not a conversation I wanted to have – my heart just wasn't in it – even though I'd guessed it was going to be inevitable sooner or later. And with only a few hours of daylight left, later was the option I was going for. I sighed and swiped my hands over my face, then gave him a resigned look. 'Just give me a couple of minutes to finish dressing, okay?'

'Go ahead,' he said, calmly moving to stand under my long beaded light, arms crossed, legs apart, like he was on guard duty or something. 'I'll wait right here.'

I shut the door carefully, resisting the urge to slam it, and leaned my head against it. Why did Finn always bring out the worst in me? Never mind my emotions felt like they were on a rollercoaster ride. Why couldn't I just have my nice quiet life back where all I had to deal with was a pack of persistent pixies? And now Finn looked like he thought I was going to make a run for it or something. Still, he'd got that right: I was. I tugged my boots on, slipped some money in my pocket and took a couple of quiet steps to the open window.

Finn's talk would have to wait until later.

My visit to Mick couldn't.

I bent and swung my leg over the low windowsill leading out onto the flat roof. My boot snagged on something *not there*. Breath catching, I jerked my leg back and felt a strange, sticky resistance, almost like I'd stepped into a large glob of chewing gum. I *looked*. The spell even looked like chewing gum, stretching out in long elastic strands from the window frame, wrapping around my boot and creeping up my calf. Crap, what the hell was Finn playing at?

'Finn,' I yelled, furious, 'get in here – now!'

The door slammed back and he burst into the room, then he stopped and stared at me in disbelief. Then a smile twitched his lips. 'Having a bit of trouble, my Lady?'

'Nice try, Finn,' I smirked, 'but I think you forgot something. Watch this!' I held up my hand and *called* the spell …

'Gen, that's really not such a—'

… the sticky spell splattered into my hand, digging into my skin, then snapped back towards the window. It jerked me off-balance and dumped me in a heap on the floor; the *chewing gum* contracting in on itself and trapping me even tighter.

'—good idea,' he finished, wincing. 'It's a snapper-snare. The more you stretch or tease, or try and *crack* the magic, the worse it gets. We – that is, me and my brothers spent years perfecting it when we were kids.' He finished with a touch of sheepish pride.

'I don't care how long it took to make it,' I spat, 'just get it off me. What the hell is it doing there anyway?'

'I put it there earlier.' he held his hands up in apology. 'Don't worry, it wasn't to catch you, Gen.' He gave me a quick grin, then knelt and took a dried-up conker-shell out of his pocket. 'When I recovered, I came round to check on you.' He plunged his hands into the sticky spell and started rolling the spiky conker-shell carefully between his palms. 'I got here just as the sucker was going. I couldn't stay, and I didn't want to leave you without any protection, just in case he decided to come back, so I set the snapper-snare.'

I huffed, watching as he coaxed the magic off me – sticky spell-traps on my window was taking this whole shining-knight thing too far. 'A standard back-off ward would've been easier.'

He grimaced. 'A ward wouldn't have held the sucker until the sun came up.'

My mouth fell open. 'The sun would've fried him!'

He looked at me and smiled, determination in his eyes. 'Of course.' Then he leaned forward and pulled the last strand of magic off my boot.

I stared at him, speechless. Somehow I'd never imagined Finn thinking like that, never mind actually doing it. Or even why he would deliberately set a trap to kill a vampire. It didn't fit with what I thought I knew about him.

Sitting back on his heels, he said cheerfully, 'Did you want to try the front door next, or can we have a sensible talk like adults?'

I shoved a hand through my hair in resignation. 'Fine, I admit it, going out the window was a bit childish.' I shuffled back and leant against the wall. 'But there really is somewhere I need to be, Finn, so can we make it quick, okay?'

'Let's start with this.' He waved, taking in both the window and me. 'When did you start inviting suckers over for a blood-fest?'

'Please don't tell me this is all because you're jealous.'

'Jealousy has got nothing to do with it. This is about business.'

'I take it this is my new boss I'm supposed to listen to?'

'Yes.'

I drew my knees up and hugged them. 'And if I don't want to,' I said quietly, 'does that mean I'm out of a job?'

'Pretty much.'

Damn.

'Gen, don't be naïve. You work for a *witch* company. These are *vampires* we're talking about. Keep going like this and it won't be long before the Witches' Council make you *persona non grata.*'

I pinched the bridge of my nose, trying to work out what would be the fastest way to end this. 'Finn, you've heard what happened at the police station,' I said, keeping my voice calm. 'So no doubt the Council know all about it by now too – the new Detective Inspector there is a witch, so she's probably told them.' And with added glee, seeing as she *really* didn't like me, but I kept that bit to myself. 'So you see, it's not like what's going on is a secret.'

Finn groaned. 'You see, that's where you're wrong. Up until now it has been: the Council don't know a thing. Friday night at the police station, Helen had permission to use a spell to keep everything under wraps, and after that fiasco with the goblin, the vampires were more than happy to agree.'

So that explained why the goblin's death hadn't made the news, and why Old Scotland Yard had been hack-free. It *didn't* explain why Finn was calling Detective Inspector Crane by her first name, as if they were old friends, or how he knew so much. And there was something else wrong with what Finn was saying, something about it all being kept under wraps—

Finn leaned over and took my hand in his and I looked at him, surprised. 'Gen, forget that for now.' An odd sadness settled on his face. 'Look, there's no other way to say this, but I know you're suffering from *salaich sìol.*'

I froze, a tight band constricting my heart. He knew I'd got 3V – *salaich sìol*, as the older fae name it … I closed my eyes, pulling my hand away from his and dropping my head to my knees. I didn't want to look at him. I didn't want him to see me. He kept on talking; his words washing over me like a gentle river, then fading away as a dark stream of pain and memory rushed into my mind.

'*I shall not allow her to enter sanctuary, troll.*' *Soft sibilant sounds echoed in her voice as a rough palm touched my fore-head.* '*The* salaich sìol *in her blood iss deeply embedded; it hass been there too long.*'

'*But she's fae, and just a child.*' *Hugh's words rumbled through me as I lay half-conscious in his arms.* '*The human tried to gut her like a fish; surely you won't refuse her aid for her injuries. Does your vow not—?*'

'*She iss …*' *for a moment doubt resonated in her voice, then she carried on firmly,* '*she may be sidhe, troll. But she doess not belong here in sanctuary, not with the vampiress' blood-taint in her. There are the lesser fae to be considered; it would be too dangerouss—*'

The rest of her words were lost as the pain rolled over me and I slipped back into the darkness.

'… just because the suckers can't trick you or mind-lock you,' Finn's quiet concern started to penetrate my mind, 'that doesn't mean you can pick and choose amongst them. I've seen before how venom addiction affects the fae.'

I tried to swallow past the ache in my throat. It didn't matter what he was saying; all that mattered was that he knew. The rest was pointless. It was over, everything was finished.

'Gen, it affects your magic too.' He stroked a gentle hand over my hair. 'Think about it, you can't do a simple *casting*, even though you can absorb spells that would knock out a fae five times your age. And then there's your Glamour. Some days it's as though there's no magic left in you, and others you almost take me under. It's been hard to resist this last couple of months.'

Briefly the scent of warm berries curled around me and I took a deeper breath, trying to anchor it in my memory, but then it was gone.

'I know you noticed it yourself,' his voice was still quiet, but he was speaking faster, sounding anxious, worried. 'Every time we got close my magic responded to yours. It was confusing, until I realised you weren't consciously using your Glamour to entice—'

A loud bang on my front door interrupted him.

'Hell's thorns, I forgot—' He jumped up. 'I phoned the Rosy Lee while you were getting dressed.'

My mind was numb, empty. I stayed where I was, my head resting on my knees, not even trying to work out what to do, not caring. Out in my lounge, voices rose and fell, but the words made no sense. The breeze brought the scents of lavender and lemon balm through the window behind me. They eddied around my shoulders with a consoling touch and a tendril of soft multi-coloured light unfurled inside me. The brownie's magic bloomed into gentle, comforting warmth that soothed and slowly eased away the darkness in my mind.

I sighed and lifted my head, rubbing away the dampness in my eyes, my conscience pricking at me. Never mind anything else; there was still something I needed to finish. I looked at my alarm clock. And I needed to do it soon.

The bedroom door opened and I looked up as Finn stood there, a serious expression on his face.

Next to him stood Detective Inspector Helen Crane. Hugh loomed behind them.

The police had come to call.

Chapter Thirty-Three

Detective Inspector Crane stood in front of my window. The afternoon sun cut through behind her, slicing to either side of her black-suited-figure, making it impossible to decipher her expression. Somehow I didn't think she'd stood there by chance.

'Ms Taylor,' she began, her voice almost without inflection, 'can you tell me your whereabouts at eleven-thirty p.m. last night?'

The question was expected – no way had I thought this a social visit – but if she was here about the headless bodies, the time was all wrong. I took a moment to think exactly where I'd been, and how much trouble the truth might cause me, but I was my father's daughter, and I was sidhe. Neither gave me the option of straight-out lying.

Finn sprang up to sit on my kitchen counter, the movement catching my eye. A half-smile wreathed his mouth, as though he were completely unconcerned, but under his shirt the muscles across his shoulders and neck were tight with tension. It didn't take much to realise the strained atmosphere had more to do with the relationship between Finn and Detective Inspector Helen Crane – whatever that was – and the fact she'd found Finn here with me than any official police business.

I frowned at the inspector. 'Why do you want to know?'

'Just answer the question, Genny,' Hugh rumbled. I looked over at him. He had folded himself down to sit Indian-style on my rug – I appreciated his attempt to look less imposing – but when you're a seven-foot-tall troll, not even sitting can manage that. His notepad was carefully balanced on his knee and he gripped one of his over-large pens between his fingers.

If I was going to have this many visitors maybe I ought to think about getting some furniture – nah, it probably wasn't worth it. I didn't want to send out the wrong impression. I was getting enough unwanted guests as it was.

A smothered cough drew my attention to the other uninvited occupant of my lounge: the ever-charming Constable Curly-hair stood to attention by my front door, her eyes flicking between me and Hugh, a happy little smirk wreathing her plump face. She looked to be the only person here enjoying herself.

'Ms Taylor?' The inspector clasped her hands and her rings chinked as if advertising her impatience.

Shrugging, I stuck my hands into the back pockets of my jeans. 'At half-past-eleven I was in a black hackney cab. I've no idea what his licence number was, but his CCTV was running, I remember seeing the red light blinking.' I rocked back on my heels. ''Course, if I'd known you were interested, I'd have made a note of it.'

Hugh rumbled a warning at my tone, and wrote something down.

'Where were you going?'

I sighed. She had to know the answer to that one. 'I had an appointment with my client, Alan Hinkley. He'd arranged for me to see Melissa Bank's body, with you.'

Her lips thinned. 'Only you never arrived at the police station. Why was that, Ms Taylor?'

Let me think. Oh yeah, I ran into a bit of trouble.

A trickle of sweat ran down my back, but I kept my voice level. 'Hinkley didn't turn up for our meeting.'

'Did you not think that strange? Or maybe consider telephoning him to find out why?'

'I would have, but I'd left my phone somewhere, and I didn't know his number.' *And don't worry*, I added silently, *he's on my to-do list – he and whoever it was sent the revenants in his place.* 'I'd been planning to contact him today.'

'That won't be possible,' she said. 'Alan Hinkley was attacked last night.'

Shock jolted through me and I crossed my arms over the sudden cold feeling in my stomach. 'Is he all right? What happened?'

'Mr Hinkley is in a coma.' She twisted the large diamond ring on her finger. 'His solicitor and a goblin guard were attacked at the same time. The solicitor is in intensive care and the goblin is dead.'

So that's where the revenants had got the bat. Alan must have been first on their list. Someone was obviously serious about stopping me from seeing Melissa's body, but if it *was* Declan – who still looked like the only candidate – Alan being attacked made even less sense.

'Genny,' Hugh broke into my thoughts, 'we need to know the details of the taxi journey to confirm your statement.'

I narrowed my eyes at him. 'You mean so you can rule me out as a suspect.'

'That's not what I said, Genny.' Hugh's brow ridges lowered over his eyes. 'But it would be better if the facts were verified.'

'Fine,' I huffed. 'I picked up the taxi from the rank at Leicester Square.' I watched Hugh as I spoke. He didn't even flinch, so they already knew I'd been to the Blue Heart. 'The taxi dropped me off under the Hungerford Bridge, on the Victoria Embankment side, at five minutes to midnight. The journey took around thirty minutes, because of the traffic.'

'Then what did you do?' The inspector's tone was brisk.

'I waited for Alan Hinkley.'

'And then what?

I shrugged. 'He didn't turn up, so I came home.'

'What time was that?'

'I'm not sure. I didn't check my watch.'

'You must have some idea of the time, Ms Taylor.'

I frowned. Maybe she was here about the revenants after all. Except, what with the fighting and the whole passing out thing, and then Malik, I really hadn't a clue what time I'd got home.

'Perhaps if I can butt in—?' Finn's voice sounded lower than normal.

I shot a glance at him and my pulse quickened. He leant forward, his arms braced on the counter on either side of him, the angles of his face seemed sharper, the moss-green of his eyes more arrogant, his horns taller. He was still Finn. Still gorgeous. Only now he had a harsh wild beauty that made him seem remote, less human than before. My breath caught in my throat as desire echoed faintly through me.

A small clinking noise dragged my attention away from him to the inspector. She was staring at him, her hand clutching the sapphire pendant at her neck.

Constable Curly-hair wasn't so circumspect. She looked as interested as a hungry vampire scenting blood.

Then it clicked. I *looked*. There was nothing to see, but whatever Finn was doing, it was deliberate, and I realised I'd felt it before – it was his own magic. Even if the inspector didn't catch on, it was so not a good idea with Hugh around. And judging by the red dust that was settling on Hugh's white shirt, he knew exactly what Finn was up to, although, oddly, he just continued to stare at his notepad.

'I came round to see Gen here last night.' Finn's voice tugged at something deep inside me. 'I was late and she'd already gone. I tried to catch up with her at Leicester Square, but missed her again, but I saw her get into the taxi. I knew she was meeting Hinkley at midnight, so I headed for the Embankment. After Hinkley didn't turn up, I made sure she got home' – a smile flitted across his face – 'and I left not long after.'

Neat, very neat. It tied everything up, without actually lying. And it all tallied with what he'd told me earlier. Only going by the expression on Detective Inspector Crane's face, she wasn't buying it.

Still gripping her pendant, she walked towards him, then stopped abruptly and turned sharply to the constable. 'That will be all, Constable Sims,' she said. 'Please wait outside.'

'But ma'am—' Constable Curly-hair's face fell. 'Don't you need me here in case you have to search the suspect?'

'What suspect?'

'Her.' As she pointed at me I caught a flash of pink at her wrist. I frowned and *looked*. The pink flashed brighter. I was right; she was wearing the rose quartz bracelet again. Had she realised not all the spells were working? Not that it mattered; she'd broken the bargain. Briefly I wondered what price the magic would extract. Then I put it out my mind.

'Ms Taylor is *not* a suspect.' Inspector Crane's teeth snapped together. 'She is not a suspect in anything. Do you understand me?'

I *looked*, and saw the inspector's spells glowing brighter than a supernova.

'Yes ma'am,' the constable said, not bothering to hide her disappointment, and she left, leaving the door ajar.

'Wait outside the *building*, Constable,' Inspector Crane called after her.

No chance of her eavesdropping then. That didn't sound good.

'And you as well, please, Sergeant Munro.'

Hugh laid his pad and pen down in front of him. 'No, I don't think so, ma'am,' he said calmly.

'That was an order, sergeant.'

'If this is no longer police business, then you cannot tell me to leave.' Hugh's words sounded like loose chippings clattering over slate. 'As a friend to both Genny and Finn, I feel that I should stay, ma'am.'

I shot Hugh a look. Nice though the support was, maybe it wasn't such a good idea to antagonise his new boss.

She glared at Hugh, then turned suddenly, ignoring him, and strode up to Finn.

Smacking her hand on his chest she cried, 'How *dare* you do this? How *dare* you give her an alibi? After everything I've done!' The magic misted round her with anger. 'You disgust me – lying to protect her, trying to *persuade* me – and for what? A psychotic sucker whore. *A sidhe!* You know what they're like, all of them – they're just out for themselves!'

Okaaay, so I really wasn't her favourite person – but *psychotic*?

'I haven't lied to you, Helen,' Finn said. The angry mist seemed to cling to him. 'Gen didn't do it.'

'Of course you'd know that, wouldn't you?' she scoffed. 'But you're thinking with your dick instead of your brain – for the Goddess' sake, you were *with* me when the call came in, Finn – you told me yourself it sounded like sidhe vengeance.'

'*Sounded*, Helen, it *sounded* like sidhe vengeance, *that's* what I said—'

I blinked. And he'd made me think he'd heard about it on the news.

'She's the only sidhe in London,' she snapped.

'You don't know that, Helen.' Finn tried to take her hand, but she batted him away. 'Hugh?' he asked, looking at the troll.

I turned to Hugh, expectant. *Were* there other sidhe around?

'Finn has a point,' Hugh rumbled quietly, 'although it is unlikely.'

Inwardly, I slumped. So it was just a misdirection.

'She was *there*.' Inspector Crane swung back to Finn. 'You've just admitted you saw her there yourself.'

'You said the bodies were found at Hammersmith Pier and that's miles away from Hungerford Bridge.'

Hugh started reading from his notebook, 'A man walking his dog early this morning called in to say he'd found a pool of blood. His dog tried to roll in it. Initial blood typing matches with the bodies found.'

Whose side are you on here, Hugh? I asked silently.

'Ask her, Helen.' Finn pointed at me. 'Ask thrice and she has to tell the truth.'

What the—? Shit, Finn, this is so not a good idea. I clamped my mouth shut to stop myself shouting at him.

'Gen.' He turned to me, emerald flecks sparking in his eyes. 'Did you at anytime last night have anything to do with the deaths and mutilation of two humans?'

I breathed an inward sigh of relief.

'No.'

He asked me again, the exact same words.

'No,' I said my answer firmer.

Hugh looked from Finn to me, a considering look on his face. My pulse sped up. Had he worked it out?

'Gen, did you at—'

'Stop it, Finn, now,' Inspector Crane shouted. 'I'll ask her myself.'

'It has to be the same question, Helen, or the geas won't hold.'

'I know that.' She glared at him. 'Remember?'

She stalked over to me, rage etched in her face. 'Did you at anytime last night have anything to do with the deaths and mutilations of two humans?'

'No,' I yelled. *Fuck, that hurt.* It felt like something had physically ripped the word from my heart. I shuddered and rubbed under my breast. I'd only had that happen twice before, but it didn't get any better.

For a moment I thought she was going to hit me, or cry, or maybe both. Then she turned away and snatched up a newspaper and a brown envelope from the window sill. She strode back to Finn and he caught the envelope as she slapped it at him. 'See this? This is what your precious sidhe's been up to.'

He opened the envelope and flipped through its contents.

She turned to face me, straightened her shoulders. 'As a senior representative of the Witches' Council, Ms Taylor, I am to inform you that in light of your involvement with the local vampire community, the Council has taken the decision to sever any association with you.'

The sick feeling roiled back in my stomach. I wanted to tell her she couldn't do that, but of course she could.

She threw down the newspaper.

The headline read **LOVE AT FIRST BITE?** Underneath it was a picture of the Earl and me. Both of us were smiling.

She carried on, 'Your employment contract with Spellcrackers.com has been terminated with immediate effect.' She swung back to Finn. 'I also have to inform you, Mr Panos, that should you decide to employ Ms Taylor after you have taken over the franchise, the franchise will revert and all monies paid will be retained in lieu of damages.'

I stared at her, stunned.

Finn jumped down from the counter. 'They can't do that, Helen – you can't let them—'

'Copies of those were sent to every council member.' She pointed at the envelope.

'So what? Doesn't Gen get a hearing, a chance to defend herself?' He pointed the envelope at her. 'Can't they see it's a set-up?'

Inspector Crane half-raised her hand, then let it drop. 'There's nothing I can do about it, Finn,' she said quietly. 'Not now.' She turned, pulled open the door and left.

I listened to the sound of her shoes clicking down the stairs, getting fainter and fainter.

Finn stood for a moment, staring after her as if he couldn't believe what she'd said. He wasn't the only one. I'd always known it was a possibility, but to have it actually happen—

Finn turned to me, his face determined. 'Gen, I'll talk to her. She's got a lot of influence. We'll get it sorted.' He glanced at Hugh as he left to follow her. 'Don't let Gen do anything stupid.'

Chapter Thirty-Four

I hugged my arms around myself and gave Hugh a shaky smile. 'Looks like I'm out of a job then.' *And out of my home*, I added silently, looking around with regret. No way could I afford the rent without the witch subsidy working at Spellcrackers gave me.

Hugh picked up his notepad, tapped his pen on the front. 'The two bodies were not human?' His voice was raised in question.

'What—? No, they were revenants. I thought you'd picked up on that.'

'They are a type of vampire.' He made a note in his pad. 'Someone wants you out of the way.'

I laughed, a short sharp burst that I cut off before I couldn't stop. 'You could say that.'

Hugh's forehead creased into concerned cracks. 'The revenants attacked you?'

'I'm okay, Hugh, really.' I gave his shoulder a reassuring pat then held my arms out. 'See, all in one piece.'

'Well, you don't look quite as skinny as you usually do.' He got slowly to his feet, knocking his head against my amber pendant.

I smiled at his diplomatic compliment.

'What I meant, Genny' – he brushed a hand carefully over his black hair and shifted away from the tinkling crystals – 'they wanted you to be out of the way physically. The bodies were left where they could be found quickly and easily. The dog-walker, the one who found the blood, said that wasn't his usual route.'

'Mind-locked,' I said.

He nodded as if I'd confirmed something. 'Inspector Crane wanted to take you in for questioning, and that would have meant you off the street for at least forty-eight hours. Now, thanks to Finn's intervention ...' He paused. 'This vampire – the one who mind-locked the dog walker – is he the one who killed the revenants?'

I hesitated, realising I'd just confirmed to Hugh I'd been hanging around with a vampire. Still, after the Earl's front page news—

'Yes, it's the same one,' I said, 'but why try and frame me up like that? He couldn't have known what was going to happen, unless— I know he didn't want me involved with this, so maybe this is his way of keeping me out of it.' I frowned as something else odd hit me. 'But then he also sent me an invitation to the Blue Heart.'

Hugh nodded thoughtfully. 'You were under the witches' protection, so sending you an invitation was the correct way to contact you. It's standard practice between the witches and the vampires; that way they meet under the old rules of hospitality.'

Of course! The hospitality thing. That was why Malik had healed me. He'd seen it as his *responsibility* to make sure I got home safe and unharmed, although it still didn't explain why he'd invited me in the first place.

'As this vampire killed the revenants, then there is no need to investigate their deaths.' Hugh continued with his note. 'I'll order the blood tests, and once they're confirmed the bodies will be burnt and the case closed.'

I nodded, understanding why. When they'd reclaimed their legal rights, the vamps agreed to abide by human laws, but only when it came to humans. They still kept their own judicial traditions, including destroying any vamps that turned feral or were considered a danger, without resorting to human law, and without fear of reprisal – and the two revenants qualified as dangerous in anyone's book, never mind mine.

I shuddered. It was the same justice Malik was planning to follow in destroying me, or rather, the *feral* Rosa me, my Alter Vamp.

'S'cuse me?' called a child's nervous voice, and a hand edged through the half-open door, dropped a white paper carrier bag on the floor and disappeared.

I blinked for a moment, baffled, then realised the bag was Finn's lunch order from the Rosy Lee. Briefly I wondered why Katie hadn't delivered it, but shrugged the thought off – it was Sunday, and what with the tourists and the Witches' Market, the café was probably busy. I'd check on her later.

'You want anything to eat, Hugh?' He shook his head and I put the bag on the kitchen counter moving the inspector's brown envelope as I did. I tipped it up and slid out the contents: four ten by eight photos. The two of the Earl bending over my hand weren't the problem. Like the one in the newspaper, it was obvious we were in a public place. They could be fobbed off as a chance meeting, something the witches probably wouldn't object to. But the one of me kissing Rio, and the other where I was sitting astride her on the floor ... well, even I had to admit the Witches' Council were probably right to think the two of us weren't discussing the weather.

I handed Hugh the pictures, trying not to wince. 'You can say I told you so if you want.'

He took them from me. 'Yes, I have seen them. There is also a video on the internet of you with this vampire.' He held up Rio's picture. 'That is what seems to have antagonised the Witches' Council the most, from what I can gather.'

My day was just getting better and better.

Hugh slid the photos back onto the counter. 'Apparently, some of the younger witches think that segregation from the vampires is the wrong way to go, particularly in the current climate. The council feel that if they don't make a stand with you, it will set a bad precedent.'

Damn. Finn with his shining-knight complex might think

he could get Inspector Crane to help me, but he had more chance of carrying soup in a sieve.

'Finn knows.' I looked up at Hugh. 'He knows about the 3V. He wants to try and help me.'

'Ah, Genny.' Hugh gave a hesitant rumble as a guilty expression crossed his face. 'There's something I should explain.'

I frowned, puzzled. 'What about?'

'I know I've always told you to keep your distance from the fae because of your *problem*.' Dust puffed from his head ridge. 'I know I said that if they were to find out they would ostracise you, but that's not entirely true. Those with good hearts – like Finn – would want to help you. I think it's time I told you this, and also to apologise for misleading you all this time.'

'But Hugh—'

'Let me finish. When I first met you, I realised you were alone and vulnerable and desperate to put your trust in someone. I also realised that if you started to mix with the fae—' He sighed, and continued, 'Well, there are some who would use you for their own gain, much like the vampires. I didn't want that to happen, so I convinced you that it was better to stay away from others of your own kind as much as possible. I'm sorry.'

'I was young, Hugh, not totally stupid,' I said, frowning. 'Why would you think I would trust someone, even another fae? I mean, it took a couple of years before I started to trust you.'

'That night I found you,' Hugh's fingers tightened around his troll-pen, 'the night when the human attacked you – well, he'd obviously picked up those church leaflets and used them to lull your suspicions. And if a human could trick you like that, then you'd be an easy mark for a fae,'

'The human didn't *trick* me, Hugh,' I snorted. 'He tried to, but I could tell he was some vamp's blood-pet, his skin was hotter than a dwarf's furnace. But when I told him to get lost, he said he'd kill the woman working in the café unless I played nice and went with him. I'd planned to Glamour him once we were outside.'

'But he poisoned you with iron, Genny,' Hugh rumbled loudly.

'Yeah.' I pulled a disgusted face. 'I admit letting him do that wasn't the smartest idea I've ever had. I sort of expected the effects to wear off a bit quicker than they did.'

'But why did you go along with me all this time if you knew I was misleading you?'

'Well, you weren't really, were you?' I said slowly. 'You were just being kind. The fae *would* shun me if they knew about my tainted blood.'

'Genny, I just explained: not all of them would.' His frown cracked even deeper.

Oh shit— Hugh didn't know! He didn't know who – or rather, *what* – my father was. The dragon at the sanctuary had told him about the *salaich sìol* in my blood, but she hadn't told him about my father … And no way could I deal with telling Hugh that little revelation just now.

'Right,' I snatched up the photos, mentally back-peddling, 'but then if some of the fae did shun me, never mind anything else, think about all the problems I'd get with the witches, and the vamps.' Hoping to distract him, I tapped the pictures and added quickly, 'Like this mess I'm in now.'

'This is what I have always been afraid of, Genny.' More red mica glinted anxiously in Hugh's hair. 'That something like this would happen. It's left you very vulnerable.'

'I'm trying to get out of it, Hugh,' I sighed, taking a cake box out of the food bag. 'There's just one more thing I need to do first before it's finished.'

Why on earth had Finn ordered cakes? Neither of us ate them. I prised up the lid and stared. It wasn't a food container, but two heart-shaped blue leather jewellery boxes. My stomach knotted: they had to be from the Earl. Tucked down beside the boxes was a note.

I unfolded the thick cream paper and read:

My dear Genevieve,

 *I believe the item within the smaller box belongs
to you. I acquired it, on your behalf, some three years
ago, when you felt the need to offer it up as security. I
understand the item has sentimental value, and so I
am returning it now, as a gesture of my esteem. I am
writing to extend you my protection at this uncertain
time and have hopes that you will look favourably upon
my offer. I also wish to assure you that my intentions are
honourable and enduring. With this in mind, the larger
box contains a gift that I trust you will appreciate.*

The Earl

My heart pounding, I grabbed the smaller box and jerked
back the lid. Tildy's black opal collar rested on the padded
cushion within. My hands were shaking as I picked it up and
ran my fingers over the five-stranded necklace. I held it to my
nose, but the precious scent of Tildy's gardenias no longer
clung to the jewels, only the sad smell of blood, old and stale
and almost bitter. I clutched the opals, blinking back tears. I
didn't have time to get upset.

The Ancient One had said she'd keep them safe, that was
the agreement. She'd decided I wasn't going to be around long
enough for her to get all her money, and had actually refused
to take *my word* that I'd pay for the spell, every month, on
the dot – which I had. And all this time I'd never known the
Ancient Bitch had sold the opals to the Earl — *shit*. Did that
mean the Earl knew about my Alter Vamp disguise? Had she
told him that's what the opals were security for, or had she
just grabbed the opportunity to cash in? The Ancient Bitch was
going to have some explaining to do. If I survived that long.

I opened the larger box, then swallowed hard. The Fabergé
Egg nestled amongst the blue velvet. It wasn't my father's; his

didn't have sapphires on it … But the egg meant that the Earl knew who my father was – who *I* was – and he wasn't planning on selling me back to my prince, so long as I accepted his offer of protection. The note was pure blackmail, however *nicely* it was couched. Only— If he'd known about me all this time, why had he waited until now before making his move?

'Genny?' Hugh's voice interrupted my thoughts. I'd almost forgotten he was there. 'Isn't that your necklace? The one I looked after for you when you were younger?'

'Yes, it is.' I took a deep breath. 'And I want you to look after it again, please Hugh.' I turned around, yanked open the fridge and took out the plastic container. It wasn't big enough to hold the blue velvet box, so I wrapped the opals carefully in some kitchen roll and tucked them next to the soap, then snapped the plastic lid closed. 'Keep it with all my other stuff.' I held the box out to him. 'Oh, and you'd better keep that too.' I indicated the egg. 'I'll need to return it.'

'Of course I'll look after your things,' he said, a small dust cloud puffing from his head ridge. He held up the Earl's letter. 'But—'

'Look, I've got to go, Hugh. There's someone I need to visit.'

'Genny.' His deep rumble made me stop. 'I don't know what you ran away from all those years ago, or what you need to do to finish this, but I do know it's something to do with the vampires. And you've come too far to give in to them now.'

I gave him a rueful look. 'Don't worry, Hugh, I'm not going to give in.' At least I hoped not. 'I'll be back before sunset. Tell Detective Inspector Crane I'll take her up on the offer of a cell, because I think I'm going to need it.'

Then tomorrow I could sort out what I was going to do with my life.

Chapter Thirty-Five

The Bloody Shamrock was closed. In the daylight the door was pitted and scared, as if it had withstood an onslaught of Beater goblins. The neon cloverleaf was unlit, and it looked like no one was home, but when I concentrated, the faint trace of vampire snagged the edge of my radar. I hammered my fist on the door and gave it a kick for good measure. I turned and scanned along the street – Shaftesbury Avenue with its busy crowds was only twenty-odd feet away – but here was deserted. There wasn't much call for day visitors, not when your main attractions were effectively dead. Or at least I hoped they still were.

I gave the door another hard thump.

There was the sound of bolts being drawn and the door opened slowly, revealing a thin slice of darkness. I shoved my shoulder against it and pushed my way into the building.

Mick stumbled away from me, a sullen look on his face. 'What'd you do that for, Genny? I was gonna let you in.'

'Yeah? Well maybe I wanted to make sure.'

His short red hair was mussed, like he'd just got out of bed – which I guessed he had going by the green silk boxers hanging off his narrow hipbones and the fluffy slippers that looked like he was wearing a couple of small furry barrels on his feet.

'You don't seem very surprised to see me,' I pointed out. 'Not going to ask me what I want or why I'm here?'

'Fiona said you'd be coming.' He hugged himself, hands clutching his arms, the suckers on his fingertips pulsing red. 'She's never wrong.'

'Let's not keep her waiting, then.'

He edged past me and re-bolted the door top and bottom, then said, 'She's upstairs.'

I followed him through the empty pub. His pale, freckled skin shone like a beacon as he picked his way through the spiky maze of upended chair legs. The place smelled of stale beer and blood. The combination made nausea roil in my stomach – or maybe that was just nerves.

He glanced back as he reached the stairs and I gave him a toothy smile.

'Bumped into your boyfriend last night,' I said, conversationally.

'I know,' Mick mumbled. His slippers made shushing sounds on the wooden treads. 'He told me he saw you at the Blue Heart.'

'He looked like he was getting all cosy with this blonde. You better watch that.'

'It was business.' He tried for *couldn't care less*, but there was a stricken sound in his voice.

Shit. Now I felt like the bad-tempered faerie ... *oh, wait, I was*, but maybe Mick deserved it. Maybe. I'd never quite worked out if he'd set his sister, Siobhan, up as bait four years ago, or if she'd just ended up a victim because of his naïveté.

We walked past the semi-circular booths to the far wall of the gallery. It looked like a dead end, but Mick waved a hand above his head and there was a soft snick, and a section of the wall slid quietly aside.

Behind was a narrow hallway, with four heavy steel doors down one side. At the fourth, Mick stopped and waved again, then he turned and glowered at me. 'I know you think I'm stupid for being with Seamus, especially after what happened with my sister.' He stuck his bottom lip out. 'Sometimes he has to do things that I don't like. But we love each other. If you had ever felt like that about anyone, then you'd understand.'

He was right: I did think him stupid, and I didn't understand

– but then, I wasn't the one in love, so I just shrugged and didn't ask him the question that popped into my mind. *Wasn't love supposed to make him happy?*

The steel door did its snick-and-slide thing.

The place was done up as an Edwardian lady's boudoir. Painted plaster roses covered the ceiling, ivory-striped silk lined the walls, and long velvet drapes suggested there might be windows behind them, though I doubted it. A huge marble fireplace dominated one side; double doors opposite presumably led to the bedroom. Someone liked their little luxuries.

In the middle of all this finery Fiona reclined on a velvet chaise lounge, looking like a beautiful painting. Her white-blonde hair spiked above her large, luminous grey eyes, and a ruby necklace dripped into the deep V of her rose silk negligee.

'You were right, it was her.' Mick sidled past me and sat in front of her, legs bent to one side. 'And she's not happy.'

She rested a pink cotton-gloved hand on his freckled shoulder, gave it a squeeze, throwing me a resigned but slightly wary look. Her makeup was still perfect, but it didn't hide the dark circles under her eyes or the map of ugly red veins that pulsed across her chest. She looked delicate and fragile, and nothing like a cold-blooded murderer.

I strode over the thick rose-coloured carpet towards her and stopped with my boots touching Mick's legs. 'Want to explain why you sent those two revenants to kill me last night?'

Mick shuffled his legs further back.

'Ms Taylor' – Fiona's fingers spasmed, digging into Mick's freckled skin – 'sometimes I *see* things that distress me, and I have to try to alter the course of what might happen.' Perspiration beaded her forehead.

'Well, I'm pretty distressed about what *did* happen, never mind the future.' I leaned over her. 'Start talking, and give me a reason not to tell the police about it.'

'Tell her what she wants to know.' Mick patted her glove,

glaring at me with a half-petulant, half-anxious expression. 'Then she'll leave us alone.'

Fiona took a shuddering breath. 'Ask your questions, Ms Taylor.'

I straightened. 'Tell me about Melissa and the spell that they all want, the one that's supposed to have killed her.'

'Melissa was Declan's little spy. He used her to keep tabs on the other Masters. Once she'd overheard them talking about the spell, then of course he wanted her to find out more.' Her gloved hand shook. 'Only she got ambitious and started holding back information, and then she died. When her mother found her, she phoned the police instead of us. It meant we couldn't get to the body. Declan searched Bobby's memories and discovered that Melissa had found the spell, but Bobby didn't know the details.'

I walked over to her dressing table, picked up a gold-backed hairbrush. 'Alan Hinkley's story about Melissa being killed by magic: I take it that was just so I'd check out her body for the spell?'

'We thought the spell had been given to her.' She watched the brush. 'Only we weren't sure how.'

Sliding the brush back onto the table, I asked, 'What does the spell do?'

'I don't know.'

'C'mon, Fiona,' I gave her a sceptical look, 'Declan must have told you.'

'Maybe he did, but I don't remember.' Her voice trembled like an old woman's. 'Memory for me is … *difficult*. Sometimes it is mine, more often it belongs to a stranger. Sometimes all my mind *sees* is the future. It is both my gift and my curse.' Her pale brows creased. 'If I know what the spell does, that knowledge is not mine at the moment.'

Mick patted her glove again.

I walked behind her chaise, lifted the edge of one curtain.

Yep, I'd been right. No windows. 'What did you *see* when you touched me?'

She twisted her head, straining to keep me in sight. 'Without Declan, Ms Taylor, I would not be able to control my ability. Neither Patrick nor Seamus is strong enough to help me. I would very quickly go insane.' She slumped down on the chaise. 'When I touched you, I *saw* that you would cause Declan's death. I will not allow that to happen.'

'So you decided that it would be much more convenient if I wasn't around.'

'It was nothing personal.'

'Great!' I snapped. 'I can't tell you how much *better* that makes me feel.' I stalked towards the double doors, heading for the room beyond. 'So how am I supposed to cause Declan's death?'

Fiona struggled up, looking anxious. 'The vampires are to Challenge each other over you. Declan would not stand down; it is not in his nature.' She clutched at Mick for balance. 'But he cannot win against the Earl or Malik.'

My stomach twisted into a tight knot. That so was not the information I wanted to hear. 'I can tell you now,' I said, 'I don't intend to be anyone's prize.'

'I don't think you have any choice in the matter,' she said softly. 'The future is decided.'

'Something else you *saw*.' I made it a statement rather than a question. Then I opened the double doors.

It was a bedroom. The rose and ivory décor continued right down to the rose silk sheets that covered the massive bed. The two vampires sprawled naked, their ivory skin gleaming in the rose-shaded lights on either side of the bed. Declan lay on his side, dark head pillowed on his arm, one knee drawn up. Next to him, lying on his front, arms and legs spread like a starfish, was one of his brothers, Patrick, I guessed. Somehow I couldn't see Mick or Seamus sharing this little ménage à trois.

I knew they would rise close to sunset, but they were lying so still, that it seemed they were more than asleep ...

'Please don't hurt them.' Fiona's slippered feet scuffed over the carpet as she hurried to stand beside me.

'Why would I harm them?'

'You are angry.' She cast a fearful look at the two brothers. 'Hurting them will not change what will happen.'

'What will then?' I demanded.

'I have lived a long time around vampires, Ms Taylor.' She sighed. 'When they want something, they usually get it. Fair means or foul. If they want you—?' She gave a delicate shrug. 'But I will keep Declan from the Challenge. I imagine that after it has happened your fate will be decided one way or another and you will no longer be a threat to us.'

'When's this Challenge supposed to happen?'

'Tonight.'

My pulse jumped.

Turning to look at her, I said, 'You know he's not going to be very happy when he wakes up and finds you tried to kill me.'

'This morning, I knew you weren't dead.' She clutched the edges of her negligée together. 'I knew then I couldn't change your future, but I thought that maybe I could change theirs.'

I narrowed my eyes. 'How?'

She puckered her lips and blew a breath towards me. 'Do you recognise the smell?'

A bittersweet scent drifted in the air. 'No.'

'She poisoned herself.' Mick put his arm round her. 'Nightshade.'

Fiona gestured at the two vampires. 'They will feed once they wake. It will take some time for their systems to neutralise the effects. It should keep them here until the night is past.'

I blinked. 'You're going to feed them both?'

'Of course.' Her lips lifted in a small smile. 'I always feed them on waking.'

'Won't they notice you're *unwell*?'

'Not until it's too late.' She leaned into Mick. 'Mick will give me the antidote once they have fed.'

She looked ill enough that I thought Mick should be giving her the antidote right now.

I waved at the bed. 'Declan lied to me.'

'Did he?' She frowned.

'Melissa wasn't a faeling.'

'No, she wasn't.' Her voice carried faint confusion. 'Did he tell you she was?'

I thought back. 'Declan told me that Melissa had fae blood in her.'

'She did,' Mick broke in. 'Bobby was always doing experiments, and we did one where he injected Melissa with my blood. Bobby said it was like she suddenly got *so* much more attractive. That's why Declan made her his spy. All of a sudden the vamps were round her like she was a bitch in heat.'

Now that was a nice image, *not!*

I stared down at the naked vampires. Declan may not have lied to me in words, but the magic didn't always take notice of semantics, only intent.

A memory edged into me.

Matilde, my stepmother, raging at my father, screaming at him to stop.

My father, drenched in blood that smelled like sweet apples, his voice calm. 'Genevieve gave me her word that she would not see the beast again.' Gripping my arm, he forced my nine-year-old self to kneel on the ground. The blood was still warm and it squelched under my knees and soaked up into my nightie. 'The waterhorse was a danger to us all. Now she will understand the result of her lack of honour.' The sleek ivory body of the kelpie was almost unrecognisable, but for patches of skin that still gleamed like pink-stained moonlight.

My father hadn't killed the kelpie; the local people had. They'd been frightened that the kelpie would drown them and steal their souls.

The kelpie would have left before they found him if it hadn't been for me. I hadn't *seen* him again, but I had gone and talked to him – for the magic, that had been enough.

A noise beside me brought me back to the present.

'Melissa wasn't killed by magic,' I said.

Fiona gasped. 'How do you know? Have you seen her body?'

I turned to her. 'I don't need to. Melissa was killed just as the police have said: her blood drained by a vampire.' I pointed at Declan. 'Tell him that. And tell him I have honoured my side of the bargain. Now he must honour his.'

She frowned. 'I don't understand.'

'Never break a bargain with a fae.' I smiled, and it was bitter. 'The magic always has its price.'

Mick gave me a sullen look. 'Go away, Genny. We don't want you here.'

I sighed. Fiona and Mick had confirmed what I'd already guessed, and if they did know about the spell, short of trying to beat it out of them, they weren't going to tell me. I'd fulfilled my obligation, but I hadn't learned anything really useful by coming here … *yet*.

Was Fiona right about what my future held? There was only one way to find out.

I clasped her arm, just above her glove, skin to skin.

Mick shouted, clamped his hands round my wrist as Fiona's eyes went wide, startled, her pulse jumping like a frightened animal under the thin skin of her throat. I held on tight, though Mick tried to pry my fingers from her flesh. She sagged, falling heavily to her knees, her mouth gasping like a waterless fish.

'Please,' she cried, her lashes fluttering on her cheeks, 'no more.'

I let her go and she collapsed, trembling into a heap of rose-coloured silk.

'Go away,' Mick shouted, shoving me back, 'just go away!'

Then he hoisted her in his arms, and tucking his head next

to hers, he murmured small comforting noises. He carried her to the bed and laid her gently between the two vampires.

She sighed and curled into Declan, cuddling up against him like he was a giant teddy bear.

'What did you see, Fiona?' I demanded.

She gazed back at me, her pupils dilated by the poison, sweat beading her forehead. 'Nothing,' she whispered. 'Nothing but fog.'

Damn.

I let myself out.

Chapter Thirty-Six

I opened the door to my flat, freezing at the metallic crash that came from my kitchen area. Heart thumping, I peered through the doorway. There was a quiet cough, followed by a popping noise. Agatha the brownie appeared on the counter next to my sink.

'Afternoon, Lady.' Her wrinkled face lifted in a tentative smile. 'I hope I'm nae disturbing thee.'

Taking a soft breath, I let the air slide back into my lungs. 'Afternoon, Agatha. Nice of you to drop in.' After all, I added to myself, everyone else does, so why should a brownie be any different?

'Och well, the wean tried to call, only thee were nae answering yon telephonic machine.'

Oh yeah, my mobile was *still* somewhere in the Blue Heart.

'Never mind, you're here now.' I gave her an enquiring look. 'Is Holly in trouble again?'

Agatha stepped diffidently along the countertop. 'Nae, Lady, she just telt me to bring thee a message.'

Through the window I could see the sun dipping lower in the sky. I needed to be safe in the police station by the time night came – the vampires could challenge each other all they wanted, but there was no way I planned on being there to see it. I tried to swallow back my impatience as I asked, 'What's the message, Aggie?'

Her brown eyes filled with worry. 'Thee's no angry with maself?'

'Why would I be angry with you, Aggie?'

'The spells.' Her fingers twisted in her floral smock. 'I dinna ken they were so many, not until thee took them.'

Narrowing my eyes, I took a step towards her. '*What* spells?' She flinched back and I stilled, not wanting to frighten her. Then I remembered Finn's little test. 'Aggie, you're not worried about all that extra magic that Finn added, are you? He was just being tricksy with me; it wasn't your fault.' I stuck my hands in the back pockets of my jeans. 'Is that why you were unhappy afterwards?'

'Maself is awfy sorry.' Her sand-coloured face creased up even more. 'I've bin worrid stoopid, thee might think I'd tried to deceive thee, Lady.'

'I'm not angry, okay?' I smiled, lips tight together. 'Now what is Holly's message?'

'The wean telt me to bring thee to her.' Her small nose wrinkled up. 'Her friend be wanting to ask thee something, Lady.'

I shook my head. 'Aggie, I'm sorry, but I just don't have the time right now. I know it's Sunday, but it would take nearly an hour to get to the restaurant and another to get back, even today.'

'Twill only take a wee minute or two.' She held out her small hand to me. 'We'll go Between – only thee will need to be quiet, mind.' She shook her hand eagerly at me, a slyness creeping into her expression. 'The Lady Meriel would be pleased if thee would come.'

Meriel of Lake Serpentine – the Lady of the local naiads, a group of water fae – and supposedly not someone to be messed with, not that I'd ever personally met her.

'Why would Lady Meriel be pleased?'

Aggie gave me a smug smile. 'The Lady be Holly's ma, o'course.'

Holly was Meriel's daughter? Well that explained why Holly had Aggie looking after her – and why it was probably a good idea to go and see what Holly wanted. No way could I afford to alienate any of the local fae, not while I still had a chance.

'Hold on two secs, Aggie.' I walked over to my computer, scribbled a note to Hugh and stuck it on the screen. When I turned back round, Aggie was peering into a cupboard. She swung round, smock billowing, a disapproving scowl on her face. 'Thee has nae food, Lady, nothin' but a jar o' sweeties and some salt.' Tufts of her hair stuck up. ''Tis nae way to be runnin' a kitchen.'

'Maybe you can help me then,' I said, an idea popping into my head. 'I've still got all those spells I took from your kitchen, Agatha, but I can't seem to make them do anything.'

'Och well,' her scowl faded, 'I telt thee, a brownie's touch goes to them that needs it. The magic will nae be leaving you until you've nae more need of it' – she patted her chest – 'for the sadness in here, Lady.'

Well, that sort of explained it … 'Thank you, Agatha,' I inclined my head, 'it was kind of you to tell me.'

'Humph.' She closed the cupboard door with a firm snap. 'Are thee ready then?' she asked, offering me her small hand.

Hesitating only slightly, I placed my hand in Aggie's. 'I still need to get back as soon as,' I warned.

'Och, I'll see you wherever, nae worries. Hold tight an' quiet, Lady.' She took a breath, lifted her foot—

A loud popping sound reverberated in my ears. Aggie's fingers squeezed mine painfully hard. My flat took on a misty hue. Pressure buffeted me as winds blew from every point. A ghostly image of a different kitchen flashed past. Then another, where the ethereal figure of a young boy sat, head bent over his colouring book. Two more unoccupied rooms and then the indistinct sight of an old man, socked feet propped on a stool, holding a china teacup to his mouth. The pressure increased, making it hard to breathe. A semi-derelict room with a broken butler's sink. A steel band clamped round my chest. A hazy, red-faced woman wiped a floury stain across her forehead with the back of her wrist. The force on my body was almost unbearable as the stronger outlines of the next kitchen took form around us: stainless steel tops, commercial ovens, stacks of white china ...

... Aggie put her foot down, released her grip on my hand. 'Here we be, safe and sound.'

I stumbled, head spinning, stomach churning like a food mixer.

She grabbed my hand again, patted it. 'There ye go.' A sudden warmth cleared my mind. 'The brownies' trail is a wee bitty fast for some, mebbe.'

I took a look around. We were in Aggie's kitchen at the restaurant. 'Well,' I gave her an impressed look, 'that's certainly one quick way to get across London.'

'Och, away with ye.' Her wrinkled face pulled up in a smile. 'Now go an' see ma wean and her friend.' She gave me a shove on the backside with her small hand. 'They're in there.'

The interior of the restaurant was dark, the blinds drawn. I stood for a moment letting my eyes get accustomed to the dimness.

Holly waved at me from the darkest corner of the room.

I took half-a-dozen steps, then my feet faltered. Her 'friend' was Louis, the French Psycho vamp from the police station.

Chapter Thirty-Seven

What was Psycho Louis doing here? More to the point, what was he doing up? The late afternoon sun was still blazing outside; I'd been counting on the vamps not being around until after dark.

'Genny,' Holly waved again, 'it's great that you could come, isn't it, Louis?'

As I got to the table, Louis half-stood and bowed his head. 'Mademoiselle, Enchanté.' He sank tiredly back. The lace at his throat and wrists was startlingly white against the rich green velvet of his jacket, and a matching velvet ribbon caught his tawny hair loosely at his nape. But the burn mark from the police's spelled silver circlet was still a livid line across his forehead; maybe healing wasn't one of his powers.

Holly clutched his arm. She'd threaded her own black waterfall of curls with green satin ribbons, and pulled her peasant blouse down to leave her creamy shoulders bare. She gave me a wide grin, her sharp, triangular teeth gleaming like phosphorescence, and I had a sudden thought that maybe Louis had bitten off more than he could swallow.

'Louis has to ask you something.' She turned an excited face to him. 'Only he doesn't speak English very well, do you?'

'Non, mon coeur.'

She giggled. 'He calls me his heart, isn't that just so cool? After you were here, me and Aggie had a real bust-up and Dad insisted—'

'Dad?' I interrupted.

'It's Dad's restaurant. I'm working fulltime now I've finished

300

school. You met him.'

Right: Mr Manager with the shiny shoes.

'Anyway' – Holly squeezed another nonexistent millimetre closer to Louis – 'Dad insisted we go and see Mother.'

'The Lady Meriel.'

'Yeah. Mother said it was okay for me to date Louis as long as he came and talked to her first.' She tugged on his arm like a child with a new toy. 'Isn't that great?'

Louis nodded back. He might not speak the language, but he appeared to have no problem understanding it – or maybe he was just interpreting Holly's enthusiasm. It wasn't hard to follow.

He broke in with a voluble torrent of words, then said in a thick accent, 'You tell pleeeze, mon coeur.'

She nodded. 'He wants to apologise for the misunderstanding in the police station. He realises now that this country is much nicer than he was told. I think some of the other vamps had a bit of a joke with him, told him that the police were all stake-happy or something.'

I gave Louis a sceptical look.

He flashed me an arrogant smirk, complete with sharp white fangs. Whatever Holly's mother had got him to promise might make him safe for Holly, but the psycho part was still there, just itching to get out. I hoped Holly's mother had made the agreement watertight – or rather, *bloodtight*.

'Anyway, Louis's not here for very long. Once he's finished his job, he's got to go back to France. Dad and Aggie aren't too happy about us seeing each other, but Mother says, what better way for me to learn about' – she lowered her voice, a deep blush colouring her cheeks – 'about sex, than with someone that's got a good three hundred years' experience?'

Louis gave a self-satisfied lift of his lips.

'And Mother's even arranged somewhere with children for Aggie, now that I'm grown up, so she'll be happy and won't end up breathing down my neck all the time.'

I thought Aggie was far more likely to breathe down Louis' neck, or maybe sic him with some of her nasty little brownie magic. But it looked like everyone was getting something they wanted, even the vampire. So what was I doing here, because it sure as hell wasn't just for Psycho Louis to apologise?

Holly opened her mouth, but Louis interrupted with an elegant lift of one shoulder that reminded me uncomfortably of Malik and said, 'I wish you to find she-witch.'

'Yeah, that's what he wants me to ask you.' Holly grinned. 'See there's this witch that used to work for his boss, only she doesn't any more, for some reason. But he's got to find her and talk to her.'

I sighed. 'Tell him I'm not a detective.'

Holly rattled away to him.

In answer, Louis reached into his jacket and produced a small photo.

'That's her,' exclaimed Holly. 'That's who he wants you to find.'

Louis held out the photo to me. 'Is this what he was asking me at the police station?'

Louis nodded, staring at me, his eyes full of disdain. 'The Earl, he want finding she-witch himself. For reward.'

So Louis hadn't developed a sudden desire for Detective Inspector Crane. I ignored his outstretched hand. 'What reward?'

He slid the photo across the table. Curiosity got the better of me and I gave it a quick glance.

It was a headshot, face on. The witch looked to be some-where in her twenties or thirties; it was difficult to put an age on her because she was so fat. She'd succumbed to sugar abuse, trying to boost her magic too far past its natural abilities. A mass of brown hair hung either side of her face and her mouth had a pinched look about it. Her bright blue eyes would have been her main feature, but the pads over her cheekbones made them look too small. I'd never seen her, only—

Louis threw another stream of words at me.

Holly gasped and leaned forward, peering at the photo. 'He says that she is a very powerful, *dangerous* witch, that she's *killed*, using *magic*. He thinks she might be hiding amongst the other witches, but she's got 3V, so she might be coming to HOPE. He wants you to see if you can find her before she kills again.'

Louis fished something else from his jacket and placed it next to the photo.

'He says the witch will not be harmed,' Holly translated. 'He just wants to talk to her. There is some information his boss needs.'

Yeah, right. Like I was going to believe that.

I looked at the piece of paper. It was a cheque, payable to me. I swallowed as I read the number of noughts. That would go way past ending my employment worries.

'He wants to know if this is enough payment. If not,' Holly squeaked, her eyes rounding like saucers, 'he says that whatever you desire he will get. More money, gems, stocks and shares, property, whatever.'

My head jerked up in surprise. *Shit.* He really was bringing out the big incentive guns. 'What's so important about this information?'

Holly looked at Louis, then reported, 'His boss has some sort of sickness and she has made a spell that makes him better.'

Of course he was after the spell, just like all the other vamps. It hadn't taken much to work that out. And now I'd discharged my debt to Declan, I didn't need to look for it, but ...

'Ask him what the spell actually does?' I told her.

Louis shook his head, lips pressed tight together, as Holly said, 'He doesn't know.'

Or wasn't about to tell me, more like! I tapped my finger on the photo. Psycho Louis was the first vamp to ask me to find a witch and not the spell – none of the other vamps had mentioned a witch. Did that mean they didn't know about her? Or— *Of course!* How stupid could I get? She was a witch, and even if they did know who or where she was, they had no way of reaching her other than through the Witches' Council – so they'd gone for the next best thing. Me.

What was it the Earl had wanted? He'd wanted me to find the spell and absorb it. And I was betting that whatever the spell did, it wasn't something cute like producing fluffy bunnies from top hats. Maybe he thought I could regurgitate it in one piece … although thinking about it, he wasn't far wrong – which made me wonder just exactly where the Earl had got his information about me. I shoved that thought aside for later.

But if Psycho Louis was here for the spell, then why was he wasting his time playing kissy-face with Holly? Okay, she was a faeling with a powerful mother, and she probably tasted good, but … Something nagged me, just at the edge of my memory.

I picked up the photo – maybe I could use it to get me into Inspector Crane's good books – and pasted on a fake smile. 'Can I have this?'

Louis nodded with enthusiasm.

I tucked it into my waistcoat pocket and stood up. 'Holly, tell him the answer's no. In fact' – I picked up the cheque, tore it in two – 'that will save you the translation.'

Louis' brows knitted together and he glared up at me. 'Meestake. You make bad meestake.'

Leaning down, I placed my hands flat on the table. 'Not in my book, mate.' I looked at Holly, clinging open-mouthed to his arm. 'I hope your mother knows what she's doing.'

I left them and strode back into the kitchen. 'Time to go, Agatha.'

'She'll be back in a couple of mins.' Mick was slouched in a heap on the floor. His red hair hung wet and dripping down his neck, and something I decided not to look too closely at was smeared across one cheek and down one side of his long coat.

'What the hell are you doing here, Mick?'

304

'I'm following you, of course,' he sniffed. 'Aggie's gone to sort out one of her kitchens. I messed it up when I came through.' He wrapped his coat tighter round him. 'Jeeesus, I hate the brownies' trail, it always makes me want to puke.'

I crouched down, frowning. 'Why are you following me?'

He looked sideways at me. 'Y'know you asked Fiona about the spell?'

'Don't tell me,' I said flatly, 'she's remembered all about it now.'

'Okay, I won't.' His bottom lip stuck out and he said petulantly, 'You should've asked me, Genny.'

'So why didn't you say something back there?'

He gave a sulky shrug. 'You weren't very nice about Seamus.'

Rolling my eyes, I said, 'Fine. Mick, I'm sorry I was nasty to you and Seamus. Now, what about the damn spell?'

He sniffed again. 'It does something to turn fae into a sort of battery pack for a vampire. The vamp gets a big boost from it; he doesn't need to touch or even feed, apparently. Specially if it's someone powerful, like you.' He swallowed, his Adam's apple bobbing in his skinny neck. 'Only it's got some hitches. It doesn't always work on faelings, or else some of them die. And the vamps still can't get us in a mind-lock.'

Fuck. I'd been right: the spell was definitely not fluffy bunny rabbits.

Then the nagging memory about Holly caught up with me.

I glanced around. It was here, in the kitchen. I'd been getting ready to *call* the brownie spells, the ones cast by Aggie and Finn. Holly had stood in the doorway, the light misting behind her. Only it hadn't been light, it had been the spell.

Holly had had the spell in her – Louis must have tasted it when he'd fed on her – the spell the vamps were looking for.

And I'd *called* it from her.

I almost laughed; I hadn't needed to find the spell. I'd had it all the time.

Holly flung herself through the swing doors. 'Louis says he'll double his offer to one million.'

Then another memory hit me. I'd seen the spell again, earlier today, in fact, when it had been misting round Finn.

Chapter Thirty-Eight

The Rosy Lee's kitchen took shape around me, the high-level grills and deep fat fryers coming into sharp focus. My feet touched tiled floor and Agatha's small hand melted from mine. I gasped for breath as my stomach tumbled in freefall. I took another step and lurched forwards, landing on my hands and knees, staring down into a face I'd hoped never again to see this close.

Gazza, the Cheap Goth, sneered up at me. For a moment I half-thought I was back in the alley with him as blood and snot bubbled round the safety pin in his broken nose. He groaned, and revulsion made me scramble backwards. Then I stopped.

Thin black rope was wrapped tight round his body in neat, equally distanced circles. A precise line of knots ran from under his chin down to his ankles. He thrashed violently, groaning again, but the sound was muffled and I realised there was something stuffed in his mouth.

What the—? Someone had trussed him up like a side of beef ready for the oven. I poked him in stunned amazement.

He made more angry sounds and the bloody snot expanded, then splat against his skin.

A noise behind me had me jerking round to see Freddie rushing into the kitchen, one of his carving knives hefted in his right hand. He rushed towards me and I dived and tucked myself under the prep counter. He swerved to follow me.

'Slow down, Freddie,' I yelled, keeping my eye on the knife.

I was almost sure he wasn't out to get me, but you don't

take chances when a twenty-stone chef is running at you brandishing over a foot of gleaming steel blade.

'Genny, thank God you're here,' he wheezed. 'I've been trying to call you.' He bent, gasping, hands on his knees. 'You weren't answering your phone.'

'I'm here now, Freddie,' I said, keeping my voice calm, 'so put the knife down, okay?'

He glanced down, obviously baffled to see the knife in his hand. It clattered to the floor. 'Sorry Genny.' He smacked his hand on his bald head. 'God knows, but I just didn't know what to do.'

I crawled out and grabbed his arm. 'Freddie, what's going on?'

'Katie didn't come in to work today. I phoned her mum, and she said Katie'd gone out with a friend last night, and rung to say she was staying over and not to worry.'

Dread twisted in my gut. 'What's Katie got to do with him?'

He took a deep breath and threw a disgusted look at Gazza by the fridge. 'This piece of shite here came strolling in with a message.' The muscles in Freddie's arm bunched under my hand. 'For you.'

'What's the message?' I shouted over the pulse thundering in my ears.

'He wouldn't tell me, said he had to tell you and only you.' Freddie's face crunched up with disgust. 'The little shite told me I could make him lunch while he waited!' He kicked Gazza on his ankle and a muffled squeal of rage came from behind the gag. 'Well, I made *him* lunch, just as he wanted.'

Freddie swung down and ripped the cloth from Gazza's mouth. 'Go on then, arsehole, give her the goddamned message.'

'Fuckinfaeriefreakansstupidbastoldman—'

Freddie slapped Gazza across the face. 'Tell her, you piece of shite.' He pointed to the carver on the floor. 'Or I'll start slicing bits off you.'

'You don't frighten me, you stupid old man! Nothing hurts any more – he told me it wouldn't. Said he'd make it all better too, whatever you did,' he sniggered. 'So you can go fuck yourself.' He stared up at me. 'And you, faerie freak, he's got big plans for you, and he said—'

I smacked my hand onto his forehead and slid into the tangled net of his thoughts. A rope of black twisted snake-like through them. Snagging it in a tendril of gold, I yanked on it and ordered, 'Just give me the fucking message!'

'The count sends his regards.' I got a brief image of Red Poet on the stage at the Blue Heart. 'He wants to offer you the staring role in his play.' Gazza's voice came out fast, excited. 'Only this time it won't be staged in the graveyard, but in the watering hole of the heart. If you're not there by midnight, he says he'll use your understudy. And it's a private audience only, so don't think about issuing any invitations.'

Shitshitshit.

Freddie thumped his hands on the counter. 'He means Katie, doesn't he? For God's sake, Genny, what does the bastard *want*?'

Gazza spewed another stream of abuse and Freddie shoved the cloth back in his mouth.

Katie.

The count, aka Red Poet – the leader of the fang-gang – had got her at the Leech & Lettuce, and I had to get her out. My heart squeezed in my chest and for a moment I couldn't think, didn't know what to do.

Then I remembered Finn and the spell. I had to find him. *Can't do two things at once.* I grabbed Freddie's arm. 'You have to phone Old Scotland Yard. You need to speak to Detective Sergeant Hugh Munro.'

He snatched up an order pad. 'He's the big red troll, isn't he?'

'Yeah, make sure you speak to him, or one of the other trolls. Lamber or Taegrin. They'll know what to do!' I shook

Freddie. 'Tell them that Katie is being held at the Leech & Lettuce in Sucker Town. It's a blood house, they'll know the one.' I watched, impatient, as he started writing it down. 'I have to find Finn first, he's in trouble too, but tell Hugh I'll meet him down there as soon as I can.'

Freddie glanced up from his careful writing. 'I saw Finn go into the office about an hour ago. Don't think he's come out yet.'

'Great! Thanks, Freddie,' I shouted as I ran out into the empty café. I pushed the closed sign to one side to turn the lock, then raced across the street to Spellcrackers.

Chapter Thirty-Nine

The door to Spellcrackers was locked. I pressed my finger to the intercom, tapping my foot with impatience.

'Spellcrack—' came a voice.

'Toni, it's me,' I called, cutting her off.

'Oh hi, Genny, hold on. I'll buzz you in.'

There was a click and I shoved open the door and dashed in. Toni stared down at me from the top of the stairs. She was eye-catchingly bright in a slim cerise sundress and purple bolero jacket, her pink and purple hair extensions curling like they belonged on the Medusa. I ran up, taking the treads two at a time.

'Hold on, Honeybee,' Toni laughed, 'what's all the rush for? You're not supposed to be at work until tomorrow.'

'Sorry, Toni,' I gasped, 'can't stop. Have to see Finn.'

She caught my arm, a sly grin on her face. 'You found out about his tail yet?'

'Later, okay?' I shook her hand off, tried to squeeze past her.

'Hey, no problem.' She winked and moved to let me through. 'You'll find the horny sex god in his office. I'm just going to double-check the entrance, those kids are driving—'

I raced to the end of the corridor and flung the door wide open. Finn was leaning back in his chair, his feet propped on a couple of box files.

'There's a spell,' I gasped, slapping my hands on his desk, 'a real nasty one, and someone's tagged you with it!'

'Hello, Gen.' He swivelled his chair round to face me.

'It's to do with the vampires, lets them steal power from us—' I could hardly get the words out fast enough.

He ran a hand through his hair and scratched behind his left horn. 'Why are you here, Gen? I left a message on your phone to stay away.'

'Dammit, Finn, didn't you hear what I just said?'

'Yes, I heard.' Sweat beaded on his forehead.

Fuck. He so didn't look so good. I *looked*. The mist clung to him like a thick second skin. 'Shit, it's all over you!'

He pushed himself out of his chair and stood up. 'I know all about the spell, Gen,' he said, sounding tired.

I blinked. 'You do?'

He came up to me and tucked a strand of hair behind my ear. 'I felt it earlier, when I tried to pull that stunt on Helen: something draining at me, sucking me dry. I didn't realise what it was then.'

My heart thudded against my ribs. Mick said the spell only killed faelings. Finn was fae. What if Mick was wrong? Swallowing back my fear, I wrapped my hand round Finn's wrist. His skin was hot and clammy. I slid gold tendrils of magic into him, searching.

'Finn, I think I can *call* the spell, take it from—'

He gave me a sad smile. 'It's too late Gen.' He lifted my chin with his forefinger and touched his mouth gently to mine. 'Way too late.'

Jagged thorns ripped through my heart, bled grief like acid juice. In the far reaches of his mind, a desolate wind scoured all before it.

Damn. What was he doing – why was he fighting me? Didn't he know I was trying to help?

I built a hedge of golden hope to keep the wind out.

Sliding my hand round Finn's neck, I pulled him down. 'Don't fight me, Finn.' I pressed my lips to his, spilling my Glamour into his mouth. 'I know how to—'

Something stung my upper arm.

Yelping, I jerked away. A pinprick of blood spotted my skin. Eyes wide, I looked at him.

'What the—?'

'I'm sorry, Gen.'

'Sorry?' I frowned, bemused, glanced at the blood again. Then back at him.

He held up something that looked like a short pen. 'I wasn't fighting you.' His voice was dull.

I couldn't feel my arm, couldn't move it. There was no pain, just spreading numbness. And then I knew what it was. He'd injected me with iron filings. They'd slip through my body, numbing me as they went, until they reached my brain ... and I'd be unconscious – or maybe worse ...

I stared at him, speechless, and lost my hold on the magic.

The wind screamed against the golden hedge, turned it brittle with despair. The mist escaped like grey smoke swirling into the sky.

Horror sliced through me. He'd been containing the spell, and now he'd let it go. Finn's face wavered, then doubled. I gazed at the two of him disappearing into the mist as the greyness filled the room.

He touched my cheek. 'You really shouldn't have come looking for me. You should've gone to Hugh. You'd have been safe there.'

Safe? My lips tried to form the question. The room tilted as I felt his arms wrap around me, then he lowered me to the floor.

'I didn't want to hurt you, my Lady.' His eyes swam through the grey. Only they weren't the moss-green I knew; there was something wrong with them. They were like algae-covered pools, waiting to suck me down. Then his tears splashed emerald chips into the greyness.

I tried to catch them with my fingers.

Green stems pushed their way into the fog, seeking for something to hold onto.

'Oh good, hon, you've done it.' The voice was female, brisk.

The fog closed over the stems, hid them from my Sight.

'Did you inject her over the heart?' the voice said.

'You should've let me stun her.' Finn's voice was harsh. 'This is too dangerous.'

'No. This way is better. If you'd stunned her, she might have *cracked* it before you'd hit her – much too risky. She's been iffy with magic lately. Too much salt in her diet.'

I had to banish the fog. I had to find the stems.

Gold light flared, formed trembling tendrils that curled into the greyness. One green shoot crept its way up through the fog.

'I told you, she's too strong. Even half out of it, she's trying to use her Glamour. It has to be the heart. Lift up her top.'

'No, I won't.' But it was more a plea than a determined denial.

'Finn, there's no way you can gainsay me, not with the spells I've tagged you with, so stop fighting and just get on with it.'

Pink and purple streamers slithered through the grey, twisting over and along the fragile green stem. The stem shivered and struggled and writhed in pain, trying to be free. But the streamers wrapped around and around, until there was nothing but a thrashing nest of brightly coloured snakes.

Feverish fingers traced over my skin.

'That's it, do it there. I'll hold her down.' Weight pressed against my ribs. 'Sorry, Honeybee, but this is going to hurt like the Nine Circles of Hell.'

The sting was a tiny, distant pain. She'd been wrong. Somewhere I laughed.

The fog bloomed with golden flowers.

Then cold iron filled my chest.

And the flowers withered.

Chapter Forty

My inner vamp sense told me sunset had long gone and night was here. My eyeballs felt like they'd been rubbed with sandpaper and my lids stuck together with Super Glue. Fear made my pulse jump in my throat. It jagged with pain. I lay frozen and listened.

I could hear a faint noise: shallow, fast breaths.

My heart pounded as my eyes snapped open. I stared, fearful, at the fuzzy greyness. Mouth dry, I blinked and the greyness resolved itself into a carved rock ceiling. Wincing, I slowly turned my head towards the light. There was a door about five feet away, steel, like the ones at the Bloody Shamrock. I sniffed, and caught a whiff of earthy dampness. I was in a cave, somewhere underground.

Why couldn't I remember what had happened?

I tried to sieve the confusion from my mind.

Venom fizzed through my veins, but its usual lust-hyped high was muted; my body felt like one big bruise. And I could smell blood. Had I been caught feeding? Was that why I felt like I'd been in a slugfest with a horde of Beater goblins? My stomach clenched in hunger and I ran my tongue over my fangs in anticipation – only I didn't have fangs, just teeth. Confusion slipped back into fear. Had I become so melded with the Alter Vamp spell that I no longer knew which body I wore? The blood snagged at my senses again. It smelled of sour blackberries.

And memory rushed back like a charging troll, smashing my fears into insignificant pieces.

Finn was somewhere nearby.

Toni the bitch witch had tagged Finn with the spell, and tied it with some sort of compulsion magic – no way would he poison me with cold iron. I visualised Toni's face, compared it with the photo Psycho Louis had shown me. Now I knew what I was looking for I could see the similarities. Toni might have lost a lot of weight, but her eyebrows and nose were still the same.

'Gen?' Finn's voice was quiet, hardly more than a whisper.

I slowly turned towards his voice. The cave room went back almost thirty feet, the ceiling sloping down to meet the floor at the end. In the gloom I could make out a body. Finn.

'Gen?' The anxious whisper came again.

I tried to say his name, but all I managed was a croak. I touched my sore throat. There was a swollen lump the size of a golf ball. *Shit.* Whichever sucker Toni had palled up with, they'd sunk their fangs into me.

I checked out my arms. I had three other bite marks: one on my right wrist and the others at the pulse points inside my elbows. I wrinkled my nose at the map of blue veins wriggling under my skin. The suckers had almost bled me dry.

No wonder I felt so depleted.

At least I still had my clothes on. I'd only been venom-fucked, nothing else.

'Are you okay?' Finn's voice was louder.

'Yeah,' I whispered. 'Give me a sec.'

I rolled onto my front, got my hands flat underneath me.

'Gen, I want you to come here to me.'

The words hit me like a hard promise, raised shivers over my skin. I got up onto my elbows and rested my head on my forearms for a moment, then dragged my legs up until I was on my knees. Panting, I peered down towards Finn. I caught the emerald gleam of his eyes.

'C'mon, Gen. I'm waiting.'

Lust twisted sharp thorns in my belly, venom fizzed in my

veins and both drew a painful gasp from my mouth. I started crawling, my hands and denim-clad knees scraping the stone, muscles protesting with aching soreness.

'My Lady, I need you.'

'I hear you,' I whispered. The soreness in my body dissipated, pushed aside by a more urgent craving. I crawled faster.

'Genny,' he crooned.

I stopped, shaking, my skin flushing with heat. The throb between my legs and at my throat was hard, insistent, almost too painful to bear. My head buzzed and the cave swam and swayed into greyness.

'Gen—'

'Dammit, Finn,' I croaked past another wave of lust, 'keep your Glamour to yourself. My body can't deal with it. I've lost too much blood.'

Silence. Then, 'I'm sorry.' His voice was soothing. 'I thought it would help.'

The desperate need inside me blunted and the aching my body had ignored returned with a gleeful vengeance. Crap. I gritted my teeth and started crawling again: slow but steady, that was the way.

Hand ... knee ... swallow ... pant.

'I don't know when she gave me the spell.' Finn's voice washed with anger. 'You know, the spell you came to tell me about? It sucks the magic out of you.'

Hand ... knee ...

'Psychic vampirism, the bitch called it. She's worked it so a sucker can bind a fae's power and use it as their own.' Fear flowed beneath the anger. 'You don't even have to know about it. No need for negotiations and bargains, just a cocktail of blood and spell and that's you.'

Swallow ... pant ...

Damn. It all fitted with what Mick had told me – and I'd a good idea that Toni had tagged me with the spell too, but for some reason it hadn't worked so well on me.

I reached Finn, my lungs gasping for air

'You need to get out, Gen,' he said quietly, staring at the ceiling.

Of course, the 'getting out' involved steel doors and solid rock, and I doubted I could blast through them with magic, even if I knew how.

'There's some sort of fight going on,' he added. 'The sucker's siphoning off my power to win.'

I tried to catch my breath as I peered through the half-darkness at him. They'd stripped him naked and staked him out, stretching his limbs to the four points. The Glamour he'd been wearing to appear more human had gone, dispersed by the gem-studded silver shackles on his wrists and ankles, or maybe he just hadn't the energy left to *hold* it. His body was broader, muscles heavier, his skin more darkly tanned than before. Sleek sable hair covered his stomach and his flanks, then smoothed like silk down his legs until it feathered over his hard cloven hooves.

Lifting my head, I crawled closer. His horns were small stubs almost hidden in his matted hair and he was covered in blood – his blood. I briefly closed my eyes as the scent of blackberries made my stomach twist with need. Hanging my head, I willed the hunger away. Deep wounds scored down Finn's chest and stomach, and bite marks punctured his skin. The familiar-looking injuries told me which sucker Toni had palled up with, which sucker was using him: *Rio*.

He turned to look at me. His face was pinched, almost feral, the bones sharp under his skin. But it was his eyes I stared at. They were dull, grey, desolate with the spell.

'You need to get undressed, Gen,' he said wearily.

'What?' My mouth fell open. That was the last thing I'd expected.

'I've been waiting for you to wake up. There's a chance you can escape using a blood door.' His gaze held mine, then he looked away again, as if it hurt him for me to see him like this.

'Only you have to go naked, in supplication. It won't work otherwise.'

I knew of blood doors. I'd even been through one once, taken by another fae. Once you activated the spell, it took you straight to the person who'd shared the ritual with you.

I frowned, slumping back on my heels. 'Don't they have to be pre-arranged?'

'You need to go to Helen.' His voice caught as he said her name. 'Ask her for aid.'

Oh right, Helen, as in Inspector Crane.

'Helen and I have performed the blood exchange. We did it when we jumped the broom before—' A spasm of pain cut him off.

They'd jumped the broom? When did that happen? And before what? Before they split up? They couldn't be still together, could they? An odd feeling slipped from beneath my heart, as though I'd lost something I never had to begin with. I shrugged it off. No wonder the inspector didn't like me. Still, priorities: escape first, pity-party later.

'Great plan,' I said, brightly. 'I'll *crack* the spells holding you.' I pulled off my T-shirt. 'Then once you're out of the shackles, I'll absorb the psychic-spell and you can take us through.' I tugged off a boot.

'Gen, *cracking* the spells isn't going to work.' He slowly turned his head back to me and gave me a shadow of his normal smile. 'I really don't want to lose any of my appendages.'

I levered off the other boot, paused as a wave of dizziness hit me. 'Then I'll absorb those spells too.'

'You can't absorb the shackles, and absorbing the spells could knock you out, or worse.'

I unsnapped my jeans. 'Who cares, Finn?' I wriggled the denim over my hips. 'If you can't carry me, you can always drag me.'

'Be realistic, Gen,' he sighed. 'You have to go to Helen and get help. You have to go alone.'

'I'm not leaving without you.'

'The sucker will be back soon, and the closer she is, the more power she can take from me.' His hands clenched. 'You need to go as soon as possible.'

I almost screamed in frustration and fear – this wasn't how it was supposed to go. Taking a deep breath, I said, 'Okay, tell me how to do it.'

'We do the ritual, then you have to stand in a circle of your own blood and *call* to Helen. Once she feels the *call*, she'll open the door.'

'What's the ritual, Finn?'

'Nothing drastic, just blood freely offered and exchanged.'

I stared at him in horror. 'You mean I drink your blood and then spill mine over the floor, then wait for your ex to answer.'

'Yes, that's pretty much it.' His eyes drifted closed. 'I think that should work.'

'What do you mean, "should"? Don't you *know*?'

'I'm working from memory here,' he murmured. 'It's not easy.'

Crap. I couldn't drink his blood. Just the smell was tempting enough. And what if it didn't work, or Helen didn't answer? He'd end up in more danger from me than the vamps we were trying to escape from. Of course, there was still my other option: I could bring out my Alter Vamp and just break his shackles ... only she wasn't strong enough to get us out of the cave, or to fight off more than a couple of other vamps. And she – *I* – would be right back to being hungry.

'You have to do it, Gen,' he said quietly. 'I can't kill the sucker, I've already tried. I can feel her in me, controlling me, feeding off me, like she's turned a tap on and I can't turn it off.' He turned his head away again.

Something about that didn't tally; I hadn't noticed the spell at all, not even after I'd taken it from Holly – nothing other than tiredness, and maybe the bad dreams—

'She's not going to let me fade—' Finn's words shattered my thoughts. He was talking about fading – letting himself die – shit, it had to be bad. 'Gen, you have to go and get help—' He was almost pleading with me.

Heart aching, I finished tugging off my jeans and briefs as another flash of dizziness hit me. 'Okay, let's do it,' I said.

He turned back to face me, hope turning the grey in his eyes back to their usual green for an instant.

'Looks like it's my turn to ride to the rescue.' I gave him a lop-sided smile.

'What are you talking 'bout, Gen?'

Leaning over, I gave him a butterfly kiss on the mouth. 'You running off to do the shining knight bit earlier when the witches kicked me out of Spellcrackers.'

He gave a weak laugh. 'If I'd known it'd impress you, I'd have tried it sooner, instead of the cheesy sex god line.'

'Don't worry; the sex god thing is pretty impressive too.' I opened my eyes wide to keep the tears from falling, grinned at him. 'Just don't tell anyone I said so.'

Chapter Forty-One

All I had to do was bleed a large enough puddle that I could stand in. I grimaced at the blue veins mapping my naked body. Getting blood out of one of them wasn't going to be easy.

'Why can't I just draw a circle in blood?' I asked.

'It doesn't work that way, Gen.' Finn gave another weary sigh. 'It's a sacrifice, a last resort thing, so no one opens a blood door without thinking seriously about it.'

Yeah, right. Heart labouring in my chest, I clambered to my feet, checked out my left wrist. Maybe I'd be lucky and the vein wouldn't have healed yet.

I raised my wrist to my mouth.

'What are you doing?' Finn was watching me.

'I haven't got a knife.'

'Use one of my horns.'

'They won't be sharp enough.'

'The spells in the restraints aren't muting my magic, they're just stopping me from getting free. And the sucker's not getting all of it; I'm holding back as much power as I can.' His chin jutted out. 'Touch one.'

I crouched near his head and gently pressed my finger to one of his horns. It quivered, its ridges scraping against my fingertip as it elongated and stiffened until it was seven inches of smooth curved horn, its tip sharp, like a whittled bone.

'You need to do it quick, Gen.' His eyes were closed again, face tight with strain.

I wrapped my hand round his horn and he groaned, low and deep. Pleasure or pain? I wasn't sure.

'Hurry.'

Gritting my teeth, I pressed my inner arm against the sharp point, pushed until it pierced the skin. Blood seeped sluggishly out of the wound. I waited for the pain, but it didn't come. Jerking my arm back, I scored a deep cut from my inner elbow to my wrist.

The blood welled slowly and I stared at it transfixed.

The tattoo on my hip throbbed like a second heart. My nostrils flared as I drew the sweet smell into my lungs. My mouth watered. The urge to rub my blood into the tattoo filled my mind like the cry of a rapacious spirit. I gazed at Finn, at the wounds on his body, and felt nothing but hunger.

And he couldn't get away.

My mouth stretched in a smile.

'Have you finished?' Finn whispered.

Suddenly appalled at my own thoughts, I scrambled back from him.

'Gen?' His horn was shrinking back down into his hair. 'What's the matter?'

'Nothing,' I looked at the floor, not wanting him to see the hunger in my face. Holding out my arm, I squeezed the wound, watched the blood trickle into a puddle the size of a teacup.

'Gen, we need to do the ritual first.'

'I'm doing it,' I muttered.

'You can't. You haven't taken my blood.'

'And I'm not going to, Finn. There's someone else I can *call* for a blood door, someone who can help us better than Helen can.'

'But you've got to go to Helen. She's the police.

'I know, but she upholds the humans' laws, Finn. We're fae. The human laws don't apply to us, not with things like this.'

'She'll still come,' he said with certainty. 'She's not going to leave me here.'

'Finn, you don't get it, do you. Helen is *police*. She has to go by the rule book whether she wants to or not.' *Look what she's just done to me*, I wanted to shout but didn't. Instead I carried on, trying to be calm. 'Technically, the vamps have done nothing wrong. She can't force her way in here, and no way is she going to start a full-scale war with the vamps, especially not on my say-so. And even if she does work out a way, by the time she gets past them and gets to you, there'll be nothing left to find. I'm sorry, Finn, but I'm not taking that chance.'

He turned his head away.

The pool of blood was the size of a plate.

'You're going to the sucker, aren't you? The one from last night.'

What if the blood door didn't work?

'Gen you don't have to do this, Take my blood, go to Helen, she'll come, I know she will.'

I looked at Finn, lying shackled to the floor. No way was I going to take his blood – if I fell into bloodlust, how was I going to stop?

'I thought you were dead,' Finn whispered. 'I thought I'd killed you. I didn't know a sidhe could survive cold iron like that.'

My heart fluttered with palpitations. I answered him without thinking. 'It's the human blood in me.'

The quick movement of his head caught my attention. 'No part of you is human, Gen, not with those eyes.'

'My mother was sidhe, my father was human.' *Or he was once*, I added silently.

'Then you would be faeling.'

'I'm not.'

After a moment he spoke again. 'They brought you in and started feeding on you. She made me watch …'

I looked at him, horror invading my mind. He wouldn't have, would he? 'What did you promise her?' I breathed, not sure if I actually wanted to know.

'I couldn't let them do that to you,' he murmured, and I heard other words echo as he spoke. *I can't kill the sucker, I've already tried. I can feel her in me, controlling me, feeding off me.*

'It's not just the spell, is it?' I whispered as shock settled cold and hard inside me. 'You took the sucker's Blood-Bond, didn't you? That's how she's draining so much power from you – she's combined them together.'

'Gen, you have to get to Helen.' He looked at me and the fear and despair on his face gave me my answer. 'She can sort everything out. Fix this.'

Rio dead was the only way to fix this, and no way was Helen Crane going to kill her.

'I know you think Helen can't do anything,' he continued, 'but you're wrong about her. Going to that sucker for help isn't the right thing for you.'

Fucking shining knight complex! Even if I got him out of this mess he'd probably still come after me, still try and rescue me, thinking I was some distressed damsel he needed to save – and he'd get himself killed, or worse. No way could I let that happen. He had to know the truth.

I squeezed the slash on my arm again, forcing more blood out, concentrating on it instead of him. 'When I said my father was human, Finn, I meant he *was* human, before he became a vampire.' I kept my tone matter-of-fact. 'So you see, there really is only one place I can go for help, Finn. And that's to the vamps.'

'That's not possible; vamps can't reproduce like that.'

'My father found my mother at a fertility rite, got her pregnant, and then after I was born, he let her fade.' Of course the story wasn't as simple as that, but it covered the basics. 'Vamps have their own magic, Finn. And the sidhe can breed with anything magic – and most things not – you know that.'

He didn't answer, and I stared blindly at my blood as it dripped onto the stony ground.

A chill crept up my spine and my heart stuttered. I closed my eyes, ran my tongue over my teeth and sniffed at the air.

A glorious miasma of pain and fear and the liquorice scent of venom had me shifting uncomfortably.

The shush, shush *of his blood rushing through his veins, the fast* da-dum, da-dum *of his heart.*

'Gen?'

My eyes snapped open.

His pulse was jumping in his throat, his skin glowing with blood heat, and I was too close for safety.

'Gen, I think it's large enough now.'

'What?' I slurred.

'The blood. You've got enough now.'

I looked down. The puddle was larger than a dinner plate. I brought my arm to my mouth and slowly licked the blood off. The sweetness muted my hunger and I sighed. Then I noticed Finn, an odd, indecipherable expression on his face.

Shit. I'd finally succeeded in frightening him.

As I staggered to my feet, the cave swung round me like a fairground ride.

'Be careful, Gen.' Finn's voice was faint in my ears.

Frowning, I half-waved my hand. There was something else. What was it? Oh yeah. 'I'll come back, okay?'

His mouth moved, but my ears were ringing and I couldn't hear him.

The blood looked wonderful. I wanted to fall back to my knees and lap it up. I dipped my toe. I felt it cool against my skin. I stepped in, then lifted my other foot and set it down.

Dark.

Cave.

Dark.

A figure.

Dark.

The woman stood, head thrown back to expose her slender throat, mouth open wide. The image flickered on and off, like a silent movie.

Thick carpet beneath my feet, smell of sex and blood in my nose, buzzing in my ears.

The vampire stood behind her, his face buried in the curve of her neck, his jaw working.

Hunger hot in my stomach, I snarled, the vamp in me clawing to get out. I pushed my wrist down towards my tattoo.

My arm stilled in midair.

A shudder rippled through the woman and she grasped the vampire's dark hair and pulled him from her neck. She reached out and took my outstretched hand in hers.

She smiled, the smile of an angel, and that smile promised me whatever I wanted. Moving closer, she pressed her body up to mine. Her skin felt slick, hot with blood. Her heartbeat throbbed, pumping sweet life from the fang marks that pierced the swollen flesh at her neck. She tilted her head to the side and offered me her throat, the smile still playing on her face.

I shoved my fingers into her glossy dark hair and fed.

Chapter Forty-Two

The blood was hot and salty and thick – human blood – with an extra kick from a recent venom hit. And when that thought finally penetrated, so did another: the vampire sucking on her neck hadn't been Malik. The blood door hadn't worked, or at least not as I'd hoped.

I dragged my mouth from her throat and shoved her away. I threw my head back and stared at the ceiling, trying to calm the exhilarated thunder of my heart. I wanted more. I felt like I could feed on her forever. Clenching my fists, I looked down at my half-finished meal: Hannah Ashby, the ladylike account-ant who'd delivered the silver invitations, aka Corset Girl, the vamp junkie from the Leech & Lettuce.

She reclined on the floor, a more normal smile on her face. 'Well, that wasn't quite as exciting as I'd imagined, but I suppose allowances should be made.' She touched her hand to her still bleeding neck and pouted. 'I really was hoping for more than a quick snatch and suck. You're sidhe – I thought faeries were supposed to be hot.'

Ignoring her, I looked round at the stone ceiling, stone floor, steel door, thick navy rug and massive oak furniture. It all appeared horribly familiar. I was still in the same under-ground place, just in a different cave room. I strode to the door and waved at it. Nothing happened. A combination of anger, frustration and fear expanded like a whirlwind inside my head. I wanted to scream and cry, punch something, anything—

I concentrated on calming my thoughts. The blood had banished the hunger and the deep slice on my arm had almost healed, the skin knitting together in a raised red scar. Now I had to get out of here.

I wiped a hand over my mouth and walked back to where Hannah was sitting on the bed. 'Let's skip the after-dinner pleasantries, shall we? Instead, why don't you tell me what I'm doing here?'

'You need help, and I like to help people.'

'*Right*. Hijacking me is being so helpful.' I stuck my hands on my hips, 'I have to tell you, it's not working for me.'

'Oh, I didn't hijack you.' She tapped her chest. 'I felt the blood door open and offered.'

'Come off it, Hannah,' I snorted, 'until now I haven't had your blood.'

Her smile turned sly. 'But you did, a tiny taste, maybe, but enough to still count.' Reaching out, she stroked her fingers across the tattoo on my hip. 'You may not be wearing the same body, but that's a minor technicality. It appears that the two of you are becoming so entwined that there is almost no separation.'

I gritted my teeth. Had the need for blood pulled her – Rosa, my Alter Vamp – from – well, wherever she was, and given Hannah an opening? Maybe the tattoo hadn't worked in the gardens because Rosa hadn't been hungry? I pushed all the questions into a dark corner in my mind; I didn't have time for them.

No use crying over spilled – well, blood, I guessed. 'Again. What do you want?' I demanded.

'I like helping people, Genevieve. I find it very rewarding.' She stood and gestured behind her at the bed. The vamp sprawled across it, one leg hanging over the edge of the mattress as if he'd been so exhausted he'd just fallen onto it without conscious thought. 'For instance, I rescued this poor lamb. His Master gave him the Gift and then left him to starve. He was going quite mad with hunger.'

'We should all be so charitable.'

'Exactly. Rio thought you'd make a nice first meal for him, only I appropriated him before that happened.' She took hold of my left arm, stroked her fingers over the almost healed skin. Her touch was gentle, hypnotic. 'And I'm sure that the four vampires Rio did finally give you to enjoyed you immensely – and they were much more effective at removing the iron poisoning from your body than just Darius would have been.' She leaned in and licked the swollen bite on my neck.

A shudder of need rippled through me.

'Without the loss of blood, you really might not have survived, even with your strange heritage.' She kissed my mouth, the faintest touch of her lips. 'My help is always free, I never ask for anything, but I always find it returns to me in such interesting ways.' She sat back down on the bed, circled her hand round Darius' ankle and smiled. 'He really was very satisfying.'

I shook my head to clear the slight wooziness brought on by her touch. Had she just told me she'd saved my life? Not that it mattered; she was after something and no doubt I'd find out what sooner or later. Until then I had other more important things to do.

'If you want to help so much, take me to Malik al-Khan,' I said flatly.

'Malik can't help you, Genevieve.' Her low, warm laugh echoed round the cave room. 'I am afraid he still dances to his Master's tune.'

So much for Plan A.

'Fine. Get me a phone then.' I waved an arm at the room. 'Or get me out of here.'

'We're underground.' She smoothed a hand over the silk sheets. 'When the goblins excavated into the rock down here mobile phones hadn't been invented, and the vamps are so archaic that as yet they haven't made provision for communications. And as for getting you out' – she sighed, standing up – 'sadly, not everything is in my power. I am, after all, just a human. We're in the middle of Sucker Town, and the vamps are gathering for the Challenge.' She moved to stand in front of the huge wooden wardrobe. 'The likelihood of you escaping and being able to get help to rescue all of your friends in time is an impossibility.'

Friends, plural? The word snagged my attention. 'You said "friends"?'

She smiled at me like I was a child. 'Well, you've more than one, haven't you?'

Katie. An anxious knot tightened in my stomach.

Hannah opened the wardrobe and placed some clothes on the bed.

I stared at them. What was I going to do if they had both Katie and Finn?

'Don't just stand there,' she chided me, and I realised what I was looking at: her Corset Girl outfit.

'Hurry up and put it on, unless you want to go out there naked.' She pulled a long blue evening dress out and held it up in front of her, her eyes sparkling. 'Beautiful, isn't it?' She stroked a hand over the shimmering silk. 'John Galliano made it especially for me.' She glanced up, a mistrustful glint in her eye. 'But don't get any ideas about it. I know I said like to help, but I draw the line at lending you an original Dior.'

Her dress was the last thing I wanted.

Chapter Forty-Three

The skyborn goblin curled her long cats' whiskers, regarding me with her blue marble-like eyes as she slid her finger down her nose. I returned the greeting. A deck of cards appeared on the blue baize card-table in front of her. She picked up the cards and shuffled the pack, the cards whizzing through her triple-jointed fingers almost too fast to see, then she carefully placed them face-down on the table.

'Hurry up, Genevieve. You need to pick a card,' Hannah shouted in my ear, trying to make herself heard over the whoops and whistles and jeering.

I pressed my lips tight together. *Now* she wanted to hurry.

The cave room had opened onto a stone-hewn corridor with a small underground stream running down the middle. Hannah had sniffed, then lifted the long silk skirt of her Dior and picked her way carefully up the slight slope, trying not to scuff her Jimmy Choos. I'd stomped along behind her in the Corset Girl outfit. Her boots were too big for me, so I'd stuffed them with tissue. The puffball skirt was itchy and scratched against my thighs, and she'd had to lace the corset so tight to stop it falling down that even my small breasts were bursting out over the top. By the time we'd reached the circular metal staircase that led upwards, my patience was running thin enough that I was ready to heave her over my shoulder and carry her. The staircase had taken us up into the empty – but noisy – interior of the Leech & Lettuce, the Blue Heart blood-pub.

There was another loud burst of sound, and Hannah nudged me. 'They've started.'

I glared at her in disbelief, snatched up the cards, and started to turn them over.

'No look, Lady,' the goblin ordered, waving her bony fingers at me.

'What the hell am I supposed to do then?' I asked.

'Just pick up half the pack, and give it to her,' Hannah said. 'Or she won't let you in.'

'Fine.' I put the cards back and cut the pack.

The goblin took them and handed me back the bottom card. 'Participant.'

'I'm not here to participate,' I snapped.

Hannah put her arm round my waist and gave me a quick hug. 'You want to save your friends, don't you? You can't do that by watching.'

'I wasn't planning to.' I shrugged out of her embrace. 'And I wasn't planning on playing games either.'

She gave me a knowing smile. 'Check your card, Genevieve.'

I turned it over. The face of the card was printed in flat grey, only as I looked, the grey swirled and eddied. What a surprise – not! I went to give it back to the goblin, but she shook her head.

'You have to keep it,' Hannah said.

Of course, I did. I stuck the card down my cleavage.

Hannah picked her own slice of the pack. Her card was painted red. 'Blood,' she announced, her face disappointed. 'Well, I suppose it's only to be expected.'

'Get a bleedin' move on, pets.' The voice came from behind us.

Tensing, I swung round to face a short, stocky vamp in black wraparounds and full goth outfit flashing his fangs in a grin. 'We ain't got the time to muck around, y'know.' He pushed past us and grabbed half the stack of cards. His card was black.

'Spectator,' called the goblin, hiking a thumb over her shoulder at the steel door behind her.

He slapped the card against it. As the door slid away into the wall, noise slammed through the opening like a tidal wave. He strutted out.

I started to head after him, but Hannah gripped my arm. 'I need to show you where to go.'

'Hurry up, then,' I snarled, my patience at an end.

Outside, Hannah led me to a tarmac walkway. I squinted, trying to shield my eyes from the glare of the huge stadium lights. To either side of me was scaffolding, and the underside of wooden planks. Another roar assaulted my ears. The planks rattled, dust filtering down between their cracks as the crowd stamped their feet. I dragged Hannah down the walkway and into an arena, where tiered seats looked down on the action, while above the tightly packed spectators hung giant plasma screens. All were showing close-ups of the two contestants in the ring. They were locked together, arms wrapped around each other like pro-wrestlers.

Then the screens switched to show a league table with a list of names. Betting odds flashed next to each name: the Earl, Rio, others I didn't recognise, and – my pulse started speeding – my own name at the bottom. Odds against me were sixty to one. Malik's name wasn't there.

I tugged on Hannah's arm and shouted at her above the noise, 'What are they betting on?'

'The winner, of course,' she shouted back.

Fuck.

A tiny Monitor goblin whizzed past our knees, blue dreads swinging, a thick wad of paper in his hand. A vampire, his own long curls falling over his face, leaned over the side of the stands and grabbed the goblin by the scuff of his boiler-suit, lifting him into the air. The vamp's mouth moved. The goblin scribbled on his pad, then thrust it at the vamp. The vamp shot an appraising look at me, nodded, and dropped the goblin. He tucked into a ball as he fell, rolled to his feet and whizzed away, his trainers flashing.

Hannah pointed at the screen. My odds had halved to thirty to one.

The vamp gave me a double thumbs-up and grinned, showing all four of his fangs.

Nice to know someone had confidence in me.

The screen switched back to the match. The two figures were apart, circling each other, arms outstretched in a fighting stance. Both were naked. The camera zoomed in on the smaller one – Rio, her dark skin gleaming like it was oiled. A close-up highlighted the pink-tinged sweat that beaded in her blue hair, moved to focus on her eyes, the whites stained a deep indigo with power, then cut downwards to her snarling lips pulled back over her fangs. Then the camera panned back out, pausing at the bloody bite wound on her shoulder before taking a fast zoom up for a bird's eye view of the whole arena.

The crowd stamped and hissed and booed.

Now the larger figure, a troll, filled the screen, his massive body glistening a dark red colour. The camera zoomed in again for the close-up. My heart caught in my throat as I recognised Hugh. I broke into a run, watching as his face grew larger above the ring. His grey eyes were clouded like a storm, his nose was chipped, his skin etched with deep cracks. Then his face was gone in a blur of movement.

The crowd jumped up as one and roared.

The screens switched to a wide-angle shot of the two of them grappling across the solid blue of the fight-ring's floor.

I ran faster, and as I reached the edge, leapt into the fight-ring—

And hit something *not there*.

I bounced back, landing on my arse. Swallowing down a scream, I crawled back to the edge and *looked*.

A shimmering dome rose up and over the ring, its bespelled wall inches from my nose. I stared in at Hugh and Rio. Hugh seemed to be winning. He was banging Rio's head against the blue floor – but as I *looked*, I saw a thin aura of grey cushioning the vamp and I realised she was using the spell to protect herself by pulling power from Finn. Hugh didn't have a chance.

My stomach lurched. That meant Finn had to be somewhere near – she needed him close to get the most from the spell. I scanned the dome, but all I see was Hugh and Rio.

And why the fuck was Hugh fighting Rio anyway?

He was supposed to be Katie's rescue party, and long gone by now.

Hannah bent over me, offered her hand. 'There's a containment-spell,' she yelled in my ear and pointed. 'If you want to get in, you have to go round to the entrance.'

I looked round. The arena was a pentagon, with only four of its sides tiered. The fifth side, the one opposite me, was flat space, with no seats, nothing – except for a lone figure in the distance.

I raced round the walkway between the dome and the stands.

'You'll need your card to get in,' Hannah's faint shout followed me.

Snatching the card from my cleavage, I held it in front of me and felt the brush of magic as I swung round the last corner and into the entrance area.

I stuck my card back between my corseted breasts and strode towards the figure.

Chapter Forty-Four

'**G**ood evening, my dear.' The Earl bowed his head, his blond hair flopping forward. Power gave his skin a translucent sheen, which matched the embroidered blue hearts that entwined in pairs down the front of his navy velvet coat. The coat cut away around his knees to show the tight leather boots that encased his legs. Whatever image he was going for, it wasn't one I recognised.

'I do appreciate the effort you've made to attend our little soirée.' He stroked his silk lapels as he cast an appraising glance over my outfit. 'And you look as delightful as ever.'

I stuck my hands on my hips, my chest heaving as I struggled for air. The corset was so not made for breathing, let alone running. 'Not sure I can say I'm pleased to be here,' I gasped. 'I've better things to do with my nights than participate in your little spats.'

For a moment he inclined his head as if listening, only there was nothing to hear. The noise from the crowd was gone, held behind the containment-spell I'd come through. The place was as quiet as the proverbial grave.

I so hoped it wasn't a bad omen.

'Shall I enlighten you as to the rules, my dear?'

'Please do,' I said, relieved my voice sounded calm, if a bit breathless, despite the anxious thudding of my heart.

'Rio has issued Challenge to me, as is her blood-right.' The Earl strolled towards the fight-ring, indicating that I should follow him. 'She wishes to usurp my position. Normally this wouldn't be a problem.' He waved a dismissive hand. 'I gave her the Gift, and I would not hesitate to take it from her, except that she has something I want.'

I snorted. 'The spell.'

'Correct, my dear.' His smile leaked charm. 'Under pre-Challenge negotiations, Rio decided which of the various facilities at her disposal she wished to utilise; she elected the satyr. I have chosen the troll.'

'All very interesting, but why don't you tell me something I don't know?'

'Certainly.' The Earl inclined his head. 'The troll came calling earlier and I managed to convince him to take up my standard.'

'You mind-locked him, in other words.'

'Partly true, but there were other factors involved. He had some colleagues with him – he appeared to be very protective of them.'

Fuck. Hugh had walked right into a trap – no, I'd *sent* him. I clenched my fists. And what had happened to Katie, was she caught too?

The Earl carried on, 'I fear that the troll will be no match for Rio, not with the magical back-up the satyr is providing for her.' He held his wrists out as though checking his nonexistent shirt cuffs. 'I wish you to remove the spell from the satyr. I understand that should be a piece of cake for you.'

Who did he think he was kidding?

'Then what happens?' I asked.

'That should be enough to allow the troll to succeed.'

Surprise made me stop. 'You want Hugh to kill Rio?' I'd sort of thought *he* would want to fight her.

'I believe that is what I said.'

'What about Hugh?' I asked.

The Earl brushed a speck of fluff off his sleeve. 'What about him?'

'It's going to take some time to obtain the spell. I want an assurance that he's going to be okay while I do it.'

'He is a troll. They are solid, dense creatures, usually very difficult to damage irretrievably.' He held a hand up as I began to speak. 'But I have a vested interest in seeing him victorious. I will "keep an eye on the situation", as I believe they say.'

Yeah, right. I pressed my lips together.

We reached the edge of the blue-floored dome. From the audience the fight-ring looked small, barely twenty feet across, but from the entrance it was more like a hundred-acre field. Hugh and Rio were small figures in the distance and Finn was still nowhere to be seen. I frowned, then realised the disparity had to be something to do with the magic containing the dome. I hurried forward.

The Earl caught my arm. 'Not so fast, my dear. We have other things to discuss first.'

Oh yeah, the blackmail bit.

'Once you have the spell, Genevieve, please bring it to me. I would hate to find my concentration slipping, thus allowing Rio to win her fight.'

I narrowed my eyes in suspicion. 'I thought you said she couldn't win without the aid of the spell.'

'My dear, I can encourage the troll to fight, but I can also make him – what shall I say? A sitting duck.' He smiled.

Fear fluttered inside me. Did he really have that much power? To make Hugh just stand there while Rio killed him? Well, that worry was for later; first I had to find Finn.

'You'd better point me in the right direction,' I said finally.

'Try not to take too long.' The Earl gestured towards his left. 'And one more thing. Please try not to injure the witch. She could still be useful.'

Of course, Toni the witch, my ex-friend, would be there. Who else would be guarding Finn while Rio, her sucker sweetie, was fighting? Only never mind not injuring the witch, how was I going to stop her harming me? After all, she was the one with all the spells hidden up her sleeves.

Chapter Forty-Five

I took a deep breath and stepped into the arena, then stopped. Hannah's boots would only slow me down now. I bent down and pulled them off as the barrier shimmered into place behind me and the Earl disappeared, as did the entrance and the distant Hugh and Rio. Damn. The magical dome had expanded even more, and once I started moving, I'd have no way of knowing where I was – or how to get out.

I started running round the outside, my bare feet slapping against the blue-rubber floor. Above me the plasma screens displayed the fight, Hugh and Rio moving in a silent, vicious ballet. After a few minutes, my lungs were screaming for air: the corset didn't leave much room. I was debating with myself whether to stop and take it off when I caught sight of a figure sitting further in towards the centre. And lying next to it was another.

Breathing and the corset could wait.

As I got closer, the sitting figure jumped to her feet. A cap of white-blonde hair shone under the stadium lights, and white shorts and a low-cut bikini top showed off her curvaceous figure. For a moment I didn't recognise her as Toni – either she'd been to the goblin hairdresser's again, or the massive head of hair she'd always sported had been a wig. I was betting on a wig; it made sense – all the time she'd spent hiding in plain sight, trying out different disguises.

Toni jerked her arm up and green light shot from her fingers.

I hurled myself to the side. The stun-spell winged my

shoulder and pain arced down my arm. Gasping, I rolled up onto my feet and kept running towards her.

She threw her arm up again.

Again I dodged, and the lightning-flash of green streaked away over my head. Now I was only feet away, close enough to see the spell-stone glowing in her hand. And close enough that this time she couldn't miss. I only had one chance: I had to *crack* the next stun-spell before it knocked me out.

I *focused*, searching for the spell's centre.

'You just don't know when to quit, do you, Hon?' Toni yelled.

My heart raced. Gold glowed under my skin. Toni swung her hand up. I could see the bright blue of her eyes. Toni had never had blue eyes in all the time I'd known her. I ducked under her arm and slammed her to the ground, forced power into the spell. She thumped me on the back, crashing the spell-stone against my body. The stone exploded like a firework, a gold-and-green fountain shooting into the air, the colours flared and tiny slivers of jade cascaded down around us.

I'd *cracked* it.

I sat up, straddling her waist. 'Sorry, *Hon*,' I laughed. 'Guess your magic's not all it's cracked up to be today.' A bad pun, but the best I could manage under the circumstances.

Toni screamed with rage and swung her other hand, aiming for my head.

'Oh no you don't'. I grabbed her wrist, then squeezed it until she dropped a hunk of jade the size of a grape. Snatching it up, I *focused* and smashed it against her forehead.

She went out in a burst of green fizzing light.

'Ouch. That's gonna leave a nasty bruise.' Finn's voice was hoarse.

I swivelled round. He was lying on his side a few feet away, his hands forced behind his back and shackled to his ankles.

'Nothing she doesn't deserve.' I shot him a fierce grin, rubbing at the aftershocks sparking along my stunned arm. Then my relief changed to worry as I took a good look at him.

His eyes were sunken, his skin pale and waxy-looking and the sleek sable hair covering his flanks had lost its sheen. The wounds down his chest and stomach had stopped bleeding, but they were still raw. His horns had shrunk to small triangular bumps, almost hidden in the matted blond of his hair. And the spell swirled through him like a malevolent grey fog.

'The bitch's got the keys,' Finn whispered.

'That's going to make it easier then.'

Toni's breathing was steady, like she was in a deep sleep. The white shorts and top were leather, and glove-smooth. I slid off her and shoved her over onto her side so I could get to the small bump in her pocket: two small silver keys, both set with crystals. I allowed myself a tiny moment of satisfaction as I tossed them in the air and, ignoring the burning sensation, caught them in my hand.

When I turned back to Finn his eyes were closed. I touched his cheek and his skin felt hot and clammy. I smiled as he opened his eyes.

'Hugh?' he whispered.

I glanced up at the nearest plasma screen. Rio had sunk her fangs deep into Hugh's neck and was worrying at him like a rabid dog, but Hugh looked unconcerned. He'd trapped her in a bear hug, his thick muscled arms crushing her torso. I guessed that neither was gaining on the other, thanks to the Earl 'keeping an eye on the situation'.

'He's holding his own just now,' I said. 'What about you?'

Finn gave me a tired wink. 'Thought I'd hang around and catch the show. That bit was the best so far.' A coughing fit shook his whole body

'Can't say I'm impressed.' I leaned over him. The gem-studded shackles were held together by a short silver chain. 'Let's get you out of these.'

'Not yet, Gen,' he whispered.

I sat back sharply on my heels. 'Why not?'

'Stupid bitch didn't realise ...' He sucked in a wheezing breath, 'the shackles are muting the spell.'

'Got it,' I said, understanding. I had to remove the spell first – the last thing I wanted was for Rio to be able to snag a last-minute magical power boost from Finn that would kill him and Hugh both.

I risked another look at the screens. Rio had Hugh face-down on the ground and was pummelling his head. I hoped the Earl's attention wasn't slipping. I pressed my lips together. Nothing I could do about it yet.

Now for the difficult bit.

The Earl might think removing the spell would be a piece of cake, but it was going to be more like trying to swallow the whole giant-sized gateau in one suffocating mouthful. I needed something to help the spell go down. The brownie's magic should do the trick – if I could get it to come out and play. I rested my hand on Finn's shoulder, wincing at the feverish heat of his skin – he certainly needed the comfort more than I did – and closed my eyes. Taking a deep breath, I *conjured* Agatha's voice in my mind.

A brownie's touch goes to them that needs it.

Pink and orange motes floated before my eyes. I pictured my kitchen, and the salt in its cardboard container. I started throwing the motes at the salt, splattering them like paint, *focusing* my will. C'mon ... *come on* ... It *had* to work. *Focus*, I told myself, chewing my lip as my stomach knotted ... There was a thud, and something stung against my legs. My eyes flew open.

The salt had arrived – but the container had split and the salt was spread like white sand across the blue-rubber floor. Still, I'd *called* it. I punched a fist in the air. One down, two to go.

I grabbed a large pinch of salt and held it to Finn's mouth. 'Open up,' I told him gently, 'it'll help unstick the spell.'

He stuck his tongue out and I touched the salt to it. He

shuddered and forced himself to swallow, pressing his lips tight together. I grimaced and hoped he wasn't going to sick it up. I watched him for a moment, then gave him some more.

I stroked Finn's arm and *called* the next thing I needed. My stash of liquorice torpedoes arrived without the plastic jar, raining down like enormous hundreds and thousands. I stuffed a handful in my mouth and sighed in relief as the sugar hit my system and made it easier to concentrate. *Calling* the vodka felt almost effortless after that. I even managed to land the bottle upright. I drank a scant mouthful, then gathered up more salt, poked it in the bottle and shook it up.

Finn watched me through half-closed eyes, a pinched, disgusted expression on his face.

I gave him a sympathetic look. 'Think of it like a margarita without the lime.'

'Hate margar—' Another racking cough interrupted his complaint.

I ignored him and when it stopped, I tipped the bottle up and trickled the salty mixture into his mouth until it was gone.

The grey fog raged and boiled around Finn. It was making me queasy. What if I tried to take the spell and it didn't work? I pressed my hands to my stomach, which felt like it was caught in a vice— Oh wait, I was still wearing the fucking corset! I yanked at the laces. Skin to skin was always better for magic anyway. I pulled the loosened corset down over my hips, taking the net skirt with it, and kicked the clothes away. The spell felt like greedy grabbing hands, wanting more, all the time. What if, rather than *absorbing* it, the spell consumed me instead?

'I'm going to undo you, Finn.' I clutched the silver keys, feeling them burn against my palm. 'I don't know what'll happen when I *call* the spell.'

He moved his head slightly in agreement. Leaning over, I unlocked the shackles and pulled them apart, freeing him. I slung them out of the way. Finn groaned in pain and curled in on himself. For an instant I saw something black at the base of his spine. His tail? Then it was gone.

Moving carefully, I lay down behind him, gently spooning along his back. His heart beat fast and shallow against my breasts, the hair on his flanks was rough against my thighs, his shoulders clammy beneath my cheek. The smell of sour berries caught at the back of my throat and I swallowed back my tears.

This *had* to work.

I hugged him tight and *called* the magic.

The grey fog surged up and over me. I opened myself to it, inviting it in. It rushed through me, spiralling fast, whirling me into a vortex. I let go of Finn and rolled, over and over, spinning the grey with my body. Gold drops sparked, running like thin golden streams through the whirlpool, draining away at its centre. I poured more gold into the vortex and the streams turned to torrents. Gasping for breath, I stopped rolling, then threw myself into reverse, forcing the torrents to funnel up from where they flooded away. The whirlpool started to slow and the gold and grey bands coalesced and stretched into long sticky strands that set like a cage of cooling sugar ... and trapped the spell. I stopped rolling and lay there for a moment, my pulse speeding with anticipation and fear.

I shattered the cage.

The spell crumbled into dust that drifted sweet into the air and I floated on a golden haze. Tiny perfect black pearls of magic floated with me.

Chapter Forty-Six

'Genny,' Katie's voice sounded urgent, 'Gennny, pleeease wake up, you've got to wake up—'

Katie?

With the after-effects of the magic still wafting through my mind, I sat up, wobbled, squinted up at her. Mascara smudged across her cheeks, her hair hung in a messy ponytail, and her jeans and vest top were creased and dirty.

I frowned and rubbed my hands over my face.

Then I stared at the vampire gripping her arm. His own blond ponytail was much neater, his grin was full of fangs, and his frilly red shirt billowed in a nonexistent breeze. My heart tripped anxiously as I recognised him: the count, aka Red Poet, the leader of the fang-gang.

He looked at me. 'Good, you're awake. I am pleased it didn't take you long to recover.'

'You're not the only one.' I scrambled to my feet, my pulse thudding. 'Only I have to admit to being disappointed that you didn't get staked for real in the *Théâtre du Grand-Guignol.*'

'Good,' he laughed, 'you have a sense of humour. Let's see if you find this funny.' He bent and kissed Katie on the forehead. She flinched and he laughed again. 'Tell your friend what it is we want, child.'

'I'm not a child,' she sniffed.

Relief settled in me: she couldn't be too badly hurt if she could still backchat him.

'Talk, child.' He shook her arm.

'He wants you to be his Blood-Bond,' she said, sneering up at him.

'Let me guess.' I bared my teeth at him. 'Katie is my incentive?'

'Good, you are smiling.' His grin widened. 'I will enjoy spending eternity with you as my slave.'

'Genny, don't do it, you mus—' Katie stopped as the blankness of a mind-lock crossed her face.

'She really is the most annoying human child,' he said. 'She never closes her mouth. But as you can see, I have not hurt her. She is my little lottery ticket.'

I looked surprised. 'You do the lottery?'

'Of course! Unfortunately for me, in my younger days I was more interested in having fun than in salting away a fortune for my future.' He sniffed disdainfully. 'You don't think I enjoy being staked, do you? The pay is good, but it takes me five humans to recover.' He grinned again. 'But now I will have you, a sidhe.' He leered at me, running his gaze over my naked body. 'And you will keep me warm at night, in more ways than one.'

Movement caught the corner of my eye.

I stuck my hands on my hips and took a deep breath, pushing my breasts out at him. 'So we're talking what, exactly? Sex, blood – and what else is part of this bargain?'

He wasn't looking at my face any more. 'That all sounds good.'

'Uh-huh.' I frowned, stroking my stomach. 'I want to know what type of sex first.'

'Sex is sex.' He took a step nearer, pulling Katie with him as he started sniffing at me like a bloodhound.

'Now that's where you're wrong.' I trailed fingers over my breasts. 'Are we talking with or without magic? What about partners? Is it going to be just me and you? Or are you into threesomes? Foursomes? Girl on girl, what?' I turned sideways and run a hand down over my hip. 'There're all sorts of things to consider.'

He licked his lips, almost panting. 'Yes. All of that.'

I waved at him, to get his attention back on my face. 'And what about getting staked for a living, are you—?'

His eyes went wide. He let Katie go as he lurched forward. Looking down at himself he touched the spreading wet stain on his shirt and opened his mouth ... but no words came out.

Katie's face lost its blank look and she stumbled, falling to her knees at my feet. She crawled behind me, shaking.

Suddenly Red Poet jerked, his limbs shaking like a rag doll's, and Katie screamed. I jumped, startled, as the vamp flew through the air and dropped, thudding onto the blue-rubber floor.

Katie screamed again and I crouched, pulling her into a hug. 'Shush, shush, it's okay, He can't hurt you now.' I patted her back, feeling her body still trembling under my hand.

Finn stood and stared down at the vampire with a satisfied expression. Bright red blood dripped off his ten-inch-long horns, trickling into his hair and down the side of his face.

Katie subsided into enthusiastic sobbing.

I glared up at him. 'Took your time, didn't you?'

He grinned back at me. 'I was enjoying the show, Gen.' Then he sank to the ground and collapsed in a heap.

Shit.

I dragged Katie over to him and slid to my knees clutching at his shoulders. He briefly opened one eye. 'S'okay, just a bit tired. Go help Hugh.'

'Is he all right?' Katie hiccoughed.

I *looked.*

He was clear of the spell. Relief winged through me.

Up on the plasma screen, Hugh and Rio were facing off, circling each other again.

I smashed the end off the vodka bottle and held it out to Katie – as a weapon against a vamp it wouldn't do her much good, but it would make her feel less helpless. 'Think you can stay here and look after him, Katie?'

She took the bottle, and cast a wary eye at Red Poet. 'He's not going to get up, is he?'

I spotted the silver shackles. 'I'll make sure he doesn't.'

She huddled next to Finn, twisting her mouth into something that nearly made it to a smile.

I grabbed the shackles and fastened them around Red Poet. I sort-of thought he was dead, but without taking his head and heart, I couldn't be sure, and no way did I have time for that.

'Genny, why are there liquorice torpedoes all over the place?' Katie asked, bemused.

'In case you fancy a snack,' I muttered, looking round. Something was missing—

'Ha ha. I get it,' Katie rolled her eyes and stuffed a couple in her mouth. 'Ask a stupid question,' she mumbled.

—Toni the witch bitch was gone. *Fuck.* I grabbed a handful of the torpedoes myself and headed off to the fight.

Chapter Forty-Seven

The Earl was waiting for me. His blond hair flopped over his forehead, as usual. His eyes were a solid blue, much like the floor. He'd removed his frock coat and boots and stood there naked, his white skin dull, corpse-like. And nude, that was really all he had that was worth commenting on.

Only I wasn't going to be the one to tell him that.

He smiled his charming smile. 'Bravo, my dear. Your removal of the spell has done the trick and now Rio is weakening.'

A map of blue veins snaked under his skin. It had been a long time since he'd fed – looked like he'd been saving himself for me. How nice was that?

I stopped a few feet away. 'What about Hugh?' I demanded.

He waved a hand above him, where the plasma screens were showing a close-up of Hugh. He was bent over, hands gripping his thighs, his black hair dusted with red, his chest heaving for air. Trails of white silicate blood ran from his neck and over his shoulders. Beneath his feet I could see the blue-rubber floor, so I knew he was still somewhere in the ring.

The tension in my stomach twisted tighter as the camera panned round and Rio came into the shot. She was on her knees, shoulders slumped, one arm hanging useless at her side.

'As you can see,' the Earl said softly, 'the outcome seems to be a sure thing, all done bar the shouting. Your troll has the upper hand.'

'Cut the crap and tell me what the deal is.'

'I find your bluntness revitalising my dear. So, as you ask, let us get onto the deal. It is as I proposed to you in my note. You will take my Blood-Bond along with the spell of course, and in exchange I will offer you my protection.'

Yep, that was pretty much what I'd expected. He wanted me for himself; he wasn't planning on selling me on. Not that his protection made any difference, seeing as it would last only as long as he did.

The Earl broke into my thoughts, almost as if he'd read my mind. 'If you have any concerns about my ability to protect you, please put them aside.' He spread his hands wide in an all-encompassing gesture. 'With our combined powers, and the spell, I sincerely doubt any other would be able to stand against me.'

Of course, he would have to be the megalomaniac type, wouldn't he?

He gave me an enquiring look. 'I take it by your silence that you have destroyed the spell?'

'You take it right,'

'Ah. I did wonder if that would happen. But worry not, for the situation is still retrievable, as you will see.'

The air *shifted*, pressure popped at the back of my head and I blinked to clear away the slight disorientation. The Earl had done his time-pause thing again.

Toni stood behind him, her face blank in mind-lock. The cap of white-blonde hair almost hid the swelling purple bruise in the centre of her forehead. In her hands, she held a short knife and an ornate silver cup, faint steam swirling above it. No doubt it contained the spell.

Time to do some bet-hedging of my own.

'Hugh,' I shouted.

'He can't hear you, my dear.'

'He can hear you though, can't he?' I kept my gaze fixed on the screen. 'Tell him to look up and wink his left eye.'

The Earl tilted his head as if listening.

Hugh's massive hands clenched and his face filled the screen, deep fissures creasing in his red skin. He bared his polished granite teeth in a growl.

'He refuses,' the Earl said, his tone indifferent.

I bared my own teeth in a smile. I hadn't expected Hugh to agree. But now I knew he was alive and we weren't just watching a recording.

Now for the rest.

I walked over to Toni and took the knife from her unresisting hand and slashed it across the raised red scar running down my left arm. Blood welled as I dropped the blade. I took the cup in my right hand. It felt cool to my fingers, so not silver then. I turned towards the Earl. 'Here's the deal. I want Rio dead, and you give me your word that you will allow all my friends – and *their* friends – to leave and go home in safety. Do that, and I'll agree your terms.'

Surprise flickered across his face. 'I had thought you would object much more strenuously.'

I hoisted the cup and offered my bloody arm. 'Do we have a deal or not?'

He inclined his head at Toni. 'Is the witch included in your negotiations?'

'No.' *She doesn't need to be*, I added silently.

He rubbed his hands. 'In that case, it is agreed.'

A chime split the air.

Above me on the silent plasma screen, Rio staggered to her feet and stood there swaying. Hugh lowered his head and charged towards her, his feet thundering across the arena. She held out her arms, as though to catch him. He crashed into her, head-butting her in the chest, knocking her backwards, and she lay broken on the blue floor as Hugh moved to stand over her.

Looking up at him, she drew her lips back in a snarl. Rio wasn't gone, not yet. Hugh turned away and I chewed my lip. I wanted him to kill her; I wanted her *dead* – it was the only way to break her Blood-Bond with Finn – but I knew Hugh would hurt inside if he did that, and I didn't want that for him. But as I watched, Hugh hesitated, his head angling to one side, then he swung back and as though the camera was rolling in slow-motion, he raised his granite foot and stamped down, crushing Rio's skull like a sledgehammer crushing an eggshell.

The screen went black.

The Earl bowed, though the action looked ungainly in his nakedness. 'And now I believe it is your turn, my dear.'

I sniffed the cup. It was mostly blood, the Earl's. The faint scent of liquorice caught my nose, and a sharp spike of bitter-ness that I recognised as the spell. I held my wrist over the cup and watched as my own blood joined with his. A ripple of power tightened within me, a small insignificant herald to the fact I was giving my life away. I put the cup to my lips, then, holding my breath, I tipped it up and drank. The liquid slid cold and sticky down my throat and settled queasily in my stomach. I drained all but the last few drops and held the cup out to him.

He took it from me and drank what was left. Power stained his skin blue and he flashed all four of his fangs in a wide grin. 'Now for the finalé.'

He *called* me.

I felt the tug inside me and knew I couldn't refuse him.

'Feels like it's my turn to provide the refreshments then.' I walked into his arms and offered him my throat as he bade me.

He struck, needle-sharp teeth piercing my neck shooting venom into my blood. The pain shocked through me. *Bastard.* He could've shielded me, but he hadn't even bothered. The venom hit my heart, making it thud fast and hard, speeding and pumping the blood through my veins and arteries.

He fed.

The Blood-Bond wouldn't let me struggle, but it couldn't stop the tears spilling down my face.

The Earl sucked on my blood until my heart was weak and my body cold and I sagged, almost lifeless, in his arms. This was what they wanted, what they all wanted: to feed until they killed. The power of life and death. Only with a human it was only ever a one-time thing. Not with a fae. Fae could be taken to the brink again and again. And the Blood-Bond would stop me from harming or killing either the Earl or myself. It would be centuries before he might finally let me fade into death.

I whimpered at the thought.

He gripped me tighter, thrusting himself against me, pushing himself into my belly. His hips jerked and his jaw worked hard and greedy at my throat.

I whimpered again, knowing it would excite him further.

Waiting...

Then I released the magic.

Tiny black pearls sheathed in golden hope flowed through my blood, and into the Earl.

I fear you have misled yourself, my dear – in my mind the Earl sounded amused – *if you feel your Glamour is a way to turn the tables. Your magic cannot harm me; why even before our Bond it would have been nothing more than a delicious appetiser.*

His amusement faded as the tiny black pearls of compulsion – the compulsion spell I'd pulled from Constable Curly-Hair's True Love bracelet – trapped him in my Glamour.

I held him there on the edge, making him feed until I felt my heart stutter and stop and my stomach clench with hunger, until I felt Rosa and her need rise inside me. I pushed him from me.

The Earl stood still, his face blank, pinpricks of gold in his pale blue eyes, staring at me with entranced adoration.

Would it work, or would the Blood-Bond still bind me in another's body?

I shoved the doubts aside and coated my hand in the last drops of blood trickling from my throat. Praying to any god that would listen, I smeared the blood over the tattoo on my hip.

The red haze clouded my body.

The compulsion broke and dissipated.

I glanced down at my creamy-white skin, tossed my long black curls over my shoulder and ran my tongue over my fangs.

The Earl's eyes opened wide—

I smiled at him.

—knowledge flooded back into his face.

I punched my fist into his chest.

And ripped out his heart.

Chapter Forty-Eight

I clutched the Earl's heart until I felt the life leave his body. I walked far enough from him that the blood spreading out from his corpse – *my* blood – wouldn't be able to reach it, then carefully placed the heart on the blue-rubber floor. I shuddered as my Alter Vamp body healed itself. I glanced up at the screens. They were black and still, and the silence told me the magic dome still shimmered above, even though I could no longer feel it. I turned full circle and searched the empty arena.

Toni had gone.

The Earl might be dead, but the spell wasn't, and Toni held its formula in her head. It wasn't over yet.

Then I sensed it: an awareness, a hint of spice in the air, and fear, anticipation, and something more, fluttered in my belly.

Malik al-Khan.

He was watching, hidden in the shadows – only there were no shadows inside the dome; the stadium lights made it as bright as day.

My silent heart thudded once. 'You can't have the witch.' My shout reverberated in the air.

A breeze teased around me, playing with the long black hair that curled over my shoulders.

'I know you're here,' I shouted again. 'You can have whatever you want, but not the witch.'

The sensation of silk slid soft over my naked skin.

'Malik al-Khan.' I held my arms out wide in offering. 'This needs to be settled.'

'*Rosa* ...' His voice whispered behind me.

I crouched and swivelled to face him.

He wasn't there.

'Or is it Genevieve?' Again the sound came from behind me.

I straightened and turned slowly, running my tongue over my fangs.

He stood perfectly still, his long black leather coat almost sweeping the ground. A pale length of flesh gleamed from his throat down to the leather trousers sitting low across his hips. The dark silk of his hair shone under the arc lights. He watched me, the obsidian-black of his eyes enigmatic.

Toni stood a few feet behind him, her face still blank with mind-lock.

'What is it you think I want?' His voice was soft.

'Me.' My voice was calm. It didn't betray the child crying in my mind. 'My agreement to come back with you.'

His long, elegant fingers brushed a wing of hair from his forehead while he studied me. 'You would sell yourself in order to destroy the spell?'

'When you put it like that,' I said, 'yes, in a heartbeat.'

Part of me didn't care. It was over anyway. I'd been running and hiding since I was fourteen, trying to stay alive, trying to stay free, but I had always known that one day my prince would find me and someone would come to take me back. Getting rid of the spell was the honey that sweetened the pill.

'If that is what you wish.' Malik turned, and beckoned Toni to him.

She walked up to stand at his side and a sunny smile broke over her face.

'You may see for yourself.' He took her hand and held it out to me like a gift. 'The spell is gone.'

I frowned, suspicion making me wary. I grasped her hand and cupped her face. Her smile didn't change. I pushed into her mind and found ... *nothing*. There was no tangled net of thoughts, no mind-lock, just nothing. Her mind was gone. She wouldn't be telling anyone anything ever again. Shock made my heart beat again. Malik hadn't just wiped her mind clean, he'd obliterated it. Nausea roiled in my gut that he could do that, that it was even possible. He touched her shoulder and she walked away into the dome.

Toni had been condemning me and every other fae the vamps might capture to an eternity of slavery.

The spell was gone.

Then the nausea dissipated and all I felt was glorious relief.

The spell was gone.

Malik would have to force me to go back, and no way was I going to make it easy.

I smiled at him, flashed my fangs. 'Looks like you're out of bargaining chips.'

'What about Rosa?'

Damn. There was always *something*, wasn't there? He wanted to destroy Rosa's body to save her soul from a demon – only it wasn't a demon, it was me. Would he still want to do that, now he knew it was me sharing her body?

I shrugged. 'What about Rosa?'

He waved towards the Earl's corpse. 'That was … unexpected.' He moved to stand in front of me and held out his hand. The pearl handle of my knife gleamed like an accusation. 'As was this, Genevieve.'

I didn't move. 'Puts you in a bit of a predicament doesn't it?' I gave him a mock sympathetic look. 'I mean, you can't kill this body, not without killing me too. It's one of those golden-egg-and-goose-type things.'

He released the blade and pressed the sharp point to my breast. The silver burned against my skin. 'Why is it,' he asked, his eyes half-lidded and his lips lifting in wry amusement, 'that I cannot take both your lives?'

'C'mon, Malik, cut the crap.' I raised my chin. 'I was a child. Children are young, not stupid. I may never have seen your face, but I recognised your touch.' *Almost from the first*, I added silently, only I hadn't wanted to admit it, not to myself, not even when my dream-mind showed me the truth. 'I'm just surprised it took *him* so long to send you after me.'

'You are right, of course.' Malik slid the blade down to rest just under my ribs.

'Nice to know the homicidal maniac hasn't forgotten me,' I said, my pulse speeding faster in my throat.

'He tasked me with bringing you back to him ten years ago.' He sighed, and the sound slipped like sorrow into my heart. 'Only I did not do as he wished.' The knife dented my flesh.

My mouth dropped open. 'What?'

'The Autarch is no longer my Master, Genevieve. He has not been so for nearly twenty years.' Cool fingers circled my left wrist. He lifted the knife and traced an ice-hot slash down my inner arm. Blood trickled in an eager rivulet to splash onto the blue floor.

I flashed back to him doing the same thing to my four-year-old self. The knife had been set with a dragon's tear, an oval of amber the same colour as my sidhe eyes. He'd taken my blood with my father's good wishes, tasted me in proxy for my prince.

As then, I stood frozen, unable to move.

Malik bent his head to my arm, licking a long firm line along the slash. He gazed at me, his pupils flaring red. 'How could I call him Master when I coveted what he owned' – he kissed his lips to mine and I tasted my own honeyed blood as his voice whispered through my mind – *'for myself.'*

Need and desire and a fledgling hope took flight inside me. He broke the kiss.

And I asked the question. 'Why did you kill Melissa?'

His expression didn't change. 'She had uncovered the witch. Once her vampire lover had realised, they would have fled again, taking the spell with them.'

So that was the information Melissa had been selling: Toni's identity. Only Malik had always known where Toni was. The trees had been gossiping about him watching Spellcrackers – watching Toni – not me. 'Why didn't you just kill the witch?'

'Genevieve.' His voice held slight impatience, 'The witch was under the protection of the Witches' Council. To do so would have violated our rules and started something I did not wish.'

'What about the spell?' I asked. 'Didn't you want it for yourself?'

'I have no need of it.'

Of course he didn't. He already had me – ever since I was four years old. 'So what happens now?' I breathed.

He reversed the knife, placed its handle in my palm and clasped his hands round mine to hold it straight and true. 'What happens now is your choice.' He spread his arms wide. The scar I'd given him bloomed rose-red against his pale skin.

I looked down at the blade, then up at his beautiful face.

And did nothing.

Malik smiled and my heart thudded in my chest. 'Genevieve.'

He whirled round, an edge of darkness swinging from his coat, and strode away, vanishing into nothingness.

Epilogue

The spell dome dissipated, leaving me standing in the much smaller car park of the Leech & Lettuce. To one side Katie, still clutching the vodka bottle, watched over Finn. On the other side sat Hugh, his head bowed, his police back-up – Constables Taegrin and Curly-hair – beside him. Behind me lay the bodies of Rio and the Earl, surrounded by a squad of Beater goblins. The tiers of seats still ringed the car park, but they were empty. The vampire audience had gone.

Hannah picked her way in her Jimmy Choos over the stony ground. 'The police will be here soon, Genevieve. I suspect that you might want to stay until your friends are safe, so I have a gift for you.' She offered me a cloak. 'It might be wise if you were to disappear before they arrive.'

I gave her a quizzical look. 'Disappear as in "not seen", or actually go away?' I asked.

'As I told you' – she smiled – 'I enjoy helping people.'

I took the cloak from her, wrapped it around me and vanished from sight.

The police arrived in force. Detective Inspector Crane in the lead, along with a whole slew of paramedics from HOPE. And as the night waned and dawn approached, all that was left were the bodies. The goblins doused them in petrol and set them alight, the acrid fumes smoking and polluting the air. When there was nothing left but ashes, they swept those into a box and marched down to the river. I followed and watched silently as the fast-flowing Thames rushed the scattered ashes down to the sea.

Now I sit in the Rosy Lee Café and stare out of the window. The heat-wave has finally broken and rain is pelting down on London's dusty streets and sluicing through the gutters.

Katie brings me an orange juice and my usual BLT sandwich with lashings of mayonnaise. She smiles and bustles away to serve the rest of the lunchtime crowd. She is still having nightmares, but it has only been a week, and the bad dreams might dim in time.

Declan kept his side of the bargain and offered the Gift to Melissa. Sadly, it didn't succeed. Two nights ago, she was cremated at a private family ceremony. Bobby, aka Mr October, was there to support Melissa's mother, all charges against him having been dropped. Alan Hinkley wasn't able to attend: he is still in a coma and Bobby is spending his nights beside his father's hospital bed, waiting for him to recover.

Constable Curly-hair is under suspension pending disciplinary action. She refused to pass on the details of Katie's abduction to Hugh, or anyone else, because of me. By the time Hugh and his back-up team arrived at the Leech & Lettuce, the sun had gone down and the Earl was waiting. Hugh is currently convalescing in the Cairngorms with his tribe.

Thanks to my boss, Stella, and her campaigning, and Finn's overwhelming evidence about Toni's activities, the Witches' Council has reinstated my contract with Spellcrackers.com. I get to keep my job, and my home – the compromise being that the witches will no longer offer me their protection, as Detective Inspector Helen Crane was entirely too happy to inform me.

Finn was taken to HOPE and then transferred to sanctuary, where he underwent the treatment to purge the *salaich siol* from his blood. Three of his brothers turned up to take him back to recuperate with his herd. As his *salaich siol* infection is so recent, the purge should be successful, but it will be another month before anyone will know for sure. We spoke briefly before he went. He plans to come back to London and take over the franchise at Spellcrackers.com, once he's well enough.

He held my hand and told me he would keep my secrets.

I don't know what that means, or how I feel about that for now, so I've tucked him away in that box in my mind, along with all the other things I'm not yet ready to think about.

Like Rosa.

And Malik.

I've heard he is still in London, but I haven't seen him.

I sip my orange juice and look at the headline in today's newspaper.

WITCH TO BE BURNT AT THE STAKE.

Toni has been quickly convicted of Melissa's murder – the motive being blackmail over the witch's secret relationship with a vampire – and as Toni can't object and Rio is dead, it's a nice neat ending for all concerned.

I push my sandwich away, no longer hungry, and watch the rain.

Read more about Genny's adventures in

THE COLD KISS OF DEATH